A·Posturing·of·Fools

Also by Brewster Milton Robertson

Rainy Days and Sundays
The Grail Mystique

A Posturing of Fools

a novel

by

Brewster Milton Robertson

8.23.06 - STONINGTON, ME

RIVER CITY PUBLISHING
MONTGOMERY, ALABAMA

Copyright 2004 by Brewster Milton Robertson.
All rights reserved under International and Pan-American Copyright Conventions. No part of this publication may be reproduced, stored in a retrieval system, or transmitted in any form or by any means electronic, mechanical, through photocopying, recording, or otherwise, without the prior written permission of the publisher.

Published in the United States by River City Publishing
1719 Mulberry St.
Montgomery, AL 36106.

This is a work of fiction. Names, characters, places, and incidents either are the products of the author's imagination or are used fictitiously.

Designed by Lissa Monroe
Cover art by Jo Patton, *Masquerade*

First Edition—2004
Printed in the United States of America

1 3 5 7 9 10 8 6 4 2

Library of Congress Cataloging-in-Publication Data

Robertson, Brewster Milton, 1929-
 A posturing of fools : a novel / by Brewster Milton Robertson.
     p. cm.
  ISBN 1-57966-051-7
 1. Pharmaceutical industry--Fiction. 2. Impotence--Treatment--Fiction. 3. West Virginia--Fiction. 4. Married men--Fiction. 5. Resorts--Fiction. I. Title.
  PS3568.O2479P67 2004
  813'.6--dc22
                           2004009901

For my wife,
Charlotte Jones Cabaniss Robertson

∾

In Memoriam
Hal Farrell
Dr. Daniel Zeluff

"The true snob never rests . . . there are always . . . more and more people to look down upon."

—Russell Lynes, "The New Snobbism," *Harper's*, 1950

NEWS FROM THE GREENBRIER

The Greenbrier is an American classic, a legendary blend of space, color and history with unlimited activities and impeccable service in the Allegheny Mountains of White Sulphur Springs, West Virginia.

Unequaled among premier resorts and conference facilities, every aspect of the hotel is monumental—from its rich history, which began in 1778, serving both the soldiers of the Civil War and the pivotal figures of modern politics, industry and society, to its sheer size and scale. With 6,500 acres, 650 guest rooms, 51 suites, 69 cottages, 10 lobbies, 30 meeting rooms, 3 golf courses, 20 tennis courts, a celebrated Culinary Apprenticeship Program, Conference Center and the $7 million Greenbrier Spa and Mineral Baths, this National Historic Landmark is both a monument to its storied past and a testament to its present stature as a modern, full-service resort.

But while the Greenbrier offers its guests a wide range of activities, amenities and services, the main pursuit of those who operate and serve the hotel is the relentless dedication to excellence.

The Greenbrier is located just off of Interstate 64 in White Sulphur Springs, West Virginia, 250 miles southwest of Washington, D.C.

Advertising copy from the Greenbrier (circa 1994)

PROLOGUE
August 1995

WHUMP!

One instant John Paul Silver and I were bumping along this bomb-pitted Bosnian back road singing a bawdy song; the next thing I knew there was a muffled explosion and I was launched skyward, tumbling ass over HUMVEE, through a cloud of dirt. Just before I landed, something thumped my chest like a 98-mph fastball. When I came to rest, I was upside down in a shell crater, the wind knocked completely out of me.

Once I recovered my senses enough to sit up, I blinked hard to clear my blurry vision. Some fifty meters farther along the rutted track, our HUMVEE was a smoldering tangle of camouflage-painted metal, its wheels spinning grotesquely in empty air.

Across the road, John Paul was crawling out of a drainage ditch, dabbing a handkerchief at an ugly gash above his eye. When he finally got his legs under him, he dusted off and started limping in my direction.

"Careful where you step, John Paul. I think we hit a mine," I called, spitting out a mouthful of dirt.

He slowed and nodded, warily picking his way across. When he'd almost made it to where I sat trying to catch my breath, he stopped dead in his tracks.

"My god, Logan, don't move!" he gasped, pointing to my upper body.

I glanced down, and a sudden wave of nausea washed over me. A jagged, six-inch piece of shrapnel was jutting out of my left breast.

"Hold still! Let me have a look." Dropping to his knees in front of me, he gingerly pulled aside the blouse of my bloodied combat fatigues to examine the fearsome-looking missile.

I caught a glimpse of bright red blood and averted my eyes, afraid of what I'd see.

"Logan Baird, you're one lucky SOB. It's hardly more than a deep scratch!" John Paul wheezed a mighty sigh of relief as he gingerly extracted the razor-sharp fragment. Incredibly, the lethal shard had been stopped short of ripping through my heart by a well-thumbed travel brochure. Wadded in the breast pocket of my cammies, I'd carried that dog-eared, coffee- and mud-stained pamphlet as a sort of good-luck charm ever since I left the States to begin my tour as an army lieutenant attached to UN peacekeeping troops outside Sarajevo.

That dear old brochure from the Greenbrier resort had actually saved my life.

It was November now, and the uneasy truce in Bosnia had been in effect since the first week in October. Just before dusk, we walked outside the squat Bosnian hut and stood side by side under a pale yellow wintry sky, pissing into the screen-covered top of the urinal pipe sticking out of the ground.

Our piss steamed in the chilling evening air and stank, sweetish and boozy, as three young women passed by, walking down the center of the muddy street. They blushed and giggled and waved.

Shit-faced drunk, we leered and waved back.

"Hotdamn, John Paul, can you believe it? We're going home," I said. "By god, we finally made it out of here."

"B'lieve it," John Paul Silver said, slurring his words a bit—still leering and smirking.

Before the war caught up to him, John Paul had been an English instructor and faculty advisor to the well-known literary magazine at a small Ohio university. As young as he was, he was only an undotted i and uncrossed t away from defending his Ph.D. dissertation. He was a lieutenant in the army reserve.

Only two years out of the university, I had been a fledgling medical writer on the daily newspaper back home in Roanoke, Virginia. Because the army would help pay for my college, I was a weekend warrior, a young lieutenant in the Virginia National Guard.

When the fighting in Bosnia broke out again, we'd both been called to active duty.

Usually the army has a way of making brain surgeons into truck drivers, but we both had been assigned to Bosnia, reporting on the UN peacekeeping force for the *Stars and Stripes*. Surviving our HUMVEE's being destroyed by the land mine with only superficial wounds, together we had walked virtually unscathed through nearly a year of some of the bloodiest fighting of the war.

"Whooeee, I could piss all the way to New York. Feels so good," I sighed. "Whatcha gonna do when you get back home, John Paul?"

I'd asked the same question at least ten times a day for the past four days. Ever since we'd gotten orders to ship back to the States, we had celebrated every night. By now I knew John Paul's answer by heart. It had become a mantra, lyrical like poetry—music to my ears.

"Gonna call Cathy and marry her. Go back to the university and teach all them dumb hick kids about great literature. Then I'm gonna write the great obscenity of an American novel about this unprintable obscenity of a war. Be the next Hemingway, by god."

Cathy was in for a big surprise. John Paul had only dated her once or twice before he was called to active duty.

"How's that for literary cussin'? Right out of *Fur'oom th' Bell Tolls*. Talk about your pure Hemingway." He hiccuped and sniggered, beaming with drunken pride over his artful avoidance of a curse word. We'd made a solemn vow to clean up our language before we shipped out for home.

Turning to catch my approval, he carelessly pointed his gushing stream toward me.

"John Paul, watch it!" I danced aside, barely avoiding getting pissed upon.

"Oops, sorry!" He laughed and kept right on talking. "Already got the title: *Carpe Diem*. Latin. Means seize the day! How you like that for a fug—for a freaking title? Seize the freaking day. Great freaking title, huh?" He smirked and pointed his member back in the right direction.

"Great title. Love that title." I meant it. It really was a great title.

"Don' forget. You're gonna write one too. We made a deal. We both oughta be dead. Never shoulda made it out of here alive. We owe Somebody up there something in exchange for our no-good fug—uh, freaking lives. You promised. We're gonna write great . . . ah . . . freaking books, right?"

He jostled me hard with his elbow, deflecting the hot stream of my urine against the side of the building. I had to stagger back again and suck in my gut to keep from getting splashed by my own piss.

"Deal's a fug—a freaking deal. Right?" He nudged me with his elbow again.

"Right. And make love and drink champagne . . . and play golf," I added as I shook the last drops off the end of my trusty trooper and zipped up my fatigues.

"That too, I guess." He gave me a skeptical look.

I took out my dog-eared Greenbrier brochure and waved it under his nose. "John Paul, ol' buddy, did I ever tell you about the Greenbrier? It's the spa to end all spas. It's the most elegant place in the whole fornicating universe. The *crème de la crème*. The whole damn place was decorated by this snooty New York broad, Dorothy Draper. A thousand rooms at least. And each room is decorated differently. She used all this freakin' wild flowery wallpaper—magnolias and stuff. At the Greenbrier they don't mow the golf courses, they manicure the sonsabit—sonsa-guns. Presidents go there and heads of state and corporate execs. It's right off the pages of F. Scott Fitzgerald or Dominick Dunne or that namedropping babe, Danielle Whatsherface. Three hundred bucks a day per person double occupancy. Their chefs aren't from Cordon Bleu. They train chefs for the bleeping Cordon Bleu. When I get back, I'm going to take Rose to the Greenbrier and do nothing but have champagne for breakfast and make early morning, sunshine-splashed love. I'm going to ravish her in the shower and on the silky percale of that big bed and on that plush green carpet and play golf twice a day for a week."

"Classy, Logan. Real classy," John Paul said, worshipfully. "May take Cathy there for a honeymoon. Great idea! Go with you and Rose—just us together."

"No, no, John Paul! You don't take anybody but the bride on your honeymoon. Besides, John Paul, take it from me, honeymoon rule number one is: Don't get married in the first place. Why ruin a perfectly good relationship?"

"I'm gonna be too godda—too doggone busy teaching and writing books to be chasing women," John Paul protested. "Marry Cathy and have my own woman right at home."

John Paul kept right on pissing.

Mostly he drank only beer. I could never understand it.

"Then honeymoon rule number two is: Don't forget the little woman." I winked.

"Right! Take Cathy. Greenbrier . . . real classy."

I fervently hoped Cathy was a black belt in karate and had at least six hands.

"John Paul, old buddy, the Greenbrier is more than classy. The Greenbrier redefines the word. Raises the freaking crossbar for every contender in the world," I said, remembering dreamily. "Slammin' Sammy Snead. You ever heard of the old Slammer?"

"Huh? Oh, yeah. He used to play goff or something, right?"

"Sheei—uh, *merde*, John Paul"—my French was lousy, but I was struggling to outdo him cleaning up my vocabulary—"the old Slammer practically invented the game. He's over eighty and still jacks it around near par."

"Yeah, well. You play goff, I'll take care of the women. But mostly we're gonna write books. You can do all of that goff stuff, too, but that doesn't count."

Beer drinkers are amazing. John Paul kept right on pissing.

"John Paul, you got no class. Golf and women—not necessarily in that order mind you—but women and golf are the only two things in life that count."

"And drinking, and don't forget writing. Deal's a deal."

"Uh-huh. But first things first, John Paul."

"Did you write Rose yet, like I told you?" He'd asked me this for at least the umpteenth time in the last five days. "No, not you. You son of a—you spawn of an unthinkable biological act, you gotta play it cute."

"I want to surprise her. The minute I hit the States, I'm going to call the Greenbrier, and then I'm going to fly to

Roanoke and walk right in and say, 'Rose honey, pack your bag and get a baby sitter. We're going to the Greenbrier."

"Serve you right if you walk in on her and she's in the sack with your best friend."

"Impossible," I said.

"Oh, no. Not so impossible. Serve you right, you seed of an unspeakable union." John Paul was really getting into the Hemingway.

"Impossible," I insisted, trying not to laugh.

"Oh? And why's that? You think you got the only pecker? Yours ain't no world record pecker you know. You want to see a real pecker?" He waved his proudly. I stepped back, out of range of his last wayward drops.

He'd finally finished pissing.

"Look, John Paul, size isn't everything. There's a real art to satisfying women."

Over John Paul's shoulder, I caught view of a young Bosnian mother walking along the muddy street carrying an infant on her hip. Nipping at her heels was a mongrel puppy. The baby looked to be less than a year old—a boy about the same age as my own baby son. Born after I landed in this Godforsaken country, my little Paul was John Paul's namesake. As yet unseen by me, Paul existed only in my heart of hearts, a chubby infant in a small snapshot.

Suddenly, I was depressed. At that moment, I looked at this fine, sensitive young Ph.D. candidate beside me and thought about our superficial conversation.

Too much death and alcohol. War brings out the worst in men.

"Gonna marry Cathy, take her to your Greenbrier Camelot." John Paul hiccupped. "Logan, baby, we gonna set this freaking world on its freaking ass."

"Too late, John Paul." I shook my head.

"Huh?" He gave me a funny look.

I looked away.

The street was lined with bomb-gutted buildings. To one side, the burned-out hulk of a Russian-built tank still reeked faintly of cordite. High above us, a single withered leaf clung to a broken branch in an artillery-blasted tree.

"The world's already been set on its rotten no-good ass," I muttered, my heart spilling out of me.

"Whatcha talkin' now, man?" John Paul asked, perplexed by my abrupt change in mood.

All at once, I'd lost my taste for frivolous chatter.

An ache deep at the back of my throat made it impossible to speak. But, it really didn't matter. I didn't have an answer anyway.

John Paul still hadn't seen the young girl and her baby.

The baby's right hand was missing—blown clean away.

On the jumbo jet flying home, my future seemed dazzling. A cocky lad of twenty-five, I had already been to two universities and survived a war. Dancing in my subconscious were images of my old nameplate waiting on my desk at the *Roanoke Times*.

LOGAN BAIRD
Medical Writer

After two years of uninspiring premed, I had grimly faced my mother's tears and switched schools to study journalism. Newly graduated from academia, I had been barely twenty-one and already employed as a medical writer at the Roanoke paper when I married my high school sweetheart, Rose Worrell, a newly graduated nurse. Like most young married couples, Rose and I had our ups and downs, but overall our marriage was mostly good.

That was before the war caught up to me and the army sent me packing off to Sarajevo.

It had been plain rotten timing that Rose was eight months pregnant with our first child the day I flew off for my year in Bosnia. On that plane coming back, my head was awhirl with visions of my fun-loving Rose and infant son welcoming me, the battle-scarred hero, at the Roanoke airport. I was ecstatic at the prospect of getting home in time to celebrate my son's first

Christmas. Visions of sugarplums—not to mention a virtual pornucopia of erotic fantasies—danced in my head.

My heart was set on a second honeymoon in the grandeur of the Greenbrier. As soon as the plane touched down at Dulles International, I called home, bubbling with enthusiasm.

"Rose, baby, I'm back. Pack your bags, we're going to the Greenbrier."

"The Greenbrier! Have you lost your mind? It's the dead of winter!" she snorted into the phone. "If you've been drinking, sober up! You've been off playing war. You've never even seen your son."

Rose's frigid reception caught me off guard.

"Which reminds me, Rose, I want to get Paul a puppy for Christmas. Every boy should have a puppy—"

"Forget the puppy, Logan. Come home. I'll teach you how to change diapers."

"Maybe we could go to Cancun or Key West. It's warmer there," I ventured, my enthusiasm undiminished. This dashing—did I mention horny?—hero was determined to take a few victory laps around the bedroom to celebrate his return from mortal combat.

"Forget Cancun. This is your son's first Christmas," Rose reminded me icily.

"Okay, then we'll go for New Year's. My folks will baby-sit. Remember our honeymoon? We had champagne for breakfast and made love on the carpet?" I persisted romantically.

"Grow up! Have you forgotten those embarrassing rug burns on my butt? And don't you dare show up here drinking. Now don't miss that plane." My bride hung up in my ear.

Back home at last, somewhat chastened—but not in the least daunted—by Rose's frigid reception, I was fairly bursting with hormonal overload. And, secretly, I was more than a little pleased Rose had taken care of her figure after the baby came. If anything, she seemed even prettier to my lusting eyes.

And, let the record show, Rose has never been into self-denial.

Once the baby fell asleep and I'd washed the baby doodie off my hands and shown her my war wound, my darling Rose relented. Momentarily, I forgot all about Cancun and the Greenbrier.

But my ecstasy was short-lived.

I was taken completely by surprise. While I had been away dutifully protecting hearth and home, with the advent of motherhood my sweet unassuming Rose had undergone a chilling metamorphosis. In my absence, my fun-loving, romantic sweetheart had been transformed into an unsmiling common hausfrau.

With each passing day, in utter disbelief, I watched as a monstrous Nurse Jekyll/Mother Hyde emerged.

To my everlasting frustration, the sweet sighs and low moans of our white-hot reunion quickly faded into Rose's oppressive preoccupation with mortgage loans and the need to increase my life insurance. My shy, maidenly Rose became a harping, world-class critic of my lackadaisical ambition. My beribboned combat fatigues packed away, I had hardly started back at the newspaper before Rose began nagging me to put aside my youthful dreams of becoming the next John Grisham—or at least a worthy rival to Tom Clancy—and quit my job as medical writer.

So, just when my karma seemed cosmically ordained, I switched careers and became a sales representative for Severance Laboratories, a firm well known for its breakthroughs in treating male erectile dysfunction.

During the ensuing transition, my relationship with Rose didn't show a lot of improvement, but I grudgingly admitted that my new career worked out far better than I expected. Not an inconsiderable contribution to that fortuitous circumstance was that I not only made a lot more money, but in the interest of my new career, I also got to play a lot of golf with doctors and pharmacists.

The downside was that the new job required a lot of travel—time away from my beautiful son. But, then, nothing is ever really perfect. Now, thinking back to my brush with death and the Bosnian infant boy with his hand blown away, I was struck by the stark realization that we are all mere paper figures caught up in some great cosmic windstorm.

And I, among all men, have been mightily blessed.

Stoically, I accepted my fate.

After all, somebody had to do it.

Cocksure and full of life, I knew just what I wanted, and, most of all, I was dead certain I knew just how to get it.

I had the answer to just about every damn thing.

Except what to do about my ailing marriage.

TUESDAY MORNING

CHAPTER ONE

Neat and slim-hipped in white designer shorts and a tangerine tank top modeling her fine matronly breasts, Rose was pretty in a conventional high-Episcopal, Junior League sort of way. She always managed to look as if she'd walked right off the pages of *Town and Country*.

"The deliveryman brought an express envelope from John Paul Silver while you were in the shower. It's on the kitchen table. I'll go get it." Rose finished buttoning her waistband and zipped her stylish silk shorts, but she made no move toward the kitchen. She stood there beaming at me with a dreamy smile on her face.

The neighbor women would never guess that barely ten minutes ago she'd been biting the pillow to keep from waking our five-year-old son with the shuddering outcries of her machine-gun orgasms.

In the bedroom, Rose was a world-class screamer.

And, she was predictable—totally mistrusting of yours truly. My darling Rose rarely let me leave for a long road trip with my libido unattended. Not that I complained. Nowadays, about the only time we really got along was in bed.

"I hate it that you have to travel so much." Rose pouted, eyes still heavy-lidded with orgasmic afterglow.

"Rose, don't blame me for that. It was your idea that I quit the paper and start peddling pills. Besides, you could still come to the Greenbrier on Friday. I've practically begged, you know." I tried to sound hopeful, but my heart really wasn't into lost causes.

For Rose, the trip to the Greenbrier was a dead issue.

She snapped back into reality. "You know I don't like it when you refer to your new profession as 'peddling pills.' Selling pharmaceuticals is a highly respected profession. Don't forget, most of our friends are doctors now."

First, last, and always, Rose was a nurse—and a medical snob. She was absolutely certain that physicians and their Junior

League wives communed daily with a white Anglo-Saxon Protestant God.

"Would you rather be out on the interstate right now, covering some head-on car wreck with arms and legs of dead drunks all over the road? Would you rather be back there in that ugly apartment with the giant cockroaches? No country club? No University Club? None of your precious member-guest outings? No Greenbrier trips to play golf? You should thank me, Logan."

"I do thank you for that." I halfway meant it. Rose had a point. I had to confess that I was guilty of a bit of class consciousness myself. The old newspaper crowd was generally a tacky bunch. We probably did run with a better class of people now. Maybe. Sometimes I wasn't all that certain. But we did belong to a better club.

Still, sometimes in the wee dark hours of the morning, stuck in some damned firetrap hotel in a place with a name like Hog Wallow, West Virginia, I thought about John Paul and that unfinished book I'd stuck in the closet, and I wondered. Then, every so often, I'd dig my attempt at the great American novel out of my closet and look at it in the cold light of day and be reminded what a pile of sentimental garbage that manuscript really was, and my vagrant pang of wistfulness would quickly pass away.

I'd said goodbye to those youthful dreams a long time ago.

"Cookie and Maryanne will be there. Why don't you let your hair down and join me Friday?" Cookie Bergmann and Maryanne Cavanaugh were wives of two young doctors I played golf with. They were in Rose's bridge club.

I'd barely gotten the words out before I wished I'd had the good sense to leave without bringing it up again.

"Oh, sure! Big shot Logan Baird. How many times do I have to tell you we can't afford it? If you'd quit spending our hard-earned money on toys for the crippled children's hospital and look at the checkbook, you'd know." She stood, feet apart, amidst our son's toy cars and Tinker toys scattered on the living room floor and brushed at a stray coil of hair stuck to the tiny beads of perspiration on her forehead. "Besides, we ought to be spending the money on our antiquated air conditioning. You don't know how bad it gets. You're in air-conditioned hotels all week."

"Rose, give it a rest! I'm tired of hearing about that. I've told you a hundred times in the last month, call the air-conditioning guy for pity's sake! While you're at it, let's get a new heat pump. Don't be so melodramatic. It's not an all-or-nothing situation."

All Rose's nonsense about our finances was pure hypocrisy. Heat pumps were advertised regularly by the electric company for bargain rates. Besides, she had just bought an expensive new Lilly Pulitzer cocktail dress. When I found it in the back of her closet, she'd had the nerve to say with a straight face, "How could I pass it up? It was a steal at $175."

Now I was rudely reminded why I didn't really care if Rose ever came to the Greenbrier with me again. The last time we were there she had whined about being bored and having nothing to wear. With a wardrobe like Rose's, not even Hillary Clinton could act bored at the Greenbrier.

"A new heat pump? Oh sure, Mr. Big Shot, who's being melodramatic now?"

I glanced at the door. I was running short on time. I had to pick up my self-important new boss, Rush Donald, at the airport.

"I'm late, late, late! Got to run. I'll call you tonight. There's plenty of time before Friday morning. I could pick you up early. I'll probably drive Rush back to the airport Friday anyway—the Charlotte flight leaves at the crack of dawn. Officially, the exhibits don't come down 'til Saturday afternoon. Rush says I can finesse Friday and Saturday night hotel charges for you on the company. Call Nanny and Grandad; they'll jump at the chance to come get Paul and take him to the farm. C'mon honey, it's not every day we common folks get a chance to have a weekend on the company at the Greenbrier. And, Rose, go ahead and order a new heat pump. It'll make you feel a lot better."

I always made certain that I made my exit looking like the good guy.

Rose ignored me. She was used to my grand gestures.

"Expense account or not, we still can't afford it. You should look at the checkbook once in awhile. And Logan, don't you go over there and act like such a big shot. My god, how much does the golf cost? A fortune—I remember. I'll bet Rush won't let you put the golf on the tab."

This was a one-way conversation.

Rose wrote the questions. Rose had the answers.

"Rose, the golf was Rush's idea for pity's sake. It's business. We play with doctors. Doctors write prescriptions for Severance Laboratories. I was number four in the country last quarter. Have you forgotten the big bonus? You pushed me into this thing of peddling pills. I'm a success, lady. I just may wind up number one this time. You'll love this next bonus. Go ahead, get the heat pump. Can't you take 'yes' for an answer?" Without putting down my briefcase, I gave her a little squeeze and tried to humor her.

Mr. Nice Guy to the end.

Still pouting, Rose pushed me away. She wasn't buying my charm. Playtime and afterglow were over now. Normally, Rose was a twice-a-week girl, Friday night and Sunday afternoon.

Tuesday was a special feature.

I patted her behind.

It really was a very nice behind.

She blushed and pushed me away again.

"Quit trying to change the subject. I'm serious."

Rose was always serious.

I edged toward the door.

"You'd better be careful, Mr. Big Shot. Rush Donald's nobody's fool. If your good doctor buddies talk too much, you're in trouble. If Rush knew you were playing golf two or three afternoons a week, you'd be looking for a job."

I was really playing almost every day, but what Rose didn't know wouldn't hurt her.

"He promoted me, remember? I'm his right-hand man now."

"Oh, sure, some promotion! Being his flunky is hardly anything to brag about. Besides, Rush knows that you should've gotten Mort's job instead of him. He knows you're way smarter than he is. Playing up to him won't help you, either. You're a fool to trust him. He'd cut your heart out if it would help him get ahead."

Rose didn't have to warn me. Secretly, I knew what she said was true. I did kiss Rush's ass shamelessly, and being his drinking buddy gave me an edge. I'd learned a lot from him, and besides it was all part of getting ahead. I knew enough to mind my p's and q's.

"Rose, you don't have the slightest notion what you're talking about. It's Rush's idea that I set up a golf match with Max and Sam while we're over there." Busy young physicians, Sam Cavanaugh and Max Bergmann both belonged to our club. My golfing buddies, they wrote a pile of prescriptions for our miracle drugs. "Playing golf with doctors is good for business."

I tried to sound confident, but what she said gave me an anxious twinge. I knew that basically Rush was a company man. He was definitely limited and had middle-management opinions about playing client golf.

"You'd best be out there making office calls. Business you get on the golf course and socializing at the club won't last." Rose sounded an awful lot like Rush. She saw no virtue in anything that wasn't paid for with suffering. Rose firmly believed it was a sin for me to enjoy my success. Too much enjoyment invoked the wrath of God, the certain cause of horrible retribution. Unless, of course, it was something she considered necessary.

Bridge and garden clubs were mandatory. Useless small appliances were fine. Frequent changes in furniture and new drapes were requirements. Increases in my life insurance coverage were a necessity. And jewelry and cocktail dresses for teas and bridge club were absolutely essential.

"Besides, now that you're making some money, we'd be better off looking for a new house and putting something aside for Paul's education instead of wasting money on a new air conditioner. But, no, you have to join the country club and the University Club, too, with your fancy new doctor friends. We're not in that league yet, big shot. And another thing. You're a father now. You never do anything with your son anymore. You spend all your time on the golf course or drinking at those damn clubs."

"That's business, honey. Don't you understand? I'm running a lot of the tabs from both clubs through the expense account. Rush is a snob. He likes the idea of doing his drinking at my clubs when he's in town. Besides, you enjoy the country club as much as I do. You take Paul to the pool practically every day. And bridge with the girls. I thought you liked that."

"Well . . . I could do without all that," she stammered. Rose was a poor liar. "I'd rather have a new house. You've got your priorities all messed up. And, speaking of Rush and the bar bill at the club, he drinks too much. And the way he looks at women when he's had a few. Remember when we went out with that government sales specialist, Hannah, after the state medical society meeting? He had his hands all over her. He was obnoxious. When you're with him, you drink too much, too. I don't like it. I don't trust him. Do you think he's faithful to Nadine?"

"Of course. He can't go to the loo without Nadine. I get sick of hearing him talking about Nadine." I hedged my assessment of his purity when he was drinking. But I meant the part about Nadine's influence. She wore the pants in Rush's family, and she had all the real brains.

"Sometimes I think she's your boss, too. You certainly make a fool of yourself trying to impress her. I see you bringing all those books home, reading up on ballet and poetry and modern art. Picasso, ugh! And those books on wine. All of it just to impress Rush's precious Nadine. In a way you've become as much a slave to Nadine as he is. Don't you feel like a prostitute, playing up to their snobbery that way?" she sneered.

"Prostitute? Sure. That's what selling is all about . . . the oldest profession. Henley Logan Baird, world-class whore! You like the money, and I like the freedom. No more nine-to-five, pounding a damn laptop." It was true. I did like the freedom. Writing was plain hard work. The *Times* and SNN had nominated me for a couple of Pulitzers but that was just going through the motions. Except for one fluky piece *Harper's* magazine had published four years ago, I'd never published anything worth mentioning.

"Besides, you're right about one thing. I am smarter than Rush. I don't intend to carry a sample bag the rest of my life. I'll get a division of my own. Let the others do the work. Drinking with Rush and getting on Nadine's good side are simply part of the game."

It was a brave speech, but I was ashamed. All the rationalization in the world didn't change things. I really didn't like having to kiss Rush's and Nadine's asses. I hated the way it made me feel.

"Don't be too sure that you're smarter than he is. A high I.Q. isn't everything. You got that one dumb article about how doctors don't know anything about art or football in—I never can remember which magazine. All I know is that nobody I know reads it."

"*Harper's* magazine, Rose. It happens to be one of the most prestigious magazines ever published. And, while you're mentioning it, your precious *Reader's Digest* picked it up. Just about everybody you know reads that. And it really wasn't about how doctors are dumb. It was about how the narrow focus of a medical education limits them. I merely pointed out that most women who fulfill their sorority-girl fantasy of marrying one wind up with a big house and nice car and a dumb clod who doesn't know which fork to use. All work and no play make doc a dull boy."

"Okay. But you're still a snob. And poo! If you were such a hotshot writer, how come you never sold anything after that? Then Rush Donald comes along and got you to read that book by H. L. Mencken, and now you don't go to church anymore. I'm sure that that awful Kirk-kee-gord you're always quoting went to hell."

Rose made the switch in subjects without even taking a breath.

My fragile ego and my endangered everlasting soul. I didn't bother to try to figure out how the two things were related. As long as she sent me through the door with my libido reduced to a whimper, the two things about me that worried Rose the most were the paid-up status of my life insurance and my immortal soul.

"Rose, don't let's start. I've got to go. Rush will be steamed if I'm late." I started through the door.

"I'm serious. Watch your drinking when you're with him. You lose control. I don't trust him. He's always making you run his expenses through your account. I don't think that's honest, and besides it makes you look bad with the company," she called to my back as I hurried down the sidewalk to the car. "Call me and let me know your room number. Let Rush pick up the checks. He's the one with the big expense account. Money doesn't grow on trees."

I put my briefcase on the back seat, slipped behind the wheel, and started to close the door.

"Anyway, Logan, don't feel too bad. We can take Paul to the beach for Labor Day weekend at my sister's with the money we'll save by my staying here."

What fun, I thought. I remembered the new "bargain dress" and struggled to keep my mouth shut—and won. Discretion was the vital ingredient in staying married to Rose. I'd learned that a long time ago.

"By the way, Rose, about the puppy for Paul. Uncle Bob's bitch has a new litter of beagles."

"I keep telling you, forget the puppy."

I started the car.

"Oh, Logan, wait! The express envelope from John Paul Silver! Hold up. I'll run get it." She ducked back inside and reappeared. Running over to the car, she pushed the envelope into my outstretched hand.

Puzzled but pressed for time, I glanced at the red and blue Express Mail envelope and reached behind me, stuffing it blindly in the outer pocket of my briefcase.

"Aren't you going to open it?"

"No time. I'm late." I closed the door.

"But, Logan, it's express. Certified or something. I had to sign for it." Her curiosity was running wild.

"It'll have to wait. I can't be late for Rush. Thanks, shug, catch you later."

"I swear, I never—" she started in, but now I was rolling up the window.

I waved and mustered a reassuring smile.

"Have a good time," she called wistfully after me.

Arms crossed beneath her breasts, she stepped away from the car as I let it start rolling back.

She didn't return my smile.

Rose never was much of a smiler.

"Bet your sweet ass I will," I muttered under my breath.

"What?" The question formed on her lips. She couldn't hear me with the window shut, but she must've seen my lips move.

I pretended not to see.

"What would you do, Rose-baby, if I left someday and kept right on going?" I mumbled to the engine's hum.

"What?" Her mouth formed the question again as she looked after me anxiously.

I waved and let the car roll on out of the driveway.

At that moment, neither of us would have believed what the next few days would bring.

CHAPTER TWO

As I sped toward the airport that morning, any twinge of guilt for my selfishness was quickly erased by fond memories of the Greenbrier.

What Rose said about me was true. I was, am, and always will be something of a snob.

I made no apology then, nor do I now.

I was brought up cloistered in a fantasy fortress of ancestral gentility. The Logans, my mother's family, were landed Southern aristocracy.

Translate that "poor but proud."

While I was still in grade school, my mother was elected president of the PTA for the entire county.

My aunt had founded the county library system.

The first book I remember my mother reading to me was Emily Post's classic on etiquette. At bedtime, she read my brother and me tales from the classics. Long before I entered first grade, I'd learned to read.

I spent my boyhood feeding chickens, weeding the garden, and milking the cow on my granny's farm. Most of the time I didn't have two nickels to rub together, but I knew how to behave anywhere.

My father was a deacon in a historic Baptist church dating back to the Revolution. He labored anonymously in the general offices of the Norfolk Southern railroad. But even though we were of modest means, when we were children my parents took my brother and me to visit cousins in Washington and New York, to Disney World, and to ballgames in Philadelphia and Cincinnati. We slept in Amtrak Pullman drawing rooms and feasted in the dining and club cars, rubbing elbows with the rich and privileged, all courtesy of my father's employee discounts with the railroad. Growing up largely unimpressed by grandeur, comfortable in the reflected aura of genteel people and cursed with a lust for the good life, I was the proverbial champagne gentleman doomed to exist on a beer budget.

Now, at age twenty-nine, I had been a correspondent on a foreign battlefield. My golf handicap was recorded in low single digits. If melted down to pure silver and pewter ingots, my collection of trophies would probably make several mortgage payments on our modest home.

Each week I pored over the pages of the *New Yorker* and the Sunday *New York Times*—how to dress and mix the perfect martini—and the latest in literature, theater, music, art, cinema, and the sex habits of the rich and famous. I learned to tiptoe artfully around the subjects of politics and religion, trilling arpeggios of ambivalence. I read Culbertson and Goren religiously and could talk intelligently about most indoor and outdoor sports in their seasons.

Now, as the representative of a major pharmaceutical manufacturer, rubbing elbows with legions of snooty doctors, nurses, and druggists, I was well prepared to get ahead.

Sales soared. Overnight, I had become a *Wunderkind*.

My new division manager had been transferred from San Francisco to Charlotte. Rush was properly mindful of my military record, my exaggerated erudition, and—most of all—my golden-boy image at the home office. Full of what I suspected were largely apocryphal tales of his long-standing intimate associations with the elegance of dining in the Garden Court at the Palace Hotel and frequent golf outings to the famous courses on the Monterey peninsula, he was anxious to impress me with his worthiness to command.

When I told him we were being sent to the Greenbrier to represent our company at this much-celebrated annual medical conference—and then it was announced that Spielberg's Dreamworks would be there shooting scenes for a major motion picture with Gwyneth Paltrow and Matt Damon and the legendary golf pro, Sam Snead—Rush tried hard to show cool indifference, but his underlying awe at the prospect had been impossible to hide.

Don't get me wrong, Rush was not alone in this state of high anticipation. Even to the most jaded, the Greenbrier is in a class all its own. I grew up a mere sixty miles across the mountains from White Sulphur Springs, West Virginia, the location of this legendary watering hole of presidents and kings. My love affair with the Greenbrier's nonpareil grandeur had begun the first time I caught its view—one rainy afternoon on a Sunday outing in a convertible Bentley touring car with my boyhood schoolmate George Cornwell and his racy, long-legged, sweet-smelling, cigarette-smoking, sensuously affluent stepmother, when I was a hormonal male animal of fifteen or sixteen.

Now, dodging traffic and cursing red lights, hurrying to meet Rush's plane and thinking back to my high school days, I tried to count the times I'd played the Greenbrier's legendary golf courses.

I gave up counting before I reached the number twenty.

I fondly remembered my father's telling of his numerous annual pilgrimages as a spectator at the Greenbrier Open, one of the more venerable stops on the PGA Tour before they changed the format and—emulating the old Bing Crosby Clambake—made it into a big pro-celebrity and renamed it the Sam Snead Spring Festival.

At my most recent peregrination to this "promenade of peacocks," having wangled my usual press pass from former colleagues at the sports desk of the *Roanoke Times*, I had taken my son to marvel at this remarkable man—now the Greenbrier's Golf Professional Emeritus—who still had the ability to score in the low seventies, though his age was now past eighty. In one of his rare expansive moods, the great Snead himself had walked over to where Paul stood beside me behind the gallery ropes on the second tee and gave my wonder-eyed five-year-old a pat on the head.

"Tell yo' papa to write something nice about me," Snead had drawled as he autographed my press pass "To Paul Baird. Your pal, Sam Snead."

All that day, every time the great man made a putt, he had winked at Paul.

With a face resembling a well-worn catcher's mitt, octogenarian Snead had gone on to shoot seventy-six.

The faded green cardboard press pass was still taped to the mirror in Paul's room.

Moreover, beyond the golf outings, I had been a registered guest at the fabled spa three years running for this same annual scientific congress of high-level researchers.

Our company, one of the top research pioneers, had just announced Virecta, a major breakthrough in the chemical synthesis of Viagra-like compounds enhancing the male erection. The whole medical world had our name on the tip of its tongue. Our champion in this arena was Dr. Ian Ferguson, the world-renown authority on hormonal research and human sexuality. He and his landmark paper on Virecta were to be the highlight of this year's research congress at the Greenbrier.

When Rush first got the news that we were going to the Greenbrier on the company tab, the unflappable, cosmopolitan Californian completely lost his poise. It was all he could do not to wet his pants when he found out he was actually going to play Snead's home course. Rush was a born fan. He loved to breathe the same air as his heroes. The fabled Greenbrier had always been his hero Slammin' Sam's home club. By his own account, Rush regularly played the Pebble Beach and Cypress Point courses at nearby Monterey with his San Francisco buddies. He'd told me that as a boy he'd once been in Sam Snead's gallery at the Crosby Clambake Pro-Am. The possibility that his hero might be shooting scenes in a Spielberg movie with Matt Damon and Gwyneth Paltrow drove him over the edge. By the time the big day arrived, my usually blasé boss man had called at least once a day for three weeks, checking on the details of getting him outfitted for the golf.

And me? Properly respectful of the power Rush had over me but now growing weary of his insufferable West Coast superiority, I was looking forward to showing him what real class was all about.

At the airport I spotted Rush before he saw me.

He was dressed in expensive dark blue Daks—all the rage in British self-belted slacks. His shirt was a nice button-down blue oxford, and his silk rep tie was the regimental stripe of the Black Watch.

Over all that, his Master's-green blazer looked spiffy until I got a load of the cartoonishly ornate emblem on the breast pocket. I was rendered momentarily speechless. It struck me that Sir Winston Churchill's nanny would never have dressed him like that to send him off to school. A caricature of the international playboy on a golf outing, a lampoon of sartorial splendor, Rush brought new dimension to the old lyric: "Just too, too and oh so very very."

Not bad, I couldn't help but muse, if you were casting the foil in a Sam Shepard play.

Then I experienced a shudder of foreboding about was to come. I could see from his face that it was a damn good thing I hadn't been late. I had already gotten to know him well enough to know that much anyway. Rush Donald took his new position—and himself—pretty seriously.

Too late to run and hide. I swallowed my pride and rushed forward as soon as I saw him searching the crowd for me.

"Rush, good to see you." It really wasn't a lie. If I played my cards right, I knew this trip would be very good for my career. All I had to do was suffer the posturings of this fool.

"I was worried. I didn't see you." He scowled, as if maybe I had purposely rendered myself invisible.

"Here, let me take that." I reached for his briefcase with the best instincts of a bright, young flunky on the way up.

"Thanks. So, how ya doin', ol' buddy?" He smiled painfully, as if his hemorrhoids were acting up.

"Doing better now that you're here," I lied with just the proper mix of humility and sincerity.

I kept trying to read the legend on the showy blazer patch.

"Hey, you're staring! Act like you've been off the farm before." He nudged me. "Pebble Beach," he said in an offhand way. "Souvenir of an old member-guest weekend. A real touch of class, don't you think?"

"Uh . . . yeah." Momentarily speechless, I choked back a laugh, recalling, in my imperfect memory, that Pebble Beach was a public links. No members—how could there be member-guest?

And, the blazer looked fresh off the rack. I could see where the tags and labels had been removed.

But, then, I supposed old souvenirs were probably a lot newer in California.

"Impressive." I chose the word carefully. Looking nervously around, I hoped desperately I wouldn't see anyone I recognized.

"Did you get the sticks?" Rush asked anxiously.

"Yeah. Gotcha all fixed up. You're gonna love this place," I enthused. "Old Slammin' Sam himself will be right there."

"Didja get the Pings and the Callaway driver?" he persisted.

I nodded. First time in my life someone had ever asked me to borrow a set of golf clubs. "Like I told you . . . the Callaway driver is mine. I won it, never used. The Pings are brand new, courtesy of the Ping salesman, personal demos, straight from the factory. Only been played with once or twice. He said if you liked 'em, he'd make you a deal."

"Did you check the color code? They are coded black, aren't they?"

Talk about beggars being choosers. Ping's color-coding system fits clubs to the individual player. They only have about ten colors to chose from.

"Uh-huh. They're the exact same clubs you hit balls with," I muttered.

"Regular shaft?"

"Yeah."

"Good, I pull-hook stiff shafts."

"So you said." I bit my tongue. Slicers sometimes have that tendency because they come over the top and smother the ball with the club face closed—a finer point of swing mechanics that I suspected would be lost on him.

"What's the bag look like? I mean it is decent isn't it? After all, we are going to play the Greenbrier."

"You're gonna use my own tournament bag. It's a Ping staff bag. The same as the regular tour pros carry. It's brand new. I won it, too, at the last Calcutta at my club."

"Thanks. I hope your bag's decent too. We both want to look respectable." He looked at me anxiously. "After all, the Greenbrier isn't some local muni track."

"Hogan staff model. Won it in my club championship a couple months back," I struggled to hold my temper. Boss or not, for a dubious twelve handicap, he was really getting on my nerves.

When he started claiming his luggage, I marveled at how much he'd packed for a four-day outing. Two large leather cases with the logo of an exclusive maker burnt into them. I collected the obviously new cases and started for the curb, but he stopped me. "Wait, my hanging bags aren't here. I'd better check with the agent."

"They're still off-loading, they'll show—" I had hardly gotten the words out of my mouth when I saw the two matching leather hanging bags moving on the carousel.

"Why don't you find a skycap? I'll bring the car around." With the two large golf bags already filling the luggage compartment, I had serious doubts that I had enough room in the car to fit in all his stuff.

By the time I brought the car, he was waiting at the curb. After some heroic manipulations we stuffed his luggage into the back seat with mine and forced the doors closed with our knees.

"Wait! I want to see the sticks," he said, as I started around to the driver's side.

"Sure." I counted to ten, retraced my steps and opened up the trunk.

"Ah, they're the blacks, all right." He admired the markings on the new Pings in the shiny-new bag. "You're right, the bag looks like the ones the pros use. Your bag's okay, too . . . I guess. I kind of wish my bag was more like Tiger Woods's. Black and white's sort of tacky, don't you think?"

Tiger Woods's bag advertised Buicks. I didn't dare tell him what I thought.

He dug into his jacket pocket and dangled a fancy bag tag in my face. "Maybe this'll help dress it up. What do you think?" He brightened.

I took a half step back and turned the slowly revolving tag so I could read it.

"Pebble Beach," I read aloud. "Impressive." My words trailed into the air as Rush stooped over and attached the bag tag. Then, to my incredulity, he fished in his other jacket pocket and came out with a second tag, bearing the emblem "The Dunes, Myrtle Beach, SC."

"That ought to get their attention," he said proudly. "Now, take me to the Greenbrier, my good man." He slid into the car.

Closing the trunk lid firmly, I got us out of there as fast as I could.

CHAPTER THREE

"Couldn't get the Caddy, huh?" Rush asked after we had made it through the city traffic and were past Salem on Route 311, the narrow rural highway heading up the mountain range that rises between Roanoke and White Sulphur Springs.

"Don't worry. The Greenbrier has plenty of caddies. You have to hire a caddy if you play there, but you can take a cart, too, if you want to ride," I said.

"No, no—the Cadillac. Remember, we talked about borrowing your brother-in-law's DeVille. It would have been a nice touch. I mean after all we are going to the Greenbrier."

"Oh? Oh, no, it didn't work out." I vaguely remembered that he had asked me several weeks ago if I knew anyone who had a fancy car. I hadn't taken him seriously. My company Buick was less than six months old. I was proud of that car. I kept it polished to a showroom shine. But, my self-esteem didn't depend on fancy cars.

Growing up, I had learned that charisma transcended the trappings of things like clothes and automobiles. My dad always managed to provide us with a good previously owned—sometimes as new as last year's model—family car. My brother and I always kept that car shining.

Dad played on the company team in the industrial baseball league. Playing industrial ball was a big deal back in the sixties and seventies. As a young man, he had played a season in the minors. A long-ball hitter, when he wasn't pitching, Dad played first base. His boss played right field. The boss drove his kids to the games in a brand new Lincoln Continental.

My dad's boss made a lot of errors and struck out a lot.

Our dad led the league in both pitching and home runs.

My envy of that fancy car disappeared when I noticed the boss's kids always wanted to ride to the games with us.

"Don't worry. We won't be the only guests arriving in Buicks or Fords. With all the corporate types at the convention, there will be a lot of company cars." I let out a tight laugh.

"I wouldn't want Dr. Ian Ferguson to think we're bums."

"Relax. We'll be better than most. Many of the big shots will be driving rentals anyway. I saw a lot of 'em back there at the airport picking up a Hertz or Avis or Budget ," I reassured him. "Don't sweat it. We pull up in front of the motor entrance, and hand the major-domo our keys. A bellman unloads our stuff. *Voila*! Two minutes after we arrive, everyone will assume we came in a chauffeured Rolls Corniche."

"Humph," he grudgingly conceded.

The drive from Roanoke through the Allegheny Mountains was spectacular. For a time, Rush fell quiet—awestruck by the vistas. He broke the silence as we started down the other side of Catawba Mountain. Catawba was the first of the four rugged ranges we had to traverse along the sixty-odd miles of narrow, winding road.

"What kind of threads did you bring?"

"A navy blazer and another suit," I answered vaguely, momentarily distracted by speculation over John Paul's express letter.

"No, no. I mean for the golf course," he snapped impatiently. "You oughta see the new slacks I bought before I left the coast. I got some shirts with the official Pebble Beach and Cypress Point logos. I picked up a few more from the Dunes at Myrtle Beach and at Pinehurst when I was working with the other reps. They're all Chemise Lacoste. That ought to be good enough for anywhere, don't you think?"

"Oh, yeah. Izod makes good shirts all right," I murmured as I stole another peek at his blazer patch.

"What did you bring for golf?" he persisted.

"Oh, don't worry, I brought plenty slacks and shirts for golf. I'm ready. Just hope the weather holds. It's cooler in the mountains." I ignored the insinuation that I might embarrass him. I'd never been called a slob around any pro shop, and that list included an impressive few.

"I brought some sweaters. They're Izod too. Those little alligators are a nice touch, don't you think?"

I had a premonition: it was going to be a long four days.

Rose had gotten me off on the wrong foot, and now I was getting more than a little tired of Rush. It took some effort, but I decided not to tell him that even though the alligator labels were currently trendy, they wouldn't correct his slice. I'd learned a long time ago that there was more to my golf game than the labels in my clothes. Nowadays, I carried a legitimate seven or eight handicap. In college, I'd played to a solid two.

I nodded absently, resisting the temptation to tell him I'd picked up a few spiffy new outfits at Wal-Mart.

"How're you hitting 'em?" I asked, trying to change the subject.

"Oh . . . well . . . you know, I haven't had a chance to play much since I moved to Charlotte. I hit some balls this weekend. It's like riding a bicycle and sex. Ben Hogan called it muscle memory. Has a lot to do with being born with natural athletic ability. You know I had a tryout with the Rams when I was in college . . . and I was on the selection committee for the Olympic synchronized swim team. That's where I met Nadine. All those horny half-naked women in the tryouts were swarming over me like flies. She couldn't stand it. Don't you dare quote me on that." He laughed. "Anyway, let's hit some balls this afternoon. I'm fighting a little too much fade. A fade's my shot. I used to be a right-to-left player, but a hook is hard to control. But I'm not worried. I'm cutting it a hair too much, but I'm hitting it a ton. Get me to the practice tee, and I'll straighten out the fade in no time. Hogan always played a fade, you know? Tiger's natural shot is left to right. Muscle memory never lets a born athlete down."

I had gotten a glimpse of him with a golf club in his hands on a recent visit when I took him to a driving range. His muscles had memorized a bunch of ugly shots.

"We'll have plenty of time to practice this afternoon," I reassured him.

I resisted explaining that there might be a slight difference between Tiger Woods's fade and his slice—like about a hundred yards, center cut. I was smart enough to know that giving the boss golf lessons is a shortcut to professional suicide. Besides, who was I to judge him? I'd lost count of the times he'd told me he shot eighty-one the last time he played Pebble Beach before he came east. I was impressed. He probably wasn't all that bad. I'd seen guys with worse swings who could shoot lights out.

"Good. And tomorrow morning before we play, too? I never go out on the course without hitting a few balls." He looked at me anxiously.

"Don't worry. I always try to hit a few balls before I play. I'd hate to cold-top my first shot into Howard's Creek with all that snooty luncheon crowd sitting up in Sam Snead's Grill at the Golf Club laughing 'til their sides hurt."

"Luncheon crowd?" He shot me a worried look.

"Oh yeah, Sam Snead's eatery overlooks the first tee."

"No kidding?" An aura of anxiety settled around him like a dark cloud, and he fell silent for a while. Slumping down in the seat, he folded his knees up against the dash into a sort of fetal position. It was a full fifteen minutes before he spoke again.

"God, I haven't been playing. I'd hate to make a fool of myself in front of your doctor buddies," he said.

"Don't sweat it. Hell, we're all in the same boat. Besides, it's no different than the smartass hecklers waiting on the first tee on Saturday at your own club."

"I guess."

"Forget all that. Who are those people to us anyway? My dad told me he saw the great Hogan himself cold-top a shot right there on sixteen tee in 1958, I think. Don't sweat it. The penalty for a bad golf shot isn't death. If you love the game, the Greenbrier courses are a joy to play. You've never seen such beautiful condition."

"Well now, don't bet on that. Don't forget, I'm used to playing Pebble and Cypress and Olympic." He brightened.

Forget? Fat chance.

"Well sure. Then you know what I mean," I replied.

I was happy to ride along in silence again. This conversation was beginning to remind me of walking through a Serbian mine field.

Finally, he straightened in his seat and ventured confidentially, "I'm going to tell you something, but you'll have to keep it under your hat for a few days."

"Sure." From his tone, I sensed he was about to let me in on something important.

"The company is going to send me to Harvard B." He paused for my reaction.

"That's great." I waited. I wasn't exactly sure what "send me" meant. But I certainly understood Harvard, and I thought the *B* stood for Business.

"I'm going to take a special three-month middle management course, and then I'm going to be transferred back to Teaneck," he said.

Teaneck was headquarters. I was dying to ask him who was going to be promoted to the vacant division manager post, but I was afraid.

"Aren't you curious who I'm recommending to take my place?" he asked.

"I was hoping it might be me," I admitted.

"Who else? Of course it's you," he laughed. "But there will be other candidates from the other divisions. And I'm sure there are some hopefuls in the home office who'd like to get back into the field. You're young and inexperienced, but you're a star. Everybody knows that. Still, I can't promise anything."

"I understand, but thanks . . . thanks a lot."

Just thinking about it, my heart was already pounding.

"The worst that will happen is that you'll be put at the head of the line for future promotions, even if there's someone political who's overdue that they have to slip into this slot. Old Rush is looking out for you, kid," he said and slid back down in the seat again. "Just make sure you don't let me down at the interviews. Show 'em I know how to pick 'em."

"Don't worry about that," I said.

"You have good taste in clothes, but it never hurts to make a better show of quality—always deal from strength," he pontificated. "Did ya notice my luggage? Hartmann."

"Huh? Oh, yeah." I squirmed, thinking about my beat-up leather duffle in the trunk, with my slightly threadbare cloth suit bag. Rush was obviously trying to tell me something.

"Take a squint at this." He waved his wrist in front of my face. Rush's expensive new watch looked like it might be the official timer for the Olympic Games.

"Real nice," I said, sliding my left hand off the steering wheel to remove my old reliable $39.95 Timex from view. I fervently wanted to tell him where to shove his goddamn Rolex.

"Fifteen hundred scoots! A real touch of class. If you're going to be management, you need to think more about your image. When they fly you up for your interview, don't screw up and make me look bad."

"Don't worry, I won't," I said.

Unless it's by comparison.

CHAPTER FOUR

Rush's new clothes and his ostentatious watch—and the way he invested so much importance in the appearance of the golf clubs, without a thought to the significance of his suspect skill in using them—set me thinking about the way I differentiated the relative value of things.

What were values, anyway?

Judging the worth of people, places, and things? The system—or more aptly the nonsystem—we use to measure the importance of things. The elusive concept we variously call quality or worth or style or good taste or, sometimes, just class.

Class?

A very elusive concept, indeed.

Like jazz, true class is an abstraction.

"If you have to ask, then you don't know what it is," Louis "Satchmo" Armstrong, the famous jazz trumpet player, was fond of saying when he was asked to explain jazz.

What would Satchmo have to say about Rush's costly watch and luggage . . . and the quiet elegance of the Greenbrier.

"Ah, man, class ain't got nuthin' to do with money. You either got it or you ain't," Satch would most likely have observed.

In the end, our personal value systems determine how we feel about ourselves. That's the true essence of class. Self-esteem is the most important thing there is.

Growing up is sometimes confusing for a boy, but even before I had entered Miss Northcross's first grade class, I understood that you should look beyond the moment and below the surface before you put a value on anything. And when it comes to people, you look for honesty and kindness and seriousness.

During my childhood my parents struggled to make ends meet. In those days, almost everybody we knew did.

I had no trouble seeing the advantages of having money.

My friend George Cornwell was my age, and his daddy owned the house we rented and the gasoline station next door, and he ran the big old country store across the road.

And, although my daddy worked hard to take care of us, I envied George because his daddy had a lot of money. George's daddy bought him Lionel electric trains for Christmas. He had a new bike with a light, a speedometer, and an electric horn.

My daddy bought my brother and me a second-rate Lionel knockoff, and my first bike was bought secondhand from Arnold Junior Overstreet's daddy. Although I knew my daddy had made a real sacrifice, I was still envious of George and ashamed of my hand-me-down bike because it wasn't new.

Even back then both the "haves" and "have nots" had something to teach me.

In contrast with the Cornwells, there was the Long family across the river.

Mr. Long had been laid off from the railroad. The Long kids didn't have any bikes—or much else for that matter.

I often wondered about how Mr. Long's kids felt.

Melvin Long was two years older than I was. His brother Charlie was in my grade.

The Long boys knew a lot about value. Once they rescued a broken pair of roller skates from the trash heap and made a wonderful racer with some cast-off two-by-fours, rusty nails, and a pair of wheels off a discarded baby carriage.

Secretly, I gladly would have traded them Arnold Junior Overstreet's secondhand bike for that homemade racer.

I'd never thought much about it before, but now, sneaking a peek at Rush's Rolex, I realized how much I'd learned from the Longs.

Sid, one of Melvin Long's older brothers, had suffered the ravages of some crippling disease and wore braces on his legs. Sid did odd jobs around the college and always liked to go to church dressed up in the preppy clothes the fraternity boys gave him. One Christmas someone from the college gave Sid a cheap wristwatch with a fancy dial. Sid was proud of that watch. It made him feel he was as good as anybody else.

Now, guiltily, I realized that even as a boy with Arnold Overstreet's secondhand bike, I'd still been a miserable snob. I remembered I had once embarrassed poor Melvin in high school by poking fun at him for having holes in his socks.

Thankfully, for a while Rush gawked, open-mouthed, as we traversed the spectacular view of the rugged Virginia mountains and valleys.

Inwardly, I smiled, watching him absently fondle his expensive watch.

"Tell me about this famous Dr. Ferguson. Have you met him?" I risked rousing him from his reveries. I wanted to get most of the business talk out of the way before we got there.

"No, but his paper on Virecta's coming out in the *New England Journal* this month—big news. Ian Ferguson, M.D., FACP, Edinburgh, Harvard, Duke, Emory . . . you name it, Ferguson's God. And, he's our ticket to fame and fortune."

I nodded. He didn't have to remind me.

"Teaneck says *Time* is doing a cover story. I wouldn't be surprised if they have a reporter here. Our research department wanted to pick up Ferguson's travel tab, but he refused. Funny, he wasn't too stuck-up to be tainted by our research grant. Last time I talked to Gert Kearns in Teaneck they were expecting the *Wall Street Journal* to break the story any day." Gertrude Kearns, M.D., Ph.D., was head of Severance's research. "By the way, I invested every spare dime I could scrape together in company stock. Better buy it now. After Ferguson reads that Virecta paper tomorrow afternoon, it'll be too late. Stock's going to go sky higher than a dot-com."

I nodded, uncomfortable at the thought of my relative poverty. I'd never bought any stock before, and against my conservative young wife's protests, I'd borrowed the staggering sum of one thousand dollars to invest. Two months ago, when the rumors of Virecta first leaked in the *New York Times*, my investment had doubled in less than a week. But, already my timid Rose was getting nervous, wanting to sell out while we were ahead.

"I didn't have much cash, but I bought all I could," I said, wracking my brain trying to think of where I could borrow some quick cash to invest behind Rose's back.

"I read somewhere that Ferguson was leaving Boston to head up a big research foundation. Where's he going?" I ventured, making idle conversation.

"Oh? I hadn't heard that. You sure?" Rush sounded doubtful.

"Pretty sure. But that was a few months back. *Time* or *Newsweek* or *Wall Street Journal* . . . *USA Today*, maybe," I said. "I can't remember the details."

"I have to call Teaneck as soon as we get to the hotel. I'll ask Gert Kearns about it."

"I wonder, does Ferguson play golf?"

"Bite your tongue! For godsakes don't ask. We don't want him to tell Teaneck we're goofing off. Besides, I don't want to get stuck with him."

His tone reminded me that I was on shaky ground. More than a little on the straight-arrow side, Rush had confided in me several times that he hadn't played much client golf as a sales rep in San Francisco because the country clubs were too exclusive and the doctors were too aloof. Besides, Nadine wore the pants. She was a couple of years older than Rush and very insecure. She saw to it that he kept his nose to the grindstone. Rush was terrified to let any of the troops see that he wasn't strictly a company man. But with me he let his hair down a bit. At odd times when he'd had a few drinks, I'd picked up enough from little confidences to know he'd cut a few corners like the rest of us.

When he first found out that a number of the other reps in our division played golf with their physicians and pharmacists, the idea bothered him. The salesman who lived near him in Charlotte told me he'd invited Rush to join him and two young pharmacists for a round on Saturday once—said Rush hit some good shots but was pretty erratic.

Telling me about it later, Rush had said that the Charlotte rep's wife invited him and Nadine over for drinks and dinner afterward but he'd declined. He said that Nadine was worried that the Charlotte man was going to try to "get social" and that Nadine was right when she said the best rule of management is familiarity breeds contempt.

Tight-assed Nadine Donald's hubby was definitely never going to be one of the boys.

"Look," he'd confided over a bottle of bourbon the last time he worked with me, "calling on doctors is the sweetest job there is. All I expect is that a man do his job. Socializing doesn't cut it with me. You got to make the calls to get the orders. I know all the tricks about goofing off. These guys can't put anything over on me."

Hearing him talk about it made me very uncomfortable.

"Well, it doesn't hurt to socialize a little. I'm top man in our division," I had responded defensively. I had a lot of long lunches at the club with doctors and hospital administrators and played business golf every chance I got. I saw no virtue in hard work if you could get the business and have fun too.

"Maybe. But give the average salesman an inch and he'll take a mile. If those other guys had it their way they'd be lying by the motel pool or out on the golf course every day." He had poured me another drink. "Besides, you have to realize that men like us are different. I see the way you move around that University Club with your doctor buddies, but how many men in the ranks of pharmaceutical sales do you suppose can do that? You and me, we work smart, use our heads."

Slowly, I was moving up in status, the rising star. My prestige in Teaneck was a known quantity. I sensed that Rush was smart enough to keep me happy.

"Sure. But I thought it might be good politics if Herman Asbury and the people in Teaneck knew you'd rubbed elbows with Ferguson on the golf course. If you get my point?" I tried to explain.

"It could backfire. Listen, Herman Asbury doesn't know jack shit about golf. And, Ferguson? Most of these academic types wouldn't know one end of a driver from the other." Rush slowly shook his head. "Let's pay our respects. Make sure Ferguson is taken care of, then keep our distance. I wouldn't want him to take any stories back to Teaneck that we were down here playing instead of looking after the store. Besides, we already have a match with those hotshot young doctor friends of yours, Max, the one I met at the University Club. Does he know you wrote that *Reader's Digest* article about what simple shits the docs are?"

"Probably not. That article's ancient history . . . been over four years now. Besides, if Max did actually read it, he saw it in *Harper's*. Max is one of the new breed of doctors. He likes opera. He wouldn't be caught dead with the *Reader's Digest*. I'll bet he could even discuss Mencken with you. Ask him. What the hell! I like the guy. We play golf, but he understands I work for Severance. He knows I need his support."

"My jury is still out on Max. I don't know if I really trust him. He's something of a smartass. Let me have a couple of drinks with a guy, and I'll tell you whether you can trust him."

"Too bad. Max never touches the stuff."

"That's my point! Never trust anybody who's afraid to take a drink."

I decided to let that one pass.

Rush sat up straight again. "How do you spell his last name?"

"Huh?"

"Bergmann. How do you spell it?"

"B-E-R-G-M-A-double N."

"That's what I thought. I'm surprised. I mean he's a member of the University Club . . . and your country club, too. Right?" He peered across at me.

"Yeah, right." I didn't exactly know what I was being asked. Or if I were being asked.

"Are all the clubs in Roanoke like yours?"

"What do you mean?"

" 'Bergmann' sounds Jewish to me."

"So?"

"Do all the local country clubs take in Hebes?"

"Hebes?"

"C'mon. Kikes. Jews."

"Jews? Sure. Why not?"

He ignored the question.

Bigots make me very uncomfortable and, job or no job, I didn't like having to act as if his bigotry didn't bother me. Besides, now I was embarrassed. I'd heard recently that one of the oldest, most prestigious country clubs in my area had never admitted Jews.

"Max Bergmann went to a Seventh Day Adventist medical school in California," I volunteered, ashamed that I felt it necessary to dignify this line of conversation.

"SDAs are worse than Jews. At least a Hebe will take a drink," he grumbled and settled back in his seat again. After a while he said, "Now that I think about it, Ingrid Bergman was Swedish. I have a hard time figuring names out. Max's buddy Cavanaugh is Irish; you can bet on that. Probably drink you under the table. What's he like?"

"Oh, I don't know. Sam Cavanaugh's about your age. He's new. Max told him you were a great guy. They're both looking forward to playing with you," I lied.

Sometimes a man will stoop really low to get ahead.

"This Bergmann. Is he pretty good on the golf course?" Rush persisted.

"Oh, we play about even. Max's very competitive. Obsessive, almost like—" I nearly slipped and said, "like me," but I caught myself. "He practices almost every day. I heard he shot even par on the back nine the other week. Finished with a seventy-six. I'm not supposed to know that. My spies told me not to give him any shots."

"Even par? What have you gotten us into?" Rush croaked. "God, he's out of our league."

"Oh, don't worry about Max. The last time I played with him, I cleaned his clock," I laughed.

"What did you shoot?" Rush shot me a suspicious look.

"Oh, probably somewhere around eighty," I hedged and decided to let the matter rest.

CHAPTER FIVE

Inevitably, Rush roused from his silence again. "Fill me in on those after-hours gambling joints you were telling me about."

He'd often complained how he missed traveling to Vegas and Reno and bragged about how good he was at the blackjack tables. In an unguarded moment, I had mentioned that I'd visited two private gaming clubs in the general vicinity of the resort.

As in every place where gambling remains off the statutory books, private after-hours clubs have been operating virtually unmolested predating the Prohibition era. Since the grand old spa attracted the crème of high-roller clientele from all over the world, it was only natural that entrepreneurial gambling interests would avail themselves of the opportunity to provide these urbane epicures some clandestine extracurricular excitement.

In my own travels I'd visited two such clubs. They operated out of magnificent old hunting lodges built on the heights overlooking the Greenbrier River gorge where the stream snaked its way through the valley. Their architecture reflected a bygone age, echoing names like Gould, Morgan, Vanderbilt, and Rockefeller—legendary robber barons who'd built exotic hideaways in picturesque, out-of-the-way places all over the world. They were mute evidence that this remote valley had always been a sort of Shangri-La, tucked into a wrinkle in the fabric of time, unaffected by wars and economic upheaval in the outside world.

I'd made the mistake of telling Rush that a few traveling men such as myself, who went to the Camellia Club strictly for the dining room, were encouraged, even given preferential treatment since we became part of the cover. Early on, I had discovered that, while my expense account couldn't afford to put me up at the Greenbrier, I could stay nearby in historic Lewisburg at a quaint old inn and drive the few miles into the river valley to eat dinner at the Camellia Club. The food was surprisingly good and the cost for drinks and dinner was affordable, but there was wide-open gambling in the back. Maintaining the appearance of a legitimate eating place was an important pretense in a state where casino operators were members of the local volunteer fire departments.

"Are you going to take me to the Azalea Club and introduce me to your buddy Charlie? Anyone can play at the tables, can't they?" Rush asked.

He meant Camellia, not Azalea. I'd gotten to be a favorite of Charlie Zaharias, the owner of the Camellia Club, and always ate there when I was in town. It was slow in the early evening, and the drinks were free in the back rooms. Charlie liked to keep up the appearance that the action was ongoing. He understood that I couldn't afford to gamble, and just for fun he sometimes took me in the back and gave me a handful of chips. The couple of times I came out a few bucks ahead, he laughed and said, "On the house," when I tried to give the chips back.

Charlie was a true gentleman. He treated me like an old friend. On one occasion he'd introduced me to a highly ranked tennis pro and the tennis star's famous lawyer-agent. I'd always treasure the memory. In my naïveté, I supposed I could be excused for telling the tale to Rush. But, secretly—fervently—I'd hoped he'd forgotten. I really didn't want to be driving him around in the hills along the wild Virginia-West Virginia border in the middle of the night, hopping from one remote gambling hideaway to another.

"Well?" he persisted.

"Huh?" I pretended to have missed the question.

"The Azalea gambling joint? I'd love to try the action. Could you get me in?"

"Maybe. I suppose I could try. But it's Camellia, not Azalea." I said, reluctantly.

"Good. I miss my trips to Tahoe. I wouldn't mind playing a little blackjack while we're here. Make our golf expenses, maybe." His voice brightened.

"Would you look at that!" Trying to divert his attention, I pointed out the window as we topped the mountain range. The view was absolutely breathtaking.

I had the uneasy feeling I hadn't heard the last of his interest in the gambling tables.

The road from Roanoke to White Sulphur Springs was a narrow, twisting, rugged roller coaster traversing a remote rural panorama through the heart of the southern terminus of the Alleghenies. A kaleidoscopic montage of weathered farmhouses of uncertain vintage balanced precariously on a patchwork of tiny rolling fields hand-hewn out of the steep forested slopes of the mountain wilderness, the vistas always reminded me of paintings by Hopper or Homer, with a hint of N. C. Wyeth and storybook trees and clouds by Maxfield Parrish.

Occasionally we passed an island of prosperity with white fences and fancy horses, but mostly there was a widely scattered sprinkling of plain buildings, with a few cattle, hogs, and sheep enclosed by rusty barbed wire strung on gnarled, hand-cut locust fence posts.

This feast for the senses was a landscape rendered in earth pigments on rough homespun canvas.

With the windows open, my senses were brought to a fine tune by the smell of honeysuckle mixed with manure and mowed alfalfa raked in neat rows standing ready to be hauled to the haymows of the ancient barns.

The sweet counterpoint of songbirds made me glad to be alive. A breeze wafting across my face reminded me that I'd promised my young son we'd go shopping for a kite.

Thinking of Paul, my thoughts turned to the last time I had laid eyes on John Paul Silver, four years ago in Bosnia—the drunken day I had told him about the Greenbrier.

Fleetingly, my curiosity wandered to the envelope stuffed in my briefcase.

CHAPTER SIX

After perhaps an hour of painstakingly negotiating the narrow switchback roads, we'd made it across the second mountain range. The trip about halfway done, we had just crossed the floor of the deep valley and passed through Paint Bank, a modest collection of houses, a few businesses and a convenience store with an island of gas pumps.

Just past the last store, the road turns sharply up the mountain. After perhaps a half-mile up the long grade, we came upon an ordinary-looking man dressed in plain khaki pants. His tie was loosened, and his sweat-soaked white business shirt was clinging soddenly in the hot, humid air. His thinning hair was almost white. Carrying, with obvious labor, a beat-up, faded red, two-gallon gasoline can, he trudged wearily up the steep mountain road.

A proud, sturdy figure, he was not exactly a fancy dude, but clearly he was not a local either. He could have been a tractor salesman, a county agriculture agent, or a school principal right out of a Norman Rockwell cover for the *Saturday Evening Post*. As we passed, he could see our back seat was jammed to the roof with baggage, and he gave us a nod and a rueful smile.

Out here, this unlucky pilgrim presented a forlorn figure in a strange land. It gave my heart a tug to see him alone and stranded so far out from civilization. I topped the rise, but before he slipped out of my view I slowed the car, feeling guilty for not stopping to give him a ride.

"What's the matter?" Rush moved quickly to an upright sitting position when I slowed the car.

"I hate to pass up that poor guy carrying the gas can. That could be me, someday . . . any day. It could be us, even, later on today," I said.

"Didn't you see how he was dressed? The guy's a bum."

"A bum? He looked okay to me. You wouldn't expect him to be wearing a suit jacket if he had to hike for gas."

"He's some local farmer. Where would we put him anyway?" Rush snapped angrily.

"I could get out and wait here while you took him to his car. Then you could come back for me. I'm sure his car's not far. We're early. Wouldn't take all that long."

Rush sniffed. "Don't be ridiculous. We don't really have room. Somebody will pick him up. Never pick up strangers. The papers are full of cases where good Samaritans get mugged or murdered. Forget the Samaritan act. Drive on."

Reluctantly I pushed the car back up to speed, but I didn't feel at all good about it. It was absurd to imagine anything sinister-looking about the man. I couldn't help but think back to one Saturday when I was about six. A man wearing dirty overalls and driving an old truck stopped by our house to see my daddy. I followed at a respectful distance when they walked out to the back yard. I sat quietly with them under the apple tree in the glider and listened while they talked baseball and drank iced tea from tall jelly glasses.

"Who was that man, Daddy?" I asked when the man's truck pulled out of the driveway.

"That was Mr. Tolley, the president of the college, Son," my daddy answered.

"Aw, Daddy, that man didn't look like no college president. Who was he, really?" My daddy hadn't gone to college. I thought he was kidding me.

"No fooling," he assured me. "You can't judge a book by its cover. And it's not correct to say *no* college president, it's *a* college president, Son. Your mother taught you better."

I knew my daddy loved me and that he believed that we men had to stick together—he'd told me that often enough—but sometimes it was hard to figure whose side he was on.

"He doesn't look like *a* college president," I grumbled. "When they see him wearing overalls, how can people tell he ain't a farmer like he looks?"

"At lunch time someday, if we walked down Main Street where a lot of the men have on regular coats and ties, do you think you would have been able to figure out that he was the one who is college president?" my daddy asked me. "Do you think Reggie Jackson wears his number forty-four when he goes downtown in Chicago? If I wore a baseball uniform with forty-four on my shirt, it wouldn't make me Reggie Jackson. Besides, Logan, Mr. Tolley's sort of a farmer, too." He laughed, and his eyes twinkled.

"You didn't tell me that," I pouted, but I knew he had a point.

"And Logan, if your mother hears you saying 'ain't' you're in deep trouble. *Ain't* ain't correct. I didn't have to go to college to learn that." He winked.

"I know, Daddy." I giggled and hugged him around the legs.

I knew that telling Rush that story would be a waste of time.

Still feeling bad about passing up the opportunity to help the man, I had driven on for perhaps a mile when we came across a dusty, old, sun-faded black—and battle-scarred—Chevy sedan temporarily abandoned at the side of the narrow two-lane. Instinctively I slowed to pass and was almost by when I noticed the familiar M.D. emblem mounted on the Massachusetts license tag. There was a small faded square sticker on the back window that bore the legend, UNIVERSITY HOSPITAL—MEDICAL STAFF, followed by the numeral 25.

"Did you see that? I'll wager that poor guy is a doctor. He's headed to the convention. I'd bet on it." I slowed the car looking for a place wide enough to turn around.

"Oh, jeezus, Logan, be serious. You're not going back to pick him up? For all we know that car is stolen or more than likely some old trade-in that belonged to a physician years ago. Didn't you get a look at him? That man's just a local redneck. Certainly didn't look like a doctor to me," he fumed. "You've got to quit playing good Samaritan. Which reminds me, you're spending a lot of time on the crippled children's ward at the hospital again."

I chose to ignore his comment about the crippled children's ward. I'd made the alcohol-fueled blunder of confiding my war story about the Bosnian baby with the missing hand.

"The car had a sticker that said University Hospital. It would be very embarrassing for him to come by our booth and see that the two representatives for Severance Laboratories had snubbed him on the road. Just imagine what that would do to sales. We aren't the only company that makes steroid hormones and antibiotics, you know."

"Shit!" Rush grudgingly conceded. He knew I had a point.

Ignoring his irritation, I turned into a narrow fire trail and backed out and started off down the mountain to where we'd seen the man.

We drove in silence, Rush pouting like a two-year-old.

When we rounded the curve at the top of the steep grade where we had first seen the man, only four or five minutes had elapsed. We were in time to see a well-used old pickup truck pull out onto the road and start toward us. When we passed the truck, the man was sitting in the truck bed on a sack of livestock feed, with the gas can wedged firmly between his feet and the tailgate.

"That was a waste of time," Rush sneered.

Without dignifying the remark, I turned around again and started back. When we passed the truck, the man looked at us and waved and smiled—a broad acknowledgment that he understood we'd come back for him. I gave him a little salute and a smile as we went by.

Rush rolled down the window and really hammed it up with a rousing thumbs-up sign right out of an old John Wayne war movie.

"I guess he can't say we didn't give it a good try," Rush said, obviously relieved that we didn't have to play Samaritan after all.

"Let's hear it for the *Spirit of St. Louis!*" I muttered.

"Huh?" My sarcasm was lost on him.

"Oh, nothing. You just reminded me of Lindberg."

"Lindberg? What are you talking about?"

"*We*," I said. "Lindberg wrote the book."

"Huh?"

He still didn't get it.

I shrugged, my annoyance subsiding.

"You're right, it does have an M.D. emblem, and the sticker says University Hospital all right. It's a Massachusetts tag. But it doesn't look like a car that any doctor worth his stethoscope would drive," Rush said, when we passed the abandoned car again.

I kept my attention on the steep, curvy road.

CHAPTER SEVEN

"Not far now," I said, pointing out the boundary sign as we crossed into West Virginia. "You're not going to believe this place. It's like another world. Back in Snead's heyday, the first hole on the Old White Course and number ten on the Greenbrier Course were on Robert Trent Jones's famous dream eighteen."

"Speaking of famous courses, I was working down at Pinehurst with Bobby Turner a couple of weeks ago." Turner was the new salesman in Raleigh. "Bobby took me over to the pro shop at the club. I bought some shirts and a blazer patch with the Pinehurst emblem on 'em. Same thing in July. I took Nadine and the kids to Myrtle Beach when I worked with Jimbo James. He drove me around the Dunes Club. What a place. Got some more shirts in the pro shop there. Ever play those courses?"

"Yeah. I've played the Dunes. Pinehurst, too. We exhibited at state medical society meetings at both places. Mort Clare let me work those meetings last year as sort of a reward for being top salesman. There's nothing on this earth like Pinehurst Number Two. Too bad you missed the Open back in '98, and the Dunes is a famous early Robert Trent Jones course."

"The Dunes is a Trent Jones course?" Rush was surprised. Trent Jones was another of Rush's heroes.

"Yeah, looks like a freaking ad for fertilizer. I love Jones's sense of fairness." I nodded, recalling the last time I'd played the Dunes. "He sets a course up so the fairway bunkers clearly establish the target areas from the teeing areas. It's a trademark. But the payback is his reverse cat-and-mouse game with the use of oversized bunkers in the landing areas in front of those huge greens. Plays hell with your depth perception. Jones is the golfer's architect . . . keeps you guessing all the time. You wouldn't believe number thirteen. Par five over water. Famous. Still on every top-eighteen-hole list I've seen." My voice trailed off as I remembered.

"Is the Dunes as good as Pinehurst?"

"Pinehurst is in a class all by itself. At Pinehurst, the Number Two Course is one all-American hole after another. There the rough is mostly bare sand, pine straw, and tree roots. And the freaking love grass. If you've never seen love grass, it's right out of hell. If you're not in the fairway, you're in jail," I said, recalling some frustrating adventures I'd had playing my errant shots out of the tall pines.

"Yeah. Turner drove me by it. I never saw so many pines," Rush admitted. "But, tell me about thirteen at the Dunes."

"A freaking monster. But fair. Robert Trent Jones gives you hard choices. You can take as much or as little of a risk as you feel up to," I said, remembering vividly. "The hole's almost a full horseshoe to the right around a huge lake. A wide, marshy inlet cuts across the fairway about two-twenty-five in front of the tee. Not even King Kong can drive across that water . . . takes a carry of perhaps three hundred fifty yards. Depending on the wind, which is always blowing from some direction down there, you have to lay up off the tee with anywhere from a three iron to a five wood. Better not get careless either. Standing there looking at that little tee shot can lull you right to sleep. You've got to be very, very straight off the tee. The lake runs all the way down the right, and there is a swamp to the left. If you hit the perfect tee shot and are right center of the fairway a few yards short of the inlet, then you've got to make up your mind. You can take the safe way and hit a five or six iron into the fat part of the fairway across the inlet and leave yourself a shot of one-eighty to one-fifty straight between the bunkers to the green. Or, if you're feeling bulletproof, you can bite off a tad more and hit anything from a deuce to a four wood to the fairway further up near the bunkers and leave yourself somewhere between an eight and a wedge for your third. Then, there's a third choice for the very brave or the goddamn fool—bite off about a two-fifty carry and go for it over water. The really good player can be rewarded if he hits two perfect shots. If you have the *cajones*, you can get really close in two and have only a little flip wedge left. The first time I played it, a guy in the foursome ahead of us dumped four perfectly hit three woods in the water trying to carry that inlet," I laughed, recollecting that day.

"Sounds like a real ball buster. I mean, if you really catch it, can you reach it in two?" Rush was enthralled.

"I seem to remember that somebody told me Mike Souchak had once gotten home in two, and with today's new equipment, I'm sure players like Tiger and Davis Love III could get home if conditions were right. But believe me, the smart player will take a par and walk to the next hole feeling like he'd dodged a bullet."

"Old Mort set you up with an opportunity to play the Dunes and Pinehurst the same year, and on the company ticket? You know the company frowns on that sort of thing." Rush didn't approve of old-timers like Mort—he was just plain jealous. Mort was a legend. All the salesmen had loved him. This spring Mort had dropped dead of a heart attack. Rush had been promoted and moved from the coast to take his place.

"Did Mort play golf with you down there?"

"No way! Mort was no golfer. He set me up with some doctors he knew. Mort knew everyone. He was a great guy," I observed fondly.

"People keep telling me," Rush begrudged. "What'd you think of him as a manager?"

It was a loaded question. I always felt uncomfortable when Rush wanted to talk about Mort. He knew he was living in Mort's shadow.

"Everybody busted ass for him." I made the point carefully.

"From what I've seen, Mort let some of 'em get by with murder. Familiarity breeds contempt. You're young. If you get into management, remember that. We're not running a fraternity, you know," he said, a little too emphatically.

"Yeah, they taught us that in Officer Candidate School," I said. "The military ain't exactly like a fraternity either, but a little team spirit never hurts when you're getting shot at." I wanted to remind him that even though I was a few years younger than he was, I was a reserve army officer and had also served as a news correspondent in combat. "Maybe Mort was soft, but before he died, his division led the nation four years in a row," I couldn't resist reminding him.

"Yeah? Well . . . " He let the thought die unvoiced, scooted down, and folded his knees up against the dash again.

"Here we are," I said as we came up on the outskirts of White Sulphur Springs. Main Street would have made a great location for the remake of *Coal Miner's Daughter*.

"My god! Is the Greenbrier actually part of this dump?" Rush asked.

I laughed.

"Just wait. We'll be there in a few minutes," I promised as we rode through the unpretentious business district. "You're in for a real treat. In an hour we'll be wearing out golf balls at the practice range."

About a quarter of a mile up ahead I could see the beginning of the old covered CSX Railway station platform, which stands across the street from the Greenbrier entrance. Now Main Street had taken on a more respectable, middle-class residential look. On our right, the modest houses gave way to a high, meticulously manicured hedge, which shut out the view of everything behind it. This triggered my anticipation. It never failed. For me, in all the world there was no place like the Greenbrier.

When we drew opposite the railroad station, I turned in between the elegant white brick columns that marked the end of the well-kept hedgerow. In its understatement, the entrance to the Greenbrier was the epitome of hauteur, light-years beyond arrogance.

The simple script on the gateposts fashioned the legend THE GREENBRIER.

In the blink of an eye we were transported into another dimension of time and space.

Rush sat bolt upright, not speaking as we moved through the briefly curving arc between the high hedgerows. It was as if the ordinary world had disappeared behind us. Moving through a leafy tunnel, we approached a gatehouse. A neatly uniformed guard stood smiling as I slowed and stopped. I opened the window, and the security man leaned forward and said, "Welcome to the Greenbrier." After giving us brief directions, he straightened, smiled, and waved us in. "Enjoy your stay, gentlemen."

The wide vista of immaculately tended grass spread before us over the long mall leading down to the stately white-columned hotel, standing like a majestic Greek temple. For me, it was one of those sights of imposing elegance that never loses its power no matter how many times, or over how many years, the experience is repeated.

Except for his sharp intake of breath as we emerged from the overhanging bower of trees and he caught the first glimpse of the buildings and grounds, Rush still hadn't make a sound. Finally, as we made our way down to the entrance, Rush said, "Did you see how the security guard turned up his nose when he looked at the car?"

I ignored the remark and pulled up short, waiting in line while the drivers of at least four other less distinguished and obviously leased automobiles—along with several Cadillacs, two Jags, a Rolls, and a Range Rover SUV—were clogging the motor entrance area, debarking passengers and luggage. Everywhere liveried attendants in their green jackets busied themselves sorting out luggage and tagging golf bags, tennis equipment, several jumping saddles, and an array of fly rods and skeet guns—putting them all into separate areas for transport to the Golf Club or the stables or the gun club at the Kate's Mountain area.

It was all so real it was unreal.

Even the grass was a richer green.

The Greenbrier's aura of mystical brightness has always given me the feeling the entire place is an enormous sound stage, with spectral klieg spotlights placed high in the branches of the ancient trees. The Homestead, the Breakers, Hot Springs, Hilton Head, and the Grand Hotel at Point Clear are superlative. Even so, they will never quite have the same magic for me.

There is an absence of tiresome ostentation, no gauche posturing of wealth. The place is entirely devoid of phoniness or pretension; the overpowering essence of old money hangs in the air like the smell of old leather.

I could almost hear the apology of new money soughing softly through the towering oaks.

Up ahead, I watched spellbound as a vaguely thirty-something heather blonde with great legs slid out of a vintage Mercedes convertible.

Absolutely stunning.

Instantly, I was transported back to a time when Kate Cornwell, my boyhood pal's long-legged stepmother, had given me my first glimpse of the Greenbrier. Big for my age at fifteen, I already had a reputation for playing football and basketball. I had skipped a grade and would be a junior at the consolidated county high school. Kate Cornwell was half George's daddy's age. I couldn't help but notice that she was always squeezing my thighs and patting me on my butt. When she drove, she hiked her dress up so the tops of her silk stockings exposed the beribboned fasteners of her garter belt. In a world of pantyhose, she was the only female I knew who wore a garter belt. She had melon breasts and the longest legs I had ever seen.

It had been fourteen years since I spent that first memorable night here, sharing a big room with George and his stepmother. After George went to sleep, I lay there in the darkness beside him pretending sleep while Kate took a shower, parading naked around the lighted bathroom with the door half-open.

When she came out of the bath she closed the door, shutting out the light and, with moonlight drifting through the window, she bent and kissed me. Then she had urged me silently into her bed.

Sitting there now, looking at the blonde, I felt an insistent stirring in my crotch as the memory came flooding back over me.

"Jeezus, look at those cars . . . and the golf equipment. Judas priest! See that? A goddamn Bentley? No, by god, a freaking Silver Cloud! We look like a couple of bums," Rush stuttered.

"Relax. We look just like everyone else. Look up ahead; there's a Toyota, a Ford, and a Chevy, last year's model."

63

"But, look at those golf bags . . . all leather. Oh, wow!"

"Yeah, and I see at least four that look worse than my old Sunday bag that I carry back home late afternoons for exercise. Don't be blinded by the fancy stuff. Chances are their owners can't play a lick."

Rush fell silent again as I let the company Buick inch slowly forward each time a car was chauffeured away to the parking area by one of the attendants. There was a quiet efficiency about the happy confusion taking place ahead of us, and all through it money was being passed from hand to hand like a greengrocer peeling the outer leaves from yesterday's lettuce heads.

Finally we reached the entrance portico, and I pulled the car to the curb. Leaving the engine idling, we both got out. I stood by the door while Rush moved to the curbside under the overhang, waiting nervously for our turn to be helped.

I suspected he didn't want the Bentley owner to see him near a Buick.

A tall, distinguished gentleman in a business suit came out of the hotel and moved around the orderly stacks of golf bags and sports equipment until finally he located whatever it was he was anxiously looking for. When he straightened, I saw him fix Rush's green blazer in his gaze and size him up. Then, he stepped across some golf equipment and touched him on the arm.

"My good man," he began and extended Rush a folded ten-dollar bill.

Rush stiffened, obviously taken aback.

Speechless and red-faced, Rush pointed in the direction of the old black man in the major-domo's coat.

"Ah. So sorry, old sport! But thanks ever so much." The man made a stiff little bow, turned, and started off in the direction of the major-domo.

When the man left, Rush's hand moved self-consciously to hide his blazer patch.

He glanced across to see if I'd caught the embarrassing exchange.

When he walked over, I didn't even crack a smile. Thoroughly occupied with waiting, I gazed off into the summer afternoon.

Rush reached in the car and found his briefcase.

"Boy . . . boy, over here," I heard someone call to a bellman. Rush's head snapped around in a knee-jerk reaction. Sheepishly, he regained his composure and glanced back toward me.

I pretended to remain oblivious, but it was all I could do to keep a straight face.

"No use my standing here. I'll go register for us both and check on Dr. Ferguson." He looked back across the top of the car again before he closed it. "Don't be chintzy with the tip. This is a class place," he ordered, anxious to take command.

"Okay, I'll find you," I replied, well aware who the cheapskate really was.

He looked nervously about, drew himself up straight, and walked inside.

My hero.

In no time, a green-jacketed attendant had efficiently unloaded our luggage onto a rolling cart and taken the car away. I explained to the waiting attendant that we might want to go to the practice range as soon as we were settled in. He tagged the golf bags and placed them in one of the stacks along with others waiting to be moved to the Golf Club. Experience told me that it wouldn't matter if it were within the hour; they would be waiting when we presented ourselves for practice.

In the lower lobby, Rush had moved away from the registration desk and was standing apart with his mouth slightly agape, awed by the quiet elegance.

"Not bad," he croaked as I approached, making a broad sweep of his hand, trying hard to act blasé. Standing on the giant black-and-white marble checkerboard floor, he looked Chaplinesque in his green blazer with the pin-on patch.

"We all set?" I asked.

"Yeah. They said that a bellman would be with us right away." He handed me a registration packet.

"What about Ferguson? He here yet?" I asked.

"No. He hasn't checked in," Rush replied.

"Leave our room numbers for him. He can call when he arrives," I suggested.

"Good idea," he conceded.

"Mr. Donald?" A bellman appeared. "If you'll help me find your luggage, I'll show you to your room, sir. Just follow me."

Before I could blink, another bellman was at my elbow. We were quickly on our way.

The elevator reached Rush's floor first.

"I'll meet you in the exhibit hall in about thirty minutes. I want to check and make sure our exhibit is here. I'd like to get it set up this afternoon and get all that out of the way, okay?" I called as he followed the porter down the hall.

As soon as the bellman had deposited my stuff in the room I quickly unpacked. I had completely forgotten about John Paul's letter until I started to hang up my jacket. I debated opening it but placed it on the desk, determined to beat Rush down to the exhibit hall.

Changing into a pair of charcoal golf slacks and a white golf shirt, I draped a pearl gray alpaca sweater across my shoulders, sleeves dangling down across my chest. The sweater had my tiny monogram in a darker gray. In a twinkling, I had transmogrified into the mysterious celebrity playboy, just flown in by corporate jet for a golf outing.

I took one approving look in the full-length mirror and headed downstairs to the mass confusion of the exhibit hall.

TUESDAY AFTERNOON AND EVENING

CHAPTER EIGHT

In the convention center, the hotel crews were hard at work.

When I arrived, the cavernous ballroom had the look of an elegantly chandeliered airplane hangar where the exploded pieces of the ill-fated starship *Enterprise* were being readied for reassembling.

As I made my way through the confusion, a few old exhibit crates were scattered throughout the hall, hulking above the more state-of-the-art paraphernalia like steles at Stonehenge. Stenciled THIS END UP and HANDLE WITH CARE, these outmoded relics required shipping in wooden crates twice as tall as king-sized Porta-Johns. Moving them from place to place was a major undertaking in scheduling, requiring heavy-freight carriers. Thankfully, the era of these awkward dinosaurs requiring strong backs and heavy equipment for setting up and taking down was mostly a bad memory.

Our Severance Labs exhibit backdrops were displayed on lightweight folding frames that collapsed into neat shipping tubes so small they would fit into automobile trunks and could be taken as luggage on airplanes, strictly space-age technology.

I went right to work, locating the manager of the hotel's convention crew, and putting twenty dollars in his hand.

Even at the Greenbrier twenty bucks still produced downright magic.

In short order, the efficient convention manager located my set of three impressive but lightweight display crates. Dispatching a neatly coveralled attendant to the mailroom to locate the five cartons of brochures, medical literature, and promotional giveaways that had been shipped to us care of booth 103, he assured me that our booth would be set up before I returned from the practice range.

Heading out, I bumped into Rush coming in. Struggling mightily to act unimpressed, he was still starry-eyed, gawking open-mouthed at the elegant surroundings.

"Oh, there you are. We're located in number . . . ah . . . " He flipped through a sheaf of papers he'd taken out of an envelope.

"Number one-o-three," I prompted and gently took his elbow. "C'mon, it's right over here. Were you able to get in touch with Dr. Ferguson?" I asked, leading him through the disorder of crates and boxes.

"No, but I talked to Gert Kearns in Teaneck. She said you were right about Ferguson leaving Harvard. Very hush-hush . . . something about a corporate position maybe. According to Gert, he's not talking."

As we negotiated the obstacle course of exhibits and exhibitors, Rush gave me a furtive once-over. By the way he opened his mouth to say something, had second thoughts, then closed it again, I could tell that my clothes passed his inspection with flying colors.

He had changed into golf slacks in a red Stewart tartan and an expensive, bright red golf shirt with "The Dunes Club, Myrtle Beach, SC," embroidered on the left breast. He kept looking back over his shoulder and down his front with the uneasy look of a man dogged by the notion he might have a wayward price tag sticking in some unexpected place. I had to turn my head away to hide my smile, remembering how the guest had mistaken him for a bellman. The long hall was lined with mirrors. Rush sucked in his belly as he stole a peek at his reflection. He was showing the beginnings of a tiny roll at the too-tight waistband. The effect was something on the order of an overstuffed chili pepper. Most of the convention clientele were doctors and salesmen, underexercised and overfed. All in all, Rush looked right at home.

"What a zoo! My god, we'll never find our exhibit in all this." He waved helplessly at the tangled clutter of packing crates and cylinders. Everywhere you looked, an army of neatly uniformed hotel staff was swarming like ants.

"Don't worry. It's all taken care of," I assured him.

"What do you mean?"

"Trust me. It's all arranged. Relax. You don't get a chance to visit the Greenbrier every day. C'mon, let's get out of here. Don't you want to have a look around?"

"We can't go running off without making sure our exhibit is here and in good shape. We have to . . ." Looking anxiously about, trying to put on his take-charge face, he was obviously at a loss as to what to do next.

"Trust me, Rush. I've taken care of everything. That's what you pay me for. Do you want to enjoy yourself or not?" I wheeled and walked away.

"Wait! Goddammit, wait! We can't leave like this." He caught up to me and pulled angrily at my elbow. "What's the matter with you? Aren't you going to help me?"

My patience was rubbing thin. "Rush, you're not listening. Take it easy. I've already located the display and supplies. It's okay. The booth is all taken care of. The exhibits open tomorrow morning at nine. Ours will be ready, and I'll be in attendance. Don't sweat it. C'mon, man, let's wander down to the Golf Club and wear out a few practice balls." I gently removed his hand from my elbow.

"Are you sure?" He seemed disappointed, somehow.

"I'm absolutely certain. Now, why don't we get the hell out of this freaking zoo?"

"Well . . . all right, I guess." He followed, glancing doubtfully back at the hall.

"C'mon, let me show you paradise." I struck out across the upper lobby, down the wide staircase to the shopping arcade.

"Let me stop by the desk and try Dr. Ferguson one more time."

He had to make certain I hadn't forgotten who was boss.

CHAPTER NINE

For the better part of the next hour I steered Rush on an informal tour of the Greenbrier.

An all-around labor of love!

We visited the movie theater and checked out the Old White Club to find out what time the band started playing. After window-shopping the posh boutiques in the shopping arcade off the lower lobby, we peeked in on the classic Roman-columned spa and pool before we walked down toward the Golf Club. Except for perhaps the Homestead a few miles across the mountains in Hot Springs, Virginia, I was convinced there was no place on earth to compare with the Greenbrier.

It was a perfect day with only little puffs of clouds. The air was sweet with the smell of newly mown grass and honeysuckle. After we passed the Laurel Tennis Club, we wandered over and watched a couple of Laurel-and-Hardy duffers sweating hard on the practice range. Chewing massive cigars, the comic pair was having a merry old time.

Their equipment was the very best money could buy. Ollie's bag tag read BERNIE FELDER over a logo for the Westchester Country Club. I couldn't see all the names on the tags on his partner's bag, but one was from the Breakers at Palm Beach. Both wore loud shirts. Bernie's slacks were printed with golf flags and his buddy's sported a pink-and-green check.

Bernie was having a hard time just getting the ball airborne. He kept cold-topping his shots, dribbling them twenty or thirty yards in front of the teeing ground, where there were perhaps fifteen balls lying in a ragged pattern.

His companion was fighting a terrible slice—a real banana ball.

Finally Bernie, who kept hitting the grounders, got the ball airborne and hit a half-decent shot.

Hardy cheered, "Way to go, Bernie. I hope you remember what you did on that one."

When we moved away and were walking across the wide parking area toward the Golf Club and pro shop, Rush scoffed, "My god, why do they bother?"

"Oh, I don't know. They looked like they were having fun. That's what it's all about. The first time I played golf, I must've taken about a hundred strokes. It got dark on me, so I had to quit on the fifth green without putting out." I laughed out loud, remembering—it was pretty much the truth.

"Did you see the way they were dressed?" Rush said with disgust. "I'd rather be caught dead."

I struggled to suppress a smile, thinking about his tack-on blazer patch.

Walking into the Golf Club, we made our way down to the pro shop. The walls were covered with pictures of Sam Snead, with and without celebrities—including several presidents.

Rush moved slowly around the shop soaking up the reflected glory.

Across the room, the striking heather blonde I'd seen when we arrived was browsing a display of straw hats. She looked vaguely thirtyish, which—given her apparent state of affluence—was probably more like forty-something going on fifty. Her devilish tennis skirt was designed to reveal an edge of lace on the pristine white panties that peeked from underneath. The flimsy silk jersey tank top struggled valiantly to restrain her marvelous monuments to the miracle of plastic surgery.

Those perky breasts and long tan legs sent me spinning off into a rich fantasy life. No matter her age, this patrician goddess was a splendid advertisement for whatever she'd been doing to be good to herself.

She caught me staring and, eyes a-twinkle, she smiled a little at the corners of her pouty mouth.

We're both irresistible, but don't let's breathe a word to another soul, the smile whispered.

"Didn't you tell me your sportswriter buddy introduced you to Sam Snead and his agent?" Rush was studying a picture of Snead.

"Alex Crim. Yeah, but that was in passing. Snead certainly wouldn't remember. I have met Alex Crim, though. She's a friend of my good friend Betty Farnsworth Gilbert. Betty's one of my heroes. She works for a doctor. I've had lunch with Betty and Alex in Roanoke a couple of times. Betty and Sam grew up in Hot Springs, a few miles east of here, across the mountains in Virginia. Sam's family worked around the golf courses at the Homestead. Alex Crim's a very nice lady and not at all stuck up."

"What's Alex look like? I heard Snead's pure hell with the ladies." Rush's voice carried across the rather crowded room. I edged away from him to examine a row of fancy golf bags, as people glared in our direction.

The resident pro frowned.

The heather blonde looked at me from the mirror where she was admiring a pert little Sam Snead straw model. She wrinkled her nose distastefully and rolled her eyes at Rush.

Red-faced, I moved across and touched Rush's arm.

"Alex Crim is a very handsome lady," I lowered my voice to a whisper. "And a good wife. Mr. Crim is a fine gentleman," I added, and quickly moved away.

Red-faced, Rush looked around and rededicated his attention to the photos on the wall.

When I looked again, the heather blonde was bending over a low shelf of golf shirts. The view was absolutely sensational.

Straightening, she caught me gawking and averted her eyes prettily. Then she wandered toward the steps, looked back, and smiled.

I was sorely afraid to check the unruly stirring at my trouser front. The show was obviously all for me. Just for a moment, I knew what it was to feel absolutely irresistible.

Rush dawdled overlong around the pro shop. I knew he was hoping that he might catch a glimpse of the ol' Slammer. I didn't have the heart to remind him that, movie or no movie, his hero spent most of his time home across the mountain in Hot Springs.

But I really didn't mind dawdling. I love browsing pro shops. For the moment, I was reminded there's none better than this one. Besides, a scattering of very good-looking women in shorts and designer frocks was browsing about. I lost all track of time.

Finally, because my fanciful preoccupations were threatening to raise embarrassing problems, I got Rush interested in hitting practice balls. A caddy appeared with our clubs on a cart, and we headed toward the practice area.

The crowd in the practice area had thinned, and the pair of chubby duffers we had watched on the walk down had just finished. As they passed by they gave us wide smiles, and Bernie waved and said, "Don't worry, we left a lot of good shots out there."

"Thanks," I smiled back. "I need all the good shots I can get."

On the range, I began as I always do, hitting three-quarter wedge shots at a fallen sycamore leaf I'd picked for a target about seventy-five yards down the range. Amazingly, the shots were smooth and crisp. After about five shots, I traded my wedge for the nine iron and glanced over at Rush. His rhythm was jerky and way too fast as, driver in hand, one right after another he was lashing at practice balls like a fat lady desperately bashing away at a pit full of rattlesnakes.

My dad once told me the legendary Jimmy Demeret said, "Show me a guy with a fast backswing, and I'll play him for a hundred bucks a hole."

"Oh, yeah!" Rush crooned as he hit one that only sliced at the tail end.

He looked over to see if I'd caught his act.

I smiled and nodded encouragement. Euphoric at being back at my favorite place, for the moment I forgave everyone for everything.

"See, that? Ben Hogan always played a fade just like that. Ben said a fade's easier to control," Rush crowed. He was actually serious.

"Yeah, I read that somewhere." I kept a straight face. "How do you like the new sticks?"

"Super . . . just super." He waggled the Callaway driver at me. "I was looking at a set like them before I left the coast. After we play a few rounds here, if you can swing a deal for me, maybe I'll buy 'em." He beamed and went back to killing rattlesnakes.

"Look at that. Looks like they should give us some shots tomorrow, Sam." A familiar voice interrupted my admiration of a particularly crisp little bullet that I'd sent flying off the face of my club. I'd changed to the nine iron, and the ball nestled close to another sycamore leaf target twenty yards further down range.

Max Bergmann and Sam Cavanaugh were in a cart.

"Rush, you remember Sam and Max," I reintroduced them.

They nodded politely, trying to hurry. By the time Max stopped the cart, Sam had already dumped some balls on the ground and was taking practice swings.

"Care to join us? We're off in fifteen minutes. We want to slip in eighteen before dark," Max asked, slipping into a new white golf glove.

"No. We have to meet someone." Rush blurted out the lie.

"Too bad," Max mumbled. Now, they both were hitting balls in the teeing spaces on the other side of Rush.

Around the pewter circuit, you learn real fast to separate duffer from golfer and both from real player.

Duffers are people who play at golf. Golfers take the game seriously and are not half bad at it.

Then there are players.

There is a quality, a certain something that you learn to spot right away. The way a person handles the equipment, and other indefinable things. If you've been around long enough, you take one look and your intuitive inner voice whispers, "player."

I looked up for a moment and watched as they both started to crank out crisp wedge shots across the meticulously manicured range.

Thwock!

There is nothing quite like the sound of a golf ball when it's struck dead-solid perfect.

Max was definitely a player, but I already knew that.

These two were in a hurry, but they were intent on a short but serious warm-up before they headed for the first tee. It was getting toward the late side of midafternoon, and my guess told me they were going to have to hustle to get in eighteen holes before dark.

Rush had stopped swinging and was watching the workmanlike way the two young doctors were mechanically cranking out efficient golf shots.

Thwock!

Now I knew for sure that Sam was a player, too.

After about twenty balls, Max stopped, walked over to the cart, and idly examined the tag on Rush's bag. "Pebble Beach! I went to med school in California. I've played all those courses at Monterey. They're spectacular. Are you from the peninsula area?" he asked, suddenly suspicious.

Rush waved in an offhand way. "Just up the road . . . San Francisco Bay."

Without a word Sam sidled closer and read the emblem on Rush's shirt.

He shot me a look. "The Dunes! Looks like they're trying to run a ringer in on us, Sam. Is that any way to treat an old friend, Logan?"

He turned back to Rush. "What's your handicap?"

"Uh . . . well, probably about a twelve when I left the coast, but I haven't been playing," he stammered.

"Looks like we got a hustler here, Sam." Max was baiting me.

I hit another shot. I wasn't about to bite.

"Whoa now," Rush protested, his face turning red. "Not me! I moved to Charlotte a few months ago, and I'm rusty as an old gate. Hitting it all over the place."

Poor Rush clearly didn't understand it was the ritual dance of making the match.

"Sounds like a con. I've run into a lot of you city slickers. Right, Sam?" Max turned to his partner. "We'll probably be needing about two shots a side tomorrow morning, Logan. Sam here used to carry a twelve, but that's ancient history. He's been in a two-year residency at Duke. You know medical residents don't have time to play golf. And back home you beat me like a clock. What are you down to now, Logan? A three?"

"Save the bullshit for someone who hasn't heard it, Max. You know I struggle playing to a ten. And I haven't been hitting 'em in the fairway lately." I chilly-dipped my next practice shot and gave him my best worried look.

"So sad," Max said, gathering up the extra clubs he had lying at his feet. He started moving toward the cart. "Sure you won't change your mind? We can get in eighteen if we hurry."

"How about it, partner?" I looked hopefully at Rush. I was dying to play.

"No, we still have work to do," Rush quickly shook his head.

"See you in the morning, then." They jumped back in the cart and headed off toward the first tee.

"Those guys swing more like pros than doctors," Rush said as he watched them leave. "I haven't been playing that much since I left the coast. Couldn't you have gotten us a game with some nice friendly amateurs who are about our speed?"

"They're not that good. I play with Max all the time back home. We play about even, and he's a nice guy. For a doctor who prescribes a lot of our drugs, he's a real nice guy. It's a business doing pleasure with him." I winked. "But don't worry. Tomorrow when we tee it up, no more nice guy. It's bloody war. Right, partner?"

"Yeah, sure," Rush agreed uncertainly before he turned and went back to hitting balls again. The sound of his club on the ball suddenly lacked the ring of enthusiasm.

I was still hitting the five iron. It was one of those rare times when everything was working. My shots were still crisp and straight and true. I was caught up in the sheer pleasure of the moment.

I noticed that Rush had stopped. When I looked up, he was watching me.

I grinned.

"Had enough?" I asked.

"Yeah, I'm feeling a little catch in my back. It hasn't acted up in a long time. I hope it isn't going to start now." He had an odd look on his face.

"No sense in overdoing it. Besides, you've spent all day riding in airplanes and automobiles. That's enough to make anybody's back stiff. Why don't you see if you can't get a rub in the spa?" I brightened at the idea.

"A rub? Oh, no. I'll be okay. Let's go back to the hotel and see about the exhibit. And I need to see if Ferguson has showed up yet." He put the clubs back in the golf bag.

We left the cart and clubs with the pro shop attendant, climbed the stairs, and exited through the old Casino, now Sam Snead's Grill. As we walked back out across the parking area heading for the hotel, the ratty old Chevy we'd seen parked beside the road on our trip across the mountains emerged into the sunlight from the overhang of giant oak trees lining the avenue leading down from the hotel. Making its way along the row of shiny-new cars, the road-worn clunker looked even more disreputable than when we'd seen it back there, abandoned alongside the country road.

When he passed, the genial driver waved and grinned recognition.

It was all so unexpected, so out of place. Both car and driver seemed totally foreign to the setting. We stopped in our tracks, turned, and watched as he approached the temporary parking spaces reserved for unloading near the entrance.

A half-dozen liveried attendants were busily loading a large collection of expensive golf equipment onto a van to be transported back to the hotel. This was routine ongoing activity. The equipment was the property of guests who had finished playing the courses and were scheduled to depart the following day. Attendants were always there, engaged in ferrying carts from the parking lot, loading and unloading equipment, and otherwise waiting to take care of arriving and departing guests.

Now, all at once a change began taking place.

Before the old rattletrap was within a wedge shot of the unloading area, a shock wave of recognition rippled through the cadre of attendants. Almost as a single entity, they dropped what they were doing and dashed toward the bag drop area, jostling each other in a race to see who would be first to attend to the man in the old car.

Rush and I both stopped dead in our tracks.

It was totally out of character for this courteous, well-ordered group to suddenly break ranks. The air of decorum at the Greenbrier was second to none anywhere, and it was rare to see any break in the dignified way the well-trained staff efficiently served the patronage.

Now, the area was alive with waving and laughing as this rabble ran to greet the car.

A small gathering of guests stood smiling at the celebration with amused curiosity.

It was something right out of a scene from an old Clark Gable safari movie—the familiar cinematic cliché of a happy gang of gun bearers racing to greet a beloved white hunter returning home from an extended absence. As the Golf Club porters jostled each other merrily, I could almost hear cries of, "Bwana, Bwana." I imagined the manicured flower beds along the immaculately paved areas replaced by a dusty tarmac and the classic white Casino building transformed into a dilapidated group of corrugated tin outbuildings standing beside a remote, red clay African airstrip.

Almost before the old car had stopped, the winner of the race was holding open the driver's door. The also-rans had the car surrounded. The driver emerged, still wearing the same seedy-looking khaki pants and the white dress shirt with the sleeves rolled up to his elbows. His run-over penny loafers hadn't seen a shine rag since the signing of the Constitution.

Totally oblivious to his lack of fashion, with no thought of apology for his beat-up car, the man enjoyed his great popularity among the staff. Calling the attendants by name, he greeted each warmly.

The attendant in charge lagged to the rear, showing great restraint, benevolently suffering the break in decorum by his overly eager charges. The major-domo stood on the periphery until the man pushed his way through the others to shake his hand and clasp him fondly about the shoulders.

The man handed the head porter his keys and stepped aside as they were passed to one of the attendants, who had been beckoned forward with a nod. This signaled the rest of the group to mind their place. Now, there was a marked straightening of jackets as a sense of comportment was restored. Expectant smiles remained on the faces as the trunk lid of the old car was opened.

I had to avert my face to hide my grin as the booty was revealed—an unbelievably disreputable canvas golf bag was held high like a priceless treasure.

The sorry condition of the bag was contrasted sharply because the set of clubs that it held were obviously new and unmistakably custom crafted. The poor old bag clearly had not been constructed for such a magnificent array of equipment. A time-honored saddle leather duffel was also extracted and, with two pair of well-worn golf shoes, was handed to the attendant who had shouldered the tattered golf bag.

The trunk lid was closed, and with a lot of waving the entire gang paraded the golf equipment back to the clubhouse. The chief attendant remained, patiently watching as the gentleman struggled mightily to extract something from his pants pocket with his right hand. Finally, he reached across with his left hand, grasped the side of the pocket, and managed to remove a green wad that looked for all the world like an oversized artichoke. The extraction of such an unbelievably large roll of cash had completely turned the pocket of his wash-faded khakis wrong side out.

I watched the benefactor peel off a large number of the bills one by one, pass them to the captain, and clasp him at the shoulder again. They shook hands before he wrestled his pants pocket back in place, waved to the crew, climbed back inside the old jalopy, and started back our way.

When the car pulled even with us, the man braked and leaned across the seat, calling out the window, "I say there, decent of you to come back to offer me a lift this afternoon. I was in a bit of a fix, you know." He spoke in cultured tones.

I nodded and smiled broadly.

"Happy to do it, sir. No problem at all," Rush, the born-again Samaritan, spoke right up.

"I don't suppose you would be looking for a game tomorrow? My partner and I have a starting time at quarter past ten," he invited. Up close, he looked to be in his late fifties.

"Sorry, we've already got a match," Rush replied curtly.

"Too bad. Glad to have bumped into you again . . . and thanks." The man straightened and let the car move forward.

As he pulled away, I noticed that, like the duffel bag, the luggage on the back seat of the car was made of fine saddle leather, but, like their owner, the bags had seen more than their share of history.

We stood there watching as the old jalopy rattled its way under the verdant overhang of trees leading back toward the hotel.

"What a boor," Rush said.

I held my tongue. Watching the happy reunion at the clubhouse had cheered me. I thought the man was courteous and friendly. Secretly, I was hoping that this might help Rush to understand that underneath all the elegance, the Greenbrier is a democratic place.

"Did you see that ostentatious wad of cash?" Rush looked at me with a reproving scowl. "You'd think he could afford a wallet at least. And the way he was dressed. Once a coal miner, always a coal miner. Nouveau riche! All the money in the world can't buy real class."

I wanted desperately to point out that the man's lack of pretension was a mark of true class. But by now I knew it would be a waste of time.

Rush turned toward the hotel. "C'mon, let's get our trunks. I'm dying for a swim in that indoor pool. It looks like an ancient Roman bath—depraved. Did I tell you I was on the selection committee for the Olympic sychronized swimming team?"

"Yeah, I believe you mentioned it." I pretended I had something in my eye.

We walked on in silence for a few minutes up the hill past the old springhouse nestled beneath a leafy canopy of giant trees. Whispering of an era when the guests rode horseback and their ladies wore organdy with ornate lace collars, the lovely structure enclosed the legendary Old White Spring. The circular, marble-columned miniature of a classic Greek temple had a little statue of a nymph dancing at the crown of its silver dome.

At the top of the rise, Rush stopped and looked back.

"Look at that. That's real class. You know, it makes me furious that a place like this, and at these prices, would allow someone driving such a junky car and dressed like a coal miner to register as a guest. That man's appearance and behavior is insulting to the other guests. What's more, I would think that they would have some standards about the quality of the golf and other sports equipment that the guests should be required to maintain." Rush was clearly bothered by the man's lack of pretension.

"I don't see why dress and equipment of other guests should bother you—"

He interrupted, "Of course, compared to most of the equipment back there, I guess we're fine ones to be complaining. I mean after all, our equipment isn't exactly all that great."

"Now wait a cotton-picking minute, Rush! Those Pings I borrowed for you are top of the line. No one—I repeat, no one here has anything better. What the hell's eating you?" I was really getting fed up now.

"Hold on . . . hold on. I don't mean to sound ungrateful. I know the clubs are okay. It's only that your golf bag isn't exactly up to standard. The bag you got for me is okay, I guess, but yours is just not top of the line. It's okay. Don't feel bad. I saw worse back there. I know you did the best you could. Did you see those dynamite new golf bags in the pro shop? I got a few hundred squirreled away. It might be a good time for me to pick up some great-looking equipment," he said, then frowned. "But I'd never be able to explain new golf clubs to Nadine."

"If you're ashamed of my golf bag, then act like you don't know me. It doesn't bother me that someone else's bag looks better. Do you think those attendants back there gave a damn about that old dude's ratty old Chevy or his tattered golf bag?" I couldn't believe that after having witnessed such an eloquent revelation of true self-esteem, it was still bothering him because my golf bag wasn't up to some of his phony, overblown standards. It was all I could do not to tell him where he could jam his shallow sense of values.

"Don't worry. You did the best you could getting me the clubs, and I appreciate it. Anyway, that guy makes us all look good."

"From the looks of the way he was greeted, I'd say that our friend has been a guest here more than once. With that wad of cash, he could damn well afford to buy a better golf bag and a Rolls Royce if he wanted to." I struggled to maintain my cool.

"Humpf! Money isn't everything," Rush sounded like a broken record. "Man's clearly got no class."

What could I say to that cockeyed logic?

Rush pouted in silence for the remainder of our walk back to the hotel.

"I'll see about Ferguson. Then I'll get my suit and go to the pool," Rush said.

"Meet you there in fifteen minutes." The prospect of seeing how he stuffed that belly into a pair of swimming trunks was fascinating.

CHAPTER TEN

By the time I arrived at the pool, most of the other swimmers were gathering up their towels and robes, ready to head back to dress for the cocktail hour.

Standing in formation in the shallow end of the pool, a lingering group of middle-aged women was going through an exercise drill with the stunning young spa instructor. Besides the exercisers, there was only a scattering of perhaps a half-dozen other men and women of assorted ages and descriptions in the pool. Rush was already in the water near the deeper end.

I waved, but he pretended not to see me. With a studied display of casualness, he climbed the ladder at the deep end and took a position at the pool's edge. No matter how hard he struggled to hold it in, his belly and love handles protruded comically over his skimpy Speedo racing suit. After a great drama of posing and lifting up on his tippy-toes, he turned around and attempted a terribly inept inward with a pike from the poolside—it's the dive the kids at the public pools call a back jackknife. He missed it badly and went in considerably short, knees bent and feet widely apart.

To anyone with half an eye, he'd never really been a diver.

When he surfaced, he looked over to see if I'd caught his act.

I waved.

He waved back.

"Come on in," his voice echoed off the lovely columns of the classic Roman setting.

I walked down to where he'd placed his towel and robe on a bench, took off my watch, and made a neat little pile of my own.

"I'm a little rusty," he called, a little louder than he needed, for the benefit of the sylph-like spa instructor. "I used to do a little diving."

Not much, I mused silently.

I walked to the deep end and dipped my toe in the water, testing the temperature. It had been a long time since I'd done any showing off in a swimming pool. I moved away from the edge of the pool and did a couple of springs off the bare tile, stretching to full height, then bending forward to touch my ankles. When I came back down, I lost my balance and nearly fell in the pool.

Rush had swum over to the ladder and was looking up at me with his mouth wide open. Witnessing my warm-up gymnastics, he saw that I knew my way around a swimming pool.

"Something tells me that I'm way too old for this." I smiled and walked back, turned around, and took a position at the pool's edge. I knew I was acting like an adolescent, but I was fed up with his insufferable superiority. I stood there for a few seconds, running my brain through the feel of the dive. Then I lifted up my arms, vaulted high, and nailed a perfect pike at the top. You allow your lift to carry the hips and feet outward so that when you reach the apex you bend forward, grasp your ankles, cradling your calves with your forearms and hands. Then you snap out without taking your eyes from a spot in the water about two feet from the poolside. That quick, fluid motion straightens the body as it follows the head and enters the water headfirst. It's a showy move. Even if you miss it a little, it looks spectacular.

I hit it dead on the button.

The spa attendant had herded her flock of women out of the pool. When I surfaced, they all clapped, and there were more than a few "oohs" and "ahs."

I waved.

The whole world loves a show-off—particularly the show-off.

Rush was still hanging on to the ladder when I swam over.

Finally he said, "You were a little over."

"Oh, well," I shrugged.

Too late now to worry about his recommending me for my promotion.

The spa instructor dismissed her flock and walked down to where we were. "That was quite athletic. You must've dove in competition?"

Her body was smoothly muscled and perfectly proportioned. Through her filmy white nylon jersey tank suit, I could see the ring of tiny little bumps around her nipples and the crinkly textured, faint shadowy triangle of her pubic hair. Each dark ringlet made a clear impression as if there were a group of tiny curlicues blind-embossed into the flimsy fabric.

A water nymph by Michelangelo.

A trifle older than I'd guessed. Still, she was a beauty—exactly what you'd expect for the classiest spa in the entire civilized world.

I wasn't exactly sure of her use of the verb *dove*, but I nodded and smiled. "A little," I said, "but I didn't have much of a career. I hit my head once, practicing alone. Lost my nerve. I'm Logan Baird, and this is Rush Donald. We're here with the medical symposium."

"Pru Sharpe," she said. "Too bad about the accident, but you're really too tall to have been a big-time diver, anyway. Still, I'll bet you were good." She smiled and moved over to the pool. With hardly a break in her stride, she sprang up and laid out a neat little front dive with a half twist that would have gotten her a best-supporting nomination in one of those old-time Esther Williams water ballet movies. When she broke water in front of the ladder, I applauded.

"Real nice. You've obviously done your turn on the springboard." I offered her a hand.

"Mostly good for showing off," she shrugged. "I'm late. Enjoy your stay. Hope I'll see you around." The water nymph grabbed her towel and trotted off toward the lockers.

The area was deserted now except for the lone figure of a woman standing down near the entrance. A flaming redhead, dressed in a khaki shirtwaist dress, she was striking. Pru Sharpe stopped and spoke before she finally moved on into the women's dressing area.

The redhead waved before she turned and left.

CHAPTER ELEVEN

When I went to check our booth, the display was all set up and ready to go. Even a pair of armchairs had been brought around, and the cartons of promotional literature were there, waiting to be unpacked. By the time Rush showed up about fifteen minutes later, I'd already opened the cartons and had almost finished laying out our brochures and other printed materials.

He didn't say hello, much less express any thanks for taking the problem of setting up the exhibit off his hands.

"No, no—let me show you." He started fussing over my neat stacks of printed materials, straightening and switching them a little here and there. Finally, after several minutes of that he stepped back to admire his handiwork.

"See?" he said with an air of proprietorship.

I wondered what he thought he'd contributed.

"The subtle art of merchandising. You'll learn after a while," he said.

I couldn't come up with a reply to that, so I changed the subject.

"What about Ferguson?" I asked.

"Oh! He's finally registered, but there's no answer when I ring his room. I left a message at the desk. They said his message light is on."

"Good," I said automatically and glanced at my watch.

We walked through the upper lobby and down the stairs to the shopping level. Standing by the elevators, I noticed the flowing *G* of the resort's well-recognized logo impressed into the smooth surface of the sand urn.

"Maybe it wouldn't hurt to check again while we're near the desk." Rush was uptight enough about tomorrow's golf. I wanted the issue of the missing Ferguson out of the way.

"Yeah," Rush agreed and stuck his cigarette right in the middle of the pristine *G*.

I resisted the urge to smooth the sand.

I looked around to other sand urns nearby. All their elegant *G*'s appeared to have been there, undisturbed, forever.

We walked around to the desk again. There was still no message.

"I think I'll go change. Dinner's six 'til nine. Give me a ring when you're ready," I said, hoping he wouldn't hurry.

"Sure. Program says there's a cocktail party in the exhibit hall. Let's go have a drink before dinner, okay?" he suggested.

We strolled back to the elevators, and Rush pushed the button.

My eye was drawn to the sand urn. The *G* had been restored. I blinked and checked the twin receptacle standing a little farther over to our right to see if we had returned to the same elevator.

The same—no doubt.

I gawked open-mouthed in appreciation and looked around.

Not a soul in sight.

"Look at that." I nudged Rush with my elbow and nodded down at the pristine surface with the elegant *G*.

"Huh? Oh, you mean the hotel logo. Is that the first time you've seen that? Better hotels do it everywhere." He pushed the button.

"I know. But, less than two minutes ago you stuck a cigarette right in the middle of that *G*. Now it's gone. The attention to detail—where else could you find that?"

"Come off it. We happened to come along when the housekeeper was making the evening rounds."

The elevator opened and we got in. When the door opened at his floor, I stuck my head out and looked at the sand urns.

"Just take a look." I pointed. "Every sand urn in the place looks like it's never been used—and not a soul in sight. Quite a trick if you ask me."

"You're embarrassing me. Don't act like such a hick," he snorted and walked away. I had to bite my tongue to keep from telling him that I hardly thought he could be the judge of that.

Watching him strut away from me down the wide hall with a cocky air—head back and a bouncy stride—it suddenly hit me.

Poor Rush. Trying to act unimpressed. New shirts, new watch, concern with the appearance of the golf equipment—on his way to John Harvard's college and staying at the Greenbrier—afraid to show weakness. The blasé facade, the false bravado. Mr. Rush Donald was out of his depth and struggling to gut it out.

Watching now called up recognition of that fear of inadequacy, that chilling, empty feeling in the gut. I had seen the same adolescent posturing in raw young officers fresh out of some ROTC detachment, hardly more than boys really, in their custom-tailored fatigues, on my first morning in Bosnia.

I'd been one of them.

But that was behind me—a rite of passage, part of becoming my own man.

Back in my room, the bed had been smoothed where I'd sat earlier to use the phone, and I noticed that the towel I'd used when I washed my hands had been replaced and the toothpaste carton I'd thrown in the trash basket had been removed.

Even the jacket I'd left lying on the bed had been brushed and was hanging in the closet.

I knew Rush had to be impressed, but he could never admit it to me. I didn't care, not really, but I fervently hoped, for the sake of my own mental health, he would eventually relax. I shuddered to think what the next three days would be like if he didn't.

I stripped, showered, fell face-down on my bed, and drifted off into a fitful dream. I was on the golf course. Rush's ball had landed in a sand trap that had been meticulously smoothed and stamped like bank paper with endless repetitions of *G*.

Rush was flailing impotently at the ball, but the sand and monogram remained undisturbed. Around the edges of the bunker, the grass was alive with snakes. I turned to discover that my caddy was the heather blonde holding a big brass embossing stamp with the initial *G*. She was stark naked and frightened of the snakes.

It became a very merry game; I was beating back the snakes with the sand trap rake as she wrapped her arms and legs around me, seeking safety in my arms. Rush kept flailing away with no result. I was brandishing the rake while the heather blonde, gloriously nude, tried to stick her tongue in my ear. She and I were thoroughly enjoying the whole thing when John Paul drove up in a golf cart and held out a red-and-blue-striped envelope.

Just as I reached to take it, I woke up.

I went into the bathroom and splashed some cold water on my face, then went to my briefcase and extracted John Paul's envelope.

Just as I was about to open the pouch, the phone rang. Still clutching the envelope, I reached across to answer.

"Hello?"

"I'm at the cocktail party in the exhibit hall. I thought you were going to meet me here for a drink before we eat."

"I'm on my way."

"Shit," I muttered aloud. Reluctantly, I put aside the letter, dressed for dinner, and headed down to baby-sit the once and future Harvard man.

By the time I arrived in the exhibit hall, the party was well underway. I guessed most of the meticulously groomed women in the room were wives—only a scattering were obviously unattached. When I finally located Mr. Excitement, he was holding court in a group of men who were drooling over a pair of beautiful women. I had to hand it to Rush, even in this room filled with attractive, expensively dressed females, these two would have stood out at a casting call for a Vegas chorus line.

At almost any place except the Greenbrier—or perhaps Nassau or the French Riviera—he would have appeared more than slightly gauche. But now I had to admit that from a distance, he looked almost dashing, in a musical-comedy kind of way. As I drew closer, however, there was an aura of newness about his attire—an uncomfortable affectedness that verged on burlesque. Dressed in a white double-breasted blazer and navy slacks, Rush's white shirt and maroon-and-white striped rep silk tie was in the best old-school tradition.

Close up, I saw the Pebble Beach blazer emblem had been replaced by the crest of the Pinehurst Hotel and Golf Club. It was easy to see that these devices were equipped with pins and clips that rendered them transferable like military insignia. I wondered if pin-on blazer patches were on sale here at the Golf Club shop or the boutiques in the shopping arcade. It would be easy to picture him at the Harvard Club sporting the Greenbrier crest on a crimson blazer.

Still, in fairness to him, I saw at least one other man and several women wearing blazers with crests or emblems.

Then, as I drew closer, I noticed that something new had been added to the equation. The white circle on his otherwise suntanned finger stood out like a beacon across the room.

Rush had dumped his wedding ring.

I took a deep breath, straightened my tie, and pressed on. Like it or not, I was stuck. As uncomfortable as I felt to be seen with him, short of faking a heart attack I could think of no way out.

"Logan, old son," he greeted me with the expansive air of a Harvard don. I surmised he'd had a drink or two in his room before he came down. He'd hardly had time to accomplish such a remarkable personality adjustment in the forty-odd minutes since I'd last spoken to him. Turning to the nearest of the women, he said, "Mimi, I'd like to introduce my budding young protégé."

I grimaced and nodded.

"Logan's my local man." Making certain everyone knew he was the boss, he introduced me to the group of salesmen who struggled to conceal their embarrassment.

I have never been very graceful around garden-variety dipshits. The two things I hate most in life are stupidity and authority. Finding them both in the same place drove me to the wall. Fighting back my frustration, I turned my attention to the women.

Mimi was wearing a dusty rose silk cocktail sheath with spaghetti straps. She had superb cheekbones, big pouty lips, a perfect nose, and the eyes of a jungle cat. She was totally feline, with seductive hips and a startling bosom that threatened to escape the bondage of the daring dress. Framed by a flowing Julia Roberts mane of dark auburn hair, her face was arresting.

Struggling not to stare, I turned as Rush was introducing the other woman.

"Ginny McKim, meet Logan Baird."

Mac . . . something? I missed the last syllable of her name, but I recognized her immediately as the woman I'd seen earlier at the pool. I guessed both women to be around my age.

"I already know Logan, but he obviously doesn't remember me," MacSomething smiled mysteriously.

She was right. I didn't.

"Oh? You must mean the pool this afternoon?"

"Before. Think back a few years."

There was something familiar about her, but I still couldn't place her. I was certain I hadn't known her very well. I could never have forgotten all of that.

"You really don't remember?"

"I'm not sure," I hedged.

Ginny edged closer and touched my arm. "Logan was a minor high school legend in Melas, where I grew up. Quarterback on the football team, a real star at basketball. He'd have done a lot better if he hadn't had to play second fiddle to the coach's son. Right, Logan?" She was looking right up into my face.

She was from Melas?

Those Kim Basinger breasts were burning holes in the sleeve of my jacket. I started to perspire. This was one very good-looking female.

"I was the practice teacher in charge of Logan's homeroom when he was starting eighth grade. I remember Hack Murphy said you could throw and kick a football farther than anybody he'd ever seen. How old were you then? Thirteen . . . fourteen?" The minty zephyr of her breath was intoxicating.

"More like twelve, I guess. I skipped third grade."

My prowess as a world-class raconteur was never more evident. Thinking back over a lifetime of dumb things I've said, this was a career high. If I ever got around to "Yep," I'd give Brian Bosworth a real run for his money.

"Only twelve? Imagine. You really were precocious. I had no idea. I was about nineteen then. I was an orphanage girl attending

Roanoke College. I married Tommy Hardison, but now my name's McKim again."

At the mention of the orphanage and Tommy Hardison, it all started coming back. When she was doing her teaching practicum, Ginny McKim had been known as something of a free spirit. Back home, that translated as "slightly out of control."

As my practice teacher, she had been only a couple of years out of high school herself—a scant six or seven years older than I at the very most.

I had fallen desperately in lust.

Then the summer I was to be a senior in high school, she had dropped out of college to marry Tommy Hardison. He was a lot older than Ginny. The descriptions of Tommy before he came back from the Vietnam War always put me in mind of an overgrown Huckleberry Finn. But his return was like a nightmare movie. He had come back from 'Nam with steel hooks replacing both hands.

Our town's first real war hero since the fifties, Tommy had had the whole town buzzing with his alcoholic escapades.

Actually, I never knew Ginny, not really. The summer before I had left for college, she became a familiar sight in the late evenings in front of Norman's Restaurant, the popular Main Street hangout in our town. Norman's was at the center of the six-block-long business section, directly across from the old Fort Lewis Hotel, where Ginny and Tommy lived in a second-floor room looking out over the marquee onto the street. There wasn't much going on in Melas in the evening when there wasn't a ball game or a new picture show playing at the modern Colonial Cineplex—or the older Melas Theater that showed classics and foreign art films. Sometimes, when Tommy was drying out from his most recent trip to the local VA hospital, Ginny would be there with him, among the die-hard, late-night hangers-on.

Tommy would disappear—binging for days or weeks. Ginny boozed with him, of course. Many nights that summer I'd seen her slightly drunk, sometimes tearful and in pitiful disarray, asking each new arrival from the local hot spots that had closed at midnight if they'd seen Tommy.

The last time I'd seen her was the summer I was home from my first year of college. She was knee-walking, half-crazy with loneliness and despair and being "helped" across to the hotel by a couple of local hard cases who obviously had more than her best interests at heart. I remember watching as Theodore, the kindly young town cop, had firmly interceded on her behalf, sending the two "Samaritans" on their way.

My hometown had a heart of gold.

I dimly remembered hearing someone say she'd finally gotten her act together, finished college, and gone off to graduate school.

I was embarrassed for her and afraid to ask if Tommy were still alive.

"I heard you'd played basketball in college, and someone told me you'd been wounded in Bosnia. Are you still living in Melas?" she asked.

"Uh-huh," I grunted at my loquacious best.

I noted that she wasn't wearing a wedding ring.

I saw that the years had been more than merely kind. Encased in the simple fitted dress, she was a knockout.

HANDLE AT YOUR OWN RISK, a neon warning flashed across my brain in lipstick pink.

"Well, well, Mimi, it would seem we've got a real folk legend on our hands," Rush interrupted. "Tell us about the time you led your college team to the national championship, right after we hear all about your Medal of Honor."

"Really! The Medal of Honor? I'm not surprised." Missing Rush's sarcasm, Ginny cooed and squeezed my arm.

"Where's the bar? Looks like I'm the only one without a drink," I quickly changed the subject.

"What would you like? I'll get it for you," Ginny volunteered.

Rush cavalierly seized upon Ginny's invitation. "Great! While you're at it, bring me a Jack Daniels on the rocks. What are you drinking, Mimi?"

"Vodka tonic—but wait. The bar's a mob scene. Let's all go help." Mimi, clearly embarrassed by Rush's bad manners, followed Ginny.

Rush and I tagged along.

"You don't sound like you're from New York, Mimi . . . more like Boston, I'd guess." Discomfited by Rush's behavior, I ventured conversation.

"Good ear. A little town named Brewster. I'm a brick mason's daughter who broke the rules and made it to Radcliffe on a scholarship. After graduation, I went to New York to find fame. I didn't become famous exactly, but I got pretty lucky, I guess," she laughed.

"A Radcliffe girl . . . small world," I said. "Rush here is headed to Harvard Business School. Our company is grooming him to be president, or some such thing."

"Logan is exaggerating. I'm not sure exactly what they've got in mind. They've never done this for anyone before, but any way you look at it, a chance to go to Harvard B is a pretty big deal." Rush preened, modestly straightening his tie.

"How exciting. I'm impressed. Harvard Business is a good credential on anybody's resume." Mimi was sincere.

Portable bars were conveniently scattered throughout the big exhibit hall for the reception. The whole place was mass confusion. Ginny led the way, still holding tight to my arm. Rush lagged behind, keeping in step with Mimi, having a hard time not looking down the front of her dress. Ginny headed straight to the nearest bar.

"Are you here with the medical meeting or on vacation?" I asked Ginny.

"Oh, no. I own a small bed and breakfast in Lewisburg. Mimi and I are old friends from my grad school days in New York. She's down on business with the hotel."

"I'm with Laurence Raphael, the designer. You know, Chuckker . . . everybody knows Chuckker. We've been waiting for centuries for a space to come open here. I flew down to try to negotiate a lease on this little piece of heaven. Ginny knows everybody here and came over to introduce me to the management. Then we got shanghaied by some drug reps," Mimi giggled.

"I can well imagine." I beamed down at Ginny with unabashed admiration.

"Mimi exaggerates. I am a local and know a bunch of folks. We were trying to make our escape and go find dinner." Ginny dismissed it all with a wave of the hand.

"Your long-lost high school teacher is too modest. She's well thought of by the Greenbrier staff," Mimi said.

"I'm impressed but not surprised. An innkeeper in Lewisburg? How long has this been going on?" I tried to add up in my head how long it had been since I'd seen her. Three years of college, a year afterwards before the Bosnian outbreak had claimed a year of my life, and the brief stint back with the newspaper syndicate before I'd started my career with the lab.

A lot can happen in nine—going on ten—years.

"I've been here almost five years, now," Ginny said, thoughtfully. "It doesn't seem possible."

"What a dream place and a dream career. Some people have all the luck," Mimi said. "In all the world, there's no place to compare."

"Don't be so sure. I've traveled all over. This dumpy town and the Greenbrier are highly overrated." Rush condescended, not at all thrilled at being upstaged by a local yokel.

"Overrated?" Mimi flared. "In all my travels, I haven't seen anything that comes close to this. Just name one place. I'd like to go there."

"That's easy. The Mark," Rush announced imperiously.

"The Mark Hopkins? Come on!" Mimi exploded in disbelief. "You've got to be kidding. The Mark is certainly a fine hotel, but so are the Plaza and the Sheraton Park. That's precisely the point. They're all hotels . . . apples and oranges. If you want to compare this with the Homestead, or even the Breakers or the Boca Raton Club, now that's different."

"This is my first trip and, frankly, I'm disappointed." Rush hedged a bit. He hadn't intended to alienate Mimi. Obviously his intent was to endear himself to her.

And, clearly, he had relegated Ginny and me to the unwashed masses.

"Oh, my, the Greenbrier management would be sorry to hear they've disappointed you," Ginny said with concern. "What's the problem?"

"For one thing, I think the Greenbrier's standards are second-rate." A faint hint of a stuffy Hahvahd Ivy League accent edged into Rush's affectation.

"Just how do you mean?" Ginny asked in disbelief.

"For instance, this afternoon we saw a perfectly disreputable-looking man unloading the rattiest golf bag I've ever seen from a car that my yardman would be ashamed to be seen in." Without confiding that he was the yardman in question, Rush recounted the scene at the Golf Club. "When I first saw him, I took him for a tradesman or maybe a handyman of the hotel staff. Personally, I think the man should've been politely reminded of the dress code when he appeared for registration. I'm from San Francisco, and I can assure you that man would not have been well received at the Mark Hopkins. And I rather imagine the pro at Cypress Point would have taken him aside and had a friendly word about the condition of his golf bag. I'm sure most of the guests here would not allow such a shabby display of dress at their own clubs back home, and that automobile would not be allowed in the members' parking lot at my own club," he concluded.

It was the first I'd heard about "his" club. I was sure he'd told me he played a public course because the clubs in the Bay area were too expensive.

"Was he all that disreputable?" Ginny glanced at me.

I shrugged. "No, not really bad at all. Perhaps he was a little the worse for wear. Poor guy had run out of gas back on Route 311 near Paint Bank and had to walk back a ways to find a gas station. We passed him on the way over."

"That golf bag looked like a reject from the Salvation Army," Rush said.

"I have to admit that his golf bag . . . shall we say, had character. It really was something in the way of a family heirloom." I smiled, remembering. "But the clubs looked to be custom-fitted, state of the art," I added to make my point.

"That's certainly more than we can say about our resident hero, Sam Snead's clubs. That old driver of his is a legend. It's been glued back together so many times, they say the Wilson Sporting Goods people offered him a fortune to replace it," Ginny laughed. "Sam wouldn't think of parting with that driver."

"This man certainly wasn't Sam Snead." Rush failed to see the humor. "That bag was a disgrace."

"The Greenbrier has a standard of decorum, but they don't impose. Occasionally a guest will come dressed inappropriately for the dining room in the evening for dinner. They tactfully call them aside and remind them of the published code. Otherwise, I grant you, during the day there may be some outlandish costumes about, but the hotel tries to keep a sense of humor. After all, not everyone is blessed with an impeccable sense of taste," Ginny defended. "I don't recognize the man you describe, but there is a longstanding list of regular guests who are somewhat unimpressed by the current fashions. You will probably see some pretty ridiculously decorated vehicles driven by newlyweds. But it would certainly never occur to someone like Steven Spielberg or Bill Gates that the appearance of their automobiles or sports equipment might validate their right to be here. As long as their manners are good and they don't annoy the other guests, it would be presumptuous of us to arbitrarily criticize their automobiles or the condition of their favorite tennis shoes."

I wanted to cheer out loud but resisted. Remembering the old adage about discretion being the better part of valor, I quietly squeezed Ginny's arm in silent approval.

Mimi giggled out loud and gave a little clap of her hands. "You think the man you saw this afternoon was bad? My boss is a disaster. The *tres* famous Raphael never wears anything but jeans, and he's not alone. At Atelier and the Ritz the *maîtres d'hôtel* always keep jackets and shirts and neckties around to accommodate him and other notoriously casual free spirits like Sam Shepard or Robert Redford. In New York, the so-called 'in' places are full of odd-looking characters in ill-fitting jackets and ties, wearing dirty sneakers. Different strokes for different folks."

"Speaking of dress codes, Rush and I were about to go in for dinner. Would you care to join us?" I spoke up, trying to ease the rising tension.

"We'd be delighted," Mimi spoke right up.

Offered the prospect of such charming company, Rush took her arm, momentarily forgetting his offended sensibilities.

Ginny led the way. "Let's head for the dining room before this mob gets the same idea."

For the moment at least, the crisis was averted.

CHAPTER TWELVE

At the dining room entrance, it didn't actually appear that we were moved past the others who had arrived ahead of us, but I noticed that the maitre d' betrayed a glimmer of recognition when he saw Ginny approaching.

Tactfully, she deferred to me.

"Good evening. Table for four?"

I nodded.

At the Greenbrier, the splendid main dining room redefines the meaning of elegance.

In the blink of an eye, we were escorted to a choice table, perfectly located the right distance from a grand piano being played by an ageless man with skin like polished African rosewood. Wearing a white dinner jacket, he was playing the love theme from *The Music Man* as part of an exquisitely sweet, intricately rendered medley of Broadway show tunes. As the evening wore on, I was delighted to find that his inexhaustible repertoire was not only harvested from show tunes but included jazz favorites and old dance standards. Just below the sound of the music, there was a hush of conversation that made a pleasant counter melody all its own.

Ginny McKim had come a long way from her orphanage days. She was right at home.

For a wide-eyed country boy who'd walked a mile to catch the school bus, so had I.

It puzzled me why Rush was threatened by the presence of the old gentleman of the mud-splattered jalopy, tattered golf bag, and everyday attire. Why was a simple lack of pretension so intimidating?

My father had worked in Norfolk Southern's general offices in a city that depended on the railroad for economic health. There were always ups and downs. But, unlike a lot of folks, my dad was lucky enough always to have steady work. Our family had suffered some lean times ourselves. Sometimes money was hard to come by, but my teenage years had been a wonderful, mixed-up time. I'd understood that better times were just around the corner—there was always the promise of that.

In bad times, everybody we knew talked of better times to come.

We'd lived outside the city, in a rambling brick house adjoining my mother's family's farm. My mother had a big old corner cupboard filled with delicate bone china, lead crystal goblets, fine antique pewter, and a complete eight-place setting of sterling silver flatware for entertaining company.

An ebony baby grand piano graced our living room.

Even when we were struggling, we kept our dignity.

"No, no, Logan! The cutting edge of the knife is always turned inward. Good manners are important, Son. A man needs to know how to act no matter where he is." My mother had taught me all Emily Post had to say about manners long before I started school.

And working for the railroad had advantages. Our family could travel on a Spartan budget practically anywhere the Amtrak ran.

"Travel broadens you," our mother had told us. It was also a lot of fun. I'd been too young to understand such things, but I soon developed a sense of comfort almost anywhere. New York's museums and Washington, with the Smithsonian and the Library of Congress, alternated with our daily routine of milking cows, slopping hogs, and hoeing the corn and beans and tomatoes, making my little brother and me curious half-breeds of a strange cosmopolitan tribe.

Railroad dining cars were a great place for a country boy to learn about menus and practice table manners. By the time I left home and headed for college, I couldn't say I really knew what I wanted, but wherever I happened to land I was pretty comfortable with who I was, and I knew how to behave anywhere.

Now, showing off for Mimi, Rush had become obviously patronizing toward Ginny and me, archly treating us as charitably tolerated peasants.

Trying hard to be blasé, even before we were seated, he asked the attendant to bring the wine list. "Since I come from the famous California wine country, I think I should order a bottle of wine.

Living next door to the celebrated wineries of Napa Valley has given me a great appreciation for the fruit of the vineyard. It's the civilized thing where I come from."

"Oh, yes. I'd love some wine, but I'm such an ignoramus. What do you suggest?" Mimi answered for us all.

"How about a California Merlot? They have a nice Greenbrier Vineyards Havens Cellars Napa Valley selection." Ginny looked eagerly around the table.

I relaxed.

That particular grape and vineyard was Rush's signature wine of the moment—right off the pages of *Gourmet*. He'd introduced me to a Havens Cellars Merlot the first time we worked together. I'd taken him to dinner at the University Club with a rising young internist named Henry Lockheart. Henry was my sometimes mentor, sometimes protégé, and drinking buddy. He loved old jazz, Hemingway, good booze, and fancy wine. Jazz, Hemingway, and bourbon likker were things I'd modestly taught Henry a lot about, but when it came to wine, I was a bumbling amateur. Henry had tried to make me his protégé—his project. He had sponsored me for membership at the University Club. The young Doctor Lockheart was chairman of the therapeutics committee at the local VA hospital. He had decided to personally make me a star in the pharmaceutical world.

I remembered well how Rush, with the proprietary air of a great connoisseur, had shared the holy secret of the Havens Cellars Merlot with Henry and me.

Henry had been quietly amused.

"Back home the Havens Cellars Merlot is a *vin ordinaire* among the common folk—more *Good Housekeeping* than *Gourmet*. It would be a good choice if one is entertaining the local PTA," Rush condescended cavalierly, eyeing the steward bringing the wine list. He wasn't about to let some glorified boardinghouse operator from the boonies of West Virginia choose the wine.

Desperately, I started searching for a way out. It was going to be a long night if I couldn't manage an excuse to split.

Quietly, the young wine steward extended the open wine list to Rush. "If the gentleman doesn't like the California selection, we have a nice Mandrielle, Castello Banfi, Tuscany."

"Um, yes. A rather amusing little provincial wine from the south of France."

"I like merlot. It tastes good, and French anything sounds risqué." Mimi giggled, her bosom jiggling into the danger zone.

"I'm sorry we don't have a French merlot. Tuscany is Italian." The young steward never cracked a smile.

"Yes, of course. The Italian Merlots are rather a plebeian choice, I think." Rush reddened, trying to finesse his geographic faux pas.

"If you're looking for a really intriguing use of merlot, then I invite your attention to our South African Rubicon, Meerlust, Stellenbosch. It's a classic Bordeaux blend of cabernet sauvignon, merlot, and cabernet franc." The apple-cheeked wine steward didn't blink.

"South African? A blend of wines? An agrarian compromise—"

"I dearly love compromise," Mimi interjected with a delightfully wicked laugh.

Nervously, I sensed the situation was getting out of hand. "Aren't we getting the cart before the horse? We should know better. Shouldn't the choice of wine depend on what we have for dinner?"

"Not necessarily," Rush's said defensively, his social acumen on trial.

"If we don't want the same entree, we could start with half-bottles. It won't matter if we all order different entrees," Ginny suggested.

"Oh, yes. Look, they have a nice selection of half-bottles." Mimi almost spilled her bosom on Rush's arm as she leaned across and pointed to the card.

"While we're mulling over our dinner selections, why don't you bring us half-bottles of the . . ." Rush was sweating now. "Pouilly-Fuisse, Louis Jadot, 1996 and . . . ah . . . Duckhorn Merlot, 1995"

Poowilly?

Fewissy?

Lewis Jad-ott?

"Will that be chilled, sir?" Expressionless, the young wine steward let the question hang. His unspoken message: pass or fail, you boorish clown.

Please, Bacchus, don't let him show his ass to the women again, I fervently implored to the first deity that popped into my head. When knee-deep in grape-colored doo-doo, my motto is any old god in a shit storm.

"Oh, it must be chilled, Rush. Who wants hot wine?" Mimi came to his rescue.

"*Certainement.*" He handed back the wine list. "Never argue with a lady."

Sir-taym-wah!

Rush's French left a lot to be desired.

"An excellent choice," the wine steward took the card.

As he left, I saw the young sommelier pass the older waiter a knowing look. There was a shadow of a smile on the distinguished-looking waiter's lips as he stepped over and presented each of us a menu, opening the elegant folios as he moved around the table.

When he had distributed the folios he began reciting several featured entrees of the day.

"Sal-mon? In the mountains of West Virginia?" Rush, in a very irritable mood now, looked up from the menu and raised an eyebrow at the waiter.

"Oh yes, sir. The chef recommends the grilled salmon prepared with lemon butter and cracked peppercorns," he concluded. The waiter pronounced "sa'mun" flawlessly.

"Frozen sal-mon doesn't sound at all worthy of your reputation. Back home at the Mark Hopkins the sal-mon is fresh daily." Rush glanced over the top of his menu at Ginny to make his point. "I'd expect the chef at the Greenbrier would stick to local mountain trout, caught fresh daily."

"There's also fresh local trout on the card, sir." With great dignity, the waiter bent forward at the waist and placed his finger at the appropriate line on the menu. "But our salmon is fresh also, flown directly from Alaska daily. As are the Chesapeake oysters and the crab."

The server paused and waited.

"I'll have the salmon. It's marvelous," Ginny said without looking at Rush.

"Make mine the salmon. I'm ravenous, folks," Mimi shrugged.

"I'll have sal-mon," I managed with a sly grin toward Ginny, hoping the cosmic architects would forgive the two-faced whore I am. I had my heart set on that promotion.

"The sal-mon all around, then. I'll be interested to see how fresh it really is," Rush pouted, his lower lip protruding. "Ask your sommelier to come back, please. I want to order white wine for the fish."

The young wine steward materialized with the half-bottles.

"I'll taste the merlot, but we're having the sal-mon and I want to change the white."

"Oh? I assure you the Pouilly-Fuisse, Louis Jadot, would be an excellent choice, but of course of the French white burgundies, the Puligny-Montrachet, Louis Jadot, might be a bit more discerning."

Upside down, I could see $76.00 listed beside the line where the sommelier had placed his finger.

Rush turned pale, and his forehead was shiny with perspiration. "Uh, well, I personally find the Pah-lig . . . that selection a bit too presumptive on the palate. How about the domestics? Perhaps a California? There's a good Beaulieu California white, but I doubt you have it here."

Bool-yeah?

"We have a Beaulieu Vineyard, Georges de Latour Cabernet Sauvignon." The steward pronounced "bow-lew" without a pause. "But our California sauvignon blancs are from other fine Napa Valley vineyards."

As soon as he'd finished pouring the merlot for the ladies, he leaned forward and pointed his finger to the listings on the card. "The Greenbrier Vineyards is a Steve Girard Selection. We have the Robert Mondavi and Cakebread Cellars too, for instance. They're all very good choices."

"Those would not be my choices of a California sauvignon blanc," Rush said, his face was getting redder at being corrected by the wine steward. "I never heard of Steve Girard or Cakebread Cellars, and I've been in every winery in the valley. I'm a San Francisco native. I travel frequently in the Napa area."

"Oh, I'm sorry, we don't have a white from the Beaulieu Wineries. The Robert Mondavi Winery is very distinguished. And, our Steve Girard selection is excellent. I personally recommend it. If you'd like, I'll bring a half-bottle—compliments of the house, of course."

"No, I'm not in an adventuresome mood. The experimentation might spoil my palate. We'll have the Mondavi." Rush, tired of being shown up, gathered his forces and took charge again.

"He personally recommends it," Rush crassly mimicked before the waiter was entirely out of earshot. "That hillbilly probably rode a mule to work."

Mimi tasted the merlot and rolled her eyes upward in delight. She raised her glass and gushed, "Rush, this is heavenly. Compliments to our worldly gourmet." She polished off the glass.

Merlot is pretty and light to the palate, but it ain't Kool-Aid. At the cocktail party, both Mimi and Rush had appeared to be getting a bit giggly. I prayed silently to a muse who didn't know me that after dinner she would find Rush irresistible and drag him off to the Old White Club to dance the night away.

When it was served, the sal-mon was superbly sa'mun.

"Admit it, Rush, the salmon was excellent," Mimi kidded.

"Whoa, let's not get carried away." He patted her hand. "Didn't it kill you the way that hillbilly waiter said 'the chef recommends it'? I wonder what sort of well-trained chef would come to a place in this Godforsaken country." Rush said, condescendingly. "Where do you ever find them?" He turned to Ginny. "Exclusively from Europe, I'm sure."

"No, the Greenbrier has its own three-year culinary apprentice program. It's famous worldwide. Created quite a stir in the industry back in the late fifties. They were the first in the country to train American chefs on site. At the moment, there are over forty chefs in the kitchen. And there are almost two hundred applications for the dozen openings they'll have for the upcoming year. Over the years, the Mark Hopkins has sent some excellent candidates," Ginny said with quiet pride.

"Forty chefs!" I was amazed.

"Interesting," Rush finally managed to mutter. "Well the salmon was certainly a nice surprise, but then, in my experience, sal-mon is like sex . . . the worst I ever had was fantastic." He was anxious to change the subject from the Mark.

"Oh, worst sex . . . fantastic. That's really priceless," Mimi giggled.

"Like an antique?" I murmured under my breath.

"Be nice," Ginny whispered and shot me a look.

"What was that?" Rush caught her whisper.

"The ice! I was suggesting Logan try the orange sherbet." Ginny gave my thigh a squeeze, accidentally brushing my groin. I was jolted by the sensuality.

"Of course. Sorbet! But not orange. Lime is best . . . cleanses the palate." Rush beamed.

After a brief discussion, we all declined.

The piano man was leaving now, replaced by a delicate-looking young woman in an elegant puce gown of iridescent satin who had already begun playing a medley of light classics on a lovely old violin. There was a little card on our table announcing that a band was appearing 8 'til 1 nightly, in the Old White Club.

Rush had already started on another bottle of Mondavi.

"We have plenty of time to have dessert and still catch the first show at the Old White. I made a reservation." He made a great show of looking at his new Rolex.

My ears had not deceived me earlier. Now his speech had taken on overtones of Ivy League. He sounded like William F. Buckley doing George Plimpton.

"I'll skip dessert, but dancing at the Old White sounds like a great idea," Mimi gushed.

"No dessert for me, either. I need to lose a few ell-bee-esses," Ginny said.

"I'd like to know where," I leered.

She put her hand over mine, beaming a thank-you smile. Leaning closer, she exuded a faint whiff of baby soap.

My breathing was a trifle labored now.

I surveyed the room, looking to see if there were any familiar faces. Even though this was an international congress of academicians and researchers—mostly medical school types—I knew there would be a fair sampling of docs from my stomping grounds along the Virginia-West Virginia border who would be combining a short holiday at the Greenbrier with a tax-deductible business expense.

As my gaze swept back across the crowded room, I caught sight of the familiar face of Dr. Rayburn, director of the Greenbrier Clinic, the full-scale medical facility located in the hotel's West Virginia wing and staffed with a cadre of highly credentialed physicians. Over the years, the clinic had built an active referral list including several hundred Fortune 500 corporations that sent their top executives for annual physicals.

I called on those diagnosticians regularly, usually late in the morning, right before lunch break. I only required ten or fifteen minutes to have my say. The pleasant young nurse in charge liked me and always tried to assemble those members of the staff who were on duty that day.

The Greenbrier Clinic exerted a symbiotic influence on several sizeable private medical groups in the surrounding area. Dr. Rayburn and his staff were often consulted and sometimes accepted diagnostic referrals. The clinic also represented a considerable source of prescribing influence to a large pharmaceutical company like ours. The affluent Greenbrier Clinic clientele usually had prescriptions to refill. The pharmacies in White Sulphur Springs and Lewisburg reflected the success of my regular presence.

It all added up to a very worthwhile investment of my time.

But it was not only Dr. Rayburn, sitting on the upper tier of the terraced room, who held my interest. Sitting at the large table with Rayburn was the genial gentleman of the battered car and tattered golf bag.

I nudged Ginny and whispered, "Look back across your right shoulder to the table where Dr. Rayburn is sitting with all those people. Do you know the gentleman in the navy blazer and the dark blue-and-green tartan slacks who looks something like an English schoolmaster?"

"I've seen him before, but I don't know who he is. If he's with Dr. Rayburn, he may be some bigwig here for an annual corporate physical." She brightened and turned back to me. "That's Alex Crim, Sam Snead's agent—the handsome woman in the ivory dress, sitting beside him. But why do you ask? Do you recognize him?"

"He's the man Rush told you about, the one who seemed to be so popular with the staff at the Golf Club this afternoon." I turned to Rush. "Do you see our mystery man back there? Looks a bit more respectable tonight, don't you think?"

Rush turned. "He's still rather seedy looking. Not at all like someone on the Fortune 500 list," he sniffed.

"He's probably one of Sam Snead's cronies. Sam's always bringing someone over here. Whoever he is, he seems to be right at home with people we consider family around here," Ginny subtly scolded Rush for his offhand judgment of the man. "Now that I think about it, I may have seen him at one of the after-hours clubs across the mountain on the river. They attract a certain adventuresome patronage."

Rush's interest perked up. "Oh, yeah, Logan was telling me about those. Give me the inside scoop. Logan says he sometimes goes to the Magnolia Club."

"You mean Camellia. So, you're friends with Charlie?" Ginny looked at me.

"No, no. I never said we're friends. I've had dinner there a couple of times. Charlie's nice to the traveling men. The food and drinks are good and not too hard on my expense account, but I do my gambling on the golf course."

"So, you travel over this way often?" Ginny perked right up.

"About every four to six weeks, depending on my schedule. I usually stay at the little inn in Lewisburg."

"Tell us what you know about the after-hours joints," Rush persisted.

"Not a lot to tell. Logan probably knows as much as I do. Over the years, I've been to both the Bluffs and the Camellia at one time or another. You can hardly live here for four years and not go. They're there for the high rollers. The Greenbrier is considered by many the premier resort in the world. Obviously, we attract the big spenders."

"Can we hoi polloi afford to play at the blackjack tables?" Rush asked.

"I think so. They wouldn't stay open if they didn't have locals who played regularly. Some come down from Charleston or over from Richmond or Roanoke. An empty house is not good for business. I understand the really big players fly in from Atlantic City or Vegas. They play high-stakes poker—mostly in private," Ginny said.

"Is it safe? I mean, are we likely to get raided?" Rush laughed to make a joke of it, but I knew he didn't want to try anything risky.

"I wouldn't worry. You'll be as safe as in your mother's kitchen. The owners are out-of-state big gambling money. The management won't tolerate any rowdy drunks—no troublemakers or loudmouths of any kind. You mustn't forget, you might see a famous actor or a foreign ambassador to the UN there. It was rumored that a former president wanted to go when he came here for some hush-hush conferences with the joint chiefs, but the big-money boys wouldn't hear of it. That nameless president already had enough problems with his image. The locals put their collective foot down. Sent word back through his security advisors that they would rather not open up a potential can of worms. Still, if the story's true, I'm sure it was an example of cooler heads prevailing. It's not often you have the power to say no to the president of the United States. Of course, it would have caused a major situation if the word had leaked in the press. And the political establishment here would have looked very bad," she confided. "You have to understand that the Greenbrier remains aloof. You're wasting your time if you ask the hotel staff—even the locals won't admit knowing what you're talking about. But you can call the clubs direct, and they'll send a private car. Or you could take a cab if you don't want to drive, but these spots are so far back in the hills they have to pipe the moonlight in. I don't want to meddle, but if you're planning on doing any more drinking, I'd recommend that you call the club of your choice for the free chauffeur," Ginny advised.

"If we let someone pick us up, we'd be stuck for the night at one place. I'm sure the Bluffs wouldn't take us to the Camellia Club if we want to make the rounds. Anyway, we have a car. We can drive if you'll draw us a map . . . after we pop in at the Old White Club, of course," Rush said.

"Thanks but I'll have to skip the Old White Club and the other too. Some of my friends on the hotel staff are having a party at the Golf Club. You're all welcome to come along if you like." I felt pressure from her knee under the table.

I gave her a closer look.

The hormonal rush of a high school freshman with a crush on his sexy young teacher came flooding back over me. As with so many women, the intervening years had only perfected her beauty. She'd been almost twenty when I was twelve or thirteen. According to my best arithmetic that made her thirty-six, maybe thirty-seven. Although demurely turned out, she exuded a latent animal sexuality that I found overpowering.

I wondered if she were involved romantically.

"Party at the Golf Club? What kind of party?" Rush wanted to know.

"Oh, just a weekly get together. We—they—celebrate birthdays . . . anything that comes along. Tonight, we're celebrating Ricky Brooks's new book. Ricky is the wine steward." Ginny nodded toward the young sommelier stationed alongside a stately column, a few tables down.

"That hillbilly wrote a book? What kind of book is that?" Rush jeered.

"Ricky writes mysteries. This is his third. Uses a pen name. He's also published a book on American wine, and his publisher is waiting on another about wines of Europe," Ginny said proudly. "He's regarded as definitive, an authority."

"Definitive! That jerk wrote a book on American wines?" Rush almost choked.

"That's right," she assured him.

"His books must not have amounted to much, or he wouldn't be working here."

"Ricky lectures regularly at Cordon Bleu." Ginny was trying to keep her temper.

"If he's so well-respected, why would he want to work here as a wine steward?" Rush scoffed. "That tells me he's lazy."

"Lazy? I'd hardly call someone who had published four books by the age of thirty lazy." Ginny's laugh was flat. "Besides, what's so wrong with working here? This is the Greenbrier."

I resisted standing up and applauding.

"Who ever heard of him? He certainly doesn't have much ambition," Rush sputtered.

"Ambition?" She raised her eyebrow. "Ambition to do what?"

"Why, to compete in the real world." Rush stuck out his chin pugnaciously.

"I wouldn't want to challenge him to a writing contest," I chimed in amicably, trying to keep the lid on the volcano.

"Don't worry, he doesn't want to be challenged. No real writer would hide out in a place like this," Rush persisted.

"Don't be so sure. The maitre d' has a law degree, from Columbia I think. He's working on a book, too. Says the real world is counter-creative. At the moment, we have quite a few advanced degrees—artists, former teachers, and other professionals—scattered about this dining room and the kitchen area and other positions on the staff. You'd be surprised." Ginny stuck her chin out right back at him.

The talk of books reminded me of the letter from John Paul, unopened in my room. Secretly, we'd both been trying to write a novel about the war for several years. At least John Paul had been working on his. I'd given up on mine. I'd never met a published novelist before. I made up my mind to go with Ginny to her party if she didn't withdraw her invitation. I'd had about all I could stand of Rush Donald for one day. I wanted to get as far away from the jerk as I could. And, to tell the truth, my groin still tingled from her touch.

"I'd like to go to the party if the invitation stands," I said.

"Of course it stands." There was a definite pressure from her knee now. "I'll have to run home and freshen up. I've been a slave all day. Besides, the party won't get started for a couple of hours. These people have to finish up here after the dining room is closed." Ginny looked at her watch and then to me. "I'll meet you on the arcade level near Draper's Cafe at nine forty-five sharp." She pushed back her chair and stood up. "I enjoyed the dinner and the company. Sure you two won't join us common folk? You'd be very welcome." She looked to Rush again.

"When we have the Old White and the Camellia? Not hardly, but thanks, anyway," Rush said through clenched teeth like a true Harvard man.

I stood like the gentleman my mama raised me to be. Reluctantly, Rush started to rise. He didn't want to look like the cavalier he was.

"Mimi?" Ginny asked.

"No, thanks. I think I'm going to tag along to the Old White and then, who knows, maybe go with Rush and try the local color after hours. Will I see you in the morning? Breakfast around nine?"

"Sounds fine. If I'm not already here, start without me. I'll find you," Ginny said and turned back to me. "I'm going to wear shorts. Be sure and bring a sweater. It gets chilly in the mountains at night. See you in a little while." She squeezed my arm and made her way across the room, threading her way in and out among the tables, nodding here and there to the guests. She was every inch a high priestess in that glamorous room.

Watching the muscles of her hips and those long straight legs, my hormones spiked into the danger zone.

I wondered if it was too late to change my mind and go to bed early.

And die not knowing what she looked like in shorts?

CHAPTER THIRTEEN

Pleading the need to make some phone calls, I tried to talk my way out of tagging along with Rush and Mimi to the Old White Club.

"Phone calls? Nonsense. Come on, don't you want to dance with me?" More than a trifle merloted and Mondavied, Mimi pulled me by the hand. I knew that Rush would be just as happy not to have me around, but the wine had Mimi in a flirty mood.

I shrugged and acquiesced, deciding it would be easier to give in and make a clean getaway at the first opportunity.

In the Old White Club, we found ourselves sitting two tables over from Max and Sam and their wives. They hailed us over before we were seated and introduced their wives to Rush. I breathed a sigh of relief that Ginny had declined coming along. Max's wife played bridge with Rose at our club. They weren't exactly best friends, but I would have had an awkward time explaining Ginny to the notoriously gossipy Cookie Bergmann.

In their early thirties, Max and Cookie were childless and very much enjoying the fruits of their early struggles getting Max through med school. They both were good-looking in that all-American, California- poster-girl and -boy sort of way. They liked the good life. They both tended to drink a little too much. Cookie was something of a free spirit and always seemed to be flirting. On occasion she made me more than a trifle uncomfortable. I knew she was trying to make Max jealous, and it wasn't that I wouldn't have liked it under other circumstances, but considering the fact that her doctor husband was a client and I needed his good will, frankly it made me nervous as hell to be around her. It was common knowledge back home that sometimes Max had gotten pretty upset with her for flirting at club parties.

It was obvious the four of them were in fine spirits, and it didn't take long to figure out why. Grinning as if he'd won the Powerball, Max said, "I hope you're ready for tomorrow, Logan. It's just like you said . . . the golf course is immaculate. I've never seen such greens. Ask Sam."

"All you have to do is figure out the line and get it started, and the putts go right in the hole. Our caddie was incredible. Knows every putt on the golf course. I only had thirty putts."

I nudged Rush. "Uh-huh, so now we're hearing the truth, and these guys were trying to hustle us for strokes. What'd you shoot, even par?"

"Don't be silly, we were only fooling around. Didn't really keep score . . . first time on the golf course," Max hedged smugly.

"Yeah, we weren't really keeping score. I played two balls on several holes. No telling what I shot, probably ninety, but I didn't care about scoring. The course is a pure joy to play," Sam said with a broad grin. I could tell he was lying. He was pretty happy with his game.

"What the hell. On golf courses like these, who cares about the score anyway? That course is a work of pure art, an aesthetic experience. I can't wait to get back out there in the morning," Max agreed. "The fairways are so good, it's impossible to catch anything but a perfect lie. Hell, the first cut of the rough is better than the fairways at Pebble, don't you agree?" He looked to Rush for confirmation.

"I haven't played here yet, but I doubt that these courses are in a class with Pebble Beach," Rush said defensively.

"I agree. I'm not talking about difficulty. Pebble is a seaside links. Grass has a hard time around salt water. Like the Old Course at St. Andrews, the fairways at Pebble are sparse. But then, you know what I mean." Max was leaning forward now, trying to catch the legend on Rush's blazer patch in the subdued light.

"Pinehurst," Rush volunteered.

"Pinehurst? You live at Pinehurst?"

"Oh, no. I live in Charlotte, but business takes me all over the Carolinas and Virginia. I was there at a big meeting in the spring. I've been back a couple of times."

"Have you played Number Two?" Max's eyes rolled back into his head in ecstasy. "Talk about a golf course I love. There's no place like Pinehurst Number Two."

"I get so sick of all this golf talk. Will you dance with me, Logan?" Cookie stood up. Even though she made me very nervous, I was more than happy to break away.

"I was a little disappointed with Pinehurst. It seemed to me to lack character. There's no rough like I know it. I don't find much inspiration in the way the fairways dissolve into sand and pine straw. Playing the west coast courses has spoiled me. Still, I . . ." The world's greatest expert was beginning to sound like a broken record.

Taking my hand, Cookie melted against me in front of the small bandstand. The combo included the ancient piano man who had played the show-tune medley in the dining room.

I have a rich fantasy life. With Cookie's pudendum burning against me, my thoughts were far away from golf. Dancing with Cookie left me feeling as though I'd been gang raped by an entire cellblock at the federal reformatory for women across the mountain at Alderson. Not that I minded as I struggled to keep my eyes off the seductive hills and valleys of her creamy décolletage, which threatened, at any moment, to escape the low-cut gown.

I kept thinking of Ginny and glancing at my watch.

When the music stopped, the ancient band leader took some slips of paper with song requests from a waiter before he began the next number. Rush was still standing at the table, talking golf to Max and Sam.

Mimi and Maryanne had gone off to find the powder room.

"I don't want to listen to this all night." Cookie squeezed my hand and pointed to the stage. "Looks like the band's taking a blow. I think I'll join the girls while they're on break. Too bad Rose isn't here. But her loss is my gain. Later, let's take this from where we left off, shall we?" She smiled and skipped away.

I stood there, reluctant to rejoin the group. Rush had gotten a drink and was getting into the roll as the well-traveled golf expert. "Of the well-known courses I've been on since I've been in this part of the country, Pinehurst doesn't compare with the Dunes at Myrtle Beach. The Dunes is a Trent Jones track. I love the way Jones sets up the landing areas with fairway bunkers. I always like to see what I'm aiming at when I stand on the tee. Of course, Jones is a sly old fox. Putting all those oversize bunkers in front of the outsized greens drives your depth perception out of kilter." I knew he'd never played Pinehurst or the Dunes and stood there aghast, listening to him plagiarizing almost verbatim what I'd told him on the trip over.

"Yeah, and how about the legendary number thirteen?" Max asked.

"Thirteen? A work of art. On every list of all-American holes I've seen. A monster. Almost a full horseshoe bending to the right around that huge lake and, if that wasn't bad enough, you have to lay up short of that wide inlet that cuts across the fairway about two-fifty in front of the tee. Not even Tiger Woods would try to drive that water. Logan has played the Dunes. We were comparing notes on the way over from the Roanoke airport. Right, Logan?"

Logan Baird: scriptwriter and notary public. Not only did he have the balls to parrot my description virtually word for word, but he also had the balls to ask me to authenticate his plagiarized account.

Cheapened by mere association, I resented his unabashed dishonesty. I knew he'd had a lot of wine earlier; still, it sickened me that he felt he had to compromise us both to exalt his image in the eyes of these strangers.

"Isn't that right, Logan?" he prompted again, impatiently.

"What's that?" I pretended not to have been listening.

"I was telling them about the Dunes at Myrtle Beach. Remember we were reminiscing about it this afternoon when we were driving over?" Rush was determined to draw me into his deception.

In the military, *quibbling* is the word used for taking liberty with the truth. Technically it isn't lying. But the officer's code is clear: Quibbling reflects unwillingness to face up to one's limitations. In some ways it is considered worse than a lie—a major flaw of character. At West Point and in OCS, quibbling is a dismissal offense.

Did ethics demand full disclosure?

Name, rank, and serial number only—if I wanted to take refuge in the Articles of War.

To be honest—and lately, I was trying very, very hard not to be—I really needed to take a good look at my own values. What did it matter that poor Rush needed to be a hero? Did it make me better than he was simply because I'd played those golf courses and my handicap was a nine?

Should be a seven . . . if I really wanted to talk about quibbling.

Truthfully, now that I was willing to look at it, wasn't I just envious? Resentful that the Rush Donalds and the Sam Cavanaughs and Max Bergmanns were all successful, and worse, that they found fulfillment in their roles?

What would it be like to be successful at what you really wanted to do?

Who was I fooling anyway? It was a role. I hated having to sell my soul for a buck, but I liked the money and the club memberships. I didn't really give a tinker's damn about pharmaceutical research or sales. I was a hero because I was half-smart, and being half-smart in a world populated with professionals who read at sixth-grade level was light-years ahead of the field. At the heart of it, I was the biggest phony of them all.

"Rush's right. The Dunes is an awesome track," I hedged artfully.

The truth might set you free, but it won't get you promoted, sayeth the soothsayer.

The soothsayer is a spineless wimp.

"I think I'll go powder my nose," I murmured and made my getaway.

I wanted to crawl under the nearest rock.

CHAPTER FOURTEEN

The band had resumed playing when I got back from the loo.

I paused at the velvet-roped entry to assess the battle situation.

The girls were back from the powder room, and Sam and Max were dancing with their wives. Rush and Mimi had returned to their own table. The waitress had brought them drinks, and they were pushing back their chairs to join the dancers. I waited until they reached the dance floor before I headed back to the table. On the way I caught a waiter and ordered a Jack Daniels on the rocks to ease the pain.

Waiting for my drink, I surveyed the dance floor. There were a number of good-looking women there. The way their bodies moved against the fabric of their seductive gowns stirred my already overactive imagination. My thoughts kept going back to Ginny. Her subtle flirting at dinner had opened the floodgates of my all-too-lusty preoccupations, leaving me with a palpable tension in my crotch.

It was still early and I had time to kill, but I wanted to get away by myself until time to meet Ginny. I resolved to make my excuses as soon as Rush and Mimi finished dancing and get the hell out of Dodge. In my head, I rehearsed my exit lines.

On the small bandstand, the ageless ebony man was squeezing out the last sweet notes of a cornet solo marvelously reminiscent of the old Bunny Berigan classic, "I Can't Get Started."

When he finished he raised the battered horn, saluting someone with a warm wave of recognition. Turning to see who it was, I caught sight of the mystery man in the navy blazer and tartan slacks, standing just inside the entryway. Beside him was Alex Crim. They both gave the old horn man a little wave and whispered something to the maitre d', who nodded and stood aside. I watched them thread their way through the tables, skirting the dance floor, slowly picking their way to the bandstand.

The soloist raised the cornet to his lips and waited patiently, tapping his foot in time as the drummer finished a solo riff.

Then the old man blew the spit out of the cornet and played the hard-driving passages of the coda. When they finished, everyone in the place started clapping.

I saw Rush and Mimi making their way back to the table and stood to hold her chair.

"Not a bad band, huh?" Rush beamed an alcoholic glow. Rush loved New Orleans-style jazz and had a collection of Lu Watters's Yerba Buena Jazz Band and the San Francisco revival of the New Orleans sound in the late thirties and forties. He was particularly fond of reminding me that Turk Murphy and Bob Scobey, from the old days around the Bay Area, had gone on to make it big in New York. He loved to regale me with tales his father had told him about the legendary banjo man, Clancy Hayes. According to Rush, Hayes had had a brief moment of fame back in the fifties for his record of "Huggin' and Chalkin'." Rush had given me an old twelve-inch album with Hayes doing great old numbers like "Ace in the Hole." He could talk for hours about how Turk Murphy had rediscovered the legendary New Orleans cornet player Bunk Johnson and had him fitted with false teeth, showcasing him with the band in smoky little Bay Area clubs.

"Not bad at all," I agreed. I meant it.

"I wonder if they know 'Ace in the Hole,' " Rush said when he was seated.

"Why don't you send a note over by our waiter," I suggested.

Rush looked back to the bandstand. He caught sight of Alex and the mystery man. They were exchanging hugs and slaps on the back, having an animated reunion with the bandleader. It was obvious they were all old friends.

"Why don't you go over and ask him?"

"Me? What's wrong with you?" I protested.

"You're better at things like that . . ." Rush's voice trailed off, watching Alex and the mystery man with the bandleader. "Look, Sam Snead's agent is making a request, so why can't you?"

I didn't say anything. I was anxious to get away, and I resented being used as his social secretary.

"Go on, Logan, ask him. Why should the hired help get preferential treatment? Besides, you know Alex. Why don't you go say hello?"

"I told you I've lunched with her, but we're hardly friends." I resisted "And I'd hardly call Sam Snead hired help. The man's a legend. Won twice as many tournaments as Nicklaus, probably more than anybody ever will. Presidents salivate to play with him. He's over eighty and big shots still dream of an invitation to play in his annual pro-am bash. They'd kill for a chance to tee it up with the ol' Slammer himself." Rush was definitely getting on my nerves.

"You can say what you want, but golf pros are still considered the help where I come from," he sniffed. "Besides, look who's with her. You saw what that redneck looked like before they cleaned him up and put a tie on him."

I wondered if he ever admitted he was wrong.

"Well? How about it?" His tone was ugly and he was becoming loud.

"How about what?" I tried to calm him down.

"The song. Go on over there. We have just as much right to make a request as she does." People were turning to stare.

"Okay. 'Ace in the Hole,' right?" I pushed back my chair and stood up. I didn't want to make a scene.

"Tell Mr. Sam I'll see him there." The cornet player was saying goodbye to Alex Crim and the mystery man as I approached.

"See you later, Archie," Alex said as they were leaving.

As she passed, she recognized me and abruptly stopped and turned.

"Ah . . . Logan, remember me, Betty's friend?" She extended her hand, struggling to recall my name.

"Logan Baird, Alex. Of course I remember." I smiled and took her hand. "Haven't seen you around Roanoke lately."

"No, we've been traveling some. Sam has a part in a movie. How's Betty?"

"Fine. I had lunch with her yesterday as a matter of fact. She told me about the movie and said to look out for you."

"Yes, but Sam's not here yet. He's on his way as we speak. You here to play golf?"

"Business with pleasure. There's a big medical convention." I winked.

"Oh, yes, Dr. Rayburn was telling us at dinner." She turned to look for companion, but he'd gone on ahead. "Sorry, I've got to run. Sam's driving over from the Roanoke airport with some movie folk. He should be arriving soon. We're meeting later at a small staff party down at the club." Alex looked over her shoulder toward the door, already starting to move backward, anxious to catch up to her friend. "Gotta run! If I don't see you around, tell Betty I said hi."

"Sure thing. Good running in to you." It seemed pretentious to tell her I would be at that party with Ginny.

When I turned back, the cornet player was standing a few steps away.

"You friends with Miz Alex?" He looked at me and smiled.

"More like a friend of a friend," I said. "You blow a great horn, Archie. That last solo was Berigan, and then there was Hackett a couple numbers back. And before that you did Ziggy Elman's solo from 'And the Angels Sing.' Can you do McPartland doing Beiderbecke or a little Satchmo?" I laughed.

"Ooo-o, yeaa-ah!" His face burst into a wide smile at the Louis Armstrong impersonation. "I can do a mean Satch. Louis was my friend."

"Ever hear of Lu Watters and Turk Murphy, or Bob Scobey? You know who Bunk Johnson was?" I asked. I couldn't resist showing off.

"Sho', man. You know that stuff?"

"Ooo-o, yeaa-ah!" My Louis wasn't quite as good as his, but for a white boy, it would pass. "I wonder if you know 'Ace in the Hole'? It's not for me. I'd rather hear you do 'And the Angels Sing' again." I nodded toward the table.

When Archie looked toward the table, Rush was studiously examining his manicure, but Mimi gave us a little wave.

"It's for the good-looking blonde with the jerk in the white coat."

"Sure. How you know 'bout that other stuff? You play horn or something?"

"No," I said. "I got a lot of records. Had 'em a long time."

"I got a lot of that old wax m'self. They don't play like that today."

"Don't sell yourself short, Archie. You play a great horn, man. And, thanks." I rolled up a pair of twenties and pressed them into his hand.

"No need, man," he said.

"Buy the boys a beer," I laughed.

"Sho'. The boys say thanks." He showed me a mouth full of teeth.

"I can't help but wonder who was that man with Alex Crim. Does he come here a lot?" My curiosity got the best of me.

"That's Mister Scotty. He's a friend of Mr. Sam's from up north somewhere."

"His last name Scott?" I asked.

"Just Scotty is all I know. I think he's a big shot. I see him with Dr. Rayburn. Down for a checkup, maybe? Ask Miz Alex, I'm sure she knows."

"Okay, I will."

"You a friend of Mr. Sam?" Archie was curious now.

"No, I've met Alex a couple of times. You know, the mutual friend?" I reminded him and changed the subject. "Ever hear of Papa Celestin?"

"Oh, man, yeah! I was born in Algiers and raised in New Orleans." It came out "Nawlins." "I played around New York a long time."

"I spend some time around New York. Where'd you play?"

"Village Vanguard or Sweet Basil. A bunch of us used to jam a lot after hours." He peered down at me.

"Man, yeah!" I said. "You really been around."

"I can't do that stuff for this crowd though." Archie frowned. "How long you here?"

"Three nights . . . maybe four."

"Stick around after closing. We're going down to the Golf Club. There's gonna be a party for the working folk. Mr. Sam'll be there. You know he likes to play the horn?" Archie laughed and waved his old cornet.

"I read that somewhere. Can he really play a horn?" I laughed.

"He's okay, but not as good with that as they say he is at hitting a golf ball." He grinned. "Man can't have everything."

"Guess not. Anyway, thanks, man. I'll be sure and catch you later." I turned and made my way back to the table.

"What'd he say?" Rush asked me before I was seated. "He gonna do it?"

"His name's Archie and he was raised around Nawlins. That's New Orleans to you Yankees. Yeah, he's gonna do it."

"Great. I forgot to ask you to find out if he knew the 'Three Nineteen Blues.' Run back and ask him before he starts the next set." Now he sounded like a marine sergeant.

"He can't play much of that stuff for this crowd. Said it would be better if maybe you ask him later, toward closing."

"Jeezus, he's trying to keep us here buying drinks. He's shilling for the house," Rush sneered. "Probably picks up some big tips from these high rollers who don't know any better. What a sweet little scam that is."

"Maybe, but I don't think so. He said he'd be glad to play some jazz later, when the crowd thins out."

"You are naïve. Anyway, run back and ask him to play 'Three Nineteen Blues.' "

I was about to tell him to drop dead when a waiter came walking up and said, "Excuse me, is either of you Mr. Baird?"

"I'm Logan Baird."

"There's a call for you, sir. There are house phones outside, down the hall to your right." He handed me a folded slip of paper.

Please call home.

"I hope you'll excuse me, Mimi. I guess I'd better go see about this. Hope I'll see you tomorrow," I told her, then looked back to Rush. "Don't worry about in the morning. I'll open our booth around eight. Remember, we tee off at eleven. So if you want to hit some practice balls, we need to go down to the pro shop around ten, I guess. Anyway, hope you two have a great evening. Sure you won't change your mind and go down to the staff party with us?"

"No way. That sounds like a waste of time. I'll see you in the exhibit hall in the morning. I do want to contact Dr. Ferguson before we go play golf." Rush didn't get up. He was not unhappy to see me go. "Gimme your car keys. We're probably going to try to find some action at the after-hours joints, after we dance for awhile."

"Ginny said you could call the clubs and they'd send a car," I reminded him. I didn't like the idea of his driving around in my company car with a snoot full of booze.

"No way. If we didn't like the place, we'd be stuck without a ride to another joint." He held out his hand. "Just gimme the frigging keys."

"The bell captain has the keys. They'll get the car when you need it." I'd had enough of him for one evening. I handed him the parking receipt for the car and left without so much as a parting nod.

I was hardly out of the place and trying to remember which way to find the nearest elevator when I heard Rush behind me in the hallway. "Logan, wait up."

Except for us, the hallway was deserted.

"Listen," he began even before he'd reached where I was standing. "I hope you understand that I . . . that my being with Mimi is . . ." He was struggling to tell me that I should not blab it around about his being with Mimi.

"Harmless recreation, good clean fun?" I helped. "Don't worry, my lips are sealed."

"It's not only Nadine. I wouldn't want this to get around to the other salesmen. People in Teaneck might misunderstand." He frowned. "And, after all, you have a stake in this too. I'm recommending you for management. Discretion is the first rule of management."

Rush's first-rules-of-management list was getting overcrowded.

"Don't worry about me." I was enjoying his discomfort, but I didn't want to remind him that I was about to head off on a little harmless recreation of my own.

"Have you heard about the old maid who found herself having to go to a new dentist?" His tone was just short of threatening now.

"I guess I'm about to hear it."

"It seems that as the dentist was bending down close and saying 'open wide,' he felt the old lady cradle his balls in the palm of her hand. When he looked at her, speechless, she smiled sweetly and said, 'Now, young man, we're not going to hurt each other, are we?'"

"Besides," he leered. "You're not exactly heading out for the nearest prayer meeting yourself. But, then, I'm sure Rose would be more understanding about your old schoolteacher."

He was way ahead of me.

I wanted to ask him if he was the dentist or the old lady, but I held my tongue. I wanted to explain to him about covering one's ass. I wanted to tell him that I was going to phone Rose to tell her about running into our old eighth-grade homeroom teacher. And I especially wanted to tell him that he was a goddamn fool. He couldn't trust me any more than I trusted him.

I didn't say anything.

"Get it?" he asked.

Without dignifying his question, I turned and left him glaring daggers into my back.

I should've felt guilty for not telling him about Sam Snead's coming to the staff party, but I didn't.

When he found out, he could eat his freaking heart out.

TUESDAY NIGHT

CHAPTER FIFTEEN

With grave misgivings about Rush's driving my company car, I left him standing in the hallway outside the Old White Club and headed directly to my room.

Safely inside, I closed the door and leaned back against its reassuring sanctuary.

I let my shoulders slump forward until my chin touched my chest and my arms dangled to my knees like a rag doll.

I breathed a long sigh of relief.

At last a moment to myself.

One thing I knew for certain: Rush was as relieved to see me go as I was glad to leave.

Now that he had assumed a pose for Mimi and Sam and Max, he'd have to play out this Hahvahd charade to the end.

I could see plainly that, for the next three days at least, I was doomed.

The scene was set. Nothing for me to do but accept my fate.

Rush Donald was a shameless social chameleon. Tonight, his precious Mark Hopkins had begun to slide into the mists of obscurity. By tomorrow night on the phone with Nadine, he would have metamorphosed into the next form of his identity. I could hear him telling everyone at Hahvahd B—and at Teaneck—of his easy familiarity with the legendary Greenbrier.

From here on, Rush would project the image of darling of the country club set.

Of course, I was practicing the same dishonesty, playing up to him and his precious Nadine.

If this was what success was all about, was getting ahead in this rat race really worth it?

Shrugging, I dismissed the thought.

For me, there was a colder reality. I'd been eyeball to eyeball with death in combat. Dishonesty will kill you; truth can set you free.

And my turn was coming.

Remembering his Chaplinesque struggles out on the practice tee this afternoon, I realized Rush was certainly no golfer. It was obvious that the snobby SOB was getting very nervous about playing tomorrow, afraid he'd show his ass. I'd seen his reaction when he caught a look at the first tee and the looming presence of Howard's Creek. Standing outside the pro shop, he'd swallowed hard when I'd pointed up to the broad reach of windows across the grill room, with the gallery of people sitting at tables enjoying the clear view of the golfers teeing off. I'd told him how my father had watched the famous golfing priest, Father Duffy or Kelly—the name eluded me now—the day after Sam Snead had shot his famous fifty-nine at the Sam Snead Festival pro-celebrity. The priest had stood there crossing himself as, one after the other, he'd dumped three balls into the water before a tittering gallery of sympathetic faithful.

Now, I relished the image of the buffoon Rush cold-topping his first shot into the creek.

Sam and Max would show no sympathy for his freaking ego. I'd bet on that.

I laughed out loud.

At least I had escaped him for the remainder of the evening.

I looked around the room. The flamboyant Dorothy Draper floral bedspread had been folded and placed on a blanket chest at the foot of the four-poster bed. The bed had been neatly turned down; foiled squares of chocolate rested on each pillow.

The softly lit interior was picture perfect, right off the pages of *Town and Country*. Spilling from the bathroom, the warm light traced a sharp trapezoidal path across the rich green carpet to the bed. Overhead, the light from the reading lamp spread a soft, indistinct circle on the ceiling. The glow from the bedside table lamp flowed up the wall, illuminating the delicate pink-and-green floral splash of the upholstery and window treatments, the unmistakable trademark of the celebrated decorator.

Since I'd left this afternoon, the room had been meticulously restored to perfect order. The items of clothing I'd strewn carelessly about the room earlier when I changed for dinner were nowhere in sight.

Fascinated, I walked to the door of the walk-in closet. When the door opened the light came on automatically, and the closet seemed almost as big as Paul's bedroom back in Roanoke. Inside, my discarded underwear, socks, and shirts had been placed in a neat pile with a laundry bag left conveniently beside the stack. The trousers to my business suit had been put on a hanger. My dress shoes were arranged on a shoe shelf positioned low against the back wall.

A guardian angel?

Lately, I desperately needed one.

It was reassuring that some invisible presence was here to straighten out the sudden disarray of my life.

I wondered what it would be like to be able to live like this—pampered and free from care.

Rags to riches, the American dream—it was a seductive thought.

Was this why I let Rush abuse me?

Did anything justify selling your soul? Deep down, the question was not comforting.

There was no one to blame but me. A flunky by any other name is still a miserable sycophant.

My reflection grimaced wryly back from the mirror on the closet door at this painful introspection.

Nagged by self-loathing, I emptied my pockets onto the top of the chest of drawers, hung up my jacket, and took off my tie. Sooner or later the Rush Donalds of this world were riding for a fall. It was my own fault I was letting Rush drag me down with him.

Beyond my injured feelings, the naked glimpse of Rush's fragile ego depressed and frightened me. His need in the dining room to be the wine connoisseur, the all-knowing bon vivant—and, again, in the Old White Club with Sam and Max and the women, his need to be the well-traveled player of famous golf courses. In his gnawing insecurity, Rush could never admit to weakness or imperfection.

All this pretension left me with a hollow feeling.

My erstwhile role model had feet of clay.

Sometimes, getting ahead could be downright shitty work. I felt incredibly soiled.

I quickly stripped, needing to feel the cleansing warmth of the shower.

In the bathroom, the towels and the cake of soap I'd used earlier had vanished and been replaced. There was nothing to betray that anyone had been here earlier.

Omens for a new beginning?

I pictured myself at Rush's precious Harvard B, rising quickly to the top. I was certainly smarter than the arrogant Mr. Donald. From what I'd seen of the top management in Teaneck, I was smarter than most—maybe all—of them. All I needed was opportunity.

I allowed myself the slightest tingle of excitement at the thought of replacing Rush as division manager when the pompous bastard left for Cambridge.

"Don't count your chickens," I could almost hear my father's wise voice counseling me.

What the hell, I countered. A little innocent woolgathering couldn't hurt.

The shower helped, but no amount of water could wash away the soiled feeling.

Stinging with lingering shame, I roughly toweled myself dry.

If this was war, I'd show 'em all.

Through the window on the far side of the room I could see, just above the silhouetted ridge of Kate's Mountain, a pale orange blush where the last faint glow of twilight was losing its struggle to hold back the deep electric-blue of the night. In the clear mountain air, the stars were so sharply etched in the evening sky they seemed painted there.

The promise of an interesting evening at the Golf Club with Ginny and the legendary Sam Snead brought my spirits a sudden lift. Rush was certain to pitch a fit when he found out that his hero had been at the party he had snubbed.

The thought gave me a perverse satisfaction. God forbid that Rush would ever suspect I knew beforehand and didn't tell.

My thoughts wandered back to Ginny. My old high school teacher was a prize.

I wondered if there were a regular boyfriend.

She had invited me to the party. But then, I was just someone from her long-forgotten past. Was it possible she was meeting a lover there?

Coming back to reality, I retrieved the telephone message.

Please call home.
Rose

In the bottom corner, the time was noted neatly: 8:25 P.M. Ginny had said 9:30. My Timex showed 8:52. Might as well get all the unpleasantness behind me.

CHAPTER SIXTEEN

I watched the minute hand on my Timex click forward to 8:53 as I dialed the phone.

Most likely little Paul would already be in bed.

Rose picked up on the second ring.

"Hi, I just got your message. I was busy helping Rush set up the exhibit. I was getting ready to call. I miss you," I lied.

"Why didn't you call earlier? Paul's already down for the night. He pitched a fit when you didn't call. I wish you'd carry your cell phone. I've been frantic to get in touch."

"What's up?" I asked, suddenly alerted by her tone. "Something wrong?"

"Oh, Logan, I hope you're sitting down."

I'd heard that "bad news" tone in voices all my life. Rose always had a flair for the dramatic, but this was different, I could tell.

I felt my knees go weak.

Someone was either badly hurt or dead.

At least she'd said Paul was safe in bed—I couldn't stand the thought of losing my son.

My father? Dad was retired but still young and vital. He was getting back to his old self after a nearly fatal toxic reaction to a ruptured appendix last year. We'd almost lost him.

The incident had put me more or less on notice of my own mortality.

I hadn't heard a newscast since noon. My god, not a crash? My brother, Jim, was a captain with a major airline. Subconsciously, I worried about him more than I cared to admit.

"Are you going to tell me?" I summoned the courage to ask and held my breath.

"Are you sitting down?"

"Damn it, Rose, just tell me!"

"Logan! Don't you dare curse me!"

"Just tell me, Rose."

"John Paul Silver is dead."

No way! A mistake. It had to be.

Side by side, we'd survived Bosnia. Friends since we were eager young correspondents fresh out of army orientation, we'd met at the Combat Lifesaver course at Fort Sam Houston in San Antonio, over a beer in the Pit, the officers' club casual bar.

In Bosnia we'd been blown all to hell in a jeep by a land mine and walked away.

We'd survived a war, brothers to the end.

I couldn't comprehend.

Mistaken identity? There must be another John Paul Silver.

John Paul was my age. Men shouldn't die that young.

"Rose, are you sure? Did you see something on TV?"

"Of course I'm sure! They called here for you."

"They? Who called?"

"His sister, Jean, and his wife."

"How? A car wreck?"

"No, nothing like that. Agranulocytosis, a blood dyscrasia. Did you know he was sick?"

"No. My god, I had no idea. I haven't heard from him since Christmas . . . maybe once in the spring."

John Paul gone?

My brain wouldn't work. Thoughts struggled like insects trapped inside the cobwebbed chamber of my head.

"Logan? Are you still there?"

"Yeah, I'm here. When did you find this out?"

"Jean called about an hour ago. And I talked to his wife, Cathy. They left a number for you to call. She said he knew he was dying. Happened pretty fast, I guess. One of his last wishes was that no one call you until it finally happened. He'd had an infection and had been on some new antibiotic . . . a side effect. Agranulocytosis. It's like leukemia, you know."

Rose was a nurse, a damn good one. A-gran-u-lo-cy-to-sis. She was very clinical when she pronounced the word.

"Yeah, Rose, I know."

After all, medicine was my life too.

CHAPTER SEVENTEEN

Numbly, I held the phone, not speaking.

John Paul. Dead at thirty-one . . . from a goddamn side effect.

When I first met him, I'd viewed John Paul as a curiosity. I'd never met a grown man who admitted to being a virgin. Talk about conduct unbecoming an officer and a gentleman. In my opinion, his celibacy was unmale, unmilitary and, most of all, downright un-American.

Myself, I'd been a precocious lad who, at age five, first played doctor with an older neighbor girl who'd already started sprouting breasts. God, I loved those little titties. If I live to be a hundred, all I have to do is close my eyes and remember, and I still get an erection. It had seemed divinely ordered that John Paul's sexual initiation should be delivered into the capable hands of such a qualified mentor.

After all, real men have a sworn duty—don't they?

His sexual baptism had become my obsession.

But—talk about the proverbial poor devil who couldn't make out in a whorehouse with a fistful of hundred-dollar bills—John Paul became my albatross.

And, my holy war.

My comic sexual odyssey with John Paul had begun when I first met him at Fort Sam Houston and discovered he was still uninitiated. A male virgin at the ripe old age of twenty-four! An anomaly worthy of Ripley's *Believe It Or Not*, here was the eighth wonder of the world walking around in an army uniform.

After San Antonio we had wound up at Fort Pickett, a Godforsaken outpost in the Virginia backwater, whose terrain had the dubious distinction of closely resembling certain strategic Eastern European landscapes.

Rose left San Antonio and went to her mother's in Roanoke to have the baby at the hospital where she'd trained.

I had worn the tires on our brand-new 1992 Sunbird convertible down to the cord, taking John Paul into Petersburg and Richmond every night, a selfless undertaking indeed.

Careful attention was given to appropriateness. Officers' clubs, country clubs, sorority mixers—I was a paragon of social consciousness.

"Why don't we get the name of a respectable call girl?" John Paul had asked me in frustration time after time. "There have got to be some very high-class pros. Remember that Heidi woman, the Hollywood socialite?"

"By god, never! Don't bring it up again," I snapped. I had my standards. I wasn't about to let a fellow officer stoop to a call girl—that would have been admitting defeat.

"I just thought I'd mention it," John Paul shrugged.

"Don't. Besides, the college girls have put all the first-class pros out of business," I explained.

In our sexual safaris, we had met dozens of good-looking women dying for romance, but John Paul was hopeless. He never even came close. He was a good-looking kid. Sort of put me in mind of Brad Pitt, but I soon became convinced he was genetically cursed.

Hereditarily unlayable.

What I suffered for that man.

I'd read Henry Miller and *Lady Chatterley's Lover*. I was a man of the world. I'd seen the uncut version of *Caligula* and *The Tiffany Minx Affair*—all the best porno flicks.

A liberated young man of the world, I'd understood such things.

Night after night, I'd get him connected, dancing in the arms of some willing young deb, clearly headed for carnal ecstasy. Then, with great subtlety and a knowing wink, I would, in the interest of our humanitarian quest, whisk her unprotesting girlfriend out of the way. It was a sacrifice; but looking back, clearing the way for John Paul was not an altogether unrewarding exercise.

Yet, without exception, when the pleasantly agreeable girlfriend and I returned expecting to find our friends in happy disarray, we'd discover her frustrated companion torn between tears and insanity with John Paul blissfully regaling the poor thing with tales about his granny's sinking spells or his sister's Barbie collection.

Talk about sacrifice for a friend. My selflessness had known no bounds. I was committing the supreme sacrifice with John Paul's dates' libidinous girlfriends all over the place. Not wanting him to feel any more a failure than he already did—and quite fatalistic about dying without having experienced life to the fullest—uncomplaining, I had persevered.

Anything for John Paul.

On the way to the war zone, in New York and the glamour cities of Europe I had trolled him like a fancy spinning lure through the nightspots with not even a nibble.

Alas, John Paul had been a proverbial phallic pariah.

By the time we hit Paris, the situation had become serious—time was running out.

With embarkation to the war zone only a few days away, clearly a reassessment of standards was in order.

It was a time to take heroic measures.

After all, this was war. A man cannot always be a hero, but he can always be a man.

I was not about to stand by and let John Paul die a virgin in a foxhole.

And, after all, placing John Paul in the care of an authentic Paris demimondaine did not amount to the same thing as stooping to a visit to some back-alley whorehouse. Paris courtesans were an intrinsic expression of a time-honored culture. These flower-like women were trained in the exotic arts of pleasing men. In Paris a demimondaine was an honorable solution. John Paul's initiation would be without compromise, really. This ancient ritual was akin to a religion—or something close, I reasoned.

At last, in Paris, John Paul had been relieved of his dangerously unhealthy condition.

But John Paul's initiation had worked better than I anticipated. I had orchestrated a disaster.

"In for a penny, in for a pound." The Brits have a nice way with words. Once initiated, no argument, no plea could persuade John Paul to leave this newly found rapture. After three nonstop days and nights, we tottered on the brink of desertion. In time of war, desertion demands death by firing squad. The way he was going, however, it looked as if the situation might never come to that. I had begun to visualize the ignominious horror of having to write John Paul's mother of his death by carnal excess.

Fortunately, the day before we were to ship out, John Paul had run out of money. I herded him off to Bosnia light in heart. After his marathon rutting, it was actually a great relief to be headed for the combat zone.

We were assigned to an outpost near Sarajevo—safe enough, if there was any safety in a constantly changing battlefield.

In Bosnia, however, John Paul's sexual enlightenment had taken on frightening dimensions.

After I'd finally gotten him laid in Paris, it was a miracle—or a nightmare—the way he'd changed. Like many a good man before him, John Paul had fallen victim to the joys of the flesh. Once he'd invented sex, he went plain fanatical over it. Newly introduced to carnal congress, John Paul was like a starving man. Bombings and shelling and snipers be damned, he had hardly arrived before he got down to the serious business of stolen pleasure.

In Bosnia there had been a plethora of willing young women. Within a fortnight, he'd found himself a girl and kept her in her dead parents' tidy farmhouse on the outskirts of the village near where we worked. Sometimes in the evenings, during a lull in the hostilities, I would crank up my jeep and drive through the dusk a few miles north and east of the ravaged city, where, in a cooperative venture with a young Army doctor, John Paul had taken over the house.

To me John Paul's bucolic mistress had seemed an altogether unremarkable physical specimen.

When I was around, the young woman lurked in the background. I don't think she had much English, an interesting situation considering John Paul taught English. Her vocabulary had consisted mainly of giggles.

Awed by the Frankenstein-like proportions of my creation, I had assumed the young woman had hidden talents. I did notice that both John Paul and his young woman always smiled a lot. And, after all, he seemed content. So, mission a bit over-accomplished and having no one else to blame, I'd kept my opinion to myself.

Together we had seen enough of the intensely bloodied combat to fear for our lives, but almost before we knew it, an uneasy truce was finally negotiated. When the smoke cleared at last, we found that we'd gotten to be brothers of a kind.

In those evenings off, we'd hoist a few drinks and talk about books and women.

For some reason I have never understood, from the beginning John Paul put me on a pedestal even though I was two years younger. In his eyes I was always a hero, a role to which I never became totally accustomed.

Still, it's nice to be a hero in someone's eyes.

The last time I saw John Paul was the evening before I left Bosnia heading back to the States. We'd gotten wasted.

After we had returned to the States, we talked frequently on the phone and corresponded regularly during our readjustment to civilian life.

John Paul had returned to the job he'd left. In less than six months, he'd called to tell me he was marrying Cathy, a former student. A girl he'd taught English, a teeny-bopper pen pal.

"I've never kissed her," John Paul had confided in Sarajevo before we headed home.

Having felt that I'd rushed into the stifling arrangement of marriage too young, I was not at all an advocate of nuptial incarceration as a sensible way of life. When he called me out of the blue a few weeks before the all-too-hasty wedding to ask me to be best man, in a self-righteously proprietary way I had reacted violently to what I considered his ill-thought-out solution to his late-blooming libido.

Alas, I'd done my job too well—but then that's an oxymoron—some things by their essence defy limitation.

However, the idea of marriage seemed excessive—entirely unnecessary.

"Damn it, John Paul, this is overkill!" I had tried in vain to talk some sense into him. Ego-wounded and totally disappointed, a dishonored—no! a failed—mentor, after I realized my advice was falling on deaf ears, without sensitivity but avoiding further recriminations, I had declined the invitation to stand beside him at the wedding.

I've always viewed weddings and funerals as shallow, social affectations that are more about society than about the true emotions of the events they commemorate. And I've always avoided them at all costs.

After a few months, John Paul's calls and letters had dwindled in their frequency. Still, over the past four years he always wrote me once a year, at Christmas. I usually jotted him a hasty responding note on my perennially belated card.

He'd kept his word and was writing his book, but it was slow going he'd said.

Ashamed, I'd confessed I'd given up, pushed my sorry manuscript to the back of my darkest closet, and traded in my laptop for a salesman's job.

Deep down, I felt I'd failed us both.

Throughout, we'd talked by phone once or twice a year at odd times—usually when I was in some damn dump of a motel in some dreary town. However, the bond between us had remained intact. He'd report the progress of his book—in numbers of pages only. We both agreed books were to be written down, not talked out. And he'd keep after me to get back to my laptop and work on my own novel again.

Secretly, in fits and starts, because of him I guess, for a time I'd taken my trusty Dell with me and spent evenings filling motel trash baskets with false starts and forgettable first lines.

It was a dark and shitty night. . . .

We were forever planning to meet somewhere for a weekend—then forever postponing the reunion due to the press of that enigmatic entity called lifeitsownrealself.

"When did he die?" Voice choked, my head spinning with memories, I roused from my reverie.

"Late yesterday," Rose replied. "His wife wants you for a pallbearer. I told her that I didn't think you could come. What's she like? She sounded awfully young."

"Oh, she is. But I never met her, remember? I didn't go to the wedding." I suffered a sharp pang, recalling how I'd turned my back on him.

You put on the ring and cut off your circulation, John Paul.

"When's the funeral, then?" I persisted, my voice husked with emotion.

"She didn't say. She didn't tell me much more than what I've told you. Mostly, I talked to his sister. She's very anxious for you to call. Tonight if you can, she said. I have the number here. Can you take it down?" Rose's voice had that awful funereal tone we learn growing up. I hated the ritual response, the phony affectation, the conditioned hand-me-down reflex that our grown-ups bequeath us to deal with death.

I picked up the pen lying on the elegant little memo pad by the phone. "Okay, shoot."

I jotted JEAN on the pad and wrote the number down beside it.

"You can't be considering going?" Rose said.

"I don't see how." I surely wasn't going to any goddamn funeral. There was no helping John Paul now. To tell the truth, I wasn't particularly anxious to make the call to his sister. "But I'll call them as soon as we hang up," I finished lamely.

"We can't afford it, anyway."

"Rose, you don't put a price tag on respecting friendship."

"Some friendship. Chasing whores—"

"Rose!"

"Don't 'Rose' me! And, why didn't you call me like you said? I've been worried."

"Worried? Don't be silly. I had to get our exhibit up." It wasn't exactly a lie. Besides, I'd only been gone a few hours. "Are you okay?"

"I'm fine. What's your room number? I thought you were going to call to let me know. I didn't know how to reach you," she whined again. Now that the bad news was out of the way, Rose reverted to her familiar accusing pout.

"I'm sorry, Rose. I've been busy. Making love was nice this morning. I miss you already." It wasn't all a lie.

"Don't give me that stuff about missing me. If you really did, you'd have called."

What could I say?

John Paul . . . dead.

I felt numb—anxious to get off the phone.

"C'mon Rose. You know how it is. We had to set up that exhibit backdrop. You remember that dinosaur our people in Teaneck shipped to the Virginia Medical Society meeting at Hotel Roanoke. My god, it's like putting together a movie set, and we don't have any tools." I felt guilty. It had become an all-around day for quibbling.

I was getting to be quite the expert.

I suddenly thought about Ginny. My watch showed 9:12.

"Rose, do you remember Ginny McKim? Our homeroom teacher in eighth grade?" I asked innocently, congratulating myself for protecting myself in case Cookie Bergmann had seen me with Ginny in the dining room.

I was developing a genuine knack for artifice.

Rush was a great teacher when it came to avoiding the truth.

"The orphanage girl? She was a college student . . . a practice teacher. My god, she married that awful Tommy Hardison. Ginny McKim was nothing more than a drunken slut. I fixed her good one time. Anyway, what about her?"

My internal warning bells started ringing.

"She's here now. Owns a local B and B. Been here for four years, she said. I ran into to her in the exhibit hall tonight. I don't know any details, but she seems to be doing well." I didn't want to overdo it. "She remembers you and said to tell you hi."

I crossed my fingers behind my back.

"Ha! She hates me. Always had it in for me. She accused me of—she made up a lie, but I got even. She must be almost forty now."

Rose loved to gloat over other women's being older or heavier than she. She'd turned thirty a few months back. It weighed on her mind.

I waited, hoping to let the subject die.

"Ginny McKim looked like hell the last time I saw her. She'd gotten fat as a hog. She must be a total wreck by now."

"It's been at least seventeen . . . maybe eighteen . . . years since the eighth grade. I wouldn't exactly say she's fat, but I didn't recognize her. She seems to be doing well here," I said, careful not to mention that Ginny McKim certainly had no weight problem. And, she certainly didn't look like hell. "Anyway, I miss you. I'll call Ohio before it gets any later. Good night."

"Don't you love me?" she whined.

"Of course! This is quite a shock. I'm not thinking straight."

"Have you been drinking?"

"Rose, for chrissake!"

"I know how it is when you're around Rush Donald. I don't trust him."

"I'm sober as a judge." Telling the truth for a change felt good. "Now let me go. I'll call tomorrow night . . . probably early, before dinner. There's a big reception on the program tomorrow night. You know how these things are."

"All right. But you know you can't go running off to Ohio to that funeral. You haven't seen him in four years, and that whole thing between you two was disgusting."

In a moment of weakness after I returned from Bosnia, I'd made the fatal mistake of telling Rose about my noble mission to oversee the deflowering of John Paul.

Rose, I discovered, had no sense of humor in the matter.

It had been a painful lesson, but one well learned.

Thanks be to my cosmic travel agent that I hadn't been so naive as to confess the details of my own sacrifices on his behalf. She would have never understood my altruism.

"Don't worry. You know how I feel about funerals," I said.

"Okay. Try to get back early Saturday afternoon. We have couples' bridge. I just wish you didn't have to travel so much," she whined again.

I was glad now I hadn't told her that I might be replacing Rush as division manager. With the new job, the travel was certain to increase. I'd be flying up to Teaneck at least once every month or so, and I'd be on the road three nights every week.

"I love you, too. I miss you, but I gotta go. Good night," I said without much feeling.

"Good night," she said as I hung up.

Too late I realized that I hadn't asked about our son.

Truly he was my pride and joy. More than anything, little Paul kept me in the marriage.

Born while I was in Bosnia, over Rose's protest we'd named him after John Paul.

Now, incredibly, John Paul was dead.

I stared unseeing out the window at the starry sky.

Automatically, I dialed the number I'd written down.

CHAPTER EIGHTEEN

"The Silver residence." The woman's voice was flat, uninflected.

"This is Logan Baird from Roanoke, Virginia. May I speak to Jean . . ." I let the question trail off. I wasn't sure if John Paul's sister was married or not and was afraid to call her "Silver."

"Oh, yes, Mr. Baird. This is Jean Silver Riley. Thank you for calling me back tonight. I regret the circumstances, but I'm glad your wife was able to find you so soon." Her voice was heavy with fatigue and sadness. John Paul had been quite close to his sister. I remembered his telling me they were orphaned early and had been reared by his grandmother.

"I don't know quite what to say. In many ways we were like brothers," I began.

"I know. You were John Paul's hero. His last request was that I call you personally to give you the news. It was important to him. He reminisced a great deal the last few weeks about your adventures in the army. I . . . Cathy and I were hoping you'd be a pallbearer."

"No . . . I can't," I stammered, momentarily off guard. "I'm sorry, but you just can't count on me. As much as I'd like to, it's impossible for me to come at all. This is so unexpected. I'm stuck at an important conference for my company. I really don't know what to say right now," I hedged, searching for excuses.

I thought I detected a sob, then silence.

"When is the funeral?"

Funerals headed a long list of things I was no damn good at. Even if I were free, I had no intention of going. I would say goodbye to John Paul in my own way and not at a funeral.

"At ten Friday morning in the college chapel. You know the university had granted him full tenure, and he found a publisher for his novel right before he got ill. He was going to surprise you." Her voice was crumbling around the edges. "It's so sad. His future looked so bright."

"A rotten waste," I agreed, running low on things to say.

I swallowed and stared out the window into the night. Across the way, I saw a light come on and the heather blonde from the golf shop entered the room. She was wearing a form-fitting gown of elegant champagne satin.

Strangely detached, I watched as Paul's sister rambled on.

"He was proud of that book. It's all about two young army officers. The more worldly of the pair is obsessed with getting the other one . . . ah . . . initiated . . . fixed up. It's hilarious. He couldn't wait for you to read it. He insisted I send you a copy as soon as it's published in the fall." Her voice was husking up, on the verge of losing control. "He called it *Carpe Diem*," she sniffled. "He said you'd understand."

"Oh, yeah, we'd talked about it. I love the title. I can't wait to read it. Give me an address. I'd like to send flowers." I knew John Paul wasn't exactly the flowers type, but I was running out of things to say.

Across the court, the heather blonde reached back with both hands and unzipped her dress. Before I could catch my breath, the dress fell in a heap around her ankles. Standing in all her glory in bikini panties and a bra, she was oblivious that her drapes were open. Her well-turned behind momentarily distracted me from my sudden melancholy.

"John Paul requested flowers be omitted. But there's a writing scholarship at the school—his pet project. I'm sure he would have liked it if you thought of that. If you have a pen, I can give you the address."

"Sure, go ahead." I wrote it down and read it back as my eyes kept straying back to the lighted window across the court.

Picking up the dress, the heather blonde tossed it across a chair before she turned and disappeared from view in the bathroom. When she appeared again at the bathroom door, she removed her bra and tossed it casually onto the chair with the dress. Now, her breasts were alive with motion. Then she leaned one hand against the doorjamb and stepped out of her panties.

I sucked in my breath. She was heather blonde all over.

"If things should work out, you could call and let us know if you can come to the service Friday. John Paul and Cathy were talking about you before he . . . he passed. He regretted that we had never met you and that he had never really gotten to know Rose. He had so much to regret. Cathy and I would be pleased to have you. I'm sure it would be a great comfort for us both to meet you at last. We have room. You could stay here with us. I lost my husband several years back. John Paul was the only man we had to lean on. But of course I understand you have other responsibilities. Still, if you could work it out . . ." Her voice grew hoarse again.

She was really getting to me now. I struggled to fight back my irritation.

Across the way the heather blonde had moved back into the bathroom and was leaning over the lavatory splashing water on her face. The view of her naked bottom was breathtaking. She straightened, put on a shower cap, and disappeared toward the tub.

"Mr. Baird? Logan? Are you still there?"

"Ah . . . yes, I'm here."

"Think about it. You don't have to commit to being a pallbearer. I understand your situation is tenuous."

"I'm really in a bind right at the moment. I don't see much hope that I can find someone to relieve me on such short notice. I'm sure you understand. This is all so sudden, but if something should work out, I'll call. I can't tell you how hard this hits me. John Paul was like a brother. Please tell Cathy I'll write or call later, in a few days after the shock is over." I recited the words, impatient to say goodbye.

"Would you like me to get Cathy to the phone? I'm sure she'd want to—"

"No!" I said abruptly. This was leading nowhere. "No, I wouldn't know what to say." I wanted to end the conversation. "I'll let you go now."

Across the way, the heather blonde stepped back into view. She was toweling herself across the back, then gently dabbing underneath her breasts and between her legs. Her legs were wide apart now, and she was being very thorough.

"He said tell you to remember *carpe diem*. It's Latin. He said you'd know what it meant." I could hear her breathing anxiously, reluctant to let me go.

"Sure. Seize the day," I murmured, remembering. "We talked about that a lot in Bosnia."

"Seize the day!" She started to cry. "He was so . . . so bright. I keep asking why."

"Sometimes it's hard to sort any of this out." I was anxious for this to end. "Anyway, try to keep your chin up. And please give Cathy my deepest sympathy. I'm sorry, I don't know what else to say," I faltered.

"Oh, my, I almost forgot. He said he'd left a letter with his attorney, Mr. Prueffer, to be mailed to you upon his death. Did you get it yet by any chance?" she asked, hopefully.

"Well, yes. Matter of fact, it came this morning before I left home. It's been a killing day. I haven't had a chance to open it," I confessed, glancing at the envelope lying on the dresser.

"I'm sorry. We—Cathy and I—wondered what he had to say. He was insistent that the lawyer handle it and that it not be mailed until he had . . . ah . . . passed." She was fishing now. I felt a pang of resentment. After all, if he'd entrusted it to his attorney instead of them, he was probably making some discreet request, or more likely it probably contained something highly personal.

The heather blonde stepped into a fresh pair of panties and was reaching for another bra.

Breathing faster now, I stood and adjusted the growing bulge in my undershorts.

"Don't worry, if there's any word for you, I'll be sure to let you know," I said.

"I know you would. Good night," Jean Silver Riley said, still reluctant to break the connection.

"Good night," I said softly and hung up.

When I looked out the window again, the heather blonde was gone.

Carpe diem!

The phone jangled me out of my reverie.

"Logan, your line's been busy. I've been trying for twenty minutes." It was Ginny.

The digital bedside clock displayed 9:21.

"Yeah, sorry. What's up?" I hoped she hadn't changed her mind about the party.

"I got caught with a minor problem after I left you."

My heart sank.

When it rains it pours, my grandmother always used to say.

"Can't you make it?"

"Oh, no, nothing that major. I'm just running behind. I got stuck down here in my friend's office, and I still want to go home and change. If you didn't want to wait here, I was wondering if you'd like to ride along with me." She left the thought hanging.

"I'd like to get out of here. I'd love the company. Give me ten minutes to get dressed?"

"Fine, the arcade at Draper's Café. I'll be waiting by the time you get there."

"Ten minutes." I hung up and sneaked a final peek across the court. The drapes were still open in the room, and the heather blonde was in the bathroom putting on her face, dressed in a long skirt and blouse.

Good night, sweetheart! Reluctantly I closed the drapes and dressed. Bone-and-navy saddle shoes, cream cotton slacks, and a pink golf shirt.

I nodded approval to the full-length mirror.

For the space of a moment, I remembered John Paul that first time, standing in the dim light of the doorway of the hotel room in Paris. He'd been naked and was still fully erect. The young Parisian girl was pulling him by the hand, urging him back into the flower-scented darkness whispering, "*Revenir, mon ami . . .*"

He had smiled sheepishly. "Go ahead. I hope you don't mind terribly if I stay awhile?"

John Paul, we thought we were bulletproof.

All at once the reality hit me hard.

An icy wind blew across the wasteland of loneliness inside my chest.

Seized by a convulsion of sobbing, I grabbed the closet door frame and held on for dear life, giving way to a devastating sense of loss.

After several minutes, the overwhelming rush of tears passed as quickly as it had begun.

Finally, I straightened and went into the bath and splashed my face. Draping the light-gray sweater over my shoulders, I crossed the dangling sleeves and knotted them loosely across my chest.

Tennis, anyone? I winked at my reflection. The man in the mirror might have stepped right out of the pages of *GQ*.

Carpe diem, mon ami!

Grabbing my key, I headed toward the elevator.

CHAPTER NINETEEN

In the lower lobby, I found Ginny waiting outside Draper's Café. The news of John Paul's death had descended on my psyche like a winter chill As I crossed the giant black-and-white checkerboard expanse of marble, Ginny's laser smile radiated a reassuring ray of warmth.

A wayward heaviness invaded my groin.

She was marvelously made. Her simple dress, slightly wrinkled now where it stretched across the seductive little declivity beneath her navel bridging the juncture of her thighs, served only to heighten the statement of her sexuality.

As soon as she heard my footsteps ringing against the hard marble floor, she ran forward and gave me a hug. It took me a little by surprise, but I held on. Then, carried away by her spontaneity, I squeezed her tightly and lifted her off her feet out of sheer appreciation of the moment. Holding her suspended above me, I buried my face between her ample breasts.

The scent was intoxicating.

When I lowered her, she slid slowly down against my body. The texture of her wispy dress moving against the satiny fabric of her slip and panties was wildly erotic. Pausing with her there for a heartbeat, my blood began to rise. The curve of her pudendum sliding hard against my penis was electric.

I felt her tense, then relax.

Finally, self-consciously, I lowered her all the way. When her feet were firmly touching the surface of the floor again, my face tarried in the hair beside her ear. It was all nicely perfumed woman in there. After another slightly awkward moment, I pulled back and we stood, still touching at belly, hip, and thigh.

I was almost afraid to look her in the eye. If this had begun as a reunion of long-forgotten acquaintances, in that moment something had changed. Before I knew quite what was happening, she kissed me sweetly on the cheek.

Impulsively, I kissed the tip of her nose and nuzzled her ear.

Carried away by the powerful sexuality of the moment, she kissed me lightly on the lips.

Two can play, I thought, letting my tongue touch her lips. Her lips parted and her tongue answered mine. Then she stopped and pulled back again. There was no rejection—she made no attempt to break the intimate communion of our bodies.

We stood there, pressed belly to belly, looking into each other's eyes.

I never wavered.

Carpe diem!

Let the game begin.

A staunch believer that our son should have the stability of a home with two parents who love him, I have always held steadfast to a commitment to maintain my marriage.

Excepting my tireless, totally unselfish sacrifice in the holy crusade to bring about John Paul's defloration, only on the rarest of occasions has worldly temptation turned my head.

However, while I maintain high standards of behavior and philosophically deplore undiscriminating sexual promiscuity, I have never believed in puritanically fanatic monogamy either. Never, for more than a few hours at a time—except perhaps to my country and to an ill-understood notion of a higher order of things—have I ever seriously considered being blindly committed to one job or one cause, and most certainly not to one woman. I hold fast to the belief that life is not a dress rehearsal and one should grab the best of it in double handfuls.

In other words, given serendipitous circumstances, on occasion I have been tempted to taste forbidden fruit.

Discretion is the better part of a lot of things. I have always considered myself a man of the highest personal discrimination. And, if on infrequent occasion I found the prospect of an interlude with a woman other than my wife tempting, I can honestly say that I have never, ever left the bed of any woman and felt remorse for having compromised my ideals.

Admittedly, on a couple of widely scattered occasions I miraculously escaped with my principles intact. One narrow brush with disaster in D.C. at the Dupont Plaza with a lusty teenage Irish chambermaid. And another time with a married lab tech I'd hired to do phlebotomies at a big convention of physicians in Atlanta. In college, there had been a brazen invitation by the randy aunt of my roommate, and even now, looking back, I sometimes wonder if I shouldn't have seized those moments too.

But then, one should never cry over spilt milk!

Indiscriminate rolls in the hay are—to my way of thinking—something for lower animals, and certainly not something I admired as a recreation. Even when I was vigorously trying to orchestrate the initiation of John Paul, except for that consummating episode in Paris when extraordinary last-ditch measures were called for, I never compromised. I only took him to places fully becoming an officer and a gentleman.

If, on occasion, I had made the supreme personal sacrifice, it was only because that seemed expedient in accomplishing my high and holy mission.

After all, John Paul was my friend.

In short, I am a man of values—a gentleman of quality.

But I cannot abide the thought of needless human suffering. In matters of humanity, I am a selfless soul, a veritable modern-day—albeit slightly hedonistic—Albert Schweitzer.

I considered the possibilities and the odds.

Never so much as at that moment had I had such high regard for the miracle of blind luck. I liked the possibilities, and the odds were interesting.

A born decision-maker, in that moment I never hesitated. The die was cast.

Carpe diem, John Paul.

Let it be written that I know when to take yes for an answer.

Finally, she pushed me slowly away. She caught her breath, and the corners of her lips flickered a Mona Lisa smile.

"Wow! What's chasing after you?"

"Just maybe, I'm very glad to see you. Can we get the hell out of here?" I blurted self-consciously.

"Sure." She gave me another look.

"Oh, I almost forgot. I don't have a car. I gave Rush my keys. I tried to talk him out of it, but he insisted." I shrugged.

"We'll take my car. After all, I know the way."

"Where are you taking me?"

"I live in Lewisburg. It's not far. Won't take long, and the party really won't be getting underway for awhile yet. C'mon, let's make our getaway while we can." She pulled me by the hand down through the shopping arcade and turned through a little corridor, and we ducked through the heavy doors out into the night.

The employees' parking lot was tucked in a stand of trees away from the view of the hotel guests. Shifting gears with the practiced competence of a veteran race driver, Ginny drove the BMW out through a back service lane that led us to old Route 60, west of the main guest entrance.

We had gone only a little way when I realized we had exited the grounds near the pedestrian crosswalk where the golfers on the Greenbrier course crossed over to continue play. Most of the course lay across the main road, on the south side of the highway. It was here, on this course, that Sam had shot his legendary fifty-nine during the Sam Snead Celebrity Pro-Am in the spring of 1959. That was before the Eisenhower administration had begun construction on the infamous underground Pentagon.

I looked across at Ginny in the reflected glow of the instrument panel of the little car. She looked younger now.

Inside the car, the air was heavy. The energy between us was a palpable thing. Her day-worn mustiness was an aphrodisiac in my heightened state.

Reaching across to move her purse on the seat, she accidentally brushed my hand.

She flinched slightly at the contact, with a sharp gasp.

For perhaps a mile, the road was lined on both sides by the fairways and riding stables. Ginny shifted up, blowing past the ramp to Interstate 64 at close to warp speed before she pushed the roadster into the rolling hills of the countryside. Within a few minutes, we started to climb, winding around the small mountain that separated White Sulphur Springs from the historic town of Lewisburg.

"Isn't it beautiful?" She nodded to where the narrow road followed the river gorge. As we moved higher, I caught occasional glimpses of moonlight sparking off the water. Reaching across, she placed her hand over mine and gave it a little squeeze, but she pulled it quickly back to the steering wheel as the lights of a car appeared from around a sharp curve.

The road suddenly reminded me of the Bosnian landscape and driving back from an evening at John Paul's house outside the village. That winding road had run beside the rapids of a small river.

We thought we were bulletproof, John Paul.

Ginny's breathing was faster now. Once, she reached forward and started to turn the radio on, then she hesitated, letting her hand fall away again.

In the reflected light of the dash, the soft curves and the heaviness of her bosom against the fitted dress were devilishly provocative. The top buttons of the simple shirtwaist dress were opened, and when she lifted her left elbow and placed it on the open window frame, the swell of her breasts drew a deep shadow line emphasizing the extravagance of their cleavage.

Carelessly askew, her skirt rode across her legs at midthigh. The smooth curve of her inner thigh gleamed smoothly where it disappeared seductively into the soft darkness underneath her dress. My thoughts drifted back to the days in her homeroom class. Her old-fashioned oak teacher's desk had been at the front of the room, centered between the row my desk was in and the one to my right. In those days teachers had to be careful—some of those antiquated kneehole desks had no modesty shield. My penis sometimes became so fully erect as I sat there sneaking peeks up her dress that I had to conceal my embarrassing condition by carrying my books awkwardly clasped in front of me when I stood to leave the room.

Many nights I had masturbated myself to sleep, obsessing over fantasies of her.

The memory filled my head with erotic images.

My mouth grew dry. My heart reverberated in my ears like a drum.

"I heard you wound up marrying Rose Worrell."

At the sound of her voice, my fantasies exploded in a puff.

"Mm," I murmured. The statement was obviously rhetorical.

We passed through an anonymous community with a homemade sign for a small, dilapidated, cinder block funeral home. The image of John Paul's unopened envelope came floating back.

I let Ginny drive in silence for perhaps a mile before I spoke again.

"Earlier, when you got the busy signal in my room, I had just gotten the message that an old friend died," I said, almost to myself, looking to change the subject away from my marriage.

"I'm sorry." She touched my hand again.

"Funny, but I'm having a hard time believing it. It's like it happened to someone else. Do you think that's strange?" I squeezed her hand.

"Oh no, I understand. It can be like that sometimes. Just shock, I guess." She squeezed back, a small gesture of understanding. "Did I know him? Was he from Melas?"

"No, a guy I knew during my tour of Bosnia," I began and blurted the abbreviated version of the whole story. When I finished, we were both laughing.

"*Carpe diem*. I love it! I bet you never told prissy Miss Rose Worrell that story."

"Sort of. Just the part about John Paul, but that was a hell of a mistake," I sobered slightly.

"I can imagine. You know, I still have trouble believing you married her. When I saw it in the paper, I was taken completely by surprise. In high school she was such a tight-assed little bitch—class president and all that. And you, well, you were something of a hellion, really. I still can't picture you two together—college must have settled you down. But then, I'm a fine one to talk. We all have our own histories. Do you have any children?"

"A son, Paul. Named him for my buddy . . . the one that just died." I stopped and cleared my throat. Talking about my marriage and John Paul's death had diminished the sexual tension between us. I wasn't sure what the evening might be leading up to, but now I knew that my wife and son, and John Paul's death, were the last things on earth I wanted to talk about.

Nothing ventured, nothing gained. I took a deep breath and started in again—might as well get Rose out of the way once and for all.

"They say opposites attract. I haven't changed a lot. Rose and I were never very much alike. I guess she has always seen me as raw material. She keeps hoping she can make me into something. Still, I have to admit I'd be back there writing the medical column and reporting car wrecks for the Roanoke paper—daydreaming of becoming the next Hemingway—if she hadn't pushed me. Each of us has a role to play, I guess."

"I'm not so sure. Take it from me, I always thought you were worth a dozen like her, but in high school you were a handful at times. In the teachers' lounge we all swapped the latest Logan Baird stories. I have to admit that you were pretty precocious. Remember the time you got caught in the reference section of the library with the Evans girl? She was much older . . . a senior." She laughed.

"Oh, come on. I was a kid, barely thirteen." It embarrassed me, remembering myself that way. But now at least the talk was taking a more interesting direction.

"Rose would have a fit if she knew you were with me. She never liked me. I'm sure you know."

"No, she's never said a word to me about not liking you," I lied.

Carelessly, she'd let her knees fall even farther apart. It made her appear vulnerable and perhaps a little wanton, and made me very nervous. I was getting aroused again—couldn't take my eyes off her. If I leaned forward a little, I knew I would be able to see the crotch of her panties. But how do you lean forward in the front seat of a BMW roadster without getting caught?

Nonchalantly, I scooted sideways and pulled my left leg up, across the seat, facing so I could see her better. I tried to be very natural about it. In the dark, I flushed at my return to such pubertal behavior.

I pretended to look upward through the windshield trying to locate the moon. "Just look how bright the moon is. Must be full." When I looked back at her, the whiteness of the satiny panties highlighted the vee of her crotch. I drew in a sharp breath and leaned back again before I became too obvious. She took her eyes off the road for an instant and shot me a questioning smile. I wondered if she suspected what my adolescent mind was up to.

"Trust me. Unless you want to start World War III at home, you won't mention me to Rose." She glanced at me.

"I think you're wrong, but I'm not looking for a fight at home. I get that without even trying. Rose never trusted me anyway." I wanted her to know my home life wasn't all that great. I knew my lines. I was rusty, but I'd played the game before.

"Probably with very good reason," she said knowingly.

"Aw, now. What makes you say that? I never should have told you about my crusade to initiate John Paul." I played along, pleased the conversation was taking an interesting turn again. "Besides, that was in a war—tomorrows were a little uncertain back then."

"Yeah, yeah, I know. *Each Dawn I Die*. It was a movie. I saw it on the late, late show. Don't bullshit me. I knew you when, remember?"

"I was only a kid."

"Some kid. Don't act so innocent with me. Just take my advice. Don't bring my name up with Rose."

At top of the long rise, we passed the Lewisburg town limit sign.

"Okay. But what happened between you two, anyway?" I wanted to get Rose out of the conversation, but I was curious now.

Ginny slowed as we started down the long grade through the neat residential outskirts.

"Let's forget it. It's not likely either one of you have ever had occasion to give me a thought," she said.

"Oh, you're wrong. I had a big crush on you in the eighth grade," I said with a self-conscious laugh. I wondered what she'd say if I told her that I still, on odd occasions, remembered sitting in that schoolroom looking up her dress.

We had turned onto a quiet side street now, and she slowed and pulled into the drive of a neat white cottage with a single garage attached. There were no lights on inside. She turned off the ignition and swiveled herself toward me, pulling her right leg up on the seat. It was almost impossible not to look at her panties now.

"Yeah, I remember. You probably knew more about my underwear than I did." She laughed and glanced down at the sprawl of her legs under the steering wheel. "Haven't changed much, have you?"

"Uh, well I . . ."

"*Carpe diem*." She winked as she opened the door and slid out of the car.

CHAPTER TWENTY

When I stepped out of the car and looked around, I saw that the area was a full notch above solid middle class—a very respectable neighborhood. There were several big Buicks, a few Lincolns, and a few foreign SUVs parked in nearby driveways. At some of the houses, the number of cars overflowed to the curbside.

Everywhere I turned there were home satellite dishes with their Martian silhouettes dark against the bright night sky. Big cars and giant TVs went hand in hand in the coal camps. Even back in the late eighties traveling in Kentucky and West Virginia with my college basketball team, I could remember seeing giant early TV dishes everywhere along the foggy hollows. Back then, traveling through those narrow West Virginia valleys, always winding along the creek beds, we'd pass through the endless succession of little towns like Keystone, Welch, and Beckley. Over into Kentucky, where there was more of the same, Harlan and Hazard and Pikeville were towns almost as famous for their high regard for basketball as they were for their legendary disregard for law and human life.

When they were working, miners always had more money than opportunity to spend it. The deeply ravined valleys were home to fast-forward technology with culture running in full reverse.

I often wondered about the families in those tumbled-down company houses—men in overalls, work-bent women in handsewn dresses, crowded around those shadowy TV screens hoping to get a glimpse of life. I guessed that when the weather was too bad for coon hunting and it was an off-night for basketball, culturally the TV was preferable to getting drunk and brawling or hanging out at the barbershop watching the preacher get his hair cut.

Looking closer, I noted a Cadillac and a brand new Lexus in a driveway further down the way. Beyond that, on the far side, at the edge of the street light's reach, an official-looking dark brown Ford Crown Victoria with a bubble light was parked at the curb.

With the law for a neighbor, it was reassuring that Ginny had security. You had to be tough and fearless—if not too bright—to be a lawman almost anywhere.

"Coming?"

"Right behind you." I kicked at a small white stone and followed. I liked the neighborhood.

By the time I'd walked around the car and started up the steps of the covered porch, Ginny had the door open and had reached inside and turned on the porch light. Stepping into the house, she held the door until I'd moved on past. When she closed the door, we were standing in the darkness with only the light from the porch beaming tiny rays down through the two little glass panes at the top of the door. Without a word she stepped up close, took my face between both her hands, and kissed me with her mouth open.

Her tongue was a lightning bolt.

My sanity went whooshing off like a skyrocket, spraying a trail of golden sparkles over the steep ridges into the night sky.

For a long time we stood there kissing. I don't know how long it lasted. I really didn't care. After awhile my hands, always with a mind of their own, moved gently over those monumental breasts, lightly at first, then as I felt her stir, more insistently.

Underneath she had on one of those flimsy little silky bras, the kind that are constructed with fifty cents worth of fabric and cost a month's salary. Her nipples were hard as nails against my fingers massaging them through the tissue-thin satiny fabric.

Sometime, perhaps light-years later, my hands moved slowly down over her hips, savoring the same erotic sensation I'd known back at the hotel when I'd lifted her and then slowly lowered her against me. The contrasting textures of her wispy dress moving against the smoother fabric of her slip and, in turn, against the fabric of her panties, drove my senses into overload. Caged inside my bikini underwear, my poor tortured manhood was awkwardly doubled under, threatening to explode. When she pushed against me, the pain was almost unbearable.

Finally, I could stand it no longer. Reaching down, I freed my struggling soldier from strangling agony and let him stretch skyward inside my bulging slacks. Then I cupped my hands underneath the curve of her buttocks and lifted her against me.

She jumped, encircled my hips with her legs, and locked them around my waist.

Lost in the moment as she rubbed herself fiercely against my imprisoned maleness through the flimsy barriers of our clothes, I felt her begin to shudder and convulse. She balled her hands into fists to keep from scratching me and dug her knuckles into my back.

As she moaned into my mouth, I could feel her shudder and release the sudden tension as she straightened her back and loosed a sigh of sheer pleasure. "Oh, yes!"

The purest, most powerful orgasms occur in nocturnal emissions—wet dreams—some self-styled sex expert had asserted in a women's magazine I'd read not long before. A gross misinformation, I realized in this moment of divine revelation.

I resolved to write the editor of that silly subversive magazine first thing the next day.

Helpless to control myself, the inside of my head exploded into a starburst of light as I ejaculated. Gushing on and on with pulsing regularity. My primordial brain recalled a scene from an awful Tommy Lee Jones film where a volcano keeps erupting higher and higher.

Then—just when I thought she was through—Ginny moaned and screamed and shuddered to orgasm again.

There's something about a screamer that I could learn to love.

Finally she lowered her legs and we both slid down the wall, exhausted, onto the throw rug in the entrance hall.

"*Carpe diem!*"

"Seize the day!"

Almost simultaneously, we gasped the words—she speaking the Latin and I the English.

We exploded in self-conscious laughter. Lying there, our clothes in total disarray, we looked at each other, letting our eyes grow accustomed to the inky darkness. Still snickering, we kissed, and each of us raised a pinky finger and hooked them together the way kids do when they've said the same thing at the same time.

She closed her eyes as she made a wish.

"What did you wish?" Ginny asked when she opened her eyes.

"Wish?"

"Yes, when two people say something simultaneously and hook their fingers like we did, they make a wish."

"Oh? Is that what that's about?"

"Yes, close your eyes and make a wish."

I closed my eyes again.

"What did you wish?"

"I can't tell. It won't come true," I said, untangling my legs. Struggling to my feet, I pulled her upright beside me.

"Oh, you devil! You knew all along." She pushed me playfully.

My eyes were better adjusted now and I looked down at the wet circle spreading across the front of my slacks.

"God! I'm ruined." I touched the sticky spot.

"Don't be silly. I haven't even begun to ruin you yet."

Ginny dropped to her knees and unfastened the tab on my slacks, unzipping and lowering them—with my semen-sodden briefs—to my ankles, and I stepped free. She held them up and examined them in a ray of the porch light.

"Don't worry about a thing. I'll have you fit for duty before we're out of the shower."

I nodded. Things were moving in a pleasant whirl.

She dabbed my undiminished manhood dry with my shorts and, still kneeling in front of me, passionately and with great tenderness she kissed the tip of my pulsing cavalier, then took me wetly into her mouth.

"Oh, my—" I sucked in a breath.

"GINNY!" A raucous voice and harsh pounding on the door shattered my ecstasy.

"Oh, no!" Ginny pulled back and gasped.

"Wha—" I began.

"Shush," she whispered and put her fingers to my lips.

"Yes? What is it?" she called and waited.

"Ginny, it's Clyde. Are you all right?" The voice was brusque, insistent.

I looked at Ginny, and she shushed me again with her finger. "I'm okay, Clyde, fine. What do you want?"

"I just wanted to know if you were all right. I saw you come in and the lights never came on. Are you sure you're okay? You got company?" The suspicious voice had a demanding, proprietary ring. I could see hands bracketing a pair of spooky eyes peering through one of the little panes in the door.

"Yes, Clyde. I have an old friend from my hometown here with me. Thanks for checking." Fighting to conceal her heavy breathing, Ginny tried not to sound annoyed.

"Are you sure? Why don't you have the lights on?" he persisted, still suspicious.

"The light in the foyer is burned out. I turned on the light back in the den."

"It's not on now. I checked around back." This Clyde person was like a bulldog worrying a bone. "Why'd you turn it off again?"

"Clyde, I appreciate your concern, but don't you think you're getting a bit personal?"

One of the shafts of light from the tiny windows in the top of the door had been almost obscured by Clyde's head peering in. Keeping in the deep shadows, Ginny pushed me around the corner into the living room, reached across, and hit the light switch. "We just finished replacing the bulb. See?"

Standing out of his view, I could see her smile and wave. She held my slacks behind her, out of sight.

"Thanks, Clyde," she said and added, "Have a good night."

"Why don't you open up and introduce me, so I can make sure. I mean you're not being coerced, are you?"

"Coerced? Clyde, this is getting very embarrassing. Do I have to call the cops to come get the rent-a-cops off of me?" She moved up to the glass and stood on her tiptoes eyeball to eyeball with him.

"I didn't mean . . . I meant . . . okay, you can't be too careful." I heard him walk across the porch and down the steps. In a moment I saw him peeking in the living room window with his hands cupped around his face against the glass, trying to see into the darkness. Naked from the waist down, my undaunted paladin still at semiattention, I quickly ducked behind a chair.

Finally, I heard him slam the car door and listened as the car drove off.

Ginny looked into the gloom and said, "All clear. How's my friend taking this?" She groped my crotch. Undiminished, the old cavalier was not at all intimidated.

"Come with me." She still had me affectionately and figuratively by the *cajones*. Her hand still sticky from my juices, she led me back through the shadows and down a little hall.

"Your obedient servant, ma'am." I followed without protest.

I blinked hard when she turned on the light in the oversized bathroom.

"Start the shower while I clean these up." She nodded toward the glassed-in shower enclosure and left, carrying my spoiled slacks and underwear.

I am quite shy by nature.

Over the years, on the few occasions that I'd been with another woman, afterward there'd been a nagging sense of insecure self-consciousness at my nakedness with a stranger.

Even with Rose, I was not exactly an exhibitionist given to casual strolls about the house, *cajones* swinging, sturdy guidon pointing to the ceiling. But now, here I was naked with a woman whom I had only known as a teacher an imperfectly remembered seventeen years ago. By any standard Ginny McKim was hardly more than a stranger to me and yet here I stood, my manhood still pointing to the sky as casually as if we'd been walking fully clothed among the stacks in the public library.

I shook my head, wondering about it all.

Within the hour, I'd chatted with my wife and been told that an old friend was suddenly dead. Even so, I felt no embarrassment for my nakedness.

I started the shower, marveling at this newfound sense of familiarity, this easy aura of intimacy.

It was almost as if Ginny and I shared a common persona, I mused romantically, testing the temperature of the water.

What adolescent saccharine poppycock, I admonished silently. I'm just plain superhorny.

What the hell? I laughed out loud. The last time I looked, the penalty wasn't death.

When, finally satisfied that I wouldn't be scalded in the shower, I turned to take off my shirt, and Ginny reentered wearing only her half slip, panties, and bra.

"All done! Your clothes will be good as new before you can say 'orgasm,' " she said.

"Orgasm," I replied.

"All right!" she said, admiring the view. "You're on."

She took off her slip and bra, then steadied herself by grabbing my arm and stepped out of her panties. Fully naked now, she hugged those unbelievable breasts with her arms and demurely looked into my face for a sign of approval.

I gently unfolded her arms and cupped her breasts in my hands. Then I bent forward and kissed her, hungrily, with my mouth open.

After a time, she pushed away without a word, pulled me into the shower, and went to work soaping me, starting with my back. The erotic exercise was driving me to the edge. Finally she turned me around and started working her way slowly down my front, torturing me by stopping to lick and bite my nipples as she went.

The sensation of her nibbling was so intense that I pulled back and bumped my head against the shower nozzle. "Ow," I winced.

"Hurt?" She looked up anxiously and kissed my nipple.

"Uh-uh," I laughed. "Not my titty, my head. The nipple felt too good."

She bit the nipple again.

This time I took my punishment like a man.

Water cascaded down around my eyes. Blindly I found her nipples and pinched.

Scrinching up my eyes against the splash, I pushed back and took in the view.

We stood there looking at each other, lost in pleasure.

Her face had softened now around her mouth and eyes. She'd taken on the appearance of a thirteen-year-old.

She lowered her gaze and, dropping to her knees, she began soaping my eager trooper. When she finished the soaping and rinsing, she started kissing and slowly licking the length of it. In no time I had to push her away. As mightily as I fought against it, it was all I could do to keep from coming again.

Now I stood her up and started my own games with the soap.

I sat on the bottom of the tub with her legs astraddle my face.

"Mm . . . yes . . there." Her hands were at the back of my head as she crushed her swollen *la praline* hard against my mouth.

She shuddered in little waves.

Finally, she pushed my head back and helped me stand.

"I can't stand this. Come on, finish me." She turned off the shower.

"Hurry," I gasped, anxious to have my turn.

We stumbled into the bedroom dabbing at each other with large towels like children, and she pulled me down on the bed on top of her.

Moving slowly in a long, sliding ecstasy, I felt myself erupting again. Rumbling out of a dark cavern from somewhere deep within the center of my primal brain, the molten silver exploded out of me.

I pushed straight out above her and remained poised there for a time. Then I slowly lowered myself onto the cushion of her breasts and lay quietly, listening to her breathing into my ear.

She whispered, "You look like that young boy in my classroom. You are so beautiful. You remind me of a Greek god." She snuggled close and put my hand back upon her breast, "You really finished me," she sighed.

"Lies, lovely lies, and promises, promises, promises," I laughed.

We lay there, holding fast to the moment. I was half asleep when she moved at last and whispered, "My leg's asleep."

I rolled off of her as she pulled the spread over us, then snuggled close again.

I lost track of time before I finally emerged from my twilight state.

I heard her stirring and felt her get up. Sleepily, I raised on my elbow and watched as she moved naked across to her dresser.

Unadorned, she was exquisite—like a romantic painting of a mythic forest nymph. Not at all self-conscious, she examined herself in the dresser mirror, turning this way and that. Her body was firm yet soft. Naked, her breasts seemed even larger, swollen—thrusting more than pouting. The areolae were huge. The size of silver-dollar pancakes. The delicate shade of pink reminded me of the lining of conch shells. Where the sun had found her body, her golden tan was splashed with a million tiny freckles. With the little creases and subtle curves and planes, with the blue network of veins underneath the almost transparent skin of her breasts and thighs, she seemed more knowing, totally wanton. Every inch a predator, this woman took no captives.

I felt myself respond again.

She caught me looking. There was no embarrassment now.

"Do you like me?"

"I more than like you."

"Yes?" She raised an eyebrow.

"I don't want to be found guilty of writing bad dialogue." I let my eyes fall away, but I knew she understood. Then I added, "Don't you know that you can't fake an erection?"

"Best dialogue I've heard in my life. Too bad you don't write some of it down." She looked at me very seriously now. "I always thought you had a wonderful gift for language. I wasn't alone. I'm sorry you don't write anymore."

"I really did try. Not much happened. I probably wrote the best car wrecks and domestic spats and book reviews at the

Times. Won an award . . . two awards. Had a piece published in *Harper's* once, at the beginning when I first got back from the war. But nothing worth mentioning after that. Besides, reporters are paid in awards, not money. Rose—ah, we got tired of credit union loans and driving secondhand cars. I decided I wanted to be something more than a newspaper flunky." I couldn't look her in the eye.

"You wanted? I heard it. You mean Rose wanted. Anyway, how old are you, not even thirty?" Her tone took a gentler quality. "Wake up! It isn't too late. Every day is the perfect day to start over. Take it from me. You're just getting started. What happened to the book you told me about earlier in the car, the one that you and your buddy John Paul promised each other? He wrote his. *Carpe Diem*, you said."

"Lighten up, Ginny. I'm too old for fairy tales." I finally met her gaze, but I left the thought unfinished.

She turned at the door and smiled. "Talk about fairy tales! Looks like I still haven't finished the job." My eyes followed hers to my still semiturgid warrior.

"Come back and let's try it out," I said.

"Save it for later. We're headed for a party, remember?"

"Oh, yeah. I seem to vaguely remember something about a party," I called to her disappearing backside.

In a minute I heard her start the shower. I sat up on the side of the bed and glanced around the room. It was a large room with a reclining chair and a table with a reading lamp over by the bay windows on the other wall. Opposite the chair, on the chest of drawers was a small portable TV. Everything a woman needed to spend her private moments away from the outside world.

When I looked back to the bay window, I noticed that the blinds in one of the smaller sidelights had not been lowered all the way. There was a crack at the bottom of perhaps a half-inch. I remembered the beady eyes peering in the darkness through the windows of the front door, and I walked straight over to the window and carefully loosed the cord and lowered the blind all the way down. Then I pulled the edge of the blind out and strained to see what was outside. In the bright moonlight, I could see a small, neatly arranged back yard and steps leading up to the back stoop at the kitchen door. The yard was fenced with a high redwood board fence for privacy. There was a gate at the right-hand corner where it joined the garage.

The gate stood slightly ajar.

Oh, well, I shrugged. If anyone were interested they would have seen quite a show.

I went in to rinse off again. Trading places, we kissed lightly as she stepped out of the spray.

The half-open gate in the back yard fence nagged me. I made a mental note to check for signs of the Keystone Kop's car when we left.

Tepid water splashing my face, I let myself luxuriate in the moment. My mind drifted to what Ginny had said about my writing and the promises I'd made John Paul. I felt a pang of envy that he'd kept his bargain and finished a book. I thought fleetingly about dragging out my half-finished manuscript.

Then my reverie turned back to those marvelous breasts with the pancake nipples.

She'd promised more.

Carpe diem, John Paul.

I'd forgotten the local rent-a-cop before we left the house.

Ginny broke the reflective silence as we turned into the little hidden service lane onto the hotel grounds. "I know you're hurting over your friend's death. I'll certainly understand if you'd rather skip the party."

"Well, yes . . . but, no. It's not that at all. I was feeling euphoric. You know, kind of dreamy." I actually had been wondering if I shouldn't dig out my laptop when I got back home.

The story line of that dusty, long-forgotten novel wasn't half bad.

"I don't know how to explain it, but I went through some sort of accelerated grieving period earlier tonight when I first got the news about John Paul. It was really strange. There was a long moment when all the grief and the pain seemed to well up in my gut and I bawled my eyeballs out. Then it passed. It was all over in a minute or two. Then, I kind of let him go. I'm certain most people would say that makes me some sort of unfeeling subspecies. Who knows, maybe I am. After I felt that one moment of deep loss back there, I told myself there's nothing I can do for him now. Maybe I am one selfish son of a bitch. They want me for the funeral . . . his wife and sister. The two of 'em really made it hard when I called. But I'm no good at that. We're such goddamn hypocrites, all of us. Special voices for funerals, prescribed periods for wearing black—all that garbage. Who makes all those silly rules, anyway?"

"Hey! Don't look at me. I know you'll always miss him, and he'll always be with you, too. You can't go around breaking into sobs at the mention of his name for the rest of your life. What's the point? Sooner or later you have to let go. If there are rules, let 'em apply to the people who play these silly games. Life is real, the poet said. Still, I know it's been a rough day." Ginny slowed as we went through a grove of trees behind the main buildings of the old hotel. Seen through the lacy overhang of leaves, the imposing buildings with their massive columns put me in mind of downtown Washington, D.C.

"You're sure about the party?" She slowed and glanced over to me.

"If John Paul were here, he'd say *carpe diem* . . . full steam ahead."

Ginny sped up again.

CHAPTER TWENTY-ONE

It was almost 11:30 when Ginny pulled into the parking area near the Golf Club. There was a scattering of stragglers, some arriving, some leaving, moving from both directions across the parking lot. Several cars loaded down with staff members were pulling in ahead of us.

A surprising number of cars of all descriptions were there, and we had to park about a full wedge shot up from the canopied portico. Grabbing her sweater off the back seat and slinging it across her shoulders, Ginny pulled a quilted bag obviously containing a bottle of booze from behind the seat before she closed the door. She handed me the bag when I came around to meet her.

A young woman in a passing group of eight or nine men and women who had apparently walked down from the hotel called, "Hi, Ginny. Mr. Webb called and said he wasn't sure if he could make it. Something came up."

"Yeah, I got the message. Thanks, Bev," Ginny called back.

In the bright moonlight, I could see Bev gawking at me, dying with curiosity to find out who I was. I sensed that Ginny was debating about making an introduction, but it would have been awkward to halt the entire group in the middle of the parking lot.

"See you inside," Ginny called as she deliberately slowed and let them move on ahead.

We followed at a leisurely pace a few yards back.

Up ahead, I could see an expensive white convertible with the top down arrogantly standing in the NO PARKING zone. I recognized the car from my regular monthly trips to the area.

The locals knew it well. It was Sam Snead's trademark. Over the past months I'd seen the famous man on several occasions, usually with the top down and always with his straw hat in place as he cruised the hotel grounds.

"Looks like Sam's already here," I said and nudged Ginny's arm.

"Sam has never been one to remain anonymous," she laughed.

"Rush Donald is going to mess his pants when he finds out that the great Sam Snead was here."

"Serves him right." She laughed. "Your stuck-up boss man thinks he's too good to rub elbows with the common folk."

"I hope he doesn't find out I knew about it and didn't tell him."

"You did? How'd you find out?"

"I bumped into Alex Crim at the Old White. I heard her tell Archie, the trumpet man."

"No fooling? Your dipshit boss man will never forgive you if he finds out. But your secret's safe with me," Ginny laughed again.

Inside we made our way back past the stairwell leading down to the darkened golf shop and entered the large grill room beyond. Across the room, the solid wall of windows overlooked the moonlit tableau of the golf course against the shadowy backdrop of the mountains in the near distance. Just below us, the lazy, meandering surface of Howard's Creek reflected a winding ribbon of silver moonlight.

The early arrivals had pulled together the small tables to accommodate larger groups. I was surprised to see that at least a hundred people had arrived before us.

In the far back corner by the window, I could see Sam Snead and his party at one of the larger tables.

I was not surprised to see that Archie had not yet arrived. The Old White Club was the last bastion of the never-say-die late-night crowd. I guessed that it was still early for him to have finished the set.

Our mystery man, Scotty, was with Sam and Alex. Once again tieless, he was wearing a white dress shirt, collar open, with an old sweater across his arm. His sleeves were rolled to the elbow, and his shirttail billowed at odd places where the belt was pulled too tight, threatening to spill outside the rumpled khaki trousers. Since I'd last seen him in the Old White, he'd reverted to the unpretentious character trudging alongside the mountain road earlier that afternoon.

No matter what he wore, Scotty had that special air that marks some men.

He and Sam were laughing hard.

"There's our mystery man back there with the ol' Slammer. He's changed back into khaki 'work pants,' as Rush called them. That's the way he was dressed this afternoon. Not stylish, I admit, but I don't see it as being any worse than some of the wild plaid Bermuda shorts outfits I saw around today. Rush would choke if he knew that guy was rubbing elbows with his hero. It would serve him right if it turned out this Scotty was some famous golf architect like Rees Jones, or one of the president's chief advisors." I grinned at the irony.

"Follow me. Maybe we'll find out." Ginny pulled me by the hand. Before I knew it, I'd been introduced to a dozen people whose names I had no chance of remembering offhand. Then, before I could protest further, we were taking seats at the table next to the Snead party.

"Sit tight." Ginny wandered off with the bottle bag.

Looking about, I did my best imitation of trying to appear at ease. I was more than a bit uncomfortable.

"Work on this." Ginny shoved a drink in my hand and headed for the woman who had spoken to her in the parking lot.

"Back in a minute," she called over her shoulder.

I sat there watching Sam Snead telling a story and laughing at his own joke. He was clearly having a grand time. Self-consciously, I looked around, awed in the presence of the legendary man.

"So you're a writer, Mr. Baird?" the young woman beside me asked, snapping me back to reality.

"No, no more. I wrote for the Roanoke paper for a couple years. Nowadays I work for a pharmaceutical manufacturer. The name is Logan."

"Ginny said you were writing a novel?"

"I have one gathering mold in the back of my closet." I searched my memory for her name. "Are you a writer?"

"Now and then, for some little magazines you never heard of . . . food and wine. And I did write a romance novel once, but take it from me, I'm no Joyce Carol Oates," she smiled.

I looked closer now. I thought I recognized her from the dining room or maybe the exhibition hall. Perhaps the cocktail reception, but I wasn't all that certain. We'd been introduced in the last five minutes, but I hadn't the foggiest notion what her name was. "I can't remember your name. Sorry, but Ginny introduced me to about a dozen people already and I've only been here for five minutes. I'm not very good at this sort of thing."

"It's Althea Richards. And don't think you're by yourself. Catching your name was easy for me because you happen to be the only person here that I don't already know."

"Oh! Then maybe you can tell me the name of the man with Sam Snead."

She twisted to look. "Sorry, that makes two of you," she laughed. "I've seen him before. Everyone calls him Scotty MacSomething-or-other, I think. He comes here with Sam to fish."

"Fish? Really? I guess I did read somewhere that he and Ted Williams had pushed a line of fishing equipment at one time. I didn't pay much attention. There's so much bull in the press."

"Oh, yes. He and the Splendid Splinter were fishing buds. Everybody kids Sam about fishing," she said. "He's damn good. Always showing up with a mess of trout at the kitchen door up at the hotel, worrying the chefs to cook 'em for him."

"No kidding." I tried to picture the famous Sam Snead with a fishing rod in his hand. But I was still wondering about her writing. "You said you wrote a novel once. Is it something I might have read?"

"I doubt it. It was entitled *Bruised Fruit*. One of those breathy, sexy—a lot of garter snaps and brassiere straps—romance things. I really doubt that you ever saw a copy or would have read it even if you did. It was written to set frustrated maiden ladies'—and young girls'—hearts aflutter."

"Sounds very racy," I said.

"Racy? It hinted strongly of kissing with parted lips, God forbid!" she laughed.

"A book before its time, I'm sure," I smiled. "Did it sell?"

"I guess it did. It was a paperback. You know, on the racks in the airports, train stations, and bus depots. Anyway, they pay a flat fee for that sort of manuscript. I was offered the princely sum of five grand. I took the money and ran."

"Too bad. They probably made a fortune and next thing you know, you'll go to the local cineplex one evening and suddenly realize that you're watching Julia Roberts playing your heroine. And your name won't be on the credit scroll."

"Oh, no. I mean, they can't do that, can they?"

"I think they probably can. Unless, of course, you retained your rights. I feel sure that whoever published the manuscript bought all rights. It's theirs. Wouldn't be the first time it happened. Did you have an agent represent you?"

"Hardly. I'd just gotten out of college and was working on the Atlanta paper writing for the women's page. It was published under the name Roxanne Roget." She raised her arms, threw back her head and laughed. "Adolescent alliteration. Stole it right off my thesaurus."

"Roxanne Roget? Not bad, but I like Althea better."

I considered her again. She was quite attractive.

Her left hand had no ring.

I stole a quick glance Ginny's way.

Althea was definitely a keeper. The night was young.

What sort of erotic spell had Ginny cast over me?

One bite of the forbidden apple and I was Don Juan.

I turned back to Althea. "Tell me about the stuff you're writing now. Food and wine. Who publishes it?"

"Oh, here and there. I sell a piece or two to magazines like *Southern Living* and *Good Housekeeping*. And, I'm on the masthead of *Gourmet* as a contributing editor," she added shyly.

"I'm impressed. What exactly do you do around here, my favorite place in all the world?"

"I'm a kind of jack-of-all-trades. I'm around to make sure that things go smoothly, oversee protocol sort of. I guess you'd say I'm like a social director or troubleshooter."

"All that responsibility must have a title. What's yours?"

Althea interrupted before I could finish.

"Talk about writers . . . see that tall, balding man standing back there near the door?" She nodded over her right shoulder.

I had no trouble identifying the person she described.

"That's Jack Saunders. He has a Ph.D. He's writing a biography of F. Scott Fitzgerald and his wife, Zelda. He taught English at Columbia and some university down in Alabama."

"Are you kidding? How can he afford to live here? I mean, is he on a big grant or something?" A single night at this place cost almost half a week's salary.

"Grant? No. His day job is a captain in the dining room," she laughed.

"A captain? You mean like a maitre d'?" I blurted in surprise.

"That's right, but not exactly a maitre d'. He wears a mess jacket and a winged collar. He's more a high-class waiter. That's during the daytime. At night he's a very fine writer with a nice advance on a book in the bank."

"A waiter with a Ph.D.? But why?"

"Don't look so surprised. I do the same. Not books anymore, but I don't do too badly at the freelance game. There are advantages. Not a bad way to live." She gestured at the room. "We have several waiters and waitresses, some husbands and wives, who have college degrees. Some have been professors. We're very choosy about who we hire. It's probably easier to get in the FBI," she said with just a little bit too much emphasis.

"I guess I sounded like a snob." I felt myself flushing.

Then I thought about it and had to laugh.

"Now that I think about it, I'm a fine one to talk. I travel into this area once a month, call on the clinic physicians and the pharmacists regularly and really can't even afford to buy a package of aspirin in the drug store. I plead guilty, your honor," I admitted.

"I didn't mean to make a big deal out of it, but we have a lot of staff here who work an eight-month season and then go to Florida for the winter. Some go to winter jobs at the CSX resort in Boca Raton. But some don't work at all in the off-season—they simply prefer to take the winter off. The money here is good. A hell of a lot better than most college professors will ever make, and living in the area is inexpensive."

"How about you? Do you only work the eight-month season? I don't mean to be impertinent, but I'm curious. What do you do with your winters?" I asked. "If it's none of my business, just say so."

"No, that's okay. I have a place in Key West. My parents are Cuban, from Havana." She pronounced it with a Spanish lilt. "Now they live in Miami. I'm writing a second book," she said, shyly.

"Another novel?"

I gave her a closer look. Her hair wasn't black but a rich, reddish brunette and she had Bambi eyes. There was a Castilian look about her I hadn't picked up before.

"No, it's a memoir. It's—well, I have a rule. I think people who talk about books they're writing usually don't finish them."

I nodded. "Probably a lot of truth in that. So you're from Cuba?" I changed subjects. My thoughts kept wandering back to John Paul, and I didn't want to talk writing anyway.

"I was born there, and my grandparents still live right outside Havana," she replied. "It's beautiful."

"But what about Castro? Isn't it kind of bad down there now?" I asked.

"It will be all right again someday." She raised her chin, but her voice lacked conviction.

Ginny had slipped up beside us while we were talking, and now she tugged on my sleeve. "Excuse us, Althea, but Bev is going to finesse us over to the Snead's table, so Logan can meet his hero," she interrupted sweetly.

"Oh, no. Really, I don't think we should; it's too obvious. I'd be mortified." I didn't budge out of my seat. "Maybe later when the party gets going. Archie is coming down, and he said that Sam likes to blow the trumpet when the boys jam after hours. Maybe we could wait. Please?"

Ginny pulled back and looked at me in surprise. "You really are shy, aren't you?"

"Yeah, I guess I am. I'm not much of an autograph hunter. If I ever got one, it would be my first. John Paul and I had our pictures taken with a famous British actor when he came to

Bosnia on tour after the truce. He'd been knighted by the queen. I was too shy to ask for an autograph then. I think I hurt his feelings." I smiled, remembering.

"My god, you posed with a knighted movie star? Your men do get around, don't they, Ginny? Some girls have all the luck," Althea kidded good-naturedly.

I don't think she believed me.

"Speak of the devil," Ginny interjected and pointed to the door. Archie and some of the band were coming in. He stopped just inside and let his eyes adjust in the dim light. Then he waved. He was looking in our general direction, but I knew he was waving at Sam. I glanced back and saw that Snead had moved further down and was talking to Alex and some other women. When I looked back again I saw that Archie was headed straight for me. He waved again. This time I waved back.

"What's the matter? You too good to wave at the hired help?" He stuck out his hand and laughed. "Or you so occupied with these beautiful women you plumb jes' don' see ol' Arch?"

"I thought you were waving at S-Sam," I stuttered.

"Arch, you ol' son, what took you so long?" The corn pone voice behind me was unmistakably Snead's. When I turned and looked up, he was standing right behind me. Alex stepped up beside him, looked down, and smiled.

A drop of sweat rolled down my back.

"Sam, I want you to meet Logan Baird," she said.

I damn near broke my shin trying to push the chair back to stand. When I finally got untangled, I shook his hand. The hand was as big as a bear's paw, and I could feel the thick, calloused pads on his fingers.

"Honored to meet you, Mr. Snead," I managed without stammering.

"Logan is Betty's friend, Sam," Alex said.

"So you're the one. Alex was telling me. We all love Betty," he said. "You play golf?"

"That's been debated in some circles. But, yes. I'm playing in the morning at eleven. I'm here for the rest of the week with the medical meeting. Sort of business and pleasure," I offered somewhat lamely.

"Eleven o'clock? In the morning?" He raised his bushy eyebrows.

"Yeah," I stammered, not sure what difference it made to him.

"You'll never make it. The band just got here, the party's just gettin' started. You really think you're going to feel like playing golf at eleven?" He chuckled.

"I couldn't get anything later, not 'til after three. Not on the Old White, anyway," I said.

"Me and Scotty have a couple of dudes flying in from Boston in the morning, and I've had 'em hold 1:08 for us. What's your handicap? Who you playing with? They any good?"

"Two of them play to about eight. The other one I'm not sure of. I'm away from home; I'll shoot around eighty. But we don't waste time hunting for lost golf balls," I said.

"You want one o'clock sharp? We'll be right behind you on every hole, so hit 'em in the fairway, or I'll be bouncing golf balls off your backs all day," he laughed.

I was about to panic. Suddenly, all I could think about was the crowd that was sure to gather up here in the grill and down by the tee when the word got out that Sam was getting ready to tee off. With us up right before, we'd be out there with a crowd almost as big as the final pairing at the Masters. I almost messed my pants just thinking about it. I could picture myself cold-topping a shot right in the middle of Howard's Creek. I was sure I was doomed. I'd never be able to face anyone again.

Sam must have seen me turning green, because he put his arm around my shoulder and said, "I'm just kidding. Scotty's pretty steady, but the pigeons he has flying in here are duffers. You ain't gonna get in our way. Whatcha say?"

"Sure, one is great. Thanks. We'll try to stay out of your way."

"You ever play the Old White? You know the course?" Sam peered down at me.

"Yeah. I'm from Roanoke. I've played over here a few times. I was in your gallery the final round this spring," I said.

"Oh, yeah. You're a writer . . . you had a little boy."

"That's right." I marveled that he remembered. "My dad said he followed you back in '59 when you were paired with Peter Thompson and Hogan."

"That was quite a day," he smiled. "We all shot sixty-six."

"My dad will never forget it. He says he saw something that day that not many people have ever seen."

"That day wasn't my best golf. I later shot fifty-nine on the Greenbrier Course, you know." He stood up straighter when he said it.

"He wasn't talking about your personal round," I said. "He said Hogan cold-topped the ball on fifteen tee that afternoon. The ball didn't even it make into the creek. He had to play his second off the cinder service road, remember?"

"That's right, he did." Sam laughed out loud. "But the son of a gun still made three. You couldn't keep him down. When we were walking off the green, I said, 'Nice three, Ben.' He nodded but never said a word. Come to think of it, the only words I ever heard Hogan say were 'I believe you're away, Sam.' " Snead never cracked a smile as he told the story.

I'd read that quote somewhere before, but hearing it now from the great man himself broke me up. I laughed until tears came to my eyes.

Pleased at his own joke, Sam gave in and laughed too.

"You ready to play some music, Arch?" Sam turned to Archie.

"I am, but it's getting mighty late. Are you gonna go back over the mountain tonight and still make it back to play by one o'clock?" Archie asked.

"Naw, we're sleeping here. Scotty has taken Top Notch Estate House. He's got all these big-shot types coming in for some kind of business meetings and a press conference. I left Steven Spielberg, Gwyneth Paltrow, and Matt Damon back at the hotel. Alex and I are staying here tonight. We start shooting Monday. I gotta fly to the coast to film a spot for ESPN next Thursday at Riviera. This is too hard on a man my age. Tomorrow's my day off. Come on, let's play some music." Sam pointed the way to a corner of the room.

He looked back and winked. "Stick around, I'll tell you some more Hogan stories."

"Did you hear that? Sam's friend has Top Notch." Althea shot Ginny a look as soon as Sam had moved away.

"That's something you gotta tell your snobbish boss man," Ginny said to me. "Some bum, this Scotty is."

"Don't keep me in the dark. I gather that Top Notch is something akin to the Taj Mahal." I smiled down at her.

"Better. Top Notch has room service from the Greenbrier. Ike and Mamie entertained family and friends there," Althea chimed in.

"Damn! What a kick. If you could have seen Rush looking down his nose at this Scotty today out front when he brought his golf sticks down, driving that beat up car. Wait 'til I tell him."

"Pardon me, sir. Are you Mr. Baird?" I turned to see a man dressed in a dark green blazer with a Greenbrier crest on the breast pocket.

"Yes, I'm Logan Baird." My heart sank. His voice fairly dripped bad news. I had heard that same inflection of doom earlier with Rose.

"I'm J. D. Sisson, Mr. Baird. Greenbrier security. We had a call from the sheriff's office. They have a Mr. Donald who's had an accident. He gave them your name. We checked and we know he's a guest here. But he's in no shape to drive."

"Are you telling me he's injured? God, how bad? There's a lady with him, I think. Is she hurt, too?"

"No, sir. It's not that. Not injured. Neither one. As I understand it, they're both kind of . . . impaired."

"Impaired? Oh, you mean slightly ploughed? How about the car?" I asked, afraid to hear the news.

"It's banged up some, they said, but it's okay to drive."

"Damn. Are they going to take him to jail?"

"No, sir. They won't let him drive, and we didn't think you'd want to leave your automobile out there all night. I have a car outside. Will you come drive him back?"

"Of course. After all, it is my car. I tried to talk him out of driving. He had no business out there. Goddamn fool wouldn't listen," I muttered.

"Come along then, sir." He turned and started for the door.

"I'm sorry, babe. I'll be back as soon as I can," I apologized to Ginny.

"Let's go." She took my arm and led the way.

"Wait. You don't have to—"

"Just shut up and follow me. I know everybody in these parts," Ginny said and smiled. "Cheer up, no one's hurt. At least we can be thankful for that."

Too bad it didn't kill the son of a bitch. I savored the thought as she led me out the door.

CHAPTER TWENTY-TWO

We followed Sisson out to the parking lot, where he'd left a dark-green Greenbrier Cadillac waiting with the motor running.

"Vanguard Security driver's parked down at the service entrance, Mr. Baird." Sisson held the door for me. "Public or private, we don't like to have the local gendarmes parked out where the guests can see them. It's not good PR. I'm sure you understand."

I nodded, tight-lipped.

"Where'd it happen, J.D.?" Ginny asked.

"From what I was told, Mr. Donald had two minor collisions. First, in the parking lot at the Bluffs and then, fleeing the scene, about a mile further down the road."

"Fleeing the scene? Shi—*merde*!" I expostulated, then amended.

"Excuse me?" The hotel security man was puzzled by the expletive.

"*Merde*! It's French, J.D.," Ginny laughed.

"I took French up at Morgantown. What's it mean?" The young security man was obviously feeling excluded from our private joke.

"Excrement," I said wryly, using a comic French accent.

"Ex-cway-mont? Is that French too?" He was really puzzled now.

"No, that's plain American," I said at my irritating best.

"I never heard of that either."

"How about just plain shit, Mr. Sisson?" I grouched unfairly. Smartass Logan Baird, educator of the unwashed masses.

"Oh." He grinned half-heartedly, looked at Ginny, and reddened. "I get it."

"Who's waiting out there, J.D.?" Ginny asked.

"Jumbo Clark with Vanguard Security is at the back gate. Clyde Goins is at the crime scene. He had to call the highway patrol, for official back-up I guess."

"Crime scene?"

J.D. shrugged like a Frenchman.

A well-deserved payback for excrement?

"I never heard of Clyde Goins calling anyone for back-up. And since when does Pauley Green call in the law to handle his problems?" Ginny sounded concerned.

"Well, Miss McKim, Mr. Donald was not being very reasonable, I understand," J.D. said hesitantly and looked my way.

"He can get that way," I nodded, then whispered to Ginny. "Rule number one: Never try to reason with a drunk."

"That's Jumbo up ahead, Mr. Baird."

When we reached the waiting Vanguard patrol car, I saw that the private rent-a-cop, Jumbo Clark, was aptly named. As we approached him, I marveled at the man's bulk, wondering if he ordered his uniforms from a tentmaker. Leaning against the company Ford picking his teeth, he looked like a baby elephant or a pregnant hippo, perhaps, or maybe the Blob from Outer Space.

"What're you doin' here, Ginny? Did Clyde call you?" Jumbo snapped.

"No, Clyde didn't call. Mr. Baird here is an old friend from home," she answered coolly. I was sure Jumbo wasn't exactly on Ginny's A list of local security agents.

"This Mr. Donald a friend of yours?" Jumbo asked me as he opened the rear door and left it standing while he waddled around to the driver's side and squeezed himself under the wheel. He went right on picking his teeth.

"You might say Rush Donald's a friend. We work for the same company, anyway," I hedged, not sure how much damage Rush had inflicted or what was waiting for me out there.

"I'll give ya one thing. From what I've heard, your buddy's a pistol." Jumbo shook his head.

"I guess I'll see you later." When I turned back to say good night to Ginny, she was already getting in the Vanguard car.

"Ginny, wait. You don't have to go. I'll take care of this." I reached for her hand and missed.

"Don't argue. Believe me, with Clyde Goins out there you need me. Get in," she said and scooted across the seat.

"What happened, exactly?" Ginny asked Jumbo as soon as we were rolling.

"I ain't been out there, but from what I hear on the two-way, this Mr. Donald made a spectacular bounce off of a brand new Cadillac when he went tearing out of the parking lot at the Bluffs about forty-five minutes ago. Never stopped. Just kept right on going. Somebody who was arriving happened to see it and told the guy on the door. The owner—I should say the driver 'cause the Caddy was rented by some doctor from out of state—and Cowboy, the bouncer, and Pauley Green, the owner, come running out, but it was too late to stop 'em. Then the doctor renting the Caddy called us." Jumbo glanced back over his shoulder through the heavy wire screen panel as he talked. "I doubt Pauley's very happy about having the state law out there."

Still picking his teeth, Jumbo liked to drive fast. And, from the way he hunched over the wheel, I was sure he was disappointed he couldn't put the siren on.

This narrow winding stretch of road wasn't exactly a straightaway on the interstate. I could see the speedometer needle bouncing near eighty. And Jumbo had a distracting habit of looking back at us as he talked.

I felt around in the dark for a seat belt.

No luck.

Digging in with my fingernails, I cringed and held on.

And I desperately tried to analyze the circumstances at hand.

Any way I looked at it, Rush was in deep ex-cway-mont.

And—to make matters worse—it was my company car, and he was my boss.

Most likely, that put me smack dab in the middle of the same pile of shit.

A delicate problem all around.

It dawned on me that on the eve of his newfound promotion and his upcoming matriculation at Hahvahd B, this was not going to look good on his employee record.

And, finally, it came rolling across my consciousness with the white-light clarity of a whiff of flatulence in an elevator with only one other occupant that all my dreams of a promotion might have just gone down the tube because my cretinous boss had gone off and gotten himself shit-faced drunk.

But wait, I rationalized. Hadn't I tried my best to reason with the arrogant bastard? After all, he was my superior officer, and he had actually demanded the use of the car, hadn't he?

In the end, I had only been following orders, hadn't I?

General Custer's hapless troops at the Little Big Horn crossed my mind.

The metaphor was not comforting.

If Rush was supposed to be the brains, where did that leave a poor SOB like me?

Up the well-known tributary without a paddle, maybe.

I wracked my head for alternatives. I'd survived worse situations—I was certain of that.

Two rules had seen me safely home from war.

Rule number one is CYA: Cover your ass.

Rule number two is: If you forget rule one, don't panic.

Not a lot of help, but at least it got my head working.

"Hold on," Jumbo warned us too late. We careened dangerously toward the edge of the steep embankment rising from the river, heading for certain disaster.

"Watch out!" I gasped.

Before I could find something to grip, I was thrown forcefully against Ginny, there was a slight shudder, and—

WHOP!

The left front wheel clipped something in the road.

Wide with abject fear, my eyes caught a glimpse of the speedometer needle wavering at eighty-five. Visions of the investigators' finding us with the needle frozen in that position when they pulled us from the river passed through my head.

"Got the fat little mutha clean!" Jumbo cackled.

Without warning, blinding headlights popped out at us from around the next curve.

Ginny gasped and grabbed my arm.

At the last instant, Jumbo jerked the wheel again and the car righted itself, narrowly making it back across the road and missing the oncoming truck by a scant millimeter.

I swallowed hard and congratulated myself for not messing my pants.

"Are you insane?" My words were lost in the blare of the truck's horn.

"Listen to him disturbing the peace! Damn crazy truck drivers! Just don't know what gets into some people." Jumbo shook his head at the disappearing image in the rearview mirror. Then he turned back to us. "Didja see that nice clean kill?"

He reminded me of a fighter pilot savoring a combat victory in an old John Wayne war movie.

I scraped myself off the side of the passenger compartment and looked over to see if Ginny was okay.

"What the hell was that all about?" I rasped.

"Possum! Gotta call Bubba. That kinky-headed Rastafarian loves his possum." Jumbo reached for the mike and pushed the button.

"Michelle, this here is Jumbo. Is Bubba still around?"

The speaker popped as the operator pushed the transmit button on the other end.

"Yeah, Jumbo, he heah. Go ahead." The heavy twang of the woman's voice crackled through the speaker.

"Tell him I just left a big fat possum lying on the south side of U.S. 60, about three hunnerd yards west of the entrance to the Camellia Club. Got him real clean. 'Ceptin' for mashin' his head a little, I din't turn a hair. If he comes straight away, he can take the kids a nice supper for tomorrow night." The speaker crackled again. "Can you hear me okay?"

"Yeah, I hear ya. Bubba's on his way. You a prince Jumbo, always was. Uh, wait, Jumbo."

"What?"

"Clyde just called in. Said he can't raise you on the two-way. I'll tell him where you are." The static was louder now. Transmission was difficult in the mountains and deep valleys.

"Okay. Tell Clyde I got Mr. Baird, and better tell him Ginny McKim's in the car," Jumbo advised.

"Ginny? Well, yeah, okay." The radio faded into noise.

"Damn radios ain't much good in these parts. We's oniest two mile outa town." Jumbo put the mike back and leaned his head back against the wire mesh partition again. "How'dja like that little piece of driving?"

"If it's okay with you, I'd just as soon you forget the possum hunting," was the only reply I could think to make.

"Same as I woulda shot him," Jumbo said proudly, oblivious to our discomfort. "I practically keep Bubba in possum and rabbit stew. Gives me something to do at night."

I got my voice back. "Gotta hand it to you, chief, you're a thrill a minute."

"Huh?"

"Sounds exciting," I said.

"Oh, ain't much. Just passes the time. Bubba's our darkie. Good as white, but all the same them black folk loves they possum," Jumbo muttered, still pumped over his kill.

"Bwana make chop-chop for good gun-bearer boy," I muttered. I'd seen *Mogambo* and *King Solomon's Mines* at least a dozen times each on late-night cable. The cable channels had some great old movies, but they didn't change the films that often.

"Huh?" Jumbo turned back again, "What's all that Boowanna stuff mean?"

"Bwana? In Africa it means 'great white hunter' to the colored folk, sort of like a big hero," I schmoozed, still holding on for dear life.

"Yeah? I never gave it much thought, but I guess I am kinda Bubba's hero at that." He turned back and straightened up in his seat.

Quietly contemplating hero status, Jumbo slowed the car a bit.

I let myself breathe again.

"Ever onct in awhile, I'll kill a cat or two to stay in practice. Hate them fu—'scuse me." He looked back at Ginny. "Breaks my heart to hit a dog, but I don't take to cats atall."

"Fill me in about what happened in the Bluff's parking lot." I was in no mood to hear about his primordial need to be the great white hunter. I had to make a plan.

"Yo' buddy hit the Caddy and run. That's 'bout the size of it."

"But you said there were two accidents?" I congratulated myself on maintaining my wits under fire.

The word "accident" rolled off my tongue like liquid silver. Instinctively I knew phrases like "hit and run" and "fleeing the scene" were bad news.

In my mind, I could already see Jumbo in a courtroom.

No sense in stacking the deck against us.

"As I get it, in his hurry to bug out, yo' bud was going too fast on that narrow dirt road and slid into a tree. Happens all the time. Them rich Yankee dudes go out there and get juiced and try to negotiate that damn road. Even cold sober that road's a bitch. You'll see. Won't he, Ginny?" Jumbo laughed, clearly enjoying the excitement.

"It's a real bitch all right." Ginny made a face and rolled her eyes at me in the dim reflection from the instrument panel.

"Clyde Goins's brother-in-law's in the wrecker business. Serves the rich bastards right," Jumbo gloated. "Nothin' personal, you unnerstan'." He shot me a look over his shoulder.

"Uh-huh." I understood all right.

"Hit and run, felony," Jumbo said happily.

Hit and run.

Felony.

This glorified night watchman knew all the words right out of *Law and Order* reruns.

"Drunk drivin' makes it worse," he went on.

Driving under the influence.

Truthfully, it wasn't the first time I'd seen Rush drunk.

Even in the few short months since he'd moved to Charlotte, he had become something of a legend among the salesmen of the division. I wasn't the only one who had had to put up with him when he'd had one too many. But he'd never really caused a bad scene with the other salesmen.

He was more careful of his image when he was out with them.

But lately, when he was with me, it had gotten worse.

And, more and more, I'd been getting his phone calls.

"How about I come ride with you for a couple of days next week, ol' buddy? Need to let my hair down. We can get one of those old square bottles"—that's what he called Jim Beam—"and solve all the world's problems."

The calls had been coming with increasing frequency in the past few months.

He was the boss. What could I do?

Still, Rose was right. I had to admit I really looked forward to it—I was always looking for an edge. Having a boss who liked to get drunk and confide all his secrets gave me an opportunity to do a little extra ass kissing.

And, up until about twenty minutes ago, it looked like it had been paying off.

Until this moment, he'd only been a minor nuisance. He'd never caused an out-and-out disaster.

But, now that I thought about it, I should have seen it coming. He'd come close enough on two separate occasions working with me in Roanoke.

Both times he'd made something of an ass of himself in front of Rose. Once at the University Club, he'd gotten snotty with the assistant manager when I took him there with Henry Lockheart. Fortunately, Henry had gone to use the john, and I tactfully told Rush to knock it off before Henry got back to the table.

The other time was at the annual Virginia State Medical Society meeting at the Hotel Roanoke. The company had sent Hannah Riker, our token female in the sales department. She was an attractive divorcee in her forties, a registered pharmacist who had once worked in procurement with the federal government. She lived in northern Virginia, right outside D.C., and spent all her time negotiating Severance contracts with Uncle Sam. Hannah was an all-around good sport—a lot of fun.

That night, Rush had gotten sloppy drunk over dinner at the hotel and acted like a fool, trying to show off for Rose and

Hannah. Out of concern, Rose and I had invited them out to the house for coffee and dessert after dinner, to give Rush a much needed opportunity to sober up.

But, dealing with drunks is tricky business.

Our good intentions had backfired. After we got to our house, Rush found some B&B in my liquor cabinet and proceeded to get drunker. In the end, when Hannah insisted she drive, Rush grabbed a flashlight out of the glove box and jumped up on the hood of her company car, loudly declaring he would light the way.

Perched up there, he struck a stupid pose as if he were a Winged Victory of Samothrace hood ornament on a Rolls or some such thing.

To humor him, we all laughed politely.

When Hannah convinced him to come on down and get in the car, he'd insisted on making a Douglas Fairbanks dismount off the hood, slipped, and ripped the seat out of his pants.

The suit was his tour de force. A brand new, expensive, raw silk number, those costly trousers had been a total loss.

The morning after both events, Rush had been remorseful and apologetic to me. More and more after similar occasions, he would be anxious to hear my account of his behavior, which I gathered he had little memory of.

When I'd fill him in, he'd usually try to laugh it off.

"Gotta stick together, ol' sport." He would nervously swear me to secrecy, punching my shoulder like Redford in *The Great Gatsby*.

He told me later that he'd ripped a sizeable chunk out of the meaty part of his ass doing the spectacular dismount. He'd slipped out to the hospital emergency room in a cab for tetanus and sutures before anyone got up the next morning.

Two days later, when I took him to the airport to catch his flight back to Charlotte, he told me about it and warned me that he'd told Nadine on the phone that he'd slipped in the tub and ripped his butt on the faucet handle. He made a joke of how she'd urged him to sue.

That incident cost him. Hannah was no pussycat. She confided to me later that she'd had the dents in the car's hood fixed and sent the bill to Rush without explanation. He had promptly remitted with a cashier's check but no word of apology—not so much as a simple how-de-do.

And Rose was right about another thing too. In the beginning, when I was with Rush, I did drink more than I should. I remember waking up one morning realizing that I'd been far too confidential the boozy night before. The lesson I'd learned from my officer buddies in Bosnia that familiarity breeds contempt kept coming back to me. If I were really honest about it now, I could thank Rose for helping me have the good sense to be more careful around him.

Being sloppy drunk was one thing. This time it sounded like he'd gone plain crazy.

I was aware that we had been traveling for about a half-hour in unfamiliar territory. Jumbo slammed on the brakes, and we went skidding off the main road onto a dirt road that led into thick woods at least twenty miles from civilization.

For a second I thought Jumbo was going to broadside us into a huge pine tree, but right at the last minute the rear end caught, and we started up the narrow rutted track at a slightly slower pace.

Too traumatized from the possum killing to even grunt, I just put out my hands to keep from smashing Ginny and braced hard against the side of the car.

"Didn't shake ya, did I? Would have been kinda embarrassing if we'd wound up hittin' that tree back there." Jumbo cackled and looked back through the wire again.

"No, Jumbo, we're okay, but take it easy, will you?" Ginny said between gritted teeth.

I kept my mouth shut. I'd had my fill of Jumbo.

Looking ahead, I strained to see into the darkness. I'd been up to the Bluffs once before about a year ago, nosing around. I'm no gambler, really. That night I'd been simply bored and curious, cruising for something to do. Once I found the place, I only had one drink at the slots, looked around a bit, and left.

Now as hard as I tried to recall the details, I didn't have a clear memory of the place or how far it was up this road. I only remembered that the narrow trail terminated in a broad clearing at the edge of a high cliff overlooking the spectacular Greenbrier River gorge. And I remembered vividly the image of the humongous Victorian hunting lodge that housed the Bluffs.

The moon had been full that night, too. It had reminded me of a set from some brooding old British horror film. The building, constructed entirely of wood, was a badly weather-faded hue of barn red. Inside, it was decorated with Tiffany lamps and crystal chandeliers and furnished with a quaint, ill-matched collection of Queen Anne, Duncan Phyfe, and Spanish country pieces. To complete the décor, the ornate flocked wallpaper was gaudy red on red.

At the time, it struck me as more early French Quarter whorehouse than late-Victorian hunting lodge.

The way the forest pressed in on the narrow tracks, the road hardly looked wide enough for two cars to pass. It was, in fact, a very tight squeeze in spots. I'd found that out for myself, the night I'd been here.

I shuddered at the thought of Rush's negotiating this narrow track with the snoot full of alcohol he'd had. I counted at least one Jack Daniels—probably more like three—two bottles of merlot, a brandy Alexander, and he was back on Jack Daniels again when I'd left him at the Old White Club.

"How much farther?" I asked, getting more anxious by the second.

"Not far. We should be coming up on them any time. I been looking for headlights between the trees. I thought we'd already reached 'em by now," Jumbo said and looked back over his shoulder again.

I put my arm around Ginny and held on tight.

"Jumbo . . . Jumbo Clark, can you read me?" The woman's voice crackling over the radio speaker startled me.

"I hear ya. Can ya hear me?" Jumbo had the mike in his hand.

Obviously they hadn't learned their radio technique from TV.

"You're breaking up, but I can hear you now," the voice got clearer. "Listen, Clyde's radio ain't working right. He asked me to tell you they'd moved that vehicle back to the parking lot at the lodge. Clyde didn't see no sense in blocking the road. It's late and a lot of folks will be heading home. 'Ceptin' for a few dents, he says the car runs all right. They're waiting up there. You still hear me, Jumbo?"

"Yeah, I hear ya, Michelle. I couldn't see no lights and was beginning to wonder what happened. Now, I see the tree they hit up ahead on the right. Must've hit it a good lick. It's broke 'bout half in two. Anyway, we're almost there. Call ya later, hon, okay?"

"Okay." The speaker went dead.

I leaned forward and peered through the windshield.

"Holy shit," I gasped.

Ginny let out a sharp breath and squeezed my knee.

The tree, a good-sized dogwood, was broken, and the top half was pushed off to the side of the road, down over a steep embankment.

The brush around it was all broken and bent down.

The way the light reflected off the greyish-green underside of the canopy of leaves, it looked like a giant broken umbrella.

"We could add destroying a dogwood to the charges. Them trees are protected by state law." For a rent-a-cop, Jumbo seemed inordinately preoccupied with crime and punishment.

The metallic taste of dread filled my mouth, and my stomach was launching jet fighter planes. Lowering my head, I peered out through the windshield, afraid of what was coming next. I could see the glint of bright lights from the top of the rise filtering through the trees ahead.

"See them lights?" Jumbo wheezed. "Din't make it far, did he?"

We'd only gone another hundred yards when we were blinded by headlights jumping out at us from a sharp bend in the road. Jumbo slowed and edged carefully past the big white Cadillac as it made its way down the narrow road.

Ginny tightened her grip on my inner thigh.

"Good thing your buddy didn't meet any traffic when he was blasting his way out of here," Jumbo laughed.

Neither Ginny nor I dignified the remark. I thought of the tree and wondered about my car.

"Not much room," I murmured in agreement.

Ginny's hand casually brushed my crotch.

Not surprisingly, my old soldier had gone AWOL.

CHAPTER TWENTY-THREE

As Jumbo rounded the curve at the top of the rise, we broke free of the tree line and came out into the abrupt glare of strong light. Mounted on poles, in trees, and high up on the eaves of the sprawling Victorian building, the vapor lights flooded the newly graveled parking area with an eerie green glow. Just as I remembered, the old building was painted red, but now, under the new vapor lights, it had a washed-out mauvish hue. In the platinum moonlight, the view from the clearing was breathtaking. The precipice was a small insular promontory at the edge of a high cliff where the river made a sharp U turn as, over the centuries, the swiftly moving current had worn a twisting course through the mountains.

Just ahead I could see two police cars at the far end, where the cliff marked a dizzying drop several hundred feet straight down to the river.

To the left of the police cars, parked against the heavy guard rail, sat my Buick. I squinted hard, but it was still too far away, and the garish vapor light threw everything into a sharply contrasting shadows and glaring lighted surfaces. From this distance the harsh light made it impossible to see any damage.

We pulled up behind a second Vanguard patrol car, and Jumbo got out.

Ginny opened the door and whispered, "This is home territory. Leave the talking to me."

I caught her arm and stopped her.

"This is my problem. I don't think you should get involved."

"Quit playing superhero. Just trust me. We're on my turf. I'll deal with the cops and you take care of your boss. Smile a lot and do a lot of listening. Don't argue with drunks. You said it yourself, remember? Get your crazy boss man calmed down, and I'll find out what we're up against, okay? If the law wants to talk to you, we just got here. You don't know anything. Don't make any serious statements about anything. And, above all, try to get Rush to keep his mouth shut. I can guarantee that Pauley Green, the guy who runs this place, doesn't want any trouble with the law any more than we do . . . maybe less. And the law doesn't want any trouble with Pauley or the spa. Bad for the local economy. We might have a standoff if the damage isn't beyond repair. Let's try to cut our losses and walk away. Just trust me." She gave my hand a little squeeze and walked me over to the highway patrol car.

A second Vanguard security guard stood talking to a young state trooper in his unmistakable Smokey Bear hat.

"What the devil you doing up here, Ginny?"

The rent-a-cop from earlier in the evening. I recognized the beady eyes.

"Hi, Clyde. Hello, George," she nodded. "I came with Mr. Baird. We were down at the Golf Club at a little get-together when they came looking for him. Logan, I'd like you to meet chief of Vanguard Security, Clyde Goins. And this is Sergeant George Rettinger of the highway patrol. Gentlemen, this is my friend, Logan Baird."

I reached out and shook the hands of both men and said, "I'd rather it had been under better circumstances, but it's nice to meet you, all the same. Where's Mr. Donald and Miss Gardner? Are they all right?"

"They ain't hurt, if that's what you mean. Mr. Donald bloodied his nose, but it didn't amount to much. Pauley took 'em upstairs to his office to use the phone. Mr. Donald was trying to get in touch with some lawyer in San Francisco, and Miss Gardner has been trying to call you." Clyde looked at Ginny.

"Before they come down, how about telling us what happened," Ginny said.

My car was only a few feet away now, and I could see an ugly dent in the left front, down low. A nasty, deep scratch ran almost the entire length of the door on the driver's side. As far as I could tell, there was no other damage to the front end. Both headlights were intact. But I knew from hearing friends talk about recent fender benders that it would cost several hundred bucks to put it back in shape, even if nothing else were wrong. Rush was going to have one hell of a time explaining this to management.

"Is that all the damage that's done to my car?" I asked and nodded in that direction.

"The front bumper's gonna have to be fixed where it hit the tree back down the road, but except for some minor scratches, there's no major body damage on the passenger side," George spoke up. "It'll drive all right. Looks a hell of a lot worse than it is. The other car, the one he hit here in the lot before he hit the tree, was a rented Caddy. It hardly showed a scratch except for a little dimple in the rear bumper. I still can't believe it didn't do more damage. According to the other driver, your friend whacked hell out of it. Too bad about your car, but all in all, he was pretty lucky."

"What's gonna happen now? If the only damage is to my company's car, then this doesn't amount to much, does it?" I saw a ray of hope and tried to minimize the whole thing. "You're not going to hold him, are you?"

"This ain't a matter of damage, it's a matter of law. Mr. Donald struck another vehicle and then knowingly fled the scene. Hit and run is pretty serious. We're talking felony now—" Clyde began.

Ginny interrupted, then turned to me. "Why don't you go find them and let 'em know we're here. No sense in Mimi being up there trying to chase me down. If I know her, she'll have everybody at the hotel and my B and B out of bed in thirty minutes. My god, we don't want this thing to become a major happening."

"Just go up those steps. The man on the door will show you where they are," the trooper said.

"Okay, but hold on a minute. I want to hear the rest. Did he make a stink?" I asked.

"You've already heard enough to make a lot of trouble," Clyde snapped. He was having a real hard time being civil.

"What's bugging you, Clyde? Michelle cut you off?" Ginny grinned.

"Aw, ain't no truth to that stupid gossip." Clyde reddened and fiddled with his tie. He cleared his throat and started in again. "Anyway, this Mr. Donald showed up here with the lady a little before eleven and played blackjack for awhile, and he dropped a couple hundred in no time at all. He wanted to write a check, and you know Pauley—cash on the barrel head. The gentleman got pretty obnoxious. He was already pretty drunk when he got here. Pauley offered him a cup of coffee and a ride home. It's standard courtesy of the house. Your friend wasn't too happy. The lady said she'd drive, so Pauley had someone show them to the parking lot. Everybody inside thought they'd left. Apparently, they started getting . . . ah . . . affectionate sitting out there in the car, and one way or another, Mr. Donald wound up in the driver's seat again before they left. Everybody inside had forgotten about 'em 'til about a half-hour later they heard the car scratch off and then the sound of metal crashing. About then, a couple of late arrivals came through the door saying that your Buick had hit the Cadillac and kept on going. Then another couple comes in and says that there's a car hit a tree down at the bottom of the steep grade. That's when someone called us. George and me was having coffee at the Old White Cafe east of town, so he come along with me."

"Where's the Caddy? Can I see the damage?" I looked around. There must have been at least seven or eight Cadillacs parked in the lot, maybe more.

"Oh, we let the doctor take it on back to the hotel. It was rented in Charleston, and we got his statement. You could hardly tell anything had hit it, just some scratches on the bumper. Anyway, he wasn't too anxious to get the lady that was with him involved. We'd had enough trouble, so we let him go. No sense in everybody staying up all night." The young trooper shrugged. "The doc won't file charges, bet on that."

Thank God for small favors, I thought.

"A damn miracle he didn't hit a car coming up the road when he scratched out of here. We get 'em all the time. People got money think they can do anything they want," Jumbo spoke up, anxious to get his two cents in.

"You right about that, Jumbo," Clyde chimed in.

I was getting the distinct feeling that we might get lynched if we didn't get out of here.

"Has he been charged—" I began, but Ginny nudged with her elbow and cleared her throat.

"Why don't you go up there and let Rush and Mimi know we're here. Get her off the phone before she has the whole world looking for me," Ginny reminded me with a gentle push. I finally got the message.

"Okay, I'll be right back," I said and went up the steps of the wide old wraparound porch and over to the heavy double oak doors with leaded sidelights. The door was locked, but a large man peered through the sidelights, out over my head. Apparently he caught a signal from one of the cops and let me in.

"I'm Logan Baird. Can you tell me how to find Mr. Donald and Miss Gardner?"

"If you'll follow me this way, sir," he said and turned toward a staircase against the wall to the left.

At the top, the steep stairwell opened into a wide hallway. I could see Rush sitting back in an office slumped in a chair while Mimi was dialing the phone, sitting behind a huge antique desk. In a chair beside the desk was a balding man who looked like an oversized Buddha.

"Where the fuck you been?" Rush growled when he saw me coming across the hallway. He stood and started toward the door.

I felt like killing the bastard, but I ignored his outburst.

"Mr. Donald, I've asked you for the last time to clean up your mouth. I don't tolerate that kind of talk in my place. I would think you'd have more respect for the lady." The Buddha stood up.

"I'm Logan Baird. Mr. Donald and I work for the same company," I said and extended my hand.

"I'm Pauley Green. I own this place." I noticed he omitted the part about how he was overjoyed to meet me.

"Hello, Mimi . . . Rush." I smiled, warmly—I hoped.

"What the fu—what kept ya? I thought maybe you were going to let me rot here all night," he started in again.

"Kept me? How was I to know you were planning on getting arrested? I was summoned out here by the police—spoiled a perfectly good party for me. If I'd had any idea you were going to play demolition derby with my company car, I'd have kept the keys to keep you out of trouble," I fired back. A man can be pushed only so far.

"Wait a minute, who the hell do you think you're talking to?"

"Did you call Nadine yet?" I gave him one more shot.

"I—are you trying to be a smartass? I told 'em to find you. These damn people won't let me drive. I'm perfectly okay to drive."

"Are you saying it was Mimi who hit the Cadillac and destroyed the tree?"

Mimi put down the phone and gave me a little wink.

"A car ran me off the road and they're trying to put the blame on me," he whined. "They insist I've been drinking. For godsakes, tell them I'm okay."

"I never argue with the law . . . no percentage in it," I said. "You want me to ask 'em to give you a breathalyzer?"

"Hell, no. But you both know that I've hardly had any. Maybe one or two. I hate people who can't hold their booze. You know that." He was really whining.

"Don't worry. If they take you to jail, I'll have you out by noon, in plenty of time for golf. I already changed our tee time to one o'clock."

I was really warming to his predicament.

"Golf? Is that all you think about? Don't you understand what I'm saying? Can't you be serious? Get me a lawyer. Did you talk to the cops? You can't let 'em lock me up." He was almost begging now.

"I heard them talking about charging you with hit and run felony. That's pretty serious. But I think they're just trying to scare you. I don't think they can hold you indefinitely without bail unless there's a death involved. I'm almost sure an attorney will back me up. It's the company's car. Maybe I should call our corporate attorney. I have the emergency number in my card case."

Logan Baird, a by-the-rules company man to the end.

He grabbed my arm. "Jeezus, are you fucking crazy? We can't let the company know."

"You didn't hurt or kill anybody did you? That'd be impossible to hide for long." I still played it straight.

"No, nothing like that. And it really wasn't the booze. I was . . . distracted." He reddened and turned to Mimi for help.

Mimi blushed and stammered, "We were, uh . . . I . . . he just lost control and the car ran off the road and hit a tree."

"There'll have to be a report," I said. "I'm not going to wind up behind the eight ball on this."

"The car is scratched up, that's all. You can tell the company you had a blowout and left the road. I'll back you up, no sweat. The insurance will take care of it," he said, seriously.

"I hope you're kidding. You are, aren't you?" I shot a sideways glance at Pauley Green.

"Hell, no. What's wrong with that?" Rush went on.

"He's kidding." I looked at Pauley, then back to Rush to remind him that there was a witness present. "Mr. Donald would never suggest that I falsify a report."

Rush reddened and looked down at his shoes.

"What do the cops say? Did you talk to them?" He finally got his voice back. "How serious is this really?"

"Serious enough to have a state cop here, too. I wanted to talk to you first. Let's go down and find out what they have in mind, okay?" I asked.

"Okay." He sounded more subdued.

I turned to Pauley and asked, "Are we square with you, sir?"

"Square." He shrugged.

"I guess you've had enough excitement from us. I'll walk down with Mr. Donald and Miss Gardner and see what the police have to say. Sorry for your inconvenience." I shook his hand again.

"Uh-huh," he grunted and shrugged again.

"Let's go down and face the music, shall we?" I waved toward the door with my open hand and stood aside while they headed for the stairs.

"Mr. Beard."

"It's 'Baird,' " I corrected and turned to face Pauley Green again.

"Mr. Baird, sir, when he sobers up, tell Mr. Donald I never want him near my place again. He got lucky tonight." His voice left no doubt he had little time for fools.

"You can count on it, Mr. Green," I said. "No hard feelings?"

"No hard feelings. Let's leave it there." He didn't bat an eye.

I nodded, shook his hand again, and followed them on down the stairs.

Ginny'd been right.

Pauley Green had just taken the world off my back.

CHAPTER TWENTY-FOUR

When we stepped out onto the porch overlooking the parking lot, Ginny and the cops seemed to be having a merry time. When they saw us, the laughing abruptly stopped and they watched in silence as Mimi, Rush, and I walked to where they stood.

Mimi stopped right outside the circle.

"Mr. Donald, we're gonna let Mr. Baird drive you and Miss Gardner on back to the hotel, sir. We'll be in touch to make a determination of charges tomorrow. But you understand, sir, you're not to leave the county without first advising us," Clyde said in his best John Wayne voice.

"Uh, yeah. What're you going to charge me with? Do I need to call a lawyer?"

"Just get a good night's sleep, sir. Plenty of time for that." Clyde turned back to me. "You can leave any time you want."

"Thanks," I said and started for the car.

"Ginny, I'll give you a lift back," Clyde offered.

"Thanks, Clyde, but I think I'd best ride with Mr. Baird. My car's at the Golf Club." Her tone was not unfriendly, but she left no room for argument.

"Okay. We'll be right behind you, just in case you have car trouble. Mr. Baird, sir, if I was you, I'd call the Buick dealer in Lewisburg tomorrow and have 'em check the car over before I headed back to Roanoke. Good night." Clyde was polite, but he made 'Mr. Baird, sir,' sound as if I were a convicted sex offender with an obsession for exposing myself to elderly nuns.

I herded them all into the car and, with Ginny's directions, we drove back to the hotel in silence. She guided us into the rear entrance, and I stopped to let Rush and Mimi out.

"See you in the morning. You can sleep in. I'll take care of the booth. Don't forget, I had our tee time moved up to one," I reminded him before he closed the door.

He started to say something, then thought better of it.

I waited until they were safely inside.

"I noticed that he didn't bother to say thanks," Ginny said when I let the car move forward.

"Mr. Perfect saying thanks to the hired help? Fat chance."

"I'm sure you figured it out. They're not going to charge him with anything. It all happened on private property, and Pauley Green isn't about to take him to court. Pauley told the doctor with the rental Cadillac that if he had any problem with the Hertz people in Charleston to have 'em call him and he'd take care of the damages. State trooper says there won't be any trouble."

"Thanks. I don't know what else to say," I replied.

When we reached the Golf Club parking lot, there were a lot of cars. The party was obviously still going strong.

"Guess I'd better get on home. Tomorrow's a busy day," she said.

"I'll follow you home," I offered.

"Don't be silly. I won't hear of it. You get some rest. If I'm going to have you here for two more nights, you're going to need it." She pulled my face down and kissed me with her mouth open. Despite everything, I felt an overpowering reaction to her again and let my hands caress her breasts. Finally she pushed me away. "Just hold that thought until tonight, okay?"

"Okay."

She opened the door, leaned back in, and kissed me lightly. I waited until she drove out of the parking lot and then drove back up to the lot nearest the main entrance. I really wasn't anxious for the staff to see my car's condition.

Back in my room, I sighed and went to the dresser where I'd placed my traveling bottles of Jack Daniels and Smirnoff on the tray beside the bucket of ice.

Even at this late hour, the ice was hardly melted.

I'd never appreciated the Greenbrier more.

I broke the seal on the Jack Black and splashed a glass half-full over the fresh ice cubes.

I'd hardly taken a sip when the phone rang.

Rush?

I started to let it ring but decided he'd just keep on calling, so I picked up.

"We need to talk. I'm coming down," he announced before I could even say hello.

I glanced at my watch. Nearly 2 A.M.

Time goes fast when you're having fun.

"You've got to be kidding, Rush. It's two in the morning. There'll be plenty of time tomorrow."

"Fuck tomorrow! We need to talk—"

"It's two o'clock, Rush, go to bed."

"Listen to me, Logan. I don't think you understand who you're talking to. I'm having a hard time trying to overlook the way you acted out there at that damn clip joint," he snarled.

"Come on, Rush. We both need to get some rest. I'm going to have breakfast around eight. Why don't you meet me in the dining room. We can talk then. Good night—"

"Goddamn you, don't hang up on me. I want to talk."

I hung up.

"I don't think you know who you're talking to either, Rush, ol' sock. Fuck with me and I'll hang your ass out to dry," I said to the empty room.

On the note pad by the telephone, I'd written JOHN PAUL SILVER.

Now, I stared at the words, trying to feel something, but I was beyond numb, beyond feeling.

"So much for *carpe diem*, John Paul," I murmured.

The phone started ringing again. It finally stopped as I finished taking off my clothes.

I polished off the drink, slipped between the cool percale sheets, and turned off the light, but my head kept reeling with a kaleidoscopic montage of shattered images.

I still couldn't believe Rush's push that I take the rap for the car.

The bastard!

Just who the hell did he think he was? At least I had witnesses to that, and Ginny had the cops in her pocket.

In the morning I'd let the rectal orifice know he didn't dare wiggle.

Gradually my anger subsided, and I drifted into a half sleep.

WHAM! WHAM! WHAM!

I sat bolt upright and stared into the darkness. The luminescent hands on the bedside clock showed 2:15.

BANG! BANG! BANG!

"Open this goddamn door, Logan!"

"Shit!" I muttered, fumbling for the light.

I found the light and retrieved the old silk kimono I'd bought in Paris during my escapades with John Paul.

Struggling to control my anger, I made my way to the door and counted to ten.

Rule number one: Stay calm. You can't reason with a drunk, I reminded myself.

"Hold on, Rush. You'll wake the whole goddamn hotel." I slowly counted to ten again before I opened the door and stepped back.

Rush charged into the room. He was waving a square bottle of Jim Beam in his hand. It was about one-third gone. "What the fuck you think you're trying to pull?"

I simply stared at him.

He looked a little green. The stink of puke and booze was overpowering.

He marched right over to the two wingback chairs flanking the reading table and sat down. Out of consideration for sleeping guests, I closed the door.

"Well?" He glared. "Wha' da fuck do you have to say?"

Rule number two: If rule one fails, kill the son of a bitch.

I merely shrugged. If the SOB wanted to talk, then by god, I'd let him. I wasn't about to dignify his shit.

He looked like hell. He'd taken off his coat and tie, and his shirttail was hanging out in the back. He tried to stare me down, but after a moment he averted his gaze.

"Le's have a li'l dring, buddy. I brought the old square bottle." He was getting a second head of steam, and his speech was already sloppy.

I shook my head.

"Aren' ya gonna say anything?"

"I was asleep. You woke me."

"Fug sleep! We gotta talk. Gotta decide about that fuggin' car."

I just looked at him.

"I need a dring. Ya sure ya won' join me?" He waved the bottle again.

I waved off his offer and looked out the window. The light was on in the honey blonde's room, but the drapes were pulled. I hoped she'd had some luck.

Rush went into the bathroom, and I could hear him dropping ice cubes in a glass. Finally he came back and sat down on the end of the bed across from me. "Why don't you jus' report that car as a parking lot incident? That way you don't even have to say you were drivin'. I'll back you up. I can say it happened at the airport," he began. His speech was better.

I gave him an icy stare.

"Don't stand there playing dumb. Say sumpthin'," he demanded.

"No."

"NO! What the fuck you mean, no?" He took a drink.

"What is it about 'no' you don't understand?"

"Don't fuck with me. You gotta do it. If the company finds out about tonight, we'll be in deep shit," he said.

"We? Not me. You. And what about the cops?" I reminded. "I don't care how you lie about what you did to the car, as long as I'm not involved. And don't look to me to swear to your story. You're on your own. But I think you'd better deal with one thing at a time. There's the hit and run."

Let the bastard suffer.

I wasn't ready to tell him that the law wasn't going to prosecute him, not ever.

"I can fix that. I'll get an attorney, and he'll keep that between me and the cops. The company won't get a whisper. Unless you rat me out." He shot me his best heavy-lidded gangster look.

I wondered if I looked properly intimidated.

Probably not.

"Why would I want to do that?" I shrugged.

"Oh, plenty of reasons. To get my job. You're ambitious too." He belched.

Now I knew what he would do for a promotion.

He sobered. I guessed he'd seen a look of recognition pass behind my eyes.

"Anyway, we could have it fixed ourselves. That way the company would never know. That's it! What do you think of that?"

"Think of what?"

"You and me, we can pay for the fucking car and the company will never be the wiser. We'll just pad our expenses a little. You know, cut a few corners here and there. What the hell, you can put down a little extra entertainment. Spread it around over a few months. Easy as pie. I'll help you. Why didn't I think of that before?"

Now, I actually was speechless.

"Well? What do think? It's foolproof."

"It's dishonest. Even if I agreed to become a thief, you're going to Harvard. You can't sign my expenses after this week."

"Well . . ." His nose was running, and he wiped it on his sleeve, then he wiped the sleeve on the side of his shirt.

He took a drink, got up, and wandered to the window, then turned back to me.

"There's this month. I still have to sign off on that. You can put down a big dinner at the University Club for several of your big-shot doctor friends. You know, a meeting of the hospital therapeutic committee or some such thing. Hundred . . . one-fifty . . . one-seventy-five. Make it one-eighty. Keep it just under two hundred. That's the magic number. No problem. It's your club. Just get them to give you a blank receipt. I'll approve it."

"Rush, you're drunk. I'm going to forget you ever asked me to conspire with you to steal from the company. If you want to pay for the car, that's okay with me. I'll never breathe a word.

You know you can count on me. But I won't do your dirty work for you."

"Listen, you Pollyanna bastard. Don't try to make me sound dishonest. You trying to blackmail me? Your ass is in my hands, you know. I don't have to recommend your promotion. Just because you think you've got me by the balls. Shit, man, I'll see to it you never work in the field again. You can't blackmail me. I'll show you."

I shrugged.

"Well?"

"Well, what?"

"Are you?"

"What?"

"Trying to blackmail me?"

"Looks to me like it's the other way around. You just threatened me with my future. Or did I hear you right?"

"Now don't take me wrong. I didn't want you to think you had me over a barrel."

"Are you finished?" I asked.

"We still need to talk," he protested.

"Good night." I looked to the door and changed the subject. "Remember what I told you about our tee time? I ran into Sam Snead at the party down at the golf club. He fixed us up with a one o'clock. He's gonna be playing too."

I bit my tongue to keep from saying, "Eat your fucking heart out, Rush, ol' buddy."

"No shit?" Despite what he'd said about golf pros being hired help, Rush brightened at the mention of his hero. "You actually talked to him? No shit? Sam Snead was at the party?"

"Yeah, the great man himself is gonna play in the group right behind us. Get some rest. I intend to have some fun this afternoon. We're at the Greenbrier, remember?"

"No shit. One o'clock. Hell, that gives us eleven hours to recuperate. No shit." He shook his head in disbelief.

I walked across and opened the door.

"What about the car?"

"If you want to handle it discreetly, I'll get an estimate tomorrow and you can give me a personal check." I wondered if I were a fool for trusting him, but I had no choice really.

"Oh, come on. You don't expect me to just take it out of my pocket. Is that any way to thank me for what I've done for you?"

"Look, I appreciate everything you've done for me. That's not the point. I know you're drunk and not thinking straight. You'll be better in the morning. We'll get a damage estimate and you can take care of it privately. The company'll never know. I'm willing to forget the entire matter."

"Fuck that shit! You'll be goddamn sorry. You could bend a little after all I've done. I'll back you."

"I said to forget it. Now let's both get some sleep."

"Goddam it, listen—"

"Listen? Rush, you listen. How about I write up a report on the whole damn thing and make a clean breast of the entire matter? You can kiss Harvard B—and your goddamn job—goodbye. I'll be in the clear. The cops'll back me up."

Sometimes I'm a better man than I want to be.

He paled.

"Aw shit, man. Can't ya take a goddamn joke?"

"No joke, Rush. I know when I'm being fucked over."

"Okay, okay! I'll handle the car. Get me an estimate and keep your mouth shut." Rush stepped back and laughed. "What the hell, can't blame a guy for trying." He slapped me on the back and hugged me around the shoulder with his free hand. "Mum's the fucking word."

I pulled away, repulsed. He smelled like rotten fish.

"Get some sleep." I tried to grin, but it made my face hurt. I just wanted him gone.

"Tee off at one, huh? Snead really fixed us up, no shit?"

"No shit. Now get some rest. We'll take those turkeys to the cleaners on the golf course tomorrow." I steered him out into the hall. I didn't want to lose the advantage now that I had him moving.

"Right. Fucking A! We'll take the grin off the faces of those cocky doctor friends of yours." He slapped me on the back again. "Think I'll skip breakfast. See ya in the exhibit hall around ten," he said and started down the hall away from the elevators.

"Rush! The other way."

"Huh?" He stopped and looked, then grinned. "Oh, yeah." He looked back in the other direction. "Yeah, right," he said and stumbled as he turned around.

I closed the door, went back to the bed, and sat there staring blankly at my doodles on the memo pad.

JOHN PAUL SILVER.

CARPE DIEM.

A-G-R-A-N-U-L-O-C-Y-T-O-S-I-S.

I was a good speller anyway.

Feeling soiled, I went in and turned on the shower.

Out of the shower, I slipped between the cool sheets again and turned out the light. The image of Ginny's incredible breasts with the jutting nipples just beginning to show the pouting womanliness of being on the down slope of thirty-five played on the big movie screen behind my eyelids.

Sexiest thing I'd ever seen.

My stalwart lancer stirred. With no respect for the fact that I was his sole life support, he was engorging again. Obviously, he functioned in a reality all his own.

The old rascal actually acted as if I existed for him and not he for me.

WEDNESDAY MORNING

CHAPTER TWENTY-FIVE

I awoke at seven-thirty feeling surprisingly alert. Through the window, I could see splashes of peach-hued early morning sunlight sparkling on the dew-jeweled, perfectly cultivated flowerbeds below. Overhead, the sky was cloudless.

Knowing full well I'd pay for it later, I pulled back the covers, rubbed my eyes, rolled out on the floor, and did twenty sit-ups, twenty crunches, and twenty leg drops.

A man should try to keep his belly flat.

As I headed for the shower, last night's scribbles CARPE DIEM and JOHN PAUL SILVER on the phone pad stabbed me in the heart.

I tore the sheet from the pad and tossed it in the wastebasket.

A brand new page for a bright new day.

Showered and shaved, I dressed in a gray silk business suit for the grand opening of the exhibit hall.

I was almost ready to go to breakfast when the phone rang.

My watch showed 8:01.

In no mood to put up with Rush's trash this early, I hesitated.

I'd left my room number in Dr. Ferguson's box, and there was Ginny. I gave in and picked up.

"Good morning. I hope I didn't wake you?" Ginny stirred an instant reaction in my groin.

"Not at all. I was heading down to breakfast."

"Marvelous. I was wondering if I might join you for coffee. I mean, you aren't meeting Rush, or anything?"

"No, thank God. I dreamed about you," I lied.

In my dreams I'd been trying to straighten broken umbrellas that kept turning into dogwood trees.

"You're a silver-tongued devil. I love it. You really do need to get back to writing fiction," she purred happily.

"There are stories I could tell." Images of last night in her bed came rushing back. The tightening in my groin was more insistent now.

"Yes," she breathed. "I was hoping for a sequel."

"Good stories always demand a sequel. What time will you get here? I'll go check on our booth and see if I can locate Dr. Ferguson while I wait."

"Oh, I'm already downstairs. How long will you be?"

"Forget the booth, I'm on my way."

"Outside the dining room. See you in a minute." She hung up.

Crossing the expanse of lobby, I could see her waving from the entrance to the dining room. Her smile was radiant. She had on a melon-colored shirtwaist dress, looking as if she'd never missed a minute's sleep in her life.

As I drew closer, I could see her panty line underneath the flimsy dress.

When I walked up to her, she took my forearms and pulled me to her. Glancing around to see that no one was within hearing distance, she whispered, "God, you certainly did grow up to be a sexy man. I can't wait to get my claws on you again. All of a sudden I don't trust myself to behave."

I'd never had a woman so blatantly, so openly aggressively in pursuit of me.

Not one I'd wanted, anyway.

My physical reaction was overpowering. Resisting the urge to pull her close and kiss her was almost more than I could handle. Certainly in a hotel of nearly seven hundred rooms we could find some nook or cranny to get lost in for thirty minutes.

"You look good enough to eat. I'm tempted to take a bite right this minute," I said. "Do you suppose we could slip off to my room?"

My errant centurion was starting to engorge again. Never again would I wonder how the porno stars could perform in front of the camera. At that moment I was sure I could make love to her at midfield in an Olympic stadium in front of a hundred thousand screaming fans.

In a hailstorm.

"Don't even think about it. I'm too tempted. It would be all over the hotel before my panties hit the carpet," she whispered. "But God, I do want you. Can't you get away tonight, after the golf?"

"Sure, but come on now. You could wander off to my room and I'll follow innocently in about five minutes. Who'd be the wiser?"

"You are indeed a dear innocent boy. How do you think your room gets put back in apple-pie order every time you start for the elevator bank?"

"By blinded slaves who've had their tongues cut out?" I answered hopefully.

"Oh, were it but true, fair Logan." She put her forearm across her brow and rolled her eyes heavenward in the best tradition of actresses of the silent screen.

"*Merde*! Foiled again." It wasn't an act. I'd never felt more frustrated in my life.

"Tonight. Meet me tonight at the Rhododendron Pool Lounge. Sixish?"

"Rats! What's your damn reputation compared to what we had last night?" I grabbed her hand and gave a little tug.

"Just cool it, Logan!" She giggled. "Tonight, okay?"

"Okay. O-freaking-kay, damn it. But, I warn you, I'm fighting for control." I made a face.

"Behave!" She gave my hand a yank and laughed.

The maitre d' walked up and saved me from acting out my death wish.

"Good morning, sir." He nodded to me. "And Miss McKim."

"Carl, this is Mr. Baird. I taught him in high school. He was my star pupil." She squeezed my arm.

"Nice to meet you, Mr. Baird," he said.

I smiled and nodded. He was about my age and tall and looked as if he might have played some basketball.

"I didn't see you and Amy at the Golf Club last night. She hasn't had that baby, has she?" Ginny asked.

"No. We were there, but it was late and we only stayed a minute. I looked for you."

"I was there earlier, but I couldn't stay long either," she said.

"Is Mr. Webb coming back soon?" he asked.

"No. He was due today, but he called and canceled. Bev told me last night."

"Too bad," he said.

"I guess something came up." Ginny shrugged, then glanced back at me. "Local stuff."

Carl shot an eye at several couples wandering toward the dining room and became all business again.

"Will you follow me, please?" He turned and led the way.

Starting down an aisle between the tables, my heart sank. Sam and Max with Maryanne and Cookie were at a table in the far corner of the large room. I thanked my cosmic guardian that I'd told Rose about Ginny last night. A good offense is usually the best defense. Still, I prayed they wouldn't spot me. I could hear Cookie now, casually dropping the news to Rose at bridge club when she got back. I made a mental note to make up a story to cover my ass when I called Rose tonight.

Ginny ordered coffee and melon, and I opted to have only coffee. Ignoring my mother's predictions of nutritional disaster, I've never been much of a breakfast eater.

"What time did you get to sleep?" I asked.

"Took me about fifteen minutes to get home and perhaps five minutes to brush my teeth and fall into bed. I was asleep before I turned out the light. I dreamed the nicest dreams of you." She smiled enigmatically.

"Me too," I lied again. It was getting easier all the time. "Tell me yours, and I'll tell you mine."

"Oh, no. I couldn't." She changed the subject. "You should get that car looked at."

"Is there a Buick dealer in town?" I asked.

"Here and also Lewisburg. Chevys, Buicks, Cadillacs, and pickup trucks. Same dealer sells them all. I could get someone to come over this morning, I'm sure. I know everybody there."

"That would be a big help. What I'd like is an official, fully itemized estimate of how much it will cost to repair the damage," I said. "I think the quicker I get the bill and a check from Rush, the better off I'm going to be. He has to leave for his precious Hahvahd right away."

"Consider it done. Are you going to be around the exhibit hall this morning?"

"I'm going to be there when it opens. Bill Moss, the company rep from Charleston, is coming down to relieve me around ten-thirty, he said. I'm going to hang around until he gets here. I want to hit some range balls, but I probably won't leave until around eleven-thirty anyway. I'm still trying to locate the elusive Dr. Ferguson. I hope I can touch base with him before we run off to the golf course. It might be embarrassing if prima donna Ferguson called the company and said, 'I looked for them, but they both were out playing golf.'"

"This morning might be a little tight on time, but I'll have the car estimate for you when you finish golfing this afternoon, all nice and official," she promised.

"That'll be a godsend. I don't want to let Rush get away from me without giving me the cash to fix my car."

"Would it help to have a copy of a police report? You know, with the official names and signatures and times and descriptions and the charges. Like 'hit and run felony with property damage' or whatever the legal terms would be?"

"Sure, but I thought you talked them into dropping charges. I didn't know they'd be making any record."

"Oh, they won't. Nothing on file. I meant you'd have the only copy. It was just an idea. I thought it might come in handy someday."

"That would be icing on the cake. Can you really do that?"

"Consider it done. I'll put it in an envelope and leave it in your box. I'll keep a Xerox in my safe at home."

"What've you got on the local law anyway? I'd hate to have you mad at me." I stole a closer look at her.

She smiled a Mona Lisa smile. I wondered if there were a subliminal warning there.

"This Ferguson . . . is he part of your company?" She changed the subject.

"No, Ferguson doesn't work for Severance. But he does research on some of our new hormones and he's famous, a world-class authority. Just finished an important study on our new miracle erection drug. He's going to report the results to these doctors tomorrow morning. His report is the *pièce de résistance* of this august meeting. There will be a big press conference. *USA Today*, *Time*, *Newsweek*, CNN, you name it. An entire world of limp penises is waiting for that report. Ferguson is God; he has a lot of influence. A good report from him will make my life a lot easier and a lot of women happier." I winked.

"I think I understand. You're supposed to help him?"

"No, not really. We—Rush and I—just wanted to make our presence known to him. Find out if he needs any support from the company. A matter of courtesy. Sort of run interference for him."

"You won't have to entertain him, will you? I guess I'm taking a lot for granted, but I was hoping I could take you home with me again." She busied herself with her food.

"Count on me. I'm free. I'll be off the golf course around five. By the time I grab a beer at the clubhouse and get back here and shower, it'll be around six. A little past, maybe. Okay?"

"I can hardly wait." She touched my arm.

"And what is this we can't wait for? Sounds exciting." Without even looking, I recognized Cookie's voice behind me.

"Good morning, Cookie." I turned and started to rise. "Care to join us for breakfast?"

"No, thanks, keep your seat. We're over there." She pointed to their table.

They all waved.

Waving back, I forced a smile.

I stood up anyway. I didn't like her peering down at me.

"Forgive Logan, he's such a clod," she purred at Ginny "I'm Cookie Bergmann, a very close friend of Logan's wife, Rose. I haven't had the pleasure."

"Forgive my manners. Cookie, allow me to present Ginny McKim. Ginny's from Melas. We went to the same high school." I felt a flush of red creeping up my neck.

"How nice. An old classmate? Tell me, Ginny, was Logan as smooth in high school as he is now? I tell Rose all the time, if he were my husband, I'd put a bell around his neck. The women at the club drool when he's around." Cookie really had her claws out.

"When I first met Logan he was only twelve. I was doing my undergraduate work for a teaching degree, and my practicum assignment was his and Rose's homeroom in eighth grade. Logan was a darling. Always into some mischief or other." Ginny smiled, unflustered.

"So? Are you here for the medical society meeting? Is your husband a physician?" Cookie oozed.

"Goodness no. I own a little B and B in Lewisburg. I came over to visit an old friend from my grad school days who's down from New York. You can imagine how delighted I was to run into Logan here last night. I hadn't seen him in ten or eleven years. We were catching up on old times."

"When I called Rose last night, she couldn't believe I'd run into Ginny. She was really pleased to hear the news. We'd all lost touch." I was squirming, but I wanted to let Cookie know that she was too late to break the news to Rose.

"How nice for you . . . and Rose." Cookie tried hard not to sound disappointed.

"Sit down, Cookie. Have a cup of coffee, won't you?" I pulled back a chair.

"I can't. I've got to be getting back to the table," she said. "So nice meeting you, Miss McKim."

Ginny cleared her throat. There was an awkward silence as we watched her go.

"The kitty's claws are showing. Kinda makes me embarrassed to be female. Women are a cold-blooded lot. I guess I shouldn't say this, but you married one of the most calculating little bitches that is ever likely to come down the pike. I had enough of Miss Goody Two Shoes, Rose Worrell, when she was in eighth grade. To her, I was only orphanage trash. If your precious Rose knew about last night, she'd cut off your balls, stuff them down your throat, and laugh all the way home from the funeral."

"Oh, I doubt she'd care." I tried to laugh, but the image brought a twinge to my gubernaculum.

"You're so naive. Hate to say it, but men don't have a chance. You're really the weaker sex." She smiled and touched my wrist. "The only difference between me and Cookie is that at least I admit that I'm an alley cat. I thought you kept your cool okay, but I could tell that Cookie had you squirming. I'm not sure whether you're feeling guilty or just plain scared of getting caught. Maybe a little of both. Me, I'm not feeling a thing except lucky and horny. I've had this silly little fantasy about you going in my head for a long time. If they'd known what went on in my head when I was practice teaching, they'd have locked me up or burned me at the stake—a modern reenactment of the witches of Salem. I can see the matron at the orphanage branding me a pedophile. I thought you were at least fifteen. I was barely nineteen myself. What the hell, you were plenty big and by orphanage standards, plenty old enough. We started young up there. Then, just when I thought I'd dreamed you up, there you were yesterday all grown up and right in front of my eyes. My lucky day. You won't remember, but even after I graduated college and got married, I used to go out to the public pool when you were lifeguard. My panties still get sticky just thinking about it. Yesterday was my lucky day all right. And by damn, tonight's another night," she laughed and gave my thigh a squeeze.

She was right. I had been squirming.

And, for that matter, after that speech, I still was.

What had I gotten myself into?

But, what the hell. I'd already done the deed. Doing it again didn't make the risk any greater.

Or the consequence of getting caught any more frightening.

"Now's your chance. If you want to bail out, I'll understand. Me, I'm going to take what I can get and ask questions later." Ginny lifted her water goblet and looked over the rim, waiting for a reaction.

I still wanted her badly. She was wrong about my not remembering her coming to the pool. I masturbated a lot back then.

"I wouldn't miss tonight for anything," I said.

A coward dies a thousand deaths, a hero only one.

"Maybe it would be a good idea if I excused myself. No sense in stirring up trouble back home. I'll make it look legit for the harpy over there," she smiled. Folding her napkin and placing it carefully on the table, she pushed back her chair and got up to leave.

"*Carpe diem.*" I lifted my water goblet in a little toast.

"*Ciao.*" She winked and was gone.

When she passed the area opposite the table where the others were sitting, Ginny gave Cookie a friendly wave.

I glanced at Cookie and the others, wondering if they were watching me.

My gubernaculum twitched when I thought about what Ginny had said about getting caught. I wondered what Rose would really do if she found out.

She wouldn't leave me. I was sure of that.

Or was I?

Rose did have a mean streak when she didn't get her way.

And I wondered what had happened between Rose and Ginny back then. They both had hinted darkly about it.

"I'm glad I caught you."

In the lobby heading for the exhibit hall, I paused to admire the spa instructor, Pru Sharpe, and her gaggle of ladies gathering to head for a workout. When I turned back around, Rush was standing at my right shoulder.

"I need a small favor," he said anxiously.

I really was in no mood to start all that mess about the car again until I could get the copy of the "official report" tucked safely away and shove a bona fide damage estimate in his hand.

He was subdued.

Nothing miraculous, though. He still neglected to say good morning.

"Good morning," he finally offered. He must have read my mind.

"Good morning," I said evenly, anxious to keep things civil.

"Listen, don't worry. It's not that damn car. I have a minor medical . . . situation. I need to see a doctor. Can you get someone at the clinic to look at me? Or even better, maybe one of the town doctors?"

"What's the problem?" I asked. I guessed he was feeling a little hung over. He didn't really look all that bad. "I think I might have some Darvoset."

"No, not that kind of problem. Ah, something else. I need to have a doctor take a look at a place that's bothering me. It's sort of personal."

When he sat down rather gingerly in the chair opposite where Ginny had been, the odor of alcohol was overpowering.

Hemorrhoids? I wondered.

"Shouldn't take long." He avoided looking me in the eye.

I looked at my watch.

The Greenbrier Clinic physicians met every morning at eight before they started doing annual physicals on corporate VIPs. An impressive list from the Fortune 500 companies sent their executives down once a year for a week, all hotel and spa amenities on the house. A great corporate perk, it also resulted in uncounted additional management meetings and trade conventions.

Understandably, the Greenbrier Clinic was not a priority call for most pharmaceutical sales reps. Aware of their far-reaching influence, I had made myself one of the few exceptions by keeping these ivory tower physicians supplied with samples for their clients and staff, along with the latest insider information. It wasn't exactly a bonanza, but I was rewarded with a steady flow of prescriptions at the local pharmacy. These highly regarded physicians were primarily diagnosticians, astute clinicians too occupied to break their schedule and entertain mere mortal drug company hoi polloi. Trying to impose Rush and his bullshit consultation into their schedule at this late hour was out of the question. I'd never be able to darken their door again.

"The Greenbrier Clinic has already started doing physicals. If we hurry, we can run downtown. Maybe we can catch one of the family docs down on Main Street before they start seeing patients." I signed the check.

"Follow me," I said, steering Rush by the elbow.

We walked across the lobby and down the steps leading to the motor entrance. It was only a short stroll to the main lot where I'd parked my poor beat-up car in the wee hours this morning.

228

"Can't you give me a hint what this is all about?" I asked as we drove along.

"I'd rather not. It's kinda personal. Don't worry. Any doc fresh out of med school can do the job." He paused and gave me a sly look. "Ginny came out there with you last night. You get into her britches?"

He kept his eyes averted when he spoke.

"Get your mind out of the gutter." I hoped I sounded offended. "Ginny McKim was my homeroom teacher when I was in the eighth grade. Just old times, that's all."

"Uh-huh, that's your story and you're sticking to it, right?" His voice carried an insinuating sneer. "I'll tell you one thing, that Mimi is a hot number, but I'm not about to get involved. Too much to lose. Still, if I wasn't married . . ."

The gentleman doth protest too much, methinks. Shakespeare was a wise old bird.

I held my tongue.

Traffic in White Sulphur Springs was light at this early hour, and we made good time.

We went through the private employee entrance into the downtown clinic, and I told Rush to wait, then went looking for Melba Noyes.

Melba was an attractive young nurse who, newly graduated from training, had followed a Greenbrier doctor down from a Midwestern university med school. The romance had faded, and the doctor eventually left. But savvy Melba, with an eye out for some unwary single millionaire at Sam Snead's Golf Academy or a promising young exec down for his corporate physical, had stayed on.

Where the Greenbrier Clinic physicians were diagnosticians and prescribed relatively little medication, the town doctors were a different breed altogether. They were as busy as the hotel docs, but for the few drug reps who would sit them out, they were a veritable gold mine.

For some reason, Melba had taken a liking to me. I frequently took her to lunch at Sam Snead's at the Golf Club, the Rhododendron Pool Lounge, or Draper's Café at the hotel, and

I supplied her with an expensive prescription for her mom. I could always count on her to slip me in to see her doctors without a wait.

She was often flirty. She'd hinted broadly that the local night life could be pretty dismal for a single girl and made it fairly obvious that I could ask her out after hours for a drink, but my better judgment had prevailed against it. I flirted back but was careful to keep my demeanor purely on a friendly level.

"Never fuck around the flag pole," was an old military adage.

I never compromised my professional status around my clientele. I'd witnessed more than a few such disasters among the ranks of my peers.

And, if that weren't reason enough, I'd also heard scuttlebutt that she had something going with one of the young ER physicians at the nearby hospital across the Virginia line in Lowmoor.

Quietly, I crept down the hall and found Melba having a cup of coffee, looking dreamily out the window of the records room.

"Hey! Remember me?" I whispered. She jumped and slopped coffee out of the cup, barely missing her spotless uniform—a gymnastic feat of Olympian proportion.

"Logan, you devil! You almost made me ruin my uniform." She giggled. Except for a slightly Roman nose, she resembled the sexy actress Charlize Theron. "I was wondering if you were here with the big medical hoopla. I was coming over to take in the exhibits this afternoon."

"Great. Come check us out. Maybe we could ride off into the sunset," I teased, maintaining the innocent flirty bond.

"Promises, promises. Just say when."

"When," I said. "But first, I have a little problem."

When I explained what I was after, Melba glanced at her watch. She looked at me doubtfully.

"Robothom just came in. He likes you. I can probably get him to take a quick peek. Is his problem surgical? You know we're limited here. Anything beyond a Band-Aid or an aspirin, we send the patient over to the miners' HMO in Lewisburg or the hospital in Lowmoor."

"He won't tell me. Touch of hypochondria more'n likely. Anyway, I don't think it amounts to much. Something for his hemorrhoids, a bad hangover maybe. Don't forget he's my boss. If you get a chance, tell him I'm a superstar, okay?"

"That'll be easy. Come on, let's go meet this ailing boss of yours."

I led her back down the long hall and introduced Rush.

"Rush here's an important guy. Our company's sending him to Harvard next week," I said, piling on the bullshit.

Lately, self-respect wasn't my strongest attribute.

"Logan's our favorite." She gave Rush the once-over while she fussed with the collar of my jacket. "We see very few pharmaceutical reps here, but Logan's a cut above the rest."

"Grab a cab back, okay? I've got to go back to the exhibit," I said, starting on my way.

"Wait." Melba gave me a hug. "Don't be such a stranger."

She raised up on her tippy-toes and pecked me on the cheek.

Rush shot us a look. He had a dirty mind.

I reddened when I looked at her. I hadn't expected her to overdo it. "Thanks, Melba. I'll find a way to make it up. Our regular lunch next month when I come. If you get a chance, come by our booth at the hotel."

She gave me a smile. "Don't think I'm not going to take you up on that lunch." Of course, it was supposed to be a show to make me look good in front of Rush, but now a free-floating anxiety nagged me not to step too far out on the ice.

"Forget lunch, Melba. Logan'll take you to dinner at the hotel. I'll hold him to it." Rush and his giant ego—he made like the big-shot boss again.

"I think I like this boss of yours," she winked and squeezed my arm.

"We have a dinner date, when I come back in October," I confirmed, but my stomach did a funny flip.

All of a sudden, my cup runneth under. I definitely could not afford to hurt Melba's feelings.

A shudder of prescience passed over me like a gust of wind.

Last night's fling with Ginny left me on shaky ground. This was a tight little community. There was no way I could have my cake and eat it too. Or could I?

October was more than a month away. A lot could happen in a month.

"Come along, Mr. Donald, and tell me what's bothering you." Melba led him back down the hall.

"Grab a cab back to the hotel when you're done," I called and got out of there.

Back at the hotel, the good-looking spa lady and another collection of amorphous female bodies were heading through the lobby. She saw me now and waved.

I waved and smiled.

Pru Sharpe. I made a mental note. Might come in handy now that it looked like I was headed for certain self-destruct.

Prodigiously pulchritudinous Pru, firmer of flabby female forms.

Watching the sensuous Pru, the warmth of Melba's hug and her lingering scent nibbled at the edges of my consciousness. Melba Noyes, fabulously, fantastically female.

An all-around auspicious day for alliteration and anticipated adultery. I savored the prospect of another evening with the glamorous, gorgeous, glandular Ginny.

Last night's orgiastic marathon had me horny as a toad.

Taking Melba out could prove problematic. I'd have to explain the situation to Ginny. She was sure to find out.

An innocent business dinner with the clinic nurse? Harmless enough. Why should that bother Ginny?

For one thing, Melba was a sexy fox, and restless, but certainly not seriously interested in me. Besides, if a friendly dinner led to a casual interlude, what the hell? The more the merrier. In for a penny, in for a pound.

Who was I to take responsibility for the whole damned universe? One night in Ginny's bed and I was all ready to orchestrate a full-scale orgy.

Carpe diem, John Paul. Let the chips fall where they may.

Earlier, I had felt a twinge of guilt when Ginny walked out of the dining room and waved to Cookie.

Guilt?

Stark raving fear more likely.

I'd looked down my nose at Rush's drunken indiscretions last night, but I was already making plans to see Ginny again.

And now Melba. Maybe Pru. Who was I to talk?

Well? The difference was that Rush got drunk and wound up with his ass in a crack.

What a pious crock of shit—the pot calling the kettle black.

Logan Baird, a regular paragon of virtue.

So? Maybe I wasn't Teflon coated, but I knew enough to avoid the booze.

Okay, John Paul. What do you have to tell me about life in the fast lane?

Careful, old sport. Don't fly too close to the sun.

The message came back, clear as a bell.

Suddenly depressed, I tried to shake my unhealthy preoccupations with morality.

What say you about morality, John Paul? You're suddenly my unwilling expert.

Screw 'em all but six and save them for the pallbearers?

"Carpe-freaking-diem," I said to a robin as I walked out into the bright sunshine. I flushed as a man in coveralls cleaning windows gave me a funny look.

Enough of these depressing preoccupations

I called Sam to tell him we were teeing off at 1:00.

Time to turn my mind to golf.

CHAPTER TWENTY-SIX

Around ten-thirty, Rush came wandering into the exhibit hall dressed in pleated white British-cut golf slacks and a slightly-too-bright-green Cypress Point golf shirt with an alligator over the left breast. Head to toe, he looked every inch the world-class duffer.

"How'd it go at the clinic? Melba get you all fixed up?" I was more than a little interested.

"All taken care of. Thanks." It was clear he'd said all he was going to say.

"Good." As curious as I was, I let it drop.

"Any word from Dr. Ferguson?"

"No, and his room doesn't answer," I replied.

"At least now we know he's here. I'm going to call Marge in Teaneck and tell her we've done everything we can to get in touch. It's really a matter of protocol, anyway."

"Good idea. I'm waiting on Bill Moss to cover the booth so we can hit the links. He was supposed to be here before now." I gave his duds an admiring look. "You look like you're ready for bear."

"Pretty classy, huh?" He beamed.

I nodded.

"As soon as I phone Teaneck, I'm going down and hit some practice balls. Wouldn't want to make a fool out of myself." He sounded a bit uptight.

Sam walked up and gave Rush an admiring look. "When you got it, you can't hide it! Logan, you think you can get away with running this ringer in on us. A circuit rider whose home tracks are Pebble Beach and Cypress and plays Pinehurst and the fabulous Dunes at Myrtle. You guys are too tough for us."

Poor Rush took the bait, hook, line and sinker. I could see him tensing up.

Sam was loving it.

"How about two a side, Logan?"

The master of psych jobs, Sam never quit.

"Okay, we'll take two a side, won't we, partner?" I played along.

"Hah! If there are any shots, you'll give 'em to us," Sam scoffed.

"Listen, you guys, give me break. I'm rusty. Logan knows I've hardly had a chance to play since I moved from the coast. Besides, I'm playing with borrowed sticks. You should be giving me strokes. Logan says you play to a nine. The best I ever played was a twelve. I'm heading down to hit a few balls right now."

"Great. Wait up. We should be hitting balls too. If I can find Max, I'm heading down that way. Gotta be careful though, when you get past thirty, you don't have the stamina you used to. Besides, I read in *Golf Digest* that if you hit too many practice balls you get arm-weary. I'm sure you know the story about Titanic Thompson, the famous hustler out in Texas who used to sucker opponents by offering to let them hit three drives off every tee and then play the best one. Titanic would double the bet on the backside. By the time they'd reached the tenth tee, the poor guy had already hit twenty-seven tee shots and was getting so arm-weary he could hardly take the club back." Sam rattled off his nonstop line of bullshit.

Rush was starting to sweat, and his hands betrayed a slight tremor.

Too much party last night.

"There's my partner now. See you guys." Sam spotted Max and headed out.

"You think he's right? Maybe I should skip hitting balls and go putt a little. Still, I really do need to hit a few to loosen up. Even the pros do that. I can't stand the thought of getting up there and dumping the ball in that damn creek in front of all those people up there in that goddamn grill looking out the window." Rush's voice cracked, and there was a hint of panic in his eye. "I wish you had better-looking equipment. I hate to look like some plumber at the public links. Did I tell you I had a kangaroo hide bag before I left the coast? Wish I hadn't sold my sticks."

He was getting on my nerves big time.

"Rush, forget the goddamn equipment. It looks okay. If you're worried about appearances, do you know who Sam Snead spent the night with?" I hoped to make a point.

"Who?"

"Our mystery man with the ratty car and golf clubs. His name is Scotty Mac . . . something, and he's flying in a bunch of Yankee big shots this morning. Your so-called bum has reserved Top Notch for an important meeting—board of directors or something." I hoped he'd get my point.

"So? What the hell's Top Notch?"

"Top Notch is one of the premier estate houses. Power brokers like Jack Welch and Bill Gates have private meetings there." I embellished the truth. "This Scotty person winters in Boca, and word is that he and Sam Snead are fishing buddies. They're playing today, right after we go off. Sam himself made our tee time. Sam ain't ashamed of Scotty's equipment, so relax."

"Am I supposed to be impressed? Money still doesn't buy you class."

"Then why are you so worried about how you dress and what kind of clubs you have?"

He gave me a second look and went pale as what I'd said sank in. "Holy shit. Sam Snead is going to play behind us? Wait'll I tell 'em back on the coast!" He stopped and began to frown. "They're going off right behind us?"

"Yeah." Now, I wished I'd held my tongue.

"Judas. I know I better hit some balls now."

"Time's awastin', Rush. Get on out of here. Just keep in mind that this ain't on national TV." I made a mental note to buy him a beer at lunch to calm him down.

"Okay, okay, I'm heading for the practice range. I hope I don't leave all the good shots on the practice tee," he muttered.

My heart sank. Sam had turned him into a regular basket case.

"For chrissake, Rush, relax. This is supposed to be fun, remember?" Looking past him, I spied my replacement down the aisle talking to the men at the Upjohn booth. "I see Bill Moss coming now. I'll be right behind you."

"Okay, but don't tell him I'm playing golf with you."

"Sure. Your secret's safe. You're in your room doing paperwork, right?"

"Right. I'm outta here."

"Do me a favor, Rush. Have them put my sticks on the cart and get me a bucket of practice balls. As soon as I can get Bill squared away, I'll change and head down that way."

We were teeing up in front of Snead. Rush wasn't the only one who didn't want to look bad.

"Sure," Rush called over his shoulder, heading out.

Watching him go, I thought about how much difference twenty-four hours can make. This time yesterday, I'd been in a state of high anticipation. Despite all his fuss about the golf clubs and his arrogance driving over the mountains, I'd kept playing up to him.

Remembering how I had buttered him up on the practice tee yesterday, trying to build his confidence so he wouldn't chicken out and spoil the golf match with Max and Sam, I felt dirty. I'd watched his god-awful swing. His stories about his prowess on the golf course were like the rest of him, manufactured out of magazines and TV.

Even though I'd stood up for myself last night, I was right back to kissing his ass again.

Why? After last night, I had him by the balls.

Once I got the promotion, I'd be in control. Free forever.

Watching him strutting in his too-new outfit, I felt angry and ashamed.

Still, no percentage in making him an enemy. He was headed to the home office. It never hurt to have a Rush Donald in your corner at the home office.

I fervently hoped the forces of the universe would somehow muster up a miracle to get Rush's tee shot at least airborne over Howard's Creek this afternoon.

Quit worrying, I told myself. After last night what else could happen?

Don't answer. I rolled my eyes heavenward.

I saw Melba heading in my direction. Every man in the place was staring. The innocence of the uniform made her look stunning.

They'd put me in jail if they knew what I was thinking.

When she spotted me, I waved. Her face brightened as she headed straight for our booth.

Go easy, I reminded myself. I didn't want to lead her on.

"Oh, I was afraid I'd missed you. I passed your boss. He said you were going to play golf," she said, slightly out of breath.

"I am, but I'm glad you caught me. Thanks for taking care of Rush this morning. I hope it was all right. I still don't have the slightest notion what the big mystery was about." I was dying to know and hoped she'd volunteer.

"That's one reason I wanted to catch you. I'm sure it's not funny to him, but it really was hilarious. I knew you'd want to know." Stifling a giggle, she looked around to see if anyone was within earshot.

"Well? So tell me."

"You're not just acting dumb are you? I mean, you really don't know what his problem was?" She gave me a close look to see if I was putting her on.

Now she was so close her bosom was pressing into my arm, and she bumped me lightly at the hip. To someone passing by it probably looked like two very good friends who hadn't seen each other in a long time, but her mouth was so close I could have kissed her without moving. Her breath was minty-delicious. My testosterone was on overload.

I was dying for a taste of those swollen bee-stung lips.

I knew now that she was being intentionally seductive. I was in no mood to play games. Where her body was touching mine, it felt like an electric current flowing into me. Her perfume was stronger than I'd remembered. I suspected she'd touched it up before she came down.

Out the corner of my eye, a flash of melon in the crowd caught my attention. When I looked again, it was gone.

"No. So help me, he didn't tell me a thing," I said.

"I guess he wouldn't. It is too embarrassing." Melba giggled again. Her breast was firm, pressing against my arm.

"Well? Don't keep me hanging," I said, looking anxiously around to see if anyone was staring. "What's his problem?"

Suddenly, the splash of melon caught my eye again. My stomach did a flip.

Ginny?

Melba had turned toward me and was fiddling with my name tag. The curve of her pudendum burned an imprint against my upper thigh. I was having a helluva time keeping my mind on the thread of the conversation.

"He wanted a tetanus booster. He had this pretty little set of teeth marks around the . . . the head of his thing," Melba was saying. She fussed with my lapels, rubbing and making damn sure that I felt more of her.

"Teeth marks? You mean his—" I suddenly realized what she was saying.

She nodded and straightened my tie. "Uh-huh." She rose up on her toes and whispered near my ear, "His skinny little penis."

I could feel the silky surface of her slip against the smooth texture of my slacks.

"Can you imagine? He was worried about tetanus. A rabies shot would have been a better choice." She giggled.

"You mean you think it was a dog?" I was having trouble following her.

"A bitch in heat. I'd bet on it." She laughed again. I had no idea shy Melba could be so outspoken.

I caught full sight of Ginny now. She was standing back in the crowd pretending to talk to a security guard. She kept glancing impatiently my way.

Involuntarily, I tried to move back a little.

When I moved, she moved. When I breathed, she jiggled. Melba was pasted against me like we were the reincarnation of Chang and Eng.

"What's she like?" Melba knew she'd lost my attention.

"Huh?" Ginny's beady glare was making me very nervous.

"The woman he was with last night. Someone got very carried away. I could see where he usually wears a ring. I assume his wife isn't here?" It was obviously a question.

"A bite. You sure?" I tried to ignore her question.

"Well? Is she here? His wife, I mean." Melba wasn't about to let the question go.

"Wife? Oh no, his wife's not here. Must have happened before he flew into Roanoke yesterday."

"Robothom said that bite was fresh. I don't think your boss is telling you everything. What were you two up to last night?"

"I left him after dinner." It wasn't exactly a lie.

I tried to catch a glimpse of Ginny again, but I'd lost her in the sea of people.

"Oh, I know all about you traveling guys . . . a woman in every town." Melba moved suggestively.

"Don't believe it," I protested, sweating now.

Seeing Ginny made me extremely nervous.

But why? I really wasn't guilty of anything.

Unless, of course, you counted submitting to rape in the middle of five hundred people.

And, after all, Ginny wasn't exactly my wife or anything.

I knew full well what Melba was leading up to, and, God help me, I couldn't help but be interested. She was making me very antsy.

I needed to get a grip.

"It's okay. You can trust me. I know the score," Melba wheedled, still welded at the hip.

She knew full well I was married and how much I loved Paul—over our regular lunches we'd become sort of confidants. I'd confessed all the sordid secrets of my unhappy life at home.

"No. Really, Melba, I don't fool around. Not like that."

"I know you are too urbane to be indiscriminately promiscuous. Still, I'm sure there are a lot of women in the hospitals and doctors' offices who are dying to go out with you."

I was getting warm around the collar, and my palms were oozing sweat. "Quit teasing, Melba. Women don't know I exist." I made a half-hearted effort to laugh.

Now Ginny was nowhere in sight.

"Oh, no! Don't stand here and tell me you don't know." She leaned back, fidgeting with my tie. "All the women up in the clinic think you're cute. How come you think we give you special treatment?" Our bellies were still touching. Sweat rolled down the crack of my butt, as she brushed her breast across my arm again. "Anyway, I think your boss got lucky last night, or unlucky if you want to look at it that way. Those little teeth marks still hadn't scabbed over. I guarantee he didn't bring those marks here from Charlotte. There are always a lot of overly amorous, bored rich women staying here for the spa program. The mountain air makes 'em horny. Unless I miss my guess, your Mr. Donald is going to be undressing in the dark for a few days when he gets back home. The good news is that he probably isn't so badly wounded that it'll cramp his style tonight." She winked broadly, patting me affectionately on the cheek.

Where the hell had Ginny gone?

"Oh, come on Melba, you don't know what a straight-laced guy he is. I'm sure it was his zipper. It happens."

"I think he's got you fooled. By the way, you owe me dinner, but if you could get free I'd cook for you. I guess tonight's out of the question?" She shot me a hopeful look.

"Afraid so. I'm on my way to play golf with my boss as soon as I can turn this thing over to my replacement." I nodded in the general direction of Bill Moss. "But don't worry. I won't forget the dinner. I'm looking forward to it."

I really meant it about the dinner—if Ginny didn't have my balls bronzed and hanging on her mantel before I left town.

No sign of her. I breathed a sigh.

I found myself wondering if I could somehow juggle both Melba and Ginny.

And I wondered if my family tree had any history of suicidal types.

"If it rains you out, I'll be in the clinic until around two." Melba wasn't giving up without a fight.

I finally managed to catch Bill Moss's eye and waved him over.

Bill nodded and came strolling up.

I let out my breath, relieved, thankful that Melba unpasted herself when I made the introduction.

After a few minutes, Melba saw that Bill wasn't going to leave, so she gave up.

"Well, I've got to get back. I'm on a break. Come visit soon." Before I saw what was coming, she took a step closer and pressed her breasts against my chest, gave me another peck on the cheek, and whispered in my ear, "Don't forget. Call if it rains. And you could call me if you find you're free after the golf. I'm in the book."

She rubbed her belly against my thigh.

"Thanks for coming to my boss's rescue." I waved as she let go of me and reluctantly walked away.

I caught sight of Ginny again, standing near the entrance and glaring my way.

She stood there for a minute and watched as Melba walked past her.

If looks could kill, I'd often heard my grandmother say.

Unless I missed my guess, tonight I'd hear the full history of Melba Noyes—chapter and verse, the gospel according to Ginny McKim.

I laughed out loud, wondering what Ginny would say when she heard that Mimi had damn near bitten the end off Rush's dick.

"What?" Bill Moss looked at me, wondering what he'd missed.

"Women," I said and shrugged.

He grunted and gave me a look. "You tappin' that?"

"I wish," I rolled my eyes. "You gonna be okay this afternoon?"

"All set. Why don't you go enjoy yourself? I got a game myself tomorrow. Appreciate your fixing me up with this gig." He slapped me on the shoulder.

"My pleasure," I smiled.

Without glancing back again, Ginny turned and left. I started after her but changed my mind, suddenly anxious to forget about women and do something important for a change.

Like, maybe get into the pockets of some overly confident doctors I knew.

"It's all yours, Bill, baby. I'm going to go wear the covers off some little white balls. Thanks for minding the store," I said.

"Fairways and greens." He winked.

I winked back and headed for my room. The last twenty-four hours had gotten far too complicated for me.

I yearned for a simpler life.

CHAPTER TWENTY-SEVEN

When I reached my room, the message light was on. The operator informed me that there was an envelope in my box and they'd send it up. Something from Teaneck, I assumed. But the bellman arrived with a thick business-sized envelope with the hotel logo on it. As soon as he left, I opened it.

A sheaf of pink carbon copies unfolded to reveal a police report and summons to appear in court.

Signed and dated, it was all there, including official-looking signatures. Official-sounding terminology like HIT AND RUN FELONY—PROPERTY DAMAGE; RECKLESS DRIVING; DRIVING WHILE INTOXICATED filled the proper spaces.

A genuine work of art.

The cover note read:

Lover,
I may have a minor problem. Call me at home as soon as you get off the golf course.
Fondly,
G.

A phone number was at the bottom.

Something about the note made me uneasy.

I wondered if she'd gotten miffed at Melba's little charade in the exhibit hall.

In no mood for cryptic messages, I picked up my cell and dialed the number Ginny left.

A woman answered, "Bed and Breakfast."

I told her who I was and asked for Ginny.

"I'm sorry, sir, she isn't in," the woman said. "Can I help you?"

"When do you expect her back?" I asked.

"She won't be back today, sir," the woman said. "I'm her manager. Can I help you?"

"No, but thanks, anyway," I murmured politely and rang off.

As soon as I broke the connection, I called the hotel operator and asked to be connected with Mimi. I was ready to hang up by the time she answered.

"Mimi, this is Logan Baird. Have you talked with Ginny this morning?"

"As a matter of fact, I just spoke to her. She had to cancel lunch. Said something important had come up. Are you going to see her tonight? What's going on?"

"Damned if I know. Guess I'll find out later. She left a note to call her after the golf. Thanks," I murmured and hung up before it turned into twenty questions.

My gaze wandered to John Paul's letter, lying where I'd left it last night, unopened by the phone.

I picked it up and walked to the window, not really wanting to open it. At the moment, I was in no mood to handle a dying declaration.

Plenty of time to read it later, I decided and placed it back near the phone.

I had almost finished dressing when the phone rang. Hoping it might be Dr. Ferguson or perhaps Ginny, I crossed the room and picked up.

"Logan Baird," I answered, absently wondering what could go wrong next.

"Oh, Mr. Baird, I'm so glad I caught you. This is Cathy Silver." She sounded more girl than woman.

"Yes, Cathy, how are you holding up? I've been in a state of shock since last night. I still can't believe it," I replied evenly, trying hard not to betray resentment at her call.

"I know it must have been a shock to you. He wouldn't let us call you when he got sick. And even though we knew it was coming, I kept thinking something would happen. It was all a bad dream. He would have turned thirty-one in December. People just don't die before they're thirty-one." Her voice broke.

"I know. It's such a waste," I said lamely.

"I hope you'll forgive me for calling you. We've never met, but I don't think you know how much you were a part of my life. You were his hero. In a strange way he felt closer to you than any of his friends up here. And, of course, you became very real to me because of that. At times, when we were first married, I almost hated you." Her voice grew faint. She was having a hard time holding it together.

I knew she was hurting, but there wasn't a damn thing I could do. I hated all this mawkish melodrama.

"Wars are good for making buddies." I sounded as intellectual as possum shit. "Last night Jean told me he'd finished his book and had found a publisher. I know that had to be a big thing in his life."

"Oh, I almost forgot. Jean said that you might make us a copy of the letter that John Paul sent you. That is, if . . ."

I knew she was grasping at straws—anything to hold on to, but I felt a hot rush of resentment now. Her request for a copy of my letter seemed tasteless. I'd never met any of these people. What the hell did they expect from me?

"No. I said I'd let you know if he had any word for you, but a copy, I doubt it. Not if it's anything too personal—you know, like man talk. And, anyway, I'm still in shock. I'm embarrassed to say I haven't even opened it yet. It's lying right here in front of me, unread," I confessed sheepishly, picking the envelope up again, idly testing its heft in my hand.

"Well, if—"

"I'm late now for a meeting with my boss. I'm sorry." I was sure my impatience was evident.

"Don't apologize. I won't keep you. And please don't misunderstand. I didn't call to pry about the letter. What I really wanted to say was that I understood if you couldn't drop everything and come to the funeral tomorrow. But if something changes and you find out you can make it, I looked up the train schedules. We're right on the main line of the CSX. It stops in White Sulphur Springs. I took the liberty of checking. I thought it might help for you to know that. There's a train late tonight that gets in here tomorrow morning. We're less than an hour to the depot in Cincinnati. I'm sure you could get a compartment and get some sleep. The funeral is at ten, and you could catch a train back there tomorrow afternoon at one-forty-five. Jean and I would be glad to reimburse you for—"

"Reimburse me? Even if I could come, I wouldn't hear of it," I struggled to hold my temper. "And you're right. I simply can't drop everything. I hope you're still not holding out hope for me. I thought I made it crystal clear. I have an important commitment here."

"But, you wouldn't have to be a pallbearer. Jean's already taken care of that. I hope you don't misunderstand. We were only hoping you might have changed your mind," she ran on hopefully, reluctant to give up. "Sometimes things change when we least expect them to. Do you want to jot down the train times? I have them here."

"No. I can get that from the desk. Besides I'm sure it's out of the question. I can't just pick up and leave here. I have a responsibility. Surely you can understand." How many times did I have to say no, I wondered, struggling now to keep the impatience out of my voice.

"I hope I didn't . . . I hope you don't think . . ." Clearly embarrassed, she was sobbing softly, floundering for words.

Now she touched a sensitive chord of guilt. With all Rush's shit, I was having a hard time with everything that was going on.

"Look, Cathy, I'm sorry." I began, "I'll call in a few days and see if there's anything I can do. By then, I'll have read the letter and maybe I will be in better shape to deal with all this. Take care. I'll be thinking about you."

"I hope you didn't mind my calling," she began again.

"No, no, not at all. I'm very glad you did," I lied. "Take care. I'll call you very soon."

"Don't forget—" she was still talking as I softly placed the phone back on the cradle.

I hefted the letter again. I had been so preoccupied yesterday morning when Rose had handed me the envelope, I hadn't given much attention to the fact that it had been sent express. It seemed to be an ordinary letter, thicker than most, but no more than three, perhaps four, sheets of paper. The clock on the bedside table showed eleven o'clock, straight up. Two hours before our starting time.

I opened it. Single-spaced, typed on white bond paper, the pages were folded around an airline ticket folio.

I unwrapped the pages and looked at the airline ticket. It was round trip from Roanoke to Cincinnati—flight numbers were filled in, but the dates were left open.

The letter was dated almost a month ago.

    Dear Logan:

    Please don't feel cheated, but by the time this reaches you, I will already be dead.
    What a corny opening line.
    Unfortunately, as unreal as it seems to me at times, it is the truth. Anyway, I have arranged for Paxton Prueffer III—a friend, who happens to be my attorney—to drop this in the post the instant I am gone. I'm sorry to dump this on you without warning, but this has been bad enough for me and I hope you can understand. I didn't want to have you calling me or coming up here and forcing me to listen to you tell me what fucking (Remember trying to clean up our vocabulary before we left Bosnia? Too late to worry now, for me anyway.) rotten luck this whole cheap little soap opera is. I have enough of that already. So—I hate to say I told you so—the lesson in this is *carpe diem*. Anyway, now that I am safely past the worst of my anguish, I am laying one last request on you. I finally finished that book that we talked about so much in Bosnia and, through a sudden whim and the most ironic of serendipities, I will be leaving a nice little chunk of money, which, I hasten to make clear, is completely separate—totally apart—from the respectable little nest egg Cathy will get. As a result, I have had a lawyer (Prueffer) draw up a special trust to fund a foundation to support young writers, and I have named you director and administrator for that trust. I

have provided that you be generously paid for your trouble—enough that you can live comfortably and be able to devote most of your time to writing your own books if you wanted.

Anyway, I won't bother here to try to explain all the ins and outs. My lawyer will do that when you get here. It's more important that you understand the circumstances and particulars of what prompted this in the first place and the essence of what I'm asking you to do for me.

To begin with, aside from you, the other benefactor of this trust will be a former student of mine, Maggie Walker. Maggie is a gifted writer and is about to finish her first novel, which she wrote while struggling to support her daughter (6) and son (5) by working in the college library and by writing book reviews for small magazines and papers. It's only fair to tell you that Maggie and I have been lovers for over two years and, had I lived, I would have divorced Cathy shortly after my book comes out. I know the most useless thing on earth is the glorification of someone else's love affair so I will spare you that, and neither will I try to justify my plan to leave Cathy, whom I will always love and value.

Remember all those great philosophical conversations we had in Bosnia? I'm still convinced that—if we distill the truth down to one final pure drop—in the end everything is motivated out of selfishness. That's not a bad thing—it just is.

If you're thoroughly at sea by now, here's a thumbnail of how all this came about. Back in the spring, right after we last talked on the phone, I got news from my agent in New York that Tallyrand-Dorsett had made an offer for my novel, *Carpe Diem*, which, as you know, is a thinly disguised fiction based on our ridiculous adventures while you were determined to bring about my sexual initiation. Before I knew it, there were three publishers bidding for the book and I finally settled on

T-D because they offered a two-book deal—the finished manuscript for the second book, a sequel based on my affair with Maggie, is in the hands of my agent as part of the foundation/trust. The royalties and subsidiary rights to both books all go to the foundation. Anyway, I was feeling so smug about my success that I wasn't going to tell you until I could mail you an autographed copy. That night, after I had celebrated with Maggie, I stayed up late thinking back over our time in Bosnia and how lucky I was to have been given a second chance—and how you had had to put aside your dreams. Ironically, I was remembering our miraculous escape from death and I was dealing heavily with my own mortality, not knowing at that moment of course that I had only three months left. So, off and on for some time, I had been toying with this idea of the foundation to help struggling writers who had laid aside their dreams (some like you, because they had to raise families) and others who were simply poor and disadvantaged.

Familiar?

So in a burst of grandiosity, the next day I went to see my insurance agent, and with some of my newfound wealth, I negotiated a cheap term policy on my life for a cool two million.

The punch line is that, less than a month later, I got this minor upper respiratory infection and my doctor put me on some exotic new analogue of a fifties antibiotic—this rather heroic measure of therapeutic overkill heightens the irony here. Being in the business, you may know that the parent drug, which still is the drug of choice for a list of exotic organisms, has a nasty record of causing agranulocytosis, which is a politically correct way of saying it all too frequently kills innocent people.

Of course, we threatened to sue and got a staggering settlement for the foundation.

That should give you some idea of what I'm asking. A quick translation of this is that the tax situation on a foundation is not burdensome and you'll have an altogether astounding bunch of money to work with. The lawyers have several scenarios worked out. But the nice part is that the starting salary of the director will be three times what I earn, and even his assistant (Maggie) will make almost twice what I made here at school plus a package of life ($2 mil) and health insurance (talk about an oxymoron), etc.

Nothing to sneeze at—if you'll pardon my pun.

Incidentally, the foundation is incorporated as a nonprofit and named for me. I told you I was selfish—translate that "egotistical to the grave."

Impressed? Don't be. Remember as you read that I am already dead.

(Too damn bad I couldn't have stayed around to do a book signing.)

So, basically here's what I'm asking. I'm enclosing an open round-trip air ticket so that you can fly up here for a few days to meet with Mr. Paxton Prueffer III of Pedigo, Spradling, McConky, Kirkwood, Snapp & Prueffer. Their business card is attached, and I encourage you to phone them without delay as soon as you read this letter to find out when the reading of the will is taking place. You need to be present at the reading to get a better grasp of what I've set in motion. And, of course, to protect my trust. (Cathy will be surprised—upset I'm sure.)

I won't ask for any empty promises—I'm not around to receive them—but write me a book, will you? And be good to Maggie. Of course, Cathy knows Maggie but she never knew about Maggie and me, and it might be she won't have to. The second book will be at least two years down the road, and the characters are put into settings not related to our life. Anyway, Cathy was not unaware that our relationship was in trouble and time has a way with things—what's the old cliché about life imitating art, or vice versa?

Besides, Cathy is young and we have no children. I have enough life insurance to leave her fairly well fixed for the rest of her life. She'll never have to worry about a thing. But, like it or not, she is acquainted with Maggie, and I have some fear things will come clear about Maggie and me when she finds out about the John Paul Silver Foundation.

As a precaution, I'm having this letter notarized in case there are any misunderstandings with the estate.

Sorry I couldn't stick around, but know I love you and I'm counting on you.

Carpe diem, friend,
John Paul Silver

The letter was fully signed and duly notarized by one Paxton J. Prueffer III, Attorney-at-Law.

I wondered what tenured English professors like John Paul made—$50,000 to $70,000 tops, I imagined. When I thought it over, I seriously doubted he made much more than $70,000.

I would make around $60,000 this year with a little luck. By at least a third, more money than most of my graduating class would pull down. Including my most optimistic expectations for top bonuses, my income with Severence Labs if I were promoted to Rush's job would be $70K a year . . . $80K tops. Plus a company car and expenses.

Not bad in this first blush of the twentieth-first century.

If John Paul was talking a minimum of $120,000 for Maggie's salary and $180,000 for me in the director's chair plus benefits, this was a fairy tale come true.

Two million life insurance? My son's education would be assured.

Maybe I would even write that book.

My heart was beating a mile a minute.

Directors of nonprofit foundations had a lot of freedom to play around, all the time for expense-paid travel and exotic golf I could ever want.

I folded the letter, rewrapped it around the ticket, and put it all back in the envelope.

Dazed, I set it back down beside the phone.

When I walked back over to the window, I realized I'd been holding my breath for some time. What would happen next? Maybe I'd shoot even par on the golf course this afternoon.

And, there was another orgy with Ginny tonight.

There has to be a limit, I laughed nervously.

I walked like a zombie out into the brave new world.

CHAPTER TWENTY-EIGHT

By the time I reached the practice range and walked over to where Rush was hitting balls, it was almost 11:30. My head was still reeling from the shock of John Paul's letter.

Watching Rush hacking desperately with the fairway metal, I was overwhelmed with the knowledge that I was free at last. He no longer held power over me.

Now, anytime I wanted, I could safely tell the rectal orifice to go do unspeakable things to himself—and, magnanimously, I would include the horse he rode in on.

Take it easy, old sock! I shook my head to rid myself of the agreeable temptation.

My father had taught me never to burn bridges. Besides, I really didn't know all that much about John Paul's foundation—not yet, anyway. Until I spoke with Prueffer, all I had was the letter of a dying man saying he'd left enough money to free me from corporate slavery.

Freedom?

Was there really ever that much freedom, anyway?

And would heroic John Paul have had so much faith in me if he'd known how I'd kissed Rush Donald's dumb fat ass, groveling shamelessly in hope of being promoted to a Mickey Mouse position of authority with all the petty expense-account dishonesty that went with it?

Watching Rush lashing pathetically at golf balls, I fought back anger, remembering that last night he had tried to solicit me to falsify reports to cover him after he wrecked my company car. I could hardly wait to show him the serious legal charges on the "accident report" that Ginny had provided.

It seemed that not so long ago I used to like myself.

Now I not only hated my job, but after last night's overpowering interlude with Ginny, I was confronted with how disillusioned I was with my marriage. Excluding the fact that Rose was a wonderful mother to our beautiful, innocent son, I couldn't think of one other redeeming thing to recommend my marriage as an estimable sociolegal institution.

Now that I thought about it, except for little Paul, I had become unhappy with my life in general up until this very moment.

Not only was I sick and tired of Rose's whining, her boring bridge parties and phony airs, but I was also fed up with playing the part of all-American husband to keep up appearances in front of those busybodies Cookie and Maryanne.

Now, watching Rush's inept hacking brought me back to the moment.

Most of all, I was unhappy with the dishonesty of my job.

I hated pandering to anal sphincters like Rush, and I wasn't all that crazy about some of those snooty, tight-assed doctors and pharmacists either.

My gaze strayed to the far end of the practice tee, where sexy heather blonde was taking a lesson from an assistant pro. My mind drifted back to last evening with Ginny.

Free love. As a newly discovered institution, I found it admirable, laudable, and downright praiseworthy.

Besides all that, I damn well liked it.

A man could run for president on a platform like that.

As a matter of fact, the sweaty episode with Ginny and John Paul's confession of his own *liaison dangereux* were the only real bright spots in my recent wars with lifeitsownrealself.

That is, if I didn't count Melba's unexpected come-on to me back in the exhibit hall.

I recollected that after John Paul's initiation in Paris, he had slapped me a high-five and laughed, "Something tells me, Toto, we're not in Kansas anymore!"

Score two for our team, John Paul!

Just thinking now about the prospect of the literary foundation brightened my outlook considerably. With an intrepid eye to this new option, I had hastily scribbled down Paxton Prueffer III, Esquire's number and stuck it in my pocket before I left the room. Ohio was an hour earlier, in the Central Time Zone. I'd brought along my cell, resolving to call this Prueffer guy before we teed off at one.

Locating a pristine white golf glove, I took it out of the cellophane and worked it onto my left hand, carefully smoothing it between the fingers as I went along. Enough of dim-witted jobs and marriages and adultery! I came here to enjoy a more serious reality. I was about to tee it up on one of the plushest, most enjoyable golf courses on the face of the earth. The prospect of a glorious afternoon on the Old White Course represented a chance to restore me to sanity.

I took my pitching wedge out of the bag and made some leisurely practice swings as I watched Rush laboring pathetically with his driver.

Thunk! His club's mishitting the balls produced a discordant sound.

"Goddamn!" Unaware that I had arrived, he stood there watching the sickening, widely curving flight of the ball.

To a golfer, a slice is the second ugliest sight in the world.

"Shit! Shit! Shit!" Rush slammed the sole of the borrowed driver into the ground.

Teeing up another ball, he repeated the performance with essentially the same result.

"Shit! Goddamn!" He slammed the sole of the driver into the ground again.

After watching this destructive tantrum twice, I could no longer hold my tongue.

"Take it easy on that club, old sport. Unless, of course, you plan on buying it."

I struggled to keep my tone light, but it didn't come off very well.

"Fuck your goddamn borrowed driver! It isn't worth a shit anyway." He didn't even glance my way.

"It may not be worth a shit to you, but it's worth about four hundred bucks wholesale to the pro back at the club," I said, barely managing to hold my temper.

"Okay, okay, you made your point," he answered with a nasty growl.

"Just take it easy. The way you're going at it, you're likely getting arm-weary, anyway. Take a break. Hit a few easy wedges to stay loose. Give me a minute to hit a few balls, and we'll grab a spot of lunch. How's a cold Corona sound?" I soothed, attempting to calm him down.

"I am not fucking arm-weary. It's these goddamn clubs. I told you to get me clubs with a stiff shaft. This driver doesn't match the swing weight of the set. I can hit the rest of the clubs okay."

He had distinctly requested regular-flex shafts. It was all I could do not to tell him he wouldn't know a stiff shaft from an electric cattle prod. And I hadn't heard the term *swing weight* used in years. But, why dignify the asshole?

I took my wedge and my five and three irons and walked out in front of the cart, tipping the heavy wire basket of practice balls onto an unblemished spot in the lush teeing area.

Methodically, I took the blade of the wedge and pulled a ball into position in front of me.

I made an easy swing and promptly shanked the ball dead right.

A shank is a slice on LSD. I hadn't shanked a shot in years.

"The asshole is freaking contagious," I muttered under my breath.

With a great sigh, I pulled another ball into position, desperately hoping I wasn't in for a long afternoon.

Thwock!

Short of orgasm, there's nothing that feels quite as good as a perfectly hit iron shot. Cheered considerably, I got down to serious work. By the time I worked my way through a half-dozen wedge shots and watched several balls fly off my five iron like photon zaps from Captain Kirk's ray gun, my mental state had greatly improved.

Euphorically, I took out the three iron and hit a couple with the same satisfying results. After watching the third long iron land in the hitting area well over two hundred yards away, I walked over to the cart, carefully wiped my irons on a damp towel, and put them in the bag.

In less than ten minutes, I'd managed to put the world behind me.

Glancing over at Rush, I saw him hit a fairly decent little wedge.

"That'll play all day long, partner!" I enthused. "C'mon. Let's grab a beer and a sandwich. We'll still have time to putt a little before we tee off."

"Just one second. I want to hit one decent shot with this fucking driver." He teed up a ball and made a great display of going through a good setup, trying to make a slow back swing. Then, lunging forward, he hit so far behind the ball that it trickled only a foot out in front of him.

It was something right out of an old W. C. Fields burlesque.

"Goddamn . . . motherfucking . . . SOB!" He pounded the driver on the ground again.

"Straight, but not far." Sam had come up behind us without my noticing.

Rush looked as if he might have a stroke.

I examined my shoe tops, struggling to suppress a near-hysterical outburst.

Without so much as a glance at Sam, Rush bent over, reteed the ball, and lashed at it again. It was wasn't exactly pretty, but this time the club head made solid contact, and the ball went sailing out into the practice area, finishing with only a trace of a fade at the end. Landing areas on the Old White Course were pretty forgiving. And a shot like that on almost any golf course wouldn't get him into a lot of trouble.

"Godawmighty, Max, did you see that? He musta hit that sucker three hundred yards at least," Sam said, facetiously.

"Perfect for a dogleg right," Max said with a straight face. "One hundred straight and two hundred right."

"Tiger Woods plays a fade," Rush snapped, defiantly.

"That was a fade?" Sam asked no one in particular. "The Tiger never hit anything that ugly in his life."

Max sniggered.

Rush was seething now.

"We're going to get some lunch. Care to join us?" Sam invited, amiably.

"No thanks. I want to hit a few more. See you on the first tee, one o'clock sharp." I waved them off. Rush's delicate mental state was bad enough already. I didn't want those scavengers upsetting him any more until after we got on the golf course.

"I don't know how you stand those two assholes. Why do you play with them, anyway?" Rush fumed as we watched them drive away.

"For one thing, it's good for business. God, country, and good ol' Severance Laboratories. A man has only one life to give to his company." I tried to keep the disgust out of my voice. "Don't pay them any attention. They're just trying to get your goat. Anyway, they wouldn't be so familiar with you if they didn't accept you as a competitor. Ignore them. Show 'em you can take it as well as dish it out."

"Humph! After this afternoon, I don't want to play with the bastards anymore. Understand? Where I come from, golf's a gentleman's game, not rough-and-tumble like a bunch of hooligans in a pool hall. Besides, everyone knows that Tiger and Jack Nicklaus—even the great Ben Hogan—hit a fade."

"You're right," I schmoozed. "My dad loves to tell about the time he was watching Hogan warm up right here, before the Sam Snead Festival back in fifty-nine. He and maybe five or six others came early and were watching the 'wee Ice Man warm up. Hogan was a perfectionist. In those days, he always carried his own shag bag of practice balls. His caddy was downrange, shagging 'em in the bag. After awhile, Hogan lit up a cigarette and picked up his driver and waved the caddy further back. This one old guy who was standing behind Hogan said, 'That's a hell of a slice you're fighting, ain't it, Ben?' My dad says Hogan was having such a hard time keeping from laughing, he thought he was going to choke. Finally, when he got control, he gave a sheepish little grin and hiked up his slacks with the back of his wrists in one of his patented mannerisms and said, 'You don't see that caddy moving, do you?' Dad said Hogan was hitting those practice shots with the precision of a brain surgeon.

Without moving a step, his caddy had been standing in the same spot catching those shots in the shag bag on the first hop all morning long."

Rush brightened. "Say, that's a hell of a story."

Something told me that the tale was about to get new life down at the Hahvahd Club.

Script by H. Logan Baird.

"C'mon, let's go get a burger and a cold Corona before we tee it up," I said.

My watch showed almost noon.

CHAPTER TWENTY-NINE

I'd entertained no thought of the possibility that at lunch we might be seated at the big window overlooking the eighteenth green and the first tee of the Old White Course. Odds against getting a golf course window table at Sam Snead's at the Golf Club are about the same as finding a black pearl in an ordinary dozen oysters on the half-shell.

But, before I knew what was happening, we were shown to a table looking directly down on the first tee.

"Great view." Rush's voice cracked a bit as he looked down at the foursome teeing off below us.

I quickly ordered a couple of Coronas.

We'd hardly been served before a murmur went through the room and diners started crowding over to look out the window.

I peered down as a very distinguished looking gentleman in his early fifties bent over to tee it up. He waved to the sizable group of spectators, who shouted encouragement. Stepping up and addressing the ball with a great deal of concentration, he promptly cold-topped it right into the serene waters of Howard's Creek. He shrugged and laughed. Before the concentric circles had fully disappeared from the creek's surface, he was back at his bag. Producing an unopened sleeve of Titleists, he broke out a glistening new ball.

A large number of the diners in the grill had left their tables and were pressing into the aisle along the window tables to get a view.

"How many's that?" a man asked.

"Five, I think," the woman in front of him said.

"Yep, number five," her nattily attired male companion chuckled.

"Whoops! There he goes, in the creek again."

The crowd howled.

"What's he lie on the tee?" a second woman asked, seriously.

"Thirteen maybe. Not sure, really," a male voice spoke up.

"The chap's about to give it another go." Now the voice was distinctly British.

Sure enough, the determined man was addressing another ball.

This time he made solid contact and hit a fairly decent shot across the short expanse of water, right down the middle of the luxuriant green fairway. After a pregnant moment of silence, the room responded with polite applause.

As the duffer raised his hands in triumph, Sam Snead appeared from the pro shop. With a sweep of his hand, the great Snead presented the player with an entire box of golf balls.

Polite little hoots and whistles punctuated the applause as the diners and outside gallery expressed appreciation for the sportsmanship.

"What a nice gesture," a woman said. "And what a good sport. I'd be mortified to stand there and make such a spectacle of myself."

"Wasn't that Sam Snead with the balls?" someone asked no one in particular.

"That was Sam all right," a voice confirmed. "Wonder if he's going to play today? I'm going to call Charlie up at the hotel and tell him to round up the gang and come down here right now if he wants to see the most perfect swing in golf." The man disappeared looking for a phone.

When I looked back at Rush, his lips were compressed into a very tight line.

"You gotta hand it to the guy, he was a good sport about it," I laughed nervously, watching Rush carefully now.

"Couldn't he have just dropped a ball on the other side? Why would anyone want to make such a public display of himself?" Rush snorted. His hands were shaking as he reached for his beer.

When the food arrived, I ordered us both another Corona. It was obvious that all these people looking down on the first tee were heavy on his mind.

After a minute, Rush looked at his watch and asked, "Is it twelve-thirty already?"

"Yeah, but relax. That poor guy just set our tee time back at least ten minutes."

"Most likely," he grunted. "Where's the men's room?"

I gave him directions, and he excused himself.

When he came back, he seemed slightly more relaxed.

Rush picked at his food. He managed only a single section of the club sandwich while he drained the second beer. "It's about ten 'til. Hadn't we better be going?" Oddly, he seemed almost anxious to get started now. The beers were apparently doing their work.

"I see two groups in front of Sam and Max down there waiting in front of our cart. That puts us third. The starter usually allows eight-minute intervals between foursomes. We don't really have to hurry, but I'm ready any time." I was happy to see him more relaxed.

"C'mon, let's go," he said. "I'd like to shut those turkeys up once and for all."

I could hardly believe my ears. The beer had done wonders, or perhaps he'd taken a pill. On the golf course, a little mild chemical tranquilization was preferable to outright drunkenness.

We went downstairs and out through the pro shop. Our caddy, Thomas, had our cart waiting behind Sam and Max. It was a perfect day for golf.

We'd reached our cart when Snead pulled his into line behind us.

Predictably, the news had gotten out. Behind the tee box, a sizable crowd had already gathered to catch a glimpse of the legendary Snead, and the numbers were increasing fast.

"Hey, Logan, see you made it okay. Great day for it, huh?" The great man got out and walked over.

"Sam Snead, meet Rush Donald." I introduced Rush to his hero, then introduced Sam and Max.

The ol' Slammer shook hands before he excused himself with a broad wink. "Looks like a great day for golf. Guess I better go round up my pigeons. Keep 'em in play, now," Snead kidded. "Remember, our group is right behind you guys."

"Get a move on, guys. We're next off," Max said anxiously, moving their cart up to the tee.

As Rush was crawling into the cart beside me, an assistant pro came out of the shop. "Which one of you gentlemen is Mr. Rush Donald?" He read the name from a memo slip.

"That's me," Rush said. "What's wrong?"

"You need to call the hotel operator. It's urgent, sir," the young pro said. "Phone's right inside. Just follow me, please."

I got out of the cart. "What's that all about?" I asked Rush, a little suspicious.

Rush shrugged. "Who knows? Back in a minute," he called over his shoulder as he disappeared into the shop, close behind the young assistant.

"What's your friend up to?" Sam asked as I pulled our cart into position.

"Who knows," I shrugged, fiddling with my new white glove. I was fastening the Velcro at my wrist when I saw Rush coming toward us with the young assistant right behind. One look at their faces gave me an uneasy feeling.

"Sorry, fellows. I can't play, something's come up," he said.

"Aw, shit, man, let it wait. Nothing's that frigging important," Sam said disgustedly.

Rush shot him a look and turned to me.

"What's the problem?" I asked him, smelling a rat. Truth was, I really didn't give a damn.

"The Teaneck office needs some stuff from me. I'm a lot sorrier than you are, believe me," Rush said, unconvincingly. Thomas was already taking his bag from the cart.

"Can we play just three?" Max asked the starter.

"Yes, sir. Three's no problem," the starter assured us. "I'd pair you up if I could. I had someone looking for a game a few minutes ago, but he seems to have disappeared."

"That's okay," Max replied.

"How do we want to make a game? Logan, you want to take us both on?" Sam grinned. He knew I wasn't about to take a sucker bet like that.

"Sure. Give me three a side, and I'll play you both best ball. Individually, I'll play you even," I said.

"Let's have a hitter if you're ready, sir," the starter said. We each selected a club and stepped out on the tee.

Max threw down a tee. It pointed to me.

"Okay. You're up, Logan."

Greatly relieved to be rid of Rush, I ignored the substantial gallery gathering for the legendary Snead. I stepped forward, teed it up, and let it rip. I caught the ball dead-solid perfect—right between the screws.

"Would you friggin' look at that?" Max whistled.

"SOB's in heat," Sam muttered under his breath.

"Eat your unclean hearts out, gentlemen." I made a little bow and retrieved my tee, doffing my cap to acknowledge the pleasant tattoo of applause from the gallery behind the tee.

"You want to lead us off, Sam?" Max glanced anxiously at the crowd.

"You're our leader, go ahead." He was definitely nervous now.

Max teed his ball and looked down the fairway, trying to ignore the spectators.

"Don't mind the gallery, Max. They're a friendly bunch." I turned and gave the throng a friendly wave. There was a conspiratorial titter of appreciation for our competitive byplay.

The gallery pressed closer now. I grinned, facetiously holding up my hands to quiet them.

Despite the pressure, Max and Sam both managed to get their drives across the creek. Max's weak pop-up landed about two hundred yards down the fairway. Sam half-smothered a worm-burning hook that rolled into the edge of the left rough.

Quietly, Sam Snead had moved up beside the tee. "You're dry at least," he said.

The gallery responded with a hearty laugh.

When I turned to get in the cart, Rush was still standing there.

"Great shot. Sorry I can't join you guys, but the job comes first." Now he didn't seem in such a hurry to leave. "Maybe I can catch you for a beer when you come in."

"See you later," I muttered, glad to be rid of the jerk.

I stopped my cart on other side of the creek and waited while Max hit his second with a fairway wood. First tee jitters behind him, he made a decent recovery and the ball came to rest up near the green.

From where his ball was half-hidden in the rough, Sam was preparing to address his shot when a loud whistle from the direction of the clubhouse caused us all to turn and look. The starter was standing at the front of the tee box signaling that he had another player ready to tee off.

"Looks like the starter is sending you a partner, Mr. Baird," my caddy observed.

I wasn't all that thrilled at the idea of having to spend the afternoon with some duffer, much less a total stranger, but anything was better than having to put up with Rush.

We patiently stood aside, watching the man address the ball and make an easy swing. In a matter of seconds, I heard the thwock of club meeting ball but lost the shot against the sun-bleached sky.

"Stand still. We're okay," Thomas cautioned, expertly following the flight of the ball. He'd hardly spoken when I heard the shot hit behind us, then saw it bounce twice before it ran up the middle of the fairway a few yards short of my ball.

"Looks likes we may have ourselves a proper partner, Mr. Baird." Thomas grinned.

"It does indeed."

It promised to be a good afternoon after all.

CHAPTER THIRTY

Sam had already hit and was standing by Max's ball near the greenside bunker when the cart with my new partner pulled up. Thomas stood by as the stranger got out, walked over to me, and stuck out his hand.

"I'm Robert Johnson. Bobby to my friends," he said. "Hope you don't mind my joining you."

"Logan Baird. Glad to have you." I shook his hand. "This is Thomas. Nice shot, by the way."

Thomas nodded and busied himself transferring Bobby's bag to our cart.

"Those shrubs are the one-fifty markers." I pointed to the edge of the fairway up ahead, about even with my ball. "You'll also find a surveyed yardage marker embedded in the center of the fairways. There's a similar bush and marker up ahead to indicate a hundred yards."

"Thanks."

I relaxed. He seemed a friendly sort, and I'd had my fill of malcontents.

Wasting no time, Bobby got down to the shot at hand.

"About one-eighty to the pin?" He looked to Thomas for confirmation.

Thomas wet his index finger and held it up, testing the wind as he surveyed the tops of the trees.

"Yes, sir. but there's a little breeze against. Can't feel it much from here."

"Five iron enough?" Bobby asked.

"If ya hit it perfect, sir, but the four might be better," Thomas suggested diplomatically.

Bobby grabbed his four and five irons. I took a good look where my ball was lying and figured 165 to the pin. I selected the five and six irons from my bag, and we walked side by side toward his ball.

Bobby was all business. He approached the shot from behind, so as to get a good line on the projected flight. His measured routine of setting up over the ball was the result of working with a good teaching pro. After a moment of debate, he dropped the five and took the four, choking down on the grip. His rhythm was smooth as silk as club head crisply met the ball.

Thwock!

The ball flew off the club head like a startled bird.

Obviously, Bobby Johnson was no stranger to the game.

"Oh, Bobby! Bobby!" He hung his head and muttered in disgust as he watched the ball start drawing a little too much left. Landing on the left front of the green, it failed to grab in time to stop from trickling into the greenside bunker.

"Too bad. It's a bastard game," I offered sympathetically.

"I seem to keep practicing the same mistakes," he shrugged with a philosophical frown as we walked up to my ball.

Handing my six iron to Thomas, I decided to hit the five, and I hit it better than I knew how. The ball covered the flag all the way to the green. It was a damn good thing I'd chosen the longer club because I still wound up a good thirty feet short of the hole.

"I must be getting old," I muttered.

"There's quite a breeze . . . nothing to do with age," Bobby grinned.

I held back a little.

Wind or not, I really was kind of fond of that shot.

I grabbed my putter, Bobby selected a small handful of clubs, and we ambled up the fairway while Sam and Max were preparing to hit their approach shots. We'd walked about fifty yards when we heard a solid thump. A muffled sound of applause drifted from the direction of the tee. I snapped my head around just as a ball rolled to a stop a scant twenty yards behind us.

"Snead." I nodded toward the yardage markers. "Nearly two-sixty-five if it's an inch. The man's over eighty years old. Can you believe that old bandit still hits the ball that far?"

"Never another like him." Bobby shook his head and grinned.

"Are these guys friends? Think we can make a game?" Bobby asked as we resumed walking to the green.

"Sure, why not? I play to an eight or nine. They play about the same. We usually play a buck four ways, automatic presses. Most you can lose is ten or twenty bucks," I said.

"What's twenty bucks? But I should warn you I carry an eleven."

"I'd take on Tiger Woods with a player who swings like you. Let's wait until we hole out before we make the game . . . partner." I winked.

At the greenside, I introduced Bobby to Sam and Max before we addressed our putts.

Max had hit a decent chip to within eight feet. The SOB wriggled in the curving putt.

Both Sam and Bobby struggled out of the sand and settled for bogey.

I had missed my long birdie attempt by a hair. I tapped in, and we halved the hole.

We set the match with Sam and Max on number two. The sun came out, and the game was on.

Don't ever let anyone tell you golf is not therapy. Standing on the practice range less than two hours ago, with John Paul's death hanging over me like a dark cloud and Rush making an all-around jackass out of himself, my emotions had been bouncing around my head like grasshoppers in a jar.

Now, I was as carefree as the hawk making lazy circles in the summer sky.

It was just damn good to be alive.

By the time we reached seven tee, we'd closed Sam and Max on the original bet. We were even on birdies, but we'd rubbed their noses in it, winning two presses before the turn.

On my individual bets, I had closed the side on the original and was ahead on two automatic presses. I would've never believed it, but when we walked off number nine, I'd double-bogied number six and was still only two over.

And Bobby was playing absolutely great.

With restrooms and a snack bar, the Old White's halfway house is between the eleventh green and number twelve tee. Play had been a little slow anyway, so we all went in to take a leak. As I came out of the restroom, a group of caddies was going in. Leaning over the water fountain, I heard Thomas inside talking to the others.

"No foolin'. I seen it with my own eyes. This Mr. Donald, the one what was on the cart with my guy, Mr. Baird, he comes down and gets the assistant, Billy Ray, to the side and slips him a fifty to bring him this faked-up message right before he's supposed to tee off. He handed Billy Ray some bullshit story about having important business. When he handed Billy Ray that fifty he was shaking like a leaf."

The youngest of the caddies spoke right up, "Lots of dem fancy genamens gets the shakes when theah's a crowd around that firs' tee. Big-shot mens take dey se'ves serious. Dey 'fraid to play the fool in front of all dem fancy folk."

"I call it jes' plain chickenshit," Thomas snickered.

Sam and Max's caddy, Lenny, chimed in. "Hell, ain't the firs' time I seen that done. A lot of folk gets nervous when they see that lunchtime crowd and that firs' shot over that li'l ol' crick. Shee-it! I don' know why they all so afraid. My li'l five-year-old girl carry that crick with a sand wedge and have room to spare."

"I've picked up a few dollahs bringing them fake phone call messages myse'f," Thomas admitted cheerfully.

"That Rush Donald fella jes' 'fraid he shit his britches standing up there on that firs' tee with everybody looking at him," another caddy spoke up. "I'm like Thomas. I calls that jus' plain chickenshit!"

"Me too," Lenny agreed.

I stood and wiped the water off my chin.

So that's why Rush was acting so relaxed and eager when he came back from the men's room at lunch.

I knew Thomas was right. Rush was chickenshit. Mr. Perfect Donald couldn't stand to let us see that his big talk about being a world-traveled golfer was just so much bull.

"I tell you something else about dat Mr. Donald. Y'all know my gal, Darlene, she work up on Main Street in Doc Robothom's office? Well she come down on her break to bring me some Kentucky Fried when Billy Ray show up to get this Donald's clubs off the cart. She whisper in my ear dat Mr. Donald be the same one come in de office to get a tetanus shot dis mawnin'. Seems lak somebody took a nip out de end of his pecker las' night. Hee, hee!" the young caddy reported.

"You don' say?" cackled Thomas. "That man sho' 'nuff a mess."

"Yessiree. The security folk say he up at the Bluffs las' night and run his car into a tree. Must be then his girl friend bit his dick."

Thomas howled, in near hysterics now. "That ol' MacDonald might have had important business after all."

Rush was already becoming a folk legend, and he'd only been there one night.

I damn near choked, suppressing a laugh.

When I turned away from the fountain, I nearly bumped into Bobby Johnson standing right behind me. Obviously, he'd overheard the whole thing.

Grinning broadly, he shrugged as he moved to take his turn at the fountain.

"I hope this Donald guy isn't your brother-in-law," he said, after we'd both teed off on twelve and were walking down to hit our second shots.

"My boss," I smiled. "If you want to know the truth, he did me a favor. I've had the SOB up to my ears in the last day and a half. It was my company car he ran into that tree last night. The best thing that's happened to me lately was his little charade back there with Billy Ray."

"If you don't mind my asking, what sort of business are you in?" Bobby asked politely.

That broke the ice. Bit by bit, as we walked along, the story of my life—the early recognition in *Harper's*, the reprint in *Reader's Digest*, the medical column with the paper, the unfinished novel and the disillusionment with writing, Rose's dissatisfaction, changing careers, Rush's heading for the special training at Harvard B, and my expectation of superseding him—it all came spilling out of me in a steady stream. Then I told him about Rush's disaster last night. I recounted my friendship with John Paul and the adventure of his sexual initiation. Then, holding my emotions in tight rein, I told him about our luck in the war and John Paul's death.

Finally, I blurted out my frustration over Rush's wanting me to cover his ass for wrecking the company car. "I detest dishonesty, and I simply cannot abide the posturing of fools. I hate feeling like I'm nothing but a whore," I said with more feeling than I intended as we walked off fifteen, highly pissed that I'd lipped out another birdie putt.

Despite the fact that we both were playing well, we only had Sam and Max one and one on the back.

"You're overreacting. It's all a preparation . . . builds character. Don't let it get you down," Bobby sympathized.

"But I don't want to wind up like Rush, paying someone fifty bucks to save my face. There's got to be more to me than that."

"I personally should thank your Mr. Donald. I wouldn't have mentioned it, but I overheard the whole thing when your boss was setting it up with Billy Ray. My crowd's behind us, back there playing with Scotty and Sam Snead. There were eight of us plus Sam, so we drew straws. I was odd man out, hanging around looking for a game. When your guy, Rush, came along with his little deception, Billy Ray told me he'd slip me into your group, but then I got caught on the cell phone and almost missed out myself."

"Then my boss did us both a favor. All right, partner!" I gave him a high-five. "We've got these turkeys on the ropes. Enough Mr. Nice Guy. Let's clean their clock."

We walked up to our tee shots. This time, I was away.

"Hit it close," Bobby urged.

I smoked it.

The rest of the way in, we both played our hearts out, but Max and Sam hung tough. Try as we might, we couldn't finish them—ding-donging back and forth, they kept pace. Then, Sam won seventeen, chipping in a gagger for birdie.

That pulled them even on the second press.

Now Bobby Johnson and I were only one up on the side.

"What about now? You still writing?" Bobby asked me as we walked onto eighteen tee.

"No. I did try to write a novel, but I gave up. It was a piece of garbage, really."

"I don't know about your novel, but there's a great need for medical writers with strong journalism experience."

"First John Paul, now you," I laughed. "Forget writing. These guys are getting serious. We got a tiger by the tail."

Eighteen is a signature hole, a picture-book par three that plays back across Howard's Creek to a monster green, situated directly below the windows of the golf club grill.

The group ahead of us had run into trouble back at sixteen, where the fairway runs along the edge of Swan Lake. Now, even though we were taking our time, we still had to wait for them on both seventeen and eighteen tee. Snead's group had been struggling all day and hadn't pushed us at all. They caught up while we were still waiting for the group ahead to clear eighteen green.

When Snead's foursome came up on the tee, Bobby made the introductions, and we shook hands all around.

Our mystery man's name was MacKenzie Brown, Scotty to his friends. His ratty golf bag was strapped proudly to the cart alongside the famous Mr. Snead's immaculate equipment. The other two players—corporate attorneys Lionel Steinweiss and Chester Morgenroth—had flown in earlier. They were staying with Scotty at Top Notch.

From stray bits of banter, I gathered there was some kind of high-level meeting tomorrow.

Their banter reeked intensity, but I was too busy wondering if a five iron would get me all the way back to the hole to pay attention to it.

"How y'all doin', Bobby?" I heard Scotty Brown ask my partner.

"These guys are tough. They can get even if they win this one, right, partner?" Bobby looked at me.

"Yeah, we have them closed on the Nassau, but the back's double. This hole can damn near make them well," I said.

Finally, the green up ahead cleared. Sam walked across and teed it up.

I had to hand it to him—if he was nervous with Sam Snead standing there, I couldn't tell. The hole was playing about 162 from where the markers were, and Sam hit it a ton. He drilled a five iron to the middle right of the giant green.

On the dance floor, but with the pin back left, still thirty feet below the hole.

"Way to go, pardner," Max applauded.

"Very nice, Alice," I conceded.

Max, who had definitely looked a little nervous when he shook hands with the great Snead, relaxed when he saw Sam on the green. He didn't get it all but managed a squibby five iron that leaked right and still trickled up on the front apron.

Even though he wasn't quite on the putting surface, Max had a surgeon's touch around the green.

"This is bloody war. Looks like we got our work cut out for us now," Bobby said.

"Plenty of room. Get inside 'em, partner," I enthused, as Bobby walked up to the tee.

"Is the five enough?" he asked.

"Hit the four," I told him. "And don't hold back."

We had to halve to win the side, and I dearly wanted to make birdie.

He nodded grimly.

Bobby hit it straight but caught it thin. The ball hit in front of the green and skipped all the way to the back fringe. He was closer than Sam but faced a delicate twenty-foot chip back to the hole.

"Smooth," I said.

"I was back there yesterday. It's like putting down a marble staircase," Max gloated.

"Confucius say, 'Everything's a marble staircase to a man with a touch like King Kong,' " I said.

"You're up, Confucius," Sam growled.

"This is a right friendly crowd," the Slammer drawled.

The banter bothered me not at all.

I was in heat, as golfers like to say.

Ordinarily I would have felt some pressure. Anyone would have been nervous with Sam Snead in the gallery. But I had been playing great all day, and there are some days when things just go right.

You get in a zone. Even before you walk up to a shot, you know it's going to be perfect.

I felt absolutely bulletproof.

If you've never been there, it's impossible to explain.

I really don't remember much about addressing the ball, but as long as I live, I will never forget that shot. The ball covered the pin all the way and hopped straight up, stopping almost in its own ball mark, five feet below the hole.

"Great shot there," the ol' Slammer drawled in open admiration.

The large gallery, gathered up by the green to watch Snead finish, burst into applause.

I turned and walked toward the cart.

"Eat your unclean hearts out, gentlemen," I said. The remark generated a small ripple of polite laughter.

Our worthy opponents were not among the ones who laughed.

Scotty Brown was waiting by our cart when Bobby and I walked off the tee. "Invite your buddies to bring their wives and come over to Top Notch about seven. We're all going to have a few drinks before we go up to the hotel for dinner," he said, nodding to include Sam and Max.

Bobby looked to me and nodded encouragingly.

"Thanks. I'll tell them. See you later."

Bobby halved Sam and Max with par. When I lined up my putt, I felt omnipotent—there was never a doubt that I'd make birdie.

We wound up winning two ways on the back. Counting birdies and the garbage, we took them for fourteen bucks apiece.

To make it sweeter, I collected over twenty bucks from each of those turkeys on the individual bets.

Money was irrelevant. Victory was everything.

Drinks were on us, of course.

But I should have known better than to relax. When we walked into the grill, Rush was waiting by the window overlooking the eighteenth green.

"Hi, guys. Let me buy you all a drink." He stood and fairly shouted across the room. He'd obviously gotten a head start already.

There was no polite way we could refuse to join him.

Drinks were served, and Sam and Max grudgingly paid off their bets. Typically, we had to sit there listening to them complain about missed opportunities and our dumb luck.

Losers always cry a lot.

Rush tried hard to push his way into the conversation, but not having been a part of the golf, he was pretty much left out in the cold. Through all the good-natured banter, I sat there praying that Bobby wouldn't think to invite Rush to MacKenzie Brown's cocktail bash. I couldn't bear the thought of getting stuck with him again tonight. I'd had enough.

Finally, Sam turned to Rush and said, "By the way, what the hell was all that about an urgent call today? You missed a great afternoon of golf."

"I'm glad you enjoyed it. Unfortunately, some of us have to work. Our clinical department in Teaneck had some crucial last-minute data to pass on to one of our researchers, Dr. Ian Ferguson, the famous endocrinologist. He's here to report his latest work on Virecta."

"What were these earth-shattering results? I hope this crucial data was worth missing a great round of golf." Max sounded skeptical.

"Dr. Ferguson will report everything tomorrow morning at ten. His paper is the highlight of the program. Sorry, I can't give you a hint," Rush gloated.

"I'm sure no one here wants to compromise your integrity," Sam scoffed. Sam was clearly unimpressed with Rush's self-importance.

"Dr. Robert Johnson, I'd like you to meet my boss, Rush Donald," I interjected to ease the strain.

"So, you're with Severance Labs, too?" Bobby offered Rush his hand. Of course, I'd already told him the truth about Rush, not that he really gave a damn.

"Are you a physician?" Rush asked.

"A physician, yes, but not a clinician anymore," Bobby nodded.

"You teach, or what?" Rush asked.

"I have taught some, but not lately. I'm really more of an administrator now," Bobby said. "I take it you must know Ian Ferguson quite well."

"Ferguson's quite a guy," Rush boasted. "I'm sort of his baby sitter for this event. Severence wants to make sure he doesn't want for anything."

"Interesting. I thought Ian insisted on working on his own," Johnson said.

"Oh, he does! I didn't mean to imply Ian was on our payroll. A man like Ian is above reproach," Rush stammered hastily.

"Actually we haven't been able to reach him since we got here," I interjected, suspecting Bobby knew Ferguson more than just by reputation.

"Oh, no, no, Logan, I talked to Ian. That's part of what my call was all about. Our research director, Gert Kearns, asked me to hunt him down and give him a message." Dumbass Rush was oblivious that I was attempting to rescue him.

Now I gave him a closer look, wondering if what he said were true. I fervently hoped it was.

"Order up. I'm buying another round and heading for the shower." I signaled for the check and got up to leave, anxious to contact Ginny.

Rush grabbed my wrist. "What's your hurry?"

"It's five-thirty. I promised Rose I'd call home." I removed his hand from my arm and headed for the vestibule where I could use my cell.

To hell with Rush Donald, anyway. I'd had enough of his dishonesty.

Ginny's line was busy. Wondering if she were trying to call me at the hotel, I went to the men's room, then tried again with the same results.

She was home at least. My watch showed 5:40 now.

Using a house phone, I called the desk for my messages.

Rose had called, and Paxton Prueffer III had left the same number I'd written down.

To my relief, the final message read, "Call G at home."

I tried again, and her line was busy still.

I headed back into the grill, anxious to get to my room, where I could use the phone in private.

When I returned, poor egocentric Rush was rattling on about Severance Laboratories' research and integrity.

Bobby stood and turned to me. "Partner, you're a hoss. We made a great team. We'll give 'em a chance to redeem themselves tomorrow."

I nodded and shook Bobby's hand.

Rush frowned.

"Don't forget, I'll see all you gents tonight at Top Notch about half past seven. I hope you'll join us, Mr. Donald. It should be a fine evening. Scotty hopes you all will come. Sam Snead will be there," Bobby said and turned to leave.

"Thanks. Wouldn't miss it for the world, would we, Logan?" Rush shook Bobby's hand and slapped him on the back.

I didn't smile or say a word.

"Half past seven, Top Notch. A hotel limo will bring you around," Bobby said.

"Thanks. We'll be there," Rush said, still shaking poor Bobby's hand.

Speak for yourself, I thought, turning to follow Bobby out the door.

"Where're you going? Stick around. Finish your drink and watch the golfers." Rush was his overbearing self again.

"I've gotta go." I waved to Max and Sam. "I enjoyed it, gentlemen. Don't forget, tomorrow, twelve-twenty-eight. Catch you later, Rush."

"Wait. Wait up, goddamn it. I'm going with you. We have to talk." I heard Rush scraping back his chair. He caught up with me as I started across the parking lot.

"What's your fucking hurry?" he panted, almost out of breath.

"I already told you. I have to call Rose." I kept right on walking.

"Go on. I'm going back and finish my drink. I'm meeting Mimi later. We'll see you in the lobby around a quarter to seven," he said.

"Don't wait. An old friend died. I have to make some calls," I hedged, determined not to get stuck with him again.

"There's nothing to do about it tonight," Rush growled. "Meet us in the upper lobby around seven," he insisted. "Don't be late. I don't want to miss seeing Sam Snead."

"I told you already. Don't count on me."

"I said seven. We'll go down together. Consider that an order." He glared. Without waiting for an answer, he turned and headed back toward the grill.

I smiled and kept walking, hoping I could still catch Ginny.

CHAPTER THIRTY-ONE

When I arrived back at the hotel, there was a sealed envelope with a local GMAC dealer's logo and another message to call "G."

As soon as I reached my room, I tried Ginny again. This time she picked up on the first ring. "Oh, Logan, honey, I was afraid I was going to miss you. Something's come up. I'm stuck for the earlier part of the evening. I thought we might work something out for later."

"Damn! Care to fill me in?" I couldn't hide my disappointment.

"It's complicated. Cleveland Webb, a big-time coal operator, buzzed into town rather unexpectedly. I go out with him sometimes when he comes. And I do have a life to consider. I mean, I'd rather be with you, but in two days you'll be gone and life goes on. Business as usual for little old Ginny. Trust me, I'm just as disappointed as you are, sugar. I might get away by ten. I was hoping you'd wait. I'll call your room sometime around ten."

"Make it ten sharp. I want to see you, but I don't want to stare at the phone all night." Erotic images of last night overcame my chagrin.

"I'll do my best. We're meeting some people. I'm late, just going out the door. I'll try to call no later than ten-thirty. Don't start without me. *Ciao!*" She rang off with a kissy sound.

"Shit," I muttered. I was left looking at the phone, my ego bleeding all over the place.

I wasn't happy. After Rush's charade, I was getting positively paranoid. And Ginny's seeing this coal mine owner tonight hurt my feelings. What the devil was I supposed to do until ten? I didn't want to get stuck with Rush, but I didn't want to just sit around and twiddle my thumbs.

My eye caught the Buick dealer's envelope sticking out from the middle of my stack of messages. I pulled it free and opened it. The single sheet of paper was a meticulously itemized estimate for repairs.

The bottom line read $4812.95!

"Holy shit!" I breathed in the empty air. That represented a month of my hard-earned income.

I folded the form into the envelope, walked to the dresser, and placed it beside my wallet.

I'd be sure to give it to Rush tonight. I wasn't about to let him off the hook.

Staring vacantly out the window, I wondered if my sexy neighbor lady were home. The reflection of the setting sun made her window a mirror. I couldn't see a thing.

My watch showed 6:15—time enough for one quick call before I showered and dressed.

I built a hefty drink from my traveling supply, took a quick swallow from the glass, walked back to the bedside table, and picked up the phone. I was in no mood to talk to Rose, but the hour was growing late.

Rose picked up on the first ring. Without bothering to say hello, she snapped, "It's about time you called. Where've you been?"

Rose's ill humor was getting to be like a broken record. I wondered what had upset her now.

"Rose, you know I was playing golf. I just got in." Marriage to Rose was very much like being American ambassador to the UN. One never knew what was coming next.

"I heard about your breakfast date."

Cookie Bergmann. I should have known.

"Rose, running into Ginny McKim in the hotel dining room is hardly a date. The woman happens to be visiting an old college chum who is staying here."

"Listen, a leopard can't change her spots. That bitch is up to her old tricks. I knew she'd make a play for you. She chases everything in pants. Ginny tried to steal Tony Wood from Avalea when I was in the eighth grade, but I knew she was screwing the whole population on fraternity row up at the college. I fixed her wagon real good. When I got through with that bitch, no decent town boy would go near her." Rose stopped to catch her breath. "I just can't understand how she wound up owning her own business and having friends who stay at places like the Greenbrier. Makes you wonder."

"Rose, calm down. I can't imagine what well-intentioned excuse Cookie invented to call and drop this tidbit of gossip on you, but I'm sure she only has your best interest at heart. And the rest of that hysterical nonsense about your sister—I don't even want to know what the hell you're talking about," I said, trying my best to sound indignant. "Now, is Paul handy to the phone? If you don't mind, I'd like to say hello to our son." I paused, waiting for a response.

"No. Paul's up the street playing with Mackie. It would take too long to get him now," she said. "Anyway, don't think you've heard the last of this, Logan Baird. If it gets back to me that you've been hanging around Ginny Hardison again, you'll regret it, I promise. I won't be made a fool of. Do you hear?" Her voice rose to a shrill shriek.

"For chrissake, just calm down, Rose. If you're so suspicious, you could still come over here. Tomorrow if you like." Reminding her that she had been invited to come along was living dangerously, but I figured it would shut her up about Ginny.

I held my breath, scared to death she might decide to come.

"You know I can't. And quit trying to change the subject. You can't trust that woman. She'd do anything to get even with me now."

Now some things were coming clearer. Both Ginny and Rose had hinted at bad blood between them last night, and I'd been too preoccupied to pay attention.

"Look, Rose, this is all nonsense. Cookie's just trying to stir up trouble. She's not happy unless she does. I'll bet she's already called everyone in your bridge club to tell them how hysterical you got when you heard the news," I said, attempting to strike a blow for the home team.

"I'm not hysterical, not at all. Do you think I'm a complete fool?"

I bit my tongue.

Some things are best left unsaid.

"Have I had any calls or messages?" I changed the subject.

"Oh, yes . . . wait a minute." She put down the phone for a few seconds, then came back on the line. "A lawyer, Paxton Preuffer, called from Ohio. He left his number. Said it was important. Said he'd be there late." Rose read the number.

I wrote it down and shuffled through the stack of messages. The numbers were the same.

"Who's this Preuffer? What's he want with you?"

"John Paul Silver's lawyer. I think it may have something to do with his will. His wife and his sister keep calling me, hoping I'll be a pallbearer."

"Don't they know you can't just drop everything and go running to Ohio?" she snorted.

I was tempted to remind her about last spring when she'd put our life on hold and gone to be a bridesmaid in her sorority sister's wedding in New Jersey. "Rose, the guy is dead. They're upset. Anything else?" I asked, maintaining my cool.

"That's it. Oh, wait. Charley Webber called wanting to know if you had a starting time for Sunday. I told him to check the pro shop. I wish you'd tell our friends that I'm not your social secretary."

"What exactly are you? It might help if I knew the rules." Almost before the words crossed my lips, I wished I'd let it go.

"What do you mean? You ungrateful—I'm your wife, the mother of your child," she wailed and started sniffling. "But I just might not be, if you don't show me more appreciation. I'm sick and tired of your being gone all the time. We have bridge club Saturday."

"Okay, okay, I'm sorry. It just seems like an unreasonable request to tell my friends not to call me at home."

"You know I didn't mean it that way," she said.

What way? I wondered but made no response.

"Well?" she said finally.

"I have to go hobnob with a couple of big-shot doctors," I said. "I'm late."

"Your father has a cold. You ought to go see him this weekend," she said, not wanting to hang up now.

"Maybe Sunday. We'll see," I replied. I loved my dad, but we argued a lot. A case of the old bull and the young bull, I reckoned. "I may have to go to Ohio in the next few days. That call from the lawyer. There may be something about John Paul's estate."

"Logan, you can't. Why you, for God's sake?" she wailed. "When will I ever get time to go see Avalea?"

Her sister was spending August at their summer cottage on the lake.

"Rose, you have a car. You can go see Avalea any time you want. I don't mind. Just pack up now and go tomorrow. It'll do you good."

"Oh, sure. And leave me stuck with the kid. What fun is that?"

"You know Nan and Grandad will take Paul any time. They fairly beg for the chance. Paul loves it out there in the country." It was the same silly game. Rose knew that, but she'd rather complain than let my folks enjoy their grandson.

"That's easy for you to say, Logan. Your folks have a life of their own. I can't just call them up and dump Paul on them any time I feel like it," she protested.

"I'll call 'em for you right now. When do you want to take him over there? Tonight? Or better still, they'll come pick him up. What time should I say? Eight tonight? Or would early tomorrow morning work better? Say around nine or ten?"

"Don't. I'd be humiliated," she protested lamely.

"They'll thank you, Rose. You know that. Just tell me what time. I'll call as soon as I hang up and have them call you and make arrangements," I persisted. It was a tired old game. What I said was all true. My parents were begging for the opportunity, but Rose would rather be a martyr and blame me for enslaving her in the role of overburdened mother.

"Don't you dare," she warned.

"Then don't blame me for not getting to see your sister," I countered.

"You know I don't want to go unless we go as a family," she whined. "Avalea and Jason wonder why you never come. It's embarrassing."

"Tell them they bore me to bleeping tears. They'll understand." I was sick to death of this. I'd been through it all before.

"You are so mean. Why don't you like them? You're just jealous. Jason makes a lot more money than you," she said.

"Maybe you're right," I said.

"I know I'm right."

"Do you want me to call my folks or not? I'm late. Late, late, late . . . gotta go!"

"No! Don't you dare. I told you, just come home early Saturday. We're hosting couple's bridge."

"I can't promise. The meeting here isn't over 'til one. I have to take the exhibit down and see that it's shipped. I told you before," I reminded. Now, I was really hoping Ginny might have Saturday afternoon free for a final farewell.

"Logan!"

"Yeah."

"I'm serious about that bitch. Don't you dare go near her, do you hear me?"

I had an eerie feeling that Rose could read my mind.

"Have a good evening. Kiss Paul for his daddy," I said. "Good night."

"Don't forget. We've got couple's bridge—"

I gently replaced the phone.

"Fuck couples bridge," I said aloud.

Lately, I was talking to myself a lot.

I looked out across the court again, and now that the sun was lower I could see the heather blonde moving casually about the room, her shapely bottom deliciously encased in a pair of satin panties. Her rounded hips rippled like little air currents moving under a collapsing silk parachute.

It pays to advertise.

I speculated but dismissed the idea. She was probably busy too.

I thought about Rose's whining over John Paul's will and my parents' baby-sitting and going to visit her sister. Rose whined over just about everything, including Ginny.

I knew I should feel some guilt about Ginny, but I didn't.

On the other hand, if I needed guilt to make me human, I certainly felt enough for neglecting my six-year-old son. Paul needed more of a father than I'd been to him. I kept resolving to do something about it, but I never seemed to get around to it. Gradually I'd stopped taking him off Rose's hands on Saturday mornings—going to the park and for ice cream and up to visit my parents, the way I had before he started kindergarten.

I had become a damn poor excuse for a father. Lately, the golf got in the way.

I'd kept putting off taking him fishing like my daddy used to do for me. Just last weekend Paul had asked me for a kite, and I had put him off.

I stood and stared again at my reflection in the mirror across the room.

A stranger stared back at me.

There used to be a daddy in there—a guy I used to like.

My real guilt had nothing to do with wanting Ginny. Neglecting my son was my real guilt, and I owned it now.

I did love my son.

Love. Just what the hell did I know of love?

I merely gave things and parceled out time and words.

Words. I was great with words.

Love. Had I ever truly loved anyone?

My parents?

My brother?

Yes, by god, I loved them all. Most important, I loved Paul. The thought of anything bad happening to my son was too painful to allow the smallest notion to tinge the edge of my consciousness.

What about Rose?

I'd loved her once in some hormonal, adolescent way.

Anyway, wasn't love supposed to be a two-way street?

Rose's dissatisfactions, her discontents, her disillusionments grew more complex with every passing day.

I tried to remember who, besides her sisters, Rose loved. I'd hardly begun before I gave up that empty exercise.

For a long time now Rose had been putting me down constantly.

I felt no guilt for having bedded Ginny. Last night Ginny had given me a whole new way of looking at myself.

She'd told me I was beautiful, talented. She said my writing mattered.

My marriage had died a long time ago, maybe even before it began. It had been running on inertia from the start. Nowadays our relationship—more an arrangement really—worked only because I traveled most of the time. If I were promoted to Rush's job, I would be traveling even more.

That suited me okay. But I knew a promotion to replace Rush would surely put me on the same treadmill he was on.

Next stop: Harvard B. Then on to Teaneck, New Jersey, maybe.

Oh, well, why not?

The thought that I might wind up just like Rush gave me a chill.

I looked in the mirror again and stuck out my tongue.

With John Paul's letter, at least I had options.

It was thrilling but scary to think I might have options now!

I raised my eyes and stared into the mirror again. A glimmer of hope for that man I used to like?

What would Rose say if she were faced with leaving Virginia? She hated John Paul. She'd be against my becoming the director of his foundation.

Divorce?

I couldn't bear the thought of losing my son.

Across the way, the heather blonde was seated now, carefully putting on her panty hose. Lifting her legs one at a time, she smoothed the calves. Finally she ran her finger around the edge and gave the crotch a little adjustment. Then she lifted up the straps of her brassiere, giving great attention to getting her breasts just so.

I felt my trusty centurion stir.

I remembered Ginny on the bed last night, her knees drawn up against her shoulders. Wide open, beckoning me.

She was noisy when she came. If she'd been faking orgasm, as the women's magazines were fond of suggesting, she'd easily take the prize.

And, the envelope please.

For the Best Performance for Faking Multiorgasmic Shudders in a One-Night Stand.

Ginny McKim! The winner! Hands down!

Guilt?

Guilt be damned.

What if Rose took a lover? I brightened. That would take care of everything.

I caught sight of myself in the mirror, and all at once I felt cheap for my rationalizations.

With both his parents running wild, where would that leave my son?

Paul was reason enough for staying in the marriage. Otherwise, I'd have taken off long ago.

Well, maybe.

I hadn't been big on confrontations or moral courage lately. Maybe I'd never been.

I glanced at my watch.

Over three hours until 10:00.

The night was young.

I stripped out of my undershorts and stepped into the shower.

Shaving carefully, the man in the mirror looked more hopeful now.

When I finished donning my best black silk suit, it was only 6:50. I went to the phone and gave the hotel operator the number that lawyer Preuffer had left.

"This is Paxton Prueffer."

"Mr. Preuffer, this is Logan Baird. I'm John Paul—"

"Oh, yes, Mr. Baird, I know who you are. I was hoping you'd call tonight. There's a lot we have to talk about. Have you received John Paul's letter and the plane tickets?"

"Yes."

"Good. When can you come up here? We shouldn't delay. The reading of the will is set for Monday at eleven. I was hoping you could come up Sunday. I'd meet you at the airport if you could."

"Sunday? I don't know. What's so urgent, anyway?" The conversation was going too fast for me.

"This foundation thing is going to land like a bomb on John Paul's wife and sister. They don't know anything about it, and they certainly don't suspect about Maggie Walker. Not that they have to. That would be a disaster, considering everything. I guess you realize Maggie Walker's middle-European, Serbian, I believe. Anyway, it will just go better if you're here to lend some credibility to the foundation. I don't want any question of contesting the will or the foundation, you understand."

Maggie Walker. Bosnian. What the hell had John Paul been up to? I had really started something when I finally got him laid that night in gay Paree.

"I accept your word for the urgency, but to answer your question, no, I really don't understand anything at all." That was the truth in the purest sense. "Right now I'm late for a meeting. Can I call you tomorrow?"

"Yes, of course. I'll be in and out of court, but almost any time you can catch me is okay," he said. "If you call between eight and ten, you'd be sure to catch me."

"All right, I'll call you in the morning. Good night, sir." I hung up.

All at once, life was getting much too complicated.

To hell with *carpe diem*. To hell with everything.

The phone rang again before I could fix myself another drink.

"Who the fuck you been talking to?" Rush oozed his usual charm.

I refused to answer.

"Well?"

"Did you call to ask me that?"

"What's eating you?"

"I always get edgy before my period." I eyed the envelope from the Buick dealer.

"Fuck you. We'll just go to MacKenzie Brown's party without you."

"I was hoping. Bye!" I hung up.

The heather blonde was dressed now and heading out the door.

Carpe diem, and here's looking at you. Have fun, you crazy kid. I blew her an imaginary kiss.

I poured myself a healthy shooter, slipped my key in my jacket pocket, and headed for the door.

WEDNESDAY EVENING

CHAPTER THIRTY-TWO

Drink in hand, I arrived downstairs and ran headlong into Rush pacing the lobby.

My all-around lucky day.

I couldn't help but wonder if he liked being treated mean.

Mimi made a dramatic entrance right behind me. Her décolletage was arresting—this woman was an original in the best New York tradition. I'd have bet my life that she had been a high-fashion model but because of her ample bosom had never quite made it to the top echelons of the profession.

None of this is to say that her startling cleavage made her in any way appear cheap.

Au contraire.

As silly as she was, Mimi would dress up any place. She was an ornament that even the Greenbrier's marketing group would gladly have recruited to pose for their tasteful brochures. Moreover, she possessed a certain unflappable panache.

Watching as she crossed the long expanse of giant black and white marble squares, I suppressed a smile, thinking about the intriguing injury to Rush's private anatomy.

"Hi, Mimi. Let's try to make tonight less eventful, shall we?" I winked.

She shot me a suspicious look and glanced at Rush.

It was all I could do to keep from laughing out loud.

I guess Rush must have shaken his head behind my back to let her know their secret was safe because she relaxed and gave me a big hug.

"What're we waiting for?" Rush growled, obviously already feeling the drinks. Grabbing Mimi by the hand, he started down the steps to the motor entrance.

I couldn't help but wonder if I'd become more like him than I wanted to admit. It was only yesterday that I had thought Rush represented everything I thought I wanted to be.

Had I sold my soul to the corporation because being a star with Severance Labs demanded little of the best of me?

In the limo, I renewed my resolve to cut loose from them at the earliest opportunity.

"Rush says we're going to Top Notch. I'm impressed. Who's this Bobby Johnson person, anyway?" Mimi bubbled, obviously excited.

"He works for Sam Snead's buddy, Scotty," I began. I debated telling them that our host was Rush's reviled mystery man.

What the hell. Maybe I should let the SOB find out for himself.

It was only a few minutes past seven when the limo dropped us at Top Notch, but the party was already in full swing. At the door, an air of conviviality overflowed the impressive setting. There must have been at least two hundred guests milling about. Probably more. Now, across the sea of well-coiffed heads, I could see that the crowd spilled into the pleasant evening, onto a broad terrace furnished with white wrought-iron tables and striped umbrellas.

Before I could make up my mind to tell Rush about Scotty, Bobby appeared at my elbow. "Logan, here you are at last. I was afraid you might not come."

He turned to Rush. "Glad you could make it, Mr. Donald."

Bobby smiled as Rush introduced Mimi. As Mimi and Rush went off looking for a drink, Bobby's eyes twinkled.

"Dr. Robothom's here. I'm sure he'll have a purely clinical interest in trying to match up that perfect model's smile with a certain row of teeth marks he examined this morning," Bobby whispered in my ear and chuckled. "You've had a busy time of it since yesterday. Is your life always this exciting?"

"No, thank God. I couldn't stand it. Where can I get one of those?" I nodded at his glass.

"Follow me." We snaked our way back through the crowded formal sitting room to one of several portable bars doing a lively trade. "Help yourself. I'll be back. I want to find Ian Ferguson. I told him about your writing background. I hope you don't mind?"

"No . . ."

He patted me on the shoulder and took off.

Over the past thirty-odd hours, my life had suddenly gotten very confusing. What possible interest could the famous Dr. Ferguson have in my ignominious writing career?

I shook my head.

Across the room, two guys who were dead ringers for Tom Brokaw and Walter Cronkite were talking to a woman who was the spitting image of Lesley Stahl. Before I could make certain my eyes weren't playing tricks on me, my stomach did a little flip as I caught a glimpse of Ginny over in the far corner near the door to the terrace. Beside her was a man in a white dinner jacket. He was wearing a ruffled shirt and one of those effeminate, crossed-under-the collar ribbons that pass for trendy formal neckwear.

The competition. Ginny's visiting big shot, no doubt.

I was hardly prepared for this.

Would Ginny think I was checking up on her?

Spinning on my heel, I ducked out of view and threaded my way back into the main room without bothering to get the drink I'd ordered. I had no intention of hanging around, trying to dodge Ginny all night.

I located another bar in a corner near the front door and asked for a double Jack Daniels on the rocks.

"Good evening, Mr. Baird." The young barman I'd met last night at the party winked as he sloshed the whiskey all the way up to the top of a double Old Fashioned glass.

"Thanks, I needed that," I said and slipped toward the door, wondering if I could make a clean getaway without causing too much stir.

I watched as limos and vans deposited load after load, a steady flow of guests. Occasionally, a few boarded for the return to dinner at the hotel. It looked easy. All I had to do was drift out the door. The next time a limo pulled up, I'd just sidle right up and hitch a ride back to the hotel. In this madhouse, who would miss me?

Best of all, I'd give Rush the slip.

But before I had a chance to make my move, I felt a hand on my arm and turned to see Bobby with a cherubic-looking white-haired gentleman dressed in a tux.

"Ian Ferguson, meet Logan Baird, the best golf partner I've had in a long time," Bobby beamed.

"I'm honored, Dr. Ferguson." I shook his hand. "I've followed your work for a long time. I'm familiar with your early work on beta estradiol and testosterone. And pregnandiol, before your original work on the early corticosteroids. I'm looking forward to hearing your paper on Virecta tomorrow," I stammered like a schoolboy.

"My paper on your remarkable new erection drug certainly won't hurt your company's stock, I can tell you that," Ferguson said.

"That's wonderful. I'm sure my division manager, Rush Donald, was delighted to hear that when you talked to him this afternoon."

"I'm sure there's some mistake?" Ferguson's face betrayed puzzlement. "The only person from Severance I've talked to this week has been Gert Kearns."

Bobby flashed a knowing glance.

"I guess I misunderstood," I mumbled, red-faced. "Is there anything we can do? I mean, if you need anything, just let us know."

"I'm fine. I told Gert not to worry. She's a fine lady and smart as a whip. She worked for me at Cambridge, but I guess you know that," he said.

I nodded.

"Is your Mr. Donald still here? I'd be glad to meet him."

"I don't see him at the moment." Embarrassed that Bobby had caught Rush in another bald-faced lie, I pretended to search the sea of guests, hoping desperately not to see him.

"I want to stop by your booth tomorrow after I read my paper. I can meet him then. Bobby tells me you were a writer before you went to work in pharmaceuticals. Are you the same Henley Logan Baird who wrote the smashing essay, 'The Magnificent Concession'? It was a send-up about the sad state of medical education that ran in *Harper's* magazine a few years back."

I couldn't believe my ears.

"As a matter of fact, I did write that, but I assure you, doctor, I meant no insult—"

"Not at all," he interrupted. "It's a marvelous piece. I read it as part of the text for my first-year lecture at Harvard Medical School."

"You read my essay to Harvard medical students?" I was flabbergasted.

I wished that Rose and Rush were here. The great Ian Ferguson knew my work—had read it to his students.

"I do indeed. You made a fine, albeit a bit wry, analysis of the common shortcomings of a medical education." He smiled. "Anyway, I haven't seen anything else by you lately. Do you still do any medical writing?"

"No, nothing like that piece. Not in several years. I worked as a journalist back then—a medical writer, the common newspaper variety. A sure way to starve to death."

"A pity. That was an exceptional piece of writing. You have an interesting mind. There's a great need for good writers with strong medical insights these days. Someone with your experience could do quite well at it. I should think a magazine piece on our work with Virecta would be attractive to top markets like the *New York Times Magazine* or even *Harper's* or the *Atlantic Monthly*, for example," he enthused. "As I recall, your piece was reprinted by the *Reader's Digest* . . . reached a wide audience. As a writer, do you realize what an influence you could be on a wide segment of our population?"

"I hadn't thought about it that way. Besides, I was just a reporter on the Roanoke paper. Cracking the big time is hard to do."

"There's a lot of national press here tonight. I saw *Time*, the *Wall Street Journal*, and the *New York Times* and *Washington Post*. All the wire services, too." He glanced over my shoulder, looking to point one out.

"I know Virecta's important, but I had no idea it was going to be anything like this big."

"I didn't mean to give the impression all this media is here about Virecta. There are bigger things going on. MacKenzie Brown is holding a big press conference tomorrow to announce his latest extravaganza. But getting back to my work with Virecta, word is getting around—" Ferguson stopped speaking, waved at someone behind me. He called over my shoulder, "Hey, Jake, come here for a second. There's someone you should meet."

When I turned, an academic-looking man was walking our way.

"Jake Chetauga with *Time*. Logan Baird is a medical writer," Ferguson introduced me.

"But—" I started to protest.

"Logan here wrote a piece for *Harper's* a few years back that I use in my classes at Harvard. Now he works for Severance Labs. I think you two should get to know each other," Ferguson persisted.

"Are you a medical writer, Mr. Chetauga?" I asked. I knew that a mention in *Time* would be a big boost for our new drug.

"Oh, no." Chetauga laughed. "Actually, I write business, but our science writer's in that jungle somewhere." He pointed vaguely into the swarm. The numbers were multiplying by the minute.

"Business?" I looked to Ferguson for a connection.

Ferguson shrugged. "Right now, I have to move on. But I am looking for a medical writer, Mr. Baird. Do you think you could come address my students at Cambridge? Perhaps we can talk about it later?"

Ferguson left the question hanging and turned to leave.

"I'd have to think about that," I murmured, standing there with my mouth open, wondering if he were serious.

"Why all this high-powered press?" I turned back to Chetauga, remembering that I thought I'd glimpsed people who resembled Tom Brokaw, Walter Cronkite, and Lesley Stahl.

"Why, I thought everyone knew. MacKenzie Brown's bought some new company. All very hush-hush—big news. Ask Dr.

Johnson here. I'm sure he knows all about it. There's a big press conference tomorrow morning." Jake turned to Bobby. "How about it, Dr. Johnson, can you give us a hint?"

"Sorry," Bobby shook his head and smiled. "I just work here."

"Besides being your boss, who is this guy Brown?" I asked Bobby. I was really curious now. I filled Jake in on yesterday's encounter on the mountain road and the celebration at the golf club. "That car he was driving had certainly seen better days. I surely would never have taken him for someone who'd be hosting a party here tonight."

"Where've you been? MacKenzie Brown is an icon. He buys a bunch of little companies and turns them into big companies. *Forbes* did a piece last year, and he just made our cover," Jake chimed in, then blurted, "Hey, look! There's Sam Snead. MacKenzie Brown and Sam are old buddies. Used to partner at the Crosby at Pebble Beach. Sam spends some time in Boca Raton in winter, and Brown winters at Palm Beach. During the summer, Brown slips up here a lot to sneak in a round of golf and fishing. This time Brown's mixing business with pleasure. Sam's just hanging out."

"Who is this Brown? Was his daddy rich?" I asked.

"Hardly," Bobby replied. "Scotty's daddy was just a dirt farmer in south Georgia. Died broke and drunk during the Depression. Scotty's uncle in Atlanta put him through some jerkwater college I never heard of. He was a fighter pilot in Korea. Shot down a bunch of MIGs. Came back from Korea a hero and got into Harvard Law on the GI Bill. After he graduated, he went to work for a Wall Street brokerage firm, and before anyone knew what was going on he'd put together a stock deal for a ragtag group of run-down private sanitaria. Overnight he wound up owning his first company, a chain of small hospitals, which he promptly sold for a fortune. After that, he was off and running. The man's a genius."

"How'd you get hooked up with him?" I asked, fascinated.

"I was his flight surgeon in Korea. He had this mistaken idea I'd saved his life. I was young and had been practicing medicine in Indiana before the war. When Scotty was putting together his first deal, he called me up out of the blue and asked me if I was interested in buying in."

"Lucky you." It sounded dumb, but I couldn't think of anything else to say. My head was still spinning from Ferguson's words. And I was extremely antsy with Ginny and her boyfriend lurking about. I was sure she didn't want to run into me here any more than I wanted her to.

I drained my Jack Daniels, considered the watery leavings, and looked at Jake and Bobby. "Anybody for a refill?"

"No, thanks. It's going to be a long evening," Bobby declined.

"How about you, Jake?" I asked.

Jake shrugged and extended his glass. "Make mine Chivas. Not even the snooty White House serves Chivas."

When I got back, Jake took his glass and wandered a few steps away to say hello to a fellow journalist.

"What did you tell Ferguson about me? Is he serious about looking for a medical writer?" I turned to Bobby.

"Ian is always serious. He's organizing a new team. I don't want to blow smoke at you, but I couldn't help but be impressed with your background and your medical knowledge this afternoon out on the golf course. I told him so. We're looking for some new talent. This new venture is a different experience for him. He's about to leave the womb of academia. I'm sure he'll talk to you about it again before he leaves. If you're interested in writing again, you should think about anything he says. I have to go pay my respects to some people across the room. I'll catch you later." He looked in Jake's direction, "Do me a favor and keep that tidbit about Ferguson under your hat until tomorrow."

He excused himself and wandered off.

Incredible, I thought, watching him leave. What was going on? Who would believe that the great Ian Ferguson had taken an interest in me? And all because Rush had been afraid to show his ass for the braggart that he was and faked a phone call to avoid stepping up on the first tee at the Old White. By this outlandish quirk of fate, I had wound up on the golf course with the partner of an international entrepreneur—who, incidentally, I had never heard of until yesterday afternoon when I'd seen him lugging a gas can on Route 311 in a remote section of the Appalachian Mountains.

And what about John Paul's literary foundation?

It didn't make sense that all of a sudden I was the man of the hour. I knew better than to take any of it too seriously. Ferguson's deal sounded like so much cocktail party bullshit, and John Paul's letter still had the ring of a cheap paperback novel.

After all, I'd heard and read enough of both in my lifetime.

I saw Rush and Mimi across the crowd, far back in the corner of the other room and was reminded that Rush was headed for Harvard.

I had it made. With what I had on the SOB now, I was surely about to get promoted.

So why was I so unsettled?

In a way I envied John Paul his book, but he was dead. I was alive and wanted more out of life than just a Library of Congress catalog number on my tombstone.

I looked around the room at all the successful people and imagined myself a rising young executive traveling on a big expense account, rubbing elbows with the high and mighty. Division managers with Severance made a nice chunk of money, and there were perks. Managers had their choice of top-of-the-line automobiles with all the extras and corporate credit cards for travel and entertainment. I didn't want Rolexes, but I liked the idea of joining a better country club. With my social connections back home, I could get in the fanciest clubs any time I could come up with the cash. To hell with medical writing or wildcat literary foundations that had to cater to a bunch of grand dames with too much bluing in their hair. I wanted to hitch my star to something solid with major medical and paid vacations and big expense accounts.

Twenty-four hours ago that was my fantasy. So why wasn't my heart going pitty-pat?

I took a big swallow of Jack Daniels and decided to forget about pipe dreams. This artificial facade had me living in a fairy tale.

When I looked out the window, I saw Melba Noyes getting out of a car with Dr. Robothom from the Main Street clinic.

The doctor also had an older woman with him. I assumed she was his wife. Melba was wearing a floral frock with spaghetti straps. It was the first time I'd seen her in anything except her uniform. She was a real piece of work.

After Melba's act in the exhibit hall, I wondered what would happen if Ginny saw us together again.

My gubernaculum gave a twitch.

I looked around desperately just as a fat lady disappeared into the loo. No place to hide.

I edged closer to Chetauga's gang and turned my back.

No luck. The next thing I knew, Melba was whispering hoarsely in my ear, "I have to go with Dr. and Mrs. Robothom to meet Dr. Rayburn and our host, but I'm not busy later. Come find me in about a half-hour, okay?"

She nuzzled my cheek and moved away.

I glanced at Jake and shrugged.

CHAPTER THIRTY-THREE

My heart sank, watching Melba disappear into the crowd. I had to get the hell out while the getting was good.

As the batender refilled my drink, I looked out at the van preparing to leave for the hotel.

Drink in hand, I turned toward the door, but before I could move, Jake blocked my way. He grabbed me by my sleeve. "Did Johnson tell you anything? Let you in on any secrets?"

"Uh-uh."

Chetauga looked suspicious and changed his tactic. "Ferguson said you were a medical writer with Severance Laboratories. You started as a journalist?"

"That was four years ago. I worked as a reporter before, and a short while after that I went to Bosnia. I work for Severance now. I'm a salesman, not a writer. The official title is professional service rep, as in salesman," I explained. "I wrote one piece for *Harper's*, and I have a medical background. Bobby and Dr. Ferguson were just putting two and one together and coming up with four."

"Word on the street is that Ian Ferguson is interviewing writers . . . has been for months. He's leaving Harvard. It's hush-hush where he's going, but it's been widely speculated about in the media. I think Ferguson somehow fits into all this MacKenzie Brown mumbo jumbo. Sounds to me like you may be on to something. We're talking megabucks, here. Aren't you interested?"

"I don't have the faintest idea what those guys have on their minds. And, yes. I guess I am curious. But things are going pretty good for me where I am," I shrugged.

"If I were you, I'd listen to anything Bobby Johnson and Ian Ferguson have to say. You heard Johnson's story. You could be on the fast track to fame," Jake said seriously.

"So tell me, what's with this press conference? Are most of these people working press?" I tried to change the subject with a casual wave at the mob of people.

"Some but not all. When Bobby Johnson sends out a release, everybody comes. You name 'em, they're all here. That's Brackett, the *New York Times*, and my competition, Walt Simmons, with *Newsweek* . . . Kelly with the *Wall Street Journal*." He nodded back at the group he'd just left. "Scotty Brown has acquired something major. Either that or he's starting something new. One or the other—that's what he does. The big press conference is tomorrow at ten, at Valley View."

Before I could ask him anything else, I looked up and Rush, with Mimi on his elbow, was bearing down on us.

"Logan, you darling. Did you ever see such a marvelous place and so many celebrities? We should call Ginny." Mimi fell all over me and gave me a sloppy kiss. She dampened her cocktail napkin with booze and dabbed at the lipstick print.

"Ginny already has a date. She's here." I tried not to sound interested.

"Oh, that bad girl!" she pouted. "Then I'll just be your date, too."

"Oh, man, whadda party!" Rush interjected loudly, grinning vacantly with an alcoholic slackness around his mouth. "Did you see Snead? My god, he wears that damn hat everywhere, no shit. Does he ever take it off? I wonder what he does with it in bed."

"Who cares?" I shrugged, ashamed to be seen with him. They both were out of control again. I knew the signs.

"Have you two met Jake Chetauga with *Time* magazine?" Trying desperately to divert them, I made the introductions and glanced wistfully toward the door.

My watch showed only 7:45—still over two hours until 10:00.

Hotel vans kept arriving and departing with an ebb and flow of guests.

Even if I had to fake a heart attack, I wasn't about to get stuck with them again tonight.

When Mimi heard the word *Time*, she and Chetauga started in on old home week. Rush moved his hand from her elbow and let it encircle her waist, obviously feeling threatened.

I started to slip off toward the bar, but Rush caught me and gave me orders for refills for them both.

Glad for a chance to move away, I headed for the bar.

On my way back, Ferguson appeared out of nowhere and asked, "Is that your Mr. Donald, over there with Jake?"

I nodded.

"Come introduce me, while I have the chance."

"Sure." It was good to have the opportunity before Rush took on any more booze.

"Dr. Ferguson, I'd like to present my division manager, Rush Donald. Next week Severance is sending Rush to Harvard B for a special course. Then he'll be reassigned to Teaneck." I laid it on thick, not wanting to pass up an opportunity to make brownie points.

"Splendid," Ferguson said. "I've been at Cambridge for some time now. There's no place like it."

"I know. Maybe you'll show me around," Rush began.

I was embarrassed. Rush was drunker than I'd suspected. I had to hand to him, though. He was a quick study. I stepped back and listened to him simper over Dr. Ferguson's work. His speech affectation made an unintended caricature of Ferguson's clipped British accent. If Ferguson was amused, he was too much the gentleman to show it. He acted as if everyone talked that way. I tried to act interested.

Time was running out on me.

I wished desperately to walk away, but I couldn't leave Ferguson like that. I kept stealing wary glances around the room with a sense of impending doom. I dreaded seeing Ginny or Melba.

"I'm sorry if I didn't return your phone messages, but I've been rather occupied," Dr. Ferguson was saying to Rush.

"I understand. I got a call from Gert this afternoon, Doctor. She wanted to know if I'd gotten up with you yet," I heard Rush say. "You know Gert. She's a worrier."

I wondered if Bobby had told Ferguson that Rush had faked the telephone message at the golf shop. It was obvious that he was trying to reconcile his lie about the phone call from Gert. I wished he had the good sense to just keep his goddamn mouth shut.

The more he talked, the deeper in he got.

Unless Gert had actually called sometime after we teed off, Rush was lying again. It was contagious, like a disease.

"Bobby said Gert gave you the new data?" Dr. Ferguson said.

The butterflies in my gut metamorphosed into 747s.

"No . . . ah . . . Bobby must have misunderstood. She said to tell you to whistle if you needed anything," Rush said, trying desperately to sound casual.

Bobby was standing behind Rush, listening intently.

Ferguson wrinkled his brow. "What time was this? I don't understand. She knows I need those figures."

"About one, a few minutes past, I guess. I got the page at the golf shop. You might know that she'd wait until just before we were scheduled to tee off." Obviously Rush was too busy covering his lie to listen. "I had to cancel the golf because of good old Gert."

"That's odd. She called me this morning."

"Huh?" Rush croaked.

"Yes. When we talked this morning about eleven, she was going to check some data for me. I was supposed to call her at home tonight. I was hoping she might have said something." Ferguson seemed genuinely puzzled.

"Er, she didn't say a word. She really didn't have much of a chance. Our conversation got cut short. She had to take another call." Rush had put his foot in it and was sweating. "You know Gert, the absent-minded professor. I'll call and get the data in the morning."

"No, no. That won't be necessary. She's expecting me to call later, after dinner." Ferguson looked at his watch.

There was a pregnant silence. Rush turned pale as a ghost.

During all this, Johnson was standing on the other side of the group listening to Rush's bullshit about the call. He caught my eye and shook his head sadly.

"Wouldn't care to give me a hint as to what's going on with you, Doctor?" Jake seized the opportunity to ask Ferguson.

"What's all this about your move? Does Brown's press conference have anything to do with that?"

"I'm here to read a paper for the medical conference," Ferguson said.

"Could that be more than just a coincidence? Just a smoke screen, maybe?" Chetauga wasn't about to let it drop.

"All I know is what I read in *Time*," Ferguson laughed. "Let's enjoy ourselves, shall we? Scotty said he played golf with the brilliant Sam Snead this afternoon. Scotty was in Sam's gallery forty years ago, the day he shot the famous fifty-nine. Said he never saw anything like it. Now there's a story for you. They have a facsimile of the scorecard in the pro shop."

Ferguson started telling the group about Snead's string of birdies during the historic round.

Rush turned to Mimi. "I'm hungry. Let's split," he said, desperately looking for an excuse to leave and trying to act as if nothing had happened. There wasn't much he could do but tough it out.

"There's plenty of food here." Mimi pointed to a buffet. She had not the slightest inkling that he had been caught in a major lie.

I moved over and whispered in his ear, "You'd better go find a phone and fix it up with Gert. She'll cover for you, I'm sure."

He shot me a look of fear. And hatred, knowing I'd caught him again in his pathological dishonesty.

Out of the dozen-odd people in the group, only four of us understood exactly what was amiss, but the energy of the lie settled over the group like the embarrassment of an inopportune belch at the communion rail.

Someone told a tired old golf joke. Ferguson pretended not to have heard it before and laughed. A tray of canapés was passed and someone else remarked about the excellence of the food and the service.

"I was here forty-two years ago when the culinary apprentice program was founded, and it already had two hundred applications. They accept only the best. The program was the first to train American chefs on site. The demand for Greenbrier graduates is overwhelming," a woman said.

"I used to summer in Europe and the Greek Islands, and I tried Majorca, but I gave them up for the Greenbrier. The spa is *tres élégante*. Doesn't get any better anywhere," another woman agreed.

"If you're talking about the service and the standard of excellence," Rush interrupted, "in my opinion, this place has slipped lately. New money has compromised this great spa's standards and traditions of taste and elegance."

"You've been here before?" Bobby asked.

I was sure that I'd told Bobby this afternoon that it was Rush's first visit.

"They always hold this conference here," Rush evaded without a blink.

"Rush is such a great kidder," I said to no one in particular. I wished I could crawl under a rock.

"The trouble with Logan is that he's easily impressed with the cost of things." Rush gave me a withering look and smiled condescendingly at the group. His speech was taking on that Hahvahd inflection again.

"You bet I am," I said, trying to lighten the mood.

That drew a polite ripple of laughter.

"No class," Rush said with the trace of a sneer. He'd turned nasty now. "Nouveau riche Americans are giving us all a bad name. With those rednecks, money is everything. Good taste and manners are things of the past."

No one laughed now.

Bobby just shook his head and gave me a weary smile.

A waiter brought another tray of drinks. It helped to relieve the tension, but an uneasiness dampened the air.

One of the women who'd attached herself asked Rush about the patch he'd had affixed to his jacket.

"Royal and Ancient," Rush said archly, his Harvard accent traded for a Scottish burr.

Bobby seemed fascinated by something on his shoe.

I glanced anxiously toward the powder room.

Ferguson leaned closer to inspect Rush's blazer emblem.

"Then you've been to St. Andrews?" Ferguson asked. There was no trace of insincerity in the question.

Ferguson wasn't trying to embarrass Rush. Instinctively I knew that he would never make cheap sport of such an easy mark.

"A shrine. Couldn't resist bringing home a patch," Rush lied. "Old club blazers are the rage in New York. They teach us at Hahvahd B to never underestimate the power of good theater in business."

I almost choked on my drink.

Bobby saw me and had to turn away to keep from laughing.

"Aye, laddie, and what did you think of the auld course?" Ferguson's voice had a sincere sense of awe.

"A bit like a cow pasture, compared to our courses over here," Rush said and everyone laughed.

"Yes, your courses are not at all the same," Ferguson agreed good naturedly.

"I loved the tradition. In Scotland, golf's a gentlemen's game. Too bad we aren't all gentlemen over here," Rush condescended. Playing the role of world traveler and bon vivant restored his wounded ego by leaps and bounds.

"I've always wanted to play St. Andrews," a stylishly turned out older gentleman said. "And, by Godfrey, you're right, golf should be a gentlemen's game."

"Don't be fooled. Golfers are a cutthroat lot. They're not all gentlemen over there, either." Dr. Ferguson smiled, still companionable but losing interest.

"At least the Scots and the Brits have respect," Rush persisted. "And they have manners."

"Yes, usually, and integrity by the cartloads." Ferguson was in no mood for an argument. The last was meant as his benediction.

The woman who had praised the Greenbrier's culinary program spoke up. "That's one thing that gives this place its charm. I love the good manners and old traditions. I find that the standards here are the best—uncompromising." Her print silk cocktail dress would have cost my last year's bonus.

"That's just the problem. The standards here are disappearing fast. Did you get a look at the old guy in the rumpled plain dress shirt with no tie and the ratty gray sweater with pushed-up sleeves?" Rush asked Ferguson. "He looks like a coal miner or a truck driver."

"That sounds just like our host, MacKenzie Brown." Bobby slapped Ferguson on the back. "Scotty and Sam Snead probably went fishing after they finished on the golf course."

Piqued, I hadn't explained to Rush that Johnson's boss was Sam Snead's friend, our mystery man.

"That old guy's our host?" Rush was incredulous.

"The one and only," Dr. Ferguson laughed.

"I . . . ah . . . ," Rush stammered. "My god, have you ever seen his golf bag?"

"As a matter of fact, yes. I played nine holes with him yesterday. That bag's something of a classic, I'd say." Ferguson laughed.

"Insulting is more like it! You really gotta have balls—er, gall to bring something like that to the Greenbrier." Rush's voice fairly shook with self-righteous indignation. "What's he trying to prove? Look at this place. Anyone who can afford this can certainly afford a decent golf bag. We're all dressed appropriately." Rush made a sweeping gesture, drunkenly slopping some of his drink. The group moved aside to avoid the spill. "And the great Sam Snead doesn't even know enough to take his hat off in the house. This is more what you'd expect at the local American Legion or VFW. Certainly not at the Greenbrier."

I moved closer, trying to shut him off, but Jake and Mimi had him sandwiched between them. Without being obvious, I nudged him in the back.

All I got for my trouble was a dirty look.

"Sam is a wee bit sensitive about being bald. And Scotty's just a country boy from Georgia. Besides, what do a golf bag and his old sweater have to do with anything? Scotty may be eccentric sometimes, but he's always a gentleman," Ferguson said. "And, after all, this is his booze and food we're enjoying."

"I'm just not used to this," Rush said lamely. "This would not be acceptable at the Mark."

Ferguson shrugged amiably then thought a moment and added with a wry smile, "You may have a point, old boy. In our own way, we're all snobs."

"Having standards doesn't make me a snob. When I'm invited to a place like this," Rush tossed his head haughtily to indicate the obvious luxury of Top Notch, "I feel I have an obligation to respect my host by being presentable for his other guests and vice versa. I think that's a matter of taste and good breeding. It has nothing to do with snobbery. It's a matter of mutual respect. And Sam Snead should be an example, not an exception. It's like Hollywood. Out there you have a bunch of ex-truck drivers and two-bit whores who've become rich overnight and they thumb their nose at good manners. They wanna start a fight when the maitre d' at Delmonico's won't let 'em in wearing blue jeans and a dirty sweat shirt. Anyway, what the hell? At the core, I guess you can't take the country out of the boy. Scotty Brown and Sam Snead just don't know any better. You can't make a silk purse out of a sow's ear. Say what you like, money can't buy class."

Nobody laughed.

I couldn't believe his tirade with Ferguson there. Rush was obviously drunk out of his mind.

"I think our host should have some prerogative in his home or at his club, don't you agree? And I personally would never think to call Scotty Brown a boor," Bobby said and walked away.

"Well," Rush hemmed. Even in his drunkenness, he understood that he'd been called a boor.

"I think I'll go make that phone call before dinner," Ferguson excused himself.

I looked around at the group as, one by one, they drifted away.

Rush looked to me. "Tell 'em," he said.

"What?" I blinked.

"Tell 'em about yesterday afternoon when this Brown guy showed up at the Golf Club in his old car and ratty golf bag waving all that money around," he said.

"Rush, don't you think you'd better try to call Gert at home? Now." I said.

"Huh?" Rush gaped at me.

Without a word, Mimi took him by the arm and urged him toward the door.

He finally got the point.

As soon as they had walked away, Ferguson came back over. He put his hand on my arm and leaned in confidentially. "As a fellow writer and a speaker, perhaps you wouldn't mind if I gave you a tip?" He looked at me with a deadly serious look.

"No, not at all," I had no idea what was coming.

"Always say 'beeta ees-tra-diol' and 'tees-tow-steerone' and 'cortico-stee-roid.' They'll never forget you." He pronounced the *e*'s with British delight and squeezed my arm

When he stepped back, his eyes twinkled.

"Never underestimate the power of good theater in business." He winked and said, "Don't forget we're going to talk again. I'll find you tomorrow morning."

Watching him walk away, I felt as if I'd just been knighted.

WEDNESDAY EVENING

CHAPTER THIRTY-FOUR

I hoped Rush would sober up before he went looking for a phone to call Gert. I shuddered, imagining her reaction if Ferguson told her about Rush's reprehensible behavior.

When I turned back, Jake had wandered over to the bar, leaving me momentarily alone. My watch showed almost 8:00. Ginny had promised to ditch her coal baron friend early. The rear terrace led directly to the street. I held out hope that she might have left without coming back through this way but was afraid to investigate because the irrepressible Melba was somewhere back in that same direction.

Outside, a hotel van sat waiting at the curb. I decided to make my getaway while I still had the opportunity.

"Jack Black, right?"

Too late. Before I could make a move for the door, Jake had reappeared and shoved another drink at me.

Wistfully, I watched the van moving away.

The flow of new arrivals had dwindled now. At the moment there were no other hotel vehicles in sight.

"Thanks," I shrugged, searching for a place to set the empty glass I already held. A waiter whisked away the discard.

"Is that dickhead really your boss?" Jake asked, looking in the direction Rush had taken.

"Not for long. They're sending him to Harvard Business as soon as he gets back to Charlotte. Severance has big plans for him."

"They're sending that asshole to Harvard?" Jake shook his head in wonder.

I shrugged. I didn't want to seem disloyal, but I wasn't about to defend the clown.

"I wouldn't sweat it. Sounds like Ian Ferguson might offer you a job."

"I'm not counting on that." I took a judicial sip of the fresh drink and sneaked a look out the window. Not another van in sight.

I still had two or three hours to kill. Ginny had estimated tenish. When I traveled the area, I sometimes freeloaded a flick at the hotel theater. The Greenbrier always got the best new releases before they played the theaters in Roanoke or Charleston. *Road to Perdition* was tonight's feature. I'd always been a Paul Newman fan. With Newman and Tom Hanks playing heavies, the film was on a lot of early Academy Award lists.

The last showing began around 9:00. Damn thing ran over two hours. If I stayed for the entire movie, I'd miss Ginny's call.

And the reviewers called the movie "edgy." The idea of an edgy film tonight didn't really turn me on. Babysitting Rush was edgy enough.

I looked nervously back into the sea of people—no glimpse of Ginny, or Melba either.

I was getting as paranoid as a priest in a porno shop. John Paul's death . . . his legacy offering a new career and freedom . . . Rush's drunken misadventures . . . my poor beat-up car . . . Ian Ferguson's surprise revelation about my *Harper's* piece and his obscure hints about my writing future . . . Rose's nonstop complaining . . . Ginny . . . my new role as an adulterer . . . the suddenly aggressive Melba . . . and . . . well, all of the above.

My poor nervous system was on overload.

Maybe I could just go to my room and catch a nap, leave a wake-up call for 10:00, and get up ready for the late, late show at Ginny's place.

Recollections of last night's erotic scenario aroused new stirrings from my overly active pituitary.

Was there an Academy Award for sexual overload? And the envelope please . . .

"Has that jerk actually been to all those places?" Jake brought me back to the moment.

"Huh?"

"Scotland, the Royal and Ancient? Has your asshole boss been there?"

"That's what he says." I shrugged.

"Personally, I think your manager is ninety-nine percent bullshit," Jake continued, amiably. "And I think you know it. But what the hey. We all have to work for a living, right?"

Chetauga seemed a decent sort. He really wasn't trying to start anything.

"Not all of us." I nodded at the room jampacked with obviously affluent people. "Or maybe these fancy men and women are just the working press."

"Those wire service factotums? Hardly," Jake laughed. "We of the esteemed fourth estate are more Marriott than Greenbrier, more draft beer than Chivas or Black Jack. You of all people ought to know that." He raised his glass.

I winked and sipped my drink, keeping a wary eye out for a hotel van.

A couple of anonymous journalist types had joined us. Except to speak to Jake and nod, the newcomers didn't say much. Standing there, turning this way and that, they sipped their booze, looking for targets of opportunity. The place fairly overflowed with expensively gowned, attractive females, their sleek haunches rippling and their bosoms pushing arrogantly against expensive summer frocks.

Apples, pears, and melons, alive, alive, oh! Maybe I'd set it to music and play it on my guitar.

I eyeballed the veritable fruit bowl of low-cut necklines, an undulating panorama of softly swelling suntanned breasts in all shapes and sizes.

I estimated well over a cool five million bucks in exclusive *couturier* creations and surgical implants milling about. With all the physicians here for the convention, many of these dazzling accouterments were most likely paid for by some poor jerk's prostate surgery. Consider the irony—all this delicious fruit at the expense of a flaccid trouser worm.

Pondering such deep insights, my head was suddenly filled with flashbacks of Ginny.

"Your Mr. Donald is a bleeding snob. He reminds me of my lace-curtain-Irish grandmother. Three-fourths of the people in this room could buy and sell the phony SOB. Who's he think he's fooling with his freaking mail-order blazer patches and Rolex knock-off? And who gives a flip if Brown wears a ratty old sweater or Sam Snead has his hat on in the house? People with real money don't need to dress up to remind other people who they are. MacKenzie Brown probably wears a Timex. Next time you get close, check it out. At least Brown knows who he is. That's what counts," Jake offered, philosophically.

"Give that phony boss of yours an enema and bury him in a shoe box," observed a slinky, attractive, and faintly dykey female hovering on the fringe of our circle.

Everybody laughed.

Dykey or not, she was a looker and had a roving eye.

AC or DC? Sometimes it was hard to tell.

Legs and an ass like that might talk me into a lesbian *ménage á trois*.

Get a grip, I cautioned myself, wondering what had happened to Max and Sam—and nosy Maryanne and Cookie.

With those bloodhounds here, the thought of Melba's roaming around loose rattled me.

Not another van in sight.

A plump, balding guy in a wrinkled khaki suit broke away from a group of working press and came wandering over.

"Jake, you old fart, how are ya?"

"Better'n I deserve, French," Jake replied.

"If Jake got what was coming to him, he'd either be dead or in jail," baldy observed.

"I'll take mercy over justice every time," Jake readily agreed.

The balding man stuck out his hand. "Jake's got no manners. I'm Pete French. I string for Associated Press out of Charleston."

"Logan Baird," I mumbled and shook his hand.

"I saw you buddying up to Ferguson and Johnson. What's Ferguson got up his sleeve?"

"Don't have the faintest," I shrugged.

"Logan here is with Severance Labs. Here for the medical convention. He used to write a medical column for the *Roanoke*

Times," Jake said. "Ferguson's trying to interest him in writing medical stuff for him."

"Word's out Ferguson's going to move." The AP guy's interest was up. "Is he hooking up with MacKenzie Brown?"

"You're talking to the wrong guy. Among his other credentials, Ferguson's a world authority on endocrinology. He's going to read an important paper tomorrow on our new erection drug, Virecta. He's also an expert on corticosteroids." Whore that I am, I pronounced it "stee-roid." I added, "He discovered our miracle synthetic cortisone, Megacorten. If he's leaving Harvard, I don't have the slightest notion what he's got up his sleeve."

"This Virecta, is that big news?" French asked.

"One pill lasts all day. Severance's stock's gone from eleven and a half to seventy-one in a month . . . a cinch to split any day now," Jake volunteered.

"A hard-on pill that lasts all bloody day? You must've made a nice piece of change. How much did you invest?" French shot me an interested look.

"Not nearly enough! My wife is saving for a new air conditioner and a bigger house." I didn't tell him that my secret stash of cash had only bought me a hundred shares at eleven and one-half.

Pete spoke up. "Wives are all the same. I finally did something permanent about mine."

Jake raised his glass. "To rich horny women, old drinking buddies, cheap legal domestic help, a damn good caddy, and hound dogs—everything to comfort a man in his hour of need."

The men clinked glasses all around.

Sweet li'l slinky-dykey was not amused.

"So, this Virecta is hot stuff, huh?" French pursued.

"Erectile dysfunction is right up there with heart disease as public enemy number one. Add allergies and you've covered three-quarters of the patients in the waiting rooms. Viagra set records for new prescriptions, but, as good as it is, any drug has limitations. There are always some patients who experience side effects, and there are precautions. Often these drugs won't help patients with radical prostate surgery. Virecta offers hope, eliminates the worst of the limitations, and lasts a lot longer."

"Wonder if that has something to do with Scotty Brown's sucking up to Ian Ferguson?" Jake mused aloud.

Absentmindedly, I watched as slinky-dykey sidled over to a stylishly attired gentleman and gave him a warm hello.

"You're writing this Virecta article for Ferguson?" Pete French was confused.

"No, no. I don't write any more. I'm in sales."

"So why not give me all the dope? I freelance to magazines. Sounds like a great article in all this," Pete said.

"Sure, catch me in the hotel exhibit hall tomorrow morning. I'll give you the full information package and you're all set," I agreed. "Best catch me early though. I'm going to play golf later."

I fished in the breast pocket of my jacket and handed him my card.

"I'll be there," French enthused.

I kept looking for a van, eager to make a break for the door.

Slinky-dykey wandered back our way, with the stylish gentleman tightly in tow.

So much for her gender orientation—for this evening at least.

"Well looky, looky. There's Cleveland Webb the Third. Mr. Wonderful himself. This must be an occasion." Jake was staring directly back over my shoulder.

I turned, and Ginny and her date were standing not more than ten feet away, at the edge of a neighboring group.

"And just who's this Cleveland Webb the Third?" someone asked, sotto voce.

"Among other things, Cleveland Webb the Third owns a lot of unmined coal. See him? Right over there with the gorgeous redhead . . . Ginny McSomething. She runs a country inn near Lewisburg." French spoke right up. "I hear Webb's backing her. Quite well, from the looks of her. Found her working in New York as a desk clerk at the Plaza. She's his protégée." French rolled his eyes. "Any way you look at it, the lady's working her way straight to the top."

Gray at the temples, Cleveland Webb the flipping Third reminded me of some faintly familiar movie actor. I felt my hackles rise as his hand casually slid down over Ginny's well-rounded buttocks and lingered for a moment. She smiled knowingly and leaned affectionately against him.

"Just look at the way the old bastard puts his hands on her." Jake had seen it too.

Thinking back on my idea of a nap in preparation for a late-night date with Ginny filled me with anger.

I was reminded of what Rose had said about Ginny's hating her.

Had Ginny played me for a fool?

CHAPTER THIRTY-FIVE

Struggling to regain my composure, I took a muscular slug of my drink and gave Webb a closer look.

Trim and decidedly well-dressed, the self-satisfied penis with legs had the slight underbite malocclusion of a bona fide Ivy. Mid-forties, perhaps? I was sure he must be older. Reminded me of the old-timey film actor, Kent Smith—the name came floating back—who played the snobby Peter Keating in the classic late, late-show, Ayn Rand's, *The Fountainhead*.

"What's this Webb do, anyway?" My voice came out a croak.

"Back in the late seventies, his pappy left him a large string of two-bit coal mines and a little pumpkin-vine railroad up near the Virginia-Kentucky line. To be around him now, you'd think the jerk owns the world. A jet-setter, hangs with the beautiful people . . . Newport and New York. Rubs elbows with Graydon and Dominick, the Kennedys and Rockefellers—that crowd. He ran for governor here in West Virginia a couple of years back. He's already had four or five wives. God only knows how many women. They fall all over him. God's gift to the female. If you don't believe it, ask him," French smirked.

"Listen, my friend, don't feel too smug. Webb just may be God's gift to the women at that," Jake said to Pete. "I caught him in the showers at the sauna this afternoon. That son of a bitch has the biggest goddamn human pecker I ever laid eyes on."

And Ginny was his steady? My equipment wasn't exactly going to get me in *The Guiness Book of World Records*.

"Size ain't everything, is it Baird?" Pete gave me a bawdy wink. "God gave ordinary men tongues. A little creativity goes a long way, right?" He slapped me on the back.

"Peetah, dahling, you're turning green with envy. I think Cleveland's the cutest ole thing. Who wants to settle for a firecracker when they can have the whole Saturn rocket?"

Slinky-dykey laughed and prowled away again, leaving her stylishly attired companion without so much as a good-bye.

"Good ol' Sylvia Wolfer. Helluva medical writer, but rumor has it she plays both sides, you know what I mean?" Pete said, watching her go.

Dykey's gentleman friend discovered something fascinating about his fingernails.

"I read in a medical journal about a guy whose penis was so big he blacked out when he got an erection because all the blood drained from his brain," I observed, snidely. The slinky Ms. Wolfer's departure left the group all males now.

That brought a polite ripple, but Jay Leno could rest easy.

"I don't want to boast," Jake picked up my lead, "but I guess you guys didn't know I took the Olympic gold in the short pecker competition in Atlanta in ninety-six. Went from a shriveled-up li'l ol' two- inch nubbin to a six-and-a-half-inch, glass-etching hard-on. I'm thinking about trying for the gold again, maybe Athens . . . wherever."

Pete slapped him on the back. "Last time I saw yours, it didn't look like it would stretch to full two inches."

The group guffawed.

"Probably won't. They measured me from the top of my scrotum on the underside, but when you think about it, that just makes my record all the more remarkable. And we were competing against a twenty-mile-an-hour head wind and the temperature was ninety-eight degrees Fahrenheit."

"How'dja do it? I mean, just standing there in the middle of the stadium. Did they give you nekkid women to look at?"

"Hell, no. This ain't no common ordinary barroom competition we're talking about. We're talking Olympic Games here. The contestants have to supply their own inspiration. It's as much a contest of the psyche and intellect as it is a physical thing. I trained on *Lady Chatterley's Lover* and Harold Robbins's *The Stallion*, and someone lent me their video of the uncut version of *Caligula*. I kept *Playboy* in the john and by my bed and spent all summer watching hard porn. And I didn't have intercourse or jack off for a whole year. Once, about six weeks before the competition, I had a wet dream. I thought I might have blown the whole thing, but I came through like a champ . . . no puns intended. Two inches flaccid to six-and-one-half-inch solid rigor mortis. You gotta be at top form to do that in front of eighty thousand screaming fans. And most of the local ladies were spreading their legs and giving the Georgia Tech competitor a look up their skirts, rooting against me. Oops, did it again! The puns are purely unintended."

"I still say not all women would be thrilled over a horse-sized dick," Pete snorted, obviously taking Sylvia Wolfer's remark to heart.

"I can tell you one thing. That redhead won't ever be satisfied with a six-inch nubbin again. See her rub up against him? I guarantee Mr. Webb has spoiled that fox for every man who ever lived," Jake fired back.

Two-faced Ginny—the slut must've had a good laugh all around. I slipped my hand in my pocket to check that my decidedly ordinary Excalibur was still intact.

"Uh-oh. Don't look now but here they come," Jake whispered.

"I'll be damned. Jake! Jake Chetauga. And Pete French. Haven't seen you two since the media broke the story on Project Greek Island." Webb looked Ivy, but he sounded West-by-God-Virginia.

"Yeah, there was CNN, *USA Today*, even the frigging BBC and that talking robot, Stone Phillips, for *NBC Dateline*." Jake acted almost glad to see the pretty boy.

I turned to leave.

"Hold on. It's early . . . fun's just starting," Jake grabbed me and whispered behind his hand.

"Jake, let me introduce you to Ginny McKim. She's one of our bright young business entrepreneurs." Webb stepped aside and urged Ginny forward. "Ginny, this is Jake Chetauga with *Time* and Pete French of the Associated Press."

Ginny nodded, studiously ignoring my presence.

As hard as I struggled to shake free, Jake held my arm in a death grip.

"I want you nice folks to meet Logan Baird." I gave up my tug of war as Jake plowed blithely ahead. When I turned back, Ginny was standing close enough to touch. "Logan's here with the medical show. His company's got a new super-hard-on pill."

Webb put out his hand. At his age, the man was a candidate for prostate trouble.

I snuck an envious peek at the bulge in his trousers. I fervently hoped that salami was as limp as his hand.

"And this is Ginny McKim." Webb nodded toward Ginny.

"Mr. Baird and I have met," Ginny said without inflection. "Nice to see you again."

Forcing a smile, I searched for an answering sign.

Ginny looked disinterestedly away.

"Great party, huh?" Webb said to no one in particular.

Contemplating how Mr. Dynamic Dipstick would enjoy a swift kick in the balls, I looked hopefully to Ginny again.

Nada.

"Yeah, but I'm playing golf in the morning. I was thinking of catching a bite at the hotel. I plan to be in bed, sober, by ten-thirty." I glanced at Ginny, still hoping for a glimmer.

Nothing. Unless you counted the suppression of a yawn.

"Nice to have met you, Mr. Webb. Good seeing you again, Miss McKim. Excuse me, I have to run." Before anyone could protest, I pulled free and headed back through the hall to find the loo.

This time the powder room was unoccupied.

Unloosing my ignominious apparatus, I could hardly bear the embarrassment as I emptied what seemed to be an endless stream of frothy urine into the commode.

Shaking my unpretentious member, I zipped and flushed.

That bitch would have just let me wait around my room all evening waiting for her call.

I splashed my face with cold water. Spitefully ignoring the urgent rattles of the doorknob, I toweled my face, roughly forcing back rage.

After a long minute I took a deep breath, drew up to my full height, and looked my reflection in the eye.

It hurt to breathe, but in spite of everything, I suddenly had to laugh out loud.

And at least I'd found out in time. I'd read that *Road to Perdition* was a good flick. At least a movie might prove distracting.

Trying on my best inscrutable Harrison Ford expression, I took a deep breath, unlocked the door, and headed out.

"Thank God!" With a look of profound gratitude, the lady waiting her turn dove past me.

The most direct exit to the vans was back through the room I'd just left, but I had no intention of going back there. Standing in the deserted hall, I gathered myself, taking a moment to formulate a battle plan.

Across the dining room to my right, I could see through the window to the terrace. The overflow of guests was a minor mob scene. Earlier I'd seen a buffet on the terrace. It was getting borderline late to slip in beneath the wire at the dining room, and the guests were attacking a groaning board of food out there. But in my present state, food was the last thing I wanted.

Two things stood uppermost in my mind. A stiff drink and a quick getaway back to the hotel.

A good plan. Even if I had to walk.

After what seemed an eternity of determinedly eeling my way back through the crowd, I finally exited through the French doors onto the brick-paved terrace.

At the Greenbrier, the influence of Dorothy Draper is ubiquitous. The terrace borders are planter boxes of geraniums. White pickets neatly fence the area. Gates swing on either side between chest-high brick columns. Here and there, umbrella-topped tables of wrought iron painted white were filled with food. From the nearest gate directly to the rear, a brick path curved around behind the bedroom wing to the garage and parking court—I was reminded that the hotel brochure stated that both Top Notch and the larger Valley View Estate House came complete with use of a distinctive Greenbrier-crested Cadillac sedan.

The remarkable spa left no need unanticipated.

Directly across the terrace from the bedroom wing, a brick walk led from the other gate back toward the front entrance where, hopefully, vans still came and went.

Aha! My escape route.

Passing the buffet, I snagged a celery stick and swallowed it damned near whole as I headed determinedly for the nearest bar.

Fresh drink in hand, I was just turning to go find a van, when the heather blonde hove into view. My hopes flared, then went a-glimmering when I saw she'd snared a dashing tuxedoed gent.

As if I hadn't had enough trouble already.

When I found a relatively quiet sanctuary out of the mob, I saw Ferguson standing with Bobby near the steps leading to the enclosed sun porch. He caught my eye and waved.

Smiling, I returned the greeting.

Nearby, Dr. Robothom and his wife were talking to our unflappable host, the infamous MacKenzie Brown, indifferently clad in khaki pants and an old sweater. At his elbow, Sam Snead—wearing his trademark hat and a fishing vest—was deeply engaged in conversation with an urbane couple in evening clothes.

My smile quickly faded as I caught a glimpse of Melba across the terrace opposite me, near the gate leading to the front. Restlessly casting her eyes about, she looked like an egret poised for flight.

Until tonight, I'd never seen her out of uniform. She was absolutely stunning.

Her outfit was as virginal as a junior high school cheerleader's, but the effect was more provocative than a courtesan's tease. Seeing her with her hair down and without her stiff nursing uniform, I realized how young she really was.

She was tall and striking in a wholesome way. The gauzy accordion-pleated peasant top of her gown showcased her maidenly breasts with a Scandinavian flare. The lance tips of her nipples struggled modestly against the wispy bodice fabric. Beneath the clingy jumper, those sculpted gymnast's legs soared all the way to her well-shaped haunches, delineated by just a tiny hint of panty line.

Sipping a champagne cocktail out of a hollow-stemmed glass that had a cherry in it, she presented the image of a little girl drinking pink party punch.

The only thing missing was a straw.

I considered the drink in my hand. Go slowly, I thought, painfully reminded of Rush's sad condition.

Around front, another van was just loading to leave. Alerted, I surveyed a path around the swarm, hastily plotting my escape.

"Hi! Looking for me?"

I blinked.

Melba materialized in front of me. Feet slightly apart, her hips thrust aggressively forward, she struck a very suggestive pose.

Déjà vu?

Remembering this morning as she had rubbed all over me in the exhibit hall, my impression of her schoolgirl innocence quickly evaporated.

Innocent little Melba?

Hardly.

Twenty-four? Maybe. But not a day over twenty-five.

Shameless trollop. Fairly begging for comeuppance. Or come-innance . . . whatever the endless variety of that experience.

Still stinging from Ginny's snub, sick to death of Rose's complaining, John Paul's sister's—not to mention his wife's—whining, and women in general, I considered.

Why not?

It would serve Ginny and Rose right.

Carpe diem, my wounded ego goaded.

CHAPTER THIRTY-SIX

"Melba. I was afraid you'd forgotten me," I lied like a politician.

"No, no. Not at all. I peeked inside a while ago and thought you'd left. I just assumed you were stuck with your boss. He seems to have made a miraculous recovery from his injury." She nudged me knowingly with a shapely hip.

I winked and bumped her back.

The scent of spring around her made me dizzy.

"The redhead . . . is that the set of pearly teeth that nibbled him last night?" she asked with a pixie grin.

"A real glutton for punishment." I smiled and nodded.

"Kiss it and make it well." She shot me a knowing look.

My traitorous eyes wandered recklessly over her maidenly décolletage.

Glancing back over the sea of people, I wished that Ginny could see me now.

"Speaking of nibbling, have you eaten yet—real food, that is?" she asked slyly.

"Not yet," I said, then whispered, "Are you stuck with them?"

"Not at all. Are you free of your boss?" she whispered back.

"Free as a bird. Think we might find a bite somewhere?" I held my breath.

"I could take you home and give you a bite . . . if you like." She lowered her eyes, then boldly looked back again.

Young? Maybe.

Naive? Perhaps.

Afraid? Never.

"Sounds too good to be true. I've about had my fill of people for one day," I said, my disposition improving by quantum leaps and bounds.

"Just give me a moment." She fished the cherry out of her glass. Holding it by the stem, she licked it with her tongue before she popped it into her mouth. Her eyes never left mine as she handed me her glass. "Get me another one of these while

I go make nice. This time, skip the cherry. They're highly overrated."

"Yeah?" I murmured, struggling mightily not to leer.

"Don't disappear." She squeezed my arm and moved away.

Do not pass Go. Go directly home with sweet young thing.

"I'll be over by the steps." I indicated the sliding doors leading back into the ell between the enclosed sun porch and the dining room. It was the most direct way back into the house.

Waiting for the barman to fix our drinks, I sneaked another peek at her.

I vividly recalled Ginny in the exhibition hall that morning as she glared daggers at Melba. I hoped Ginny and Cleveland Colossalcock were still in the front part of the house because I was going to promenade Melba right out through the front door.

This young goddess made Ginny look slightly faded—if you'd looked as closely as I had.

Sour grapes? Perhaps. But he who laughs last, laughs best.

From rejection to redemption in one roll of the dice.

Gloating, I kicked a wayward olive and sent it flying against the ankle of a nearby matron. Startled, she glanced around.

Looking over her head, I practiced my best thousand-yard stare.

Careful not to spill our drinks, I inched my way to the steps and watched while Melba made her apologies to the Robothoms.

Dr. Robothom caught my eye and waved.

Mrs. Robothom looked a trifle anxious. The doctor said something to his wife, and she brightened.

I wondered what Melba had told them. I'd worked hard to gain Robothom's trust. With his influence at the neighboring hospital, the good doctor was one of my staunchest supporters. I certainly didn't want to compromise my credibility.

I waved back—a drink in each hand—and smiled.

Melba strolled over, and I handed her the drink.

"What did you tell them? About me, I mean."

"I told them you were going to get me some Megacorten for my mom's asthma."

"Brilliant. C'mon, let's make tracks out of here." I turned to go inside.

"No. Let's not fight our way through that mob," she protested. "Let's just go out the gate and around the walk."

"Sorry, but I need to leave word with someone. Indulge me. Only take a second." I took her elbow and guided her into the crowded sun porch.

It was almost 8:30 now. The flow of vans was picking up again. A steady exodus of guests was heading back to the hotel as I led my prize flower back through the house into the front room, fervently hoping that Ginny was still around.

Vengeful anticipation dulled vestigial guilt I felt for using Melba this way. And watching heads turn as we made our way through the crowd did wonders for my failing ego.

Bingo!

I'd been holding my breath, afraid that Ginny might have left. When we turned the corner, I let it out in triumph.

Ginny and old prodigious poker, Cleveland Jackhammer III, were still standing with Jake and Pete over near the front entrance.

When I spotted them, I slowed and stopped, pretending to look around for my fictitious associate.

I paused, hoping Ginny would look our way.

I watched her clinging to Lord Powerpole. His hand still rested proprietarily near the top of her ample derrière.

They were still touching lightly at thigh and hip.

I edged a few steps closer.

No flash of recognition. She pretended to ignore my existence.

Finally, I walked to the edge of the group and waited until there was a lull in the conversation.

"Excuse me, Jake. Have you seen Rush?" I asked, playing out my charade.

He looked over and shook his head.

"If he comes back, would you just tell him I'll call him in the morning?"

Then he saw Melba and his mouth dropped open.

"Okay, but what's your hurry?" Jake couldn't take his eyes off of Melba. "Aren't you going to introduce us to your friend?"

"Melba Noyes, I'd like to present Mr. Jake Chetauga of *Time* magazine, and this is Mr. Pete French of the Associated Press. And this is Mr. Cleveland Webb . . . the Third. I believe you already know Ginny McKim."

Webb spoke right up, "Hello, Melba, long time no see." "You're looking lovely. I must tell Ben Robothom to let you out of the clinic more often."

"Hello, Ginny. Why, thank you, Cleveland." Melba was chilly to Webb's flirty overture.

Ginny's eyes kept cutting back and forth between Webb and Melba as if she were trying to follow a volley at Wimbledon.

Reflexively, she tightened her grip on Webb's elbow, but Mr. Suave'n'debonair's attention was directed entirely toward Melba.

Ginny jerked his arm. The tiny muscles in her jaw tightened unattractively.

Melba ignored Webb and snuggled closer to me.

Mammothmast had been around the block more than once or twice. I was quite sure of that.

Was there some history here?

Had my wounded ego done me in?

Ginny tugged his arm again. "Clevie, honey, c'mon."

"What's your hurry?" Webb snapped.

Old Donkeydong was still giving Melba his best Robert Redford gaze.

Melba squeezed my hand, her eyes pleading sweetly.

"You work in the clinic, Melba?" Pete French wanted to keep her around.

She nodded. "Not here at the hotel. The one downtown."

"I've been thinking about a physical. How do I make an appointment?" Pete bored in.

"It's not complicated. Just give us a call. We're in the book."

"I hadn't thought of that," Pete said.

That got a laugh.

"Of course, you know there're rules about nurses dating the patients, Pete," Jake said.

"What a drag," Pete said.

Everyone laughed but Ginny. Looking over Jake's shoulder at the pictures hanging on the wall, she pretended a tired disinterest in it all.

My eyes caught her reflection in the window glass. Her attention wandered back toward Melba, until she saw me watching her and quickly looked away.

Then, self-consciously, she glanced back at me. I met her eyes, still hoping for some sign. Her lip curled slightly with disdain.

She tossed her head and moved closer to Webb, encircling his waist possessively with her arm.

Eat your jealous heart out, I responded with a wolfish grin.

Ginny shot Melba another withering look and beamed me a ray of death.

It was all I could do to keep from laughing out loud.

Game, set, and match!

Ginny grabbed Webb's hand and gave it a jerk.

"Cleveland, I'm starving," she whined.

He pulled away, still resisting.

"That reminds me. I'm long overdue for my physical. I'll stop by in the morning and make an appointment," Webb said to Melba.

"I'm sure Helen'll be glad to take care of it," Melba said politely. "Tomorrow's my day off."

"Well? Friday then?" Webb persisted.

Ginny shot him a disgusted look.

Jake and Pete and slinky-dykey looked nervously at each other.

Clearly, Webb didn't mind living on the edge.

"Ready, Logan, honey?" Melba pleaded.

"*Ciao!* Got to run." I lifted my glass with a parting flair.

David Mamet would have been impressed as we skipped hand-in-hand merrily out the door.

Outside, three vans were waiting now. Melba pulled me around the line of people, and we found the third one completely empty.

Melba pulled me in behind her. "Do we have to wait, Andy? We're in a hurry."

"No problem, Miss Melba," the driver said, pulling out around the other vans and heading for the hotel.

"If you're really hungry, I may surprise you. I have hidden talents. In the kitchen, I mean." Her breath was soft on my cheek.

"Where do you live?" I asked.

"Not far, really. But I came with the Robothoms. Do you have a car?"

"Yeah. Rush Donald banged it up last night, remember?"

"Oh, yeah. Does it still run okay?"

"I guess. It just doesn't look so hot."

"Who cares? Have it brought around." She giggled and snuggled closer.

Her breast pushed against my bicep, and she left it there. Casually, she squeezed my hand, then moved it across, pressing it deep into her lap, atop the inner part of her thighs. Her legs relaxed, parting just a little. Through the filmy fabric, I could feel the outline of her panties where they curved down between her legs.

Against my forearm, her pudendum was firm and flat.

The silky feel of fabric against fabric drove me up the wall.

Melba cleared her throat with a purring sound and stirred just ever so lightly, pushing my hand lower against her crotch.

In the darkness, she opened her mouth to me.

An unambiguous contract of intimacy was sealed.

CHAPTER THIRTY-SEVEN

Waiting at the main motor entrance for my car to be brought around, Melba asked, "What do you know about Ginny McKim?"

"She's from my hometown, Melas. It's near Roanoke. She was a practice teacher when I was in high school. Until yesterday, I hadn't seen her in years."

Melba thought that over for a moment.

"Do you like her?"

"I hardly know her."

After our cool exchange back at Top Notch, that answer would have passed muster if I had been hooked up to a polygraph.

"How well do you know Webb?" I asked, curious to see her reaction.

"Well enough to know better!" She gave a snort.

"I noticed Ginny wrapped herself around him like a vine, inappropriate for her position in the community and the setting. She looked daggers at you when Webb made that pass at you back there."

"Ginny definitely doesn't like me. I went out with Cleveland before he started dating her. She thinks he's still trying to date me."

"She's obviously right about that." I'd hardly begun speaking before I was sorry I'd opened my mouth. I didn't want to hear anything more about this legendary lord a-leaping.

"Cleveland thinks he's God's gift to women. I only went out with him once, maybe twice. He's a creep. For a while he pestered me to go out again, but not lately. She's welcome. I don't know how she stands the dork. She just sticks with him because he's her sugar daddy. He set her up in business. When sweet Ginny first came here, she had us fooled. We all liked her. When it became obvious that Cleveland Webb was her sponsor, we soon found out what a two-faced bitch she is. Now everyone in the area despises her. Ginny is vindictive. Just plain goddamn mean. She got one girl fired at the hotel because she thought her precious sugar daddy was coming on to her. Cleve had the girl moved to some plush job with a hotel in Charleston. Everybody is laughing behind the bitch's back now, but they're still afraid. Ginny knows that Cleve is trying to get his hand up the dress of every good-looking female in the place."

"Can Webb make it difficult for you?" I asked sympathetically. I felt relieved knowing that she didn't like the SOB, but now I wanted to change the subject.

"Difficult for me? Not at all. I work for Ben Robothom. He doesn't give a hoot about Webb. He answers to his partners. Nobody in our clinic likes Webb anyway."

"I like Dr. Robothom. Thanks to you, he's been good to me." I squeezed her hand.

"I don't know if you know it, but you're one of our chosen few. We don't see very many pharmaceutical salesmen. The girls at our clinic think you're . . . nice. They'd simply die if they knew we were together." She snuggled closer and pressed my hand lower.

"I wouldn't want . . ." A cold knot formed in my stomach. I thought about Rose and Ginny and felt a chill. The last thing I wanted was to become an item among the clinic staff.

"Don't worry. I know you're married. I know how catty older women can be. You don't have to worry. I'll never tell." She hugged my arm conspiratorially.

"Look, it might be better if we just go out to the Camellia Club and get something to eat. Charlie Zaharias's usually nice to me. And he's discreet." Soberly considering the consequences of being seen with her, I was having second thoughts.

"Forget that. Trust me . . . it's okay." She tugged my sleeve, urging me toward the curb as the driver pulled my car up under the portico and came around to hold the door for her.

"It doesn't look like it's been wrecked—" she began.

"Wait 'til you see the other side." I started to pull her around to show her the damage.

"No, let's go. There'll be time enough for that." She moved to where the attendant stood holding the door.

When she slipped into the front seat, her dress slid awry. I caught just a flash of panty as she swung her legs inside. They were a delicious shade of pale peach. My fleeting desire to maintain a professional decorum went skittering off into that vast wasteland that lately served as a wrecking yard for my good intentions.

Melba caught me looking, but she didn't avert her gaze. She lifted her hips and gave the skimpy skirt of her dress a futile tug.

What's a poor girl to do? her heartbreaking smile implored.

Making a great fuss over seeing that she was tucked safely inside, I carefully closed the door.

Logan Baird . . . ever the perfect gentleman.

We didn't speak until we'd passed the gatehouse.

"Which way?" I asked as we approached the main entrance, across from the railroad station.

"Back toward town." She hugged my arm and wriggled closer.

I turned onto the deserted street, toward the cluster of stores and gas stations that marked the business section a few blocks up ahead. The main drag runs down the center of a small collection of undistinguished buildings, alongside a rocky creek and the CSX railroad.

"Slow down and turn left at the next street," she directed and squeezed my thigh.

I turned onto a street lined with an oddly matched collection of nondescript homes.

To my everlasting shame, I considered the neighborhood with a patronizing air. The setting reminded me of the poor but honest working-class residential sections of the East Bottom section of Melas, near the meatpacking plant. Doctors, lawyers, merchants, miners—there was almost no class distinction here. In these coal mining mountain towns, the people were a tight society and stuck together. I guessed we were heading north and slightly west. There were only a few widely scattered street lights. I kept peering into the darkness expecting the street to come to a dead end. I calculated we were were near where the fairways of number four and five of the Old White Course looped back in a westerly direction.

"See up ahead on the right? The light on the porch of the big white house." Melba squeezed my leg. Her hand had moved casually up higher on my thigh as we drove along the quiet street. Now it imposed brazenly against my rapidly engorging penis. "Turn in and drive around back."

The house was two-story, noticeably bigger than most of its neighbors. In the rear, a parking area ran back through the trees, alongside a large wooden garage. The garage stood back, well away from the house.

"Pull in beside my little bug." She pointed to a shiny-new yellow VW convertible parked beside the narrow flight of stairs that ran up the side of the garage. At the top of the steps there was a small landing with a covered stoop. A bright red geranium in an earthen pot balanced on the railing. Over the door, there was one of those garish yellow insect-repellent bulbs.

"Ta-da! Home sweet home. What d'ya think?" she said nervously.

"Very secluded."

"That's a cop-out! A euphemism for 'no class' if I ever heard one. West-by-god-wah-ginny is from a different planet, ain't it?" She increased her not-so-innocent pressure on the temporary headquarters for my brain.

In one instant, she revised my entire opinion of the neighborhood.

"Belongs to Dr. Sobel. He's semiretired two blocks back on Main. Mrs. Sobel mothers me, but she doesn't pry into my personal life," Melba said with heavy emphasis. "Come on. I'm dying for a drink."

Trailing her up the narrow stairs, I purposefully lagged two steps behind to catch the view.

By the time I reached the top, she stood waiting, just inside the darkened door.

"I don't have company very often. I hope you won't mind the mess." She seemed a trifle anxious.

"Don't be silly." I brushed close by her, fleetingly recalling the darkened entrance hall of Ginny's house the night before.

The living room was surprisingly large. In the center, a grouping of completely tasteless overstuffed furniture—a three-piece rose-beige sectional sofa and two chairs with oversized ottomans, all arranged around a triangular faux modern cocktail table—dominated the room.

Everywhere I turned, old-fashioned whatnot shelves of every description overflowed with trinkets and figurines.

Lace doilies graced the backs of the chairs and sofa.

Decidedly more Haverty's than Dorothy Draper or Martha Stewart.

"The furniture belongs to Mrs. Sobel." She was way ahead of me.

Most of the bric-a-brac were random, tasteless things—souvenirs of proms, carnivals, senior trips—obviously keepsakes of major events in her still-young life. On the sofa and chairs were scattered an array of silly, adolescent pillows emblazoned with the names of cities or places, and several stuffed animals rested here and there. She moved to the sofa, picked up an amazingly large pink panda and hugged it.

"Okay, so most of the tacky shit is mine. Can I help it if I'm still just a teeny-bopper at heart? Want to play high school principal and naughty cheerleader?" She winked lewdly.

Logan Baird, child molester.

"Let me take your jacket and tie." She moved to help.

I shrugged out of the jacket and tie and let her put them on a hanger.

"I'll hang them in my bedroom closet. Come fix us a drink before I give you the tour." She led the way across a small dining ell with a pass-through door opening into a neat kitchen with up-to-date paraphernalia.

"I love to cook. Keeps me busy." Prattling self-consciously, she hung the hanger on a cabinet knob. She opened a pantry door near the sink, revealing a well-stocked liquor supply on a shelf above the boxes of cereals, cake mixes, and baking supplies. "You be bartender. I'm not much of a drinker. Fix me a light gin and tonic and help yourself, okay?" She searched my face for a sign of approval.

"One gin and tonic coming up." I gave her a friendly hug and looked around at the apple-pie perfection of her kitchen. "You were kidding about the mess, right?"

"Not really. I'll bet your wife keeps a nice home for you."

There it was—out in the open. Sooner or later, I knew it was bound to come. I had never lied about my marriage. I wasn't about to start now. Anyway, she knew I was married. Might as well tell it all. With the hungry kiss and the unabashed groping in the van still burning my senses, I suspected she had more than fixing our dinner on her mind.

"Rose is a good housekeeper. But we have a son. Our house is rarely as neat as this unless Rose is having her bridge club over. Rose plays bridge a lot."

"Here the doctors' wives all play bridge. I suppose I ought to learn," she chattered on nervously. When she handed me the ice tray, her hands betrayed a slight tremble.

"Do you play bridge with Rose?"

"Sometimes, but only under threat of divorce," I laughed. "Frankly, cards bore me. Besides, I'm ususally on the road."

"They have bridge lessons for the employees at the hotel. I've been invited, but cards don't excite me much, either."

I twisted the plastic ice tray to loosen the cubes while Melba opened a cabinet and located a slender Collins glass. Dropping ice cubes in the glasses, I splashed a dollop of gin in one. She set a bottle of tonic on the counter.

"How old is your son?" She seemed determined to run the entire gamut of my family show and tell.

"Five . . . soon be six." An icy bead of sweat trickled slowly down my spine.

Was this some kind of pass-or-fail game?

"Is he Logan Jr.? Logan's a beautiful name."

"His name's John Paul." Tiny mouse teeth of guilt nibbled the margins of my lust.

"John Paul Baird." She smiled. "A man could run for president with a name like that."

"Never thought of that." I was feeling quite uncomfortable now.

"Do you ever take your family with you on the road?"

"Not lately. My marriage isn't working too well."

The understatement of the new century.

I watched her as I filled her glass with tonic. I wondered if I'd flunked or passed.

Reaching over, she turned on the oven and set the thermostat. Then she took a foil-covered platter out of the fridge. Peeling back the foil she unveiled two filet mignon steaks richly marbled with veins of fat. Turning back to the fridge, she removed a plate with two potatoes wrapped in foil and placed it beside the steaks on the counter by the stove.

"I precooked the potatoes for about forty minutes," she explained. "It's a trick one of the chefs at the hotel taught me."

Both chef and entrée were inarguably prime.

"Clever," I marveled at her ingenuity, among other things.

"The problem with your marriage. Is that because you're gone so much?"

"No, not really. The opposite, I'm afraid."

Her brow wrinkled into a frown. "I don't think I understand."

"Simple. If I weren't gone most of the time, we probably would've divorced a long time ago. We never should have married in the first place. We were high school sweethearts. All that hearts and flowers stuff only works in romance novels."

"I guess you're right," she sighed. "You're probably too good for her anyway."

"Hold on. Don't read me that way. She's a darn good mother. She just married the wrong guy. Okay?" I suddenly realized it was true. It was wrong to lay the blame entirely on Rose.

She shook her head. "You're something else." "I'll put your jacket in the closet and freshen up. Be right back." She grabbed the hanger and disappeared into the hall.

"Hey, wait. Where's the necessary?" I called after her.

"The what?" Melba stuck her head back around the corner.

"The powder room." I put my knees together and burlesqued dire distress.

"Oh! Down here at the end of the hall on the left. You can't miss it. The stereo is in the living room. Put on something very, very romantic." Her voice floated back from down the corridor.

It didn't take a genius to figure that the stereo didn't belong to old Doc Sobel's wife. In contrast to the middle-class furnishings, the components were state-of-the-art. I found a pair of Sinatra CDs and added a saccharine Kenny G to the changer—a full hour and a half of melodic aphrodisia. I pushed PLAY and adjusted the volume.

"I get along without you very well, of course I do . . . ," Sinatra reminded me.

Dedicated to Ginny, with a tender afterthought for Rose, my dear ball-busting wife.

I went back into the kitchen to build myself a drink.

Melba's collection of liquor seemed to run to Scotch and Canadian blends. I was about to settle for a half-filled bottle of George Dickel when I found an unopened bottle of Jack Black hidden at the back of the shelf. In a far corner of the cabinet, I discovered a set of double Old Fashioned glasses emblazoned with the Greenbrier *G*. I dropped in three cubes and sloshed the liquor on the rocks. When I put the ice tray away, I peeked in the refrigerator and saw a tossed salad in a glass mixing bowl covered with Saran wrap.

I picked it up and gave it a closer look.

Dewy fresh.

With two potatoes already half-done.

The truth finally dawned on me.

I needed a brain transplant.

The refrigerator was Melba's hope chest. Tonight was my lucky night. My watch showed 8:59. The night was young, and I felt absolutely bulletproof.

Swishing the Tennessee sour mash whiskey around the glass with a little motion of my wrist, I sniffed the bouquet, took a big swallow of the mellowed liquor, and rolled it around inside my mouth. The ripe fruity potion warmed me like the morning sun.

Taking another swallow, I headed for the loo.

The only illumination in the dim hallway was a narrow sliver of light from her bedroom, the door slightly ajar directly opposite the bathroom. As I fumbled for the bathroom light switch, a flicker of movement in the bedroom attracted my attention. Avoiding the light, I stepped closer and peered through the crack. I couldn't find her at first, but then I caught a movement in the mirror on the dresser and glimpsed her reflection. She had arranged my jacket and tie on a wooden hanger and was turning to hang it in the closet.

I turned back to the john, emptied my bladder, washed my hands, and checked my teeth. I opened the medicine chest and looked for some mouthwash.

Listerine . . . the oral liquid equivalent of granny's lye soap.

I put down my glass, took out the tube of toothpaste, squeezed out a little dab, and rubbed my teeth.

A sly old dog should always be prepared on a night like this.

Turning off the light, I stepped back into the darkened hall.

"When your lover has gone . . ." Sinatra drifted down the shadowed passageway.

The slender opening in her boudoir door beckoned what Freud would term my voyeurself.

Valiantly, I resisted.

Then, just as I turned to retreat back down the hall, there was another flicker of movement through the narrow cleft.

I edged closer to catch a better view.

Logan Baird, skulking pervert, didn't even say goodbye to his voyeurself.

My eyes had trouble adjusting at first. She'd cut off the overhead light and switched on the frilly lamp on the stand beside her bed. I couldn't find her in plain view, so I checked the mirror again. My vision adjusting to the light, I made her out. Wearing a half slip, panties, and strapless bra, she was standing in front of her closet carefully inspecting her dress for spots. Reassured the garment was unsoiled, she hung it on the rod.

I watched her balance on one foot and then the other as she removed her shoes and bent to place them on a shoe rack on the wall of the closet. The outline of her panties was clearly defined as the satiny fabric of the slip moved across them when she bent over, twisting this way and that, adjusting the shoes on the rack.

With a deft maneuver, she twisted the strapless brassiere around until the fasteners faced the front. Unfastening the bra, she placed it on the vanity bench. She pulled the slip off and laid it beside the bra.

Moving to the night stand beside her bed, she opened the drawer and took out a diaphragm kit. She unzipped the kit, carefully removed the long-handled inserter, and placed it on the bed. Then she took out the diaphragm, held it up against the soft peach lampshade, and gave it a careful look. When she was satisfied with its condition, she picked up the inserter, sat down on the side of the bed, affixed the diaphragm in position, and placed the apparatus back on top of the plastic kit. Finally, she removed the cap from a tube of spermicidal jelly and placed the tube beside the bag before she swung her feet up on the bed, lay back, raised her knees to her chest, and slipped off her panties. Her pubic triangle was an almost colorless shadow.

There were no secrets between us now.

Legs lifted and knees bent, she was displayed in all her glory.

There was an immediate and overpowering stirring in my groin. She was a feast for my prurient eyes. Ordinary as it might be, my stalwart old campaigner had a mind all his own. Totally unprepared for the compelling sensuality, I felt the blood rushing to my groin.

With exquisite care—in slow motion it seemed—she picked up the inserting device and the tube and carefully applied the jelly in long stripes up and down the creases of the diaphragm. Then she lifted her bottom even higher while she inserted the device.

"It never entered my mind . . ." In the living room, Sinatra was poking fun at me.

I'd never seen anything so overpoweringly erotic in my life.

She wiped the tube and the inserter, carefully zipped the bag, and replaced it all in the nightstand drawer. Wiping her hands on a tissue, she picked up her panties, went to the closet, and tossed them in. Back at the dressing table, she opened a large jar and removed one of those little premoistened wipes that women use to remove makeup. Lifting her right foot to the vanity stool and standing with her legs apart, she carefully cleansed herself. She repeated the entire ritual with a fresh wipe, the strokes slower and more sensual now.

Watching herself in the mirror, her eyes flicked in my direction.

"I see your face before me . . . ," Old Blue Eyes cautioned from down the hall.

Heart in throat, I backed out of the slice of light spilling across my face.

I held my breath.

Without so much as a blink of her eye, she returned to the task at hand. Taking her time, she dried herself on a little hand towel. When she'd finished, she lowered her leg and leaned forward to look at her face. She wrinkled her brow in a frown when she examined her nose. She paused, took another tissue and blotted her lipstick. Her eyes flicked to the partially opened door again, but I was out of the light. Now, she quickly resumed her ritual. Browsing her perfumes and colognes, she lifted and rejected a series of fancy bottles before she found the one she was looking for.

Removing the glass stopper, she touched it to each ear lobe.

As an afterthought, she dabbed inside her wrists before she replaced the stopper in the elegant bottle.

Her breasts were absolutely breathtaking—everything they'd promised under the peasant blouse. The outer area of the areolae were tight circles of the faintest pink, and the nipples were a slightly darker shade of the same delicate blush. Perfect little cones, they looked like tiny baby teats. It wasn't so much their size as it was their perfection of proportion and the solid thrust of their mass that caused me to draw in my breath sharply as I took them in.

Leaning forward again, she shook the perfume up against its glass top. Removing the stopper again, she drew a line under each breast. Then, she brushed the stopper lightly along each side of of her crotch, spreading her legs to get back around and all the way under.

When she was done she looked into the mirror again, did a pirouette, and raised her arms with mischievous delight.

She moved back out of my direct vision again, but I followed her in the mirror as she went to the closet and started searching through the clothes hanging from the racks.

Touching myself, I could feel where my juices had soaked through my slacks. My poor penis, painfully engorged and unnaturally bent, was trapped awkwardly in my underwear.

One final look at the seductive swell of her backside as she leaned into the closet, and I retreated regretfully into the bathroom to repair the damage and try to regain my composure.

"I'll never be the same . . ." Sinatra came muted through the bathroom door.

CHAPTER THIRTY-EIGHT

Sponging myself with a towel as best I could, I dried my bikini shorts and the large damp area where I'd leaked through my slacks. In the light, I found no glaring evidence showing through pants.

Happiness is wearing black pants on a hot date.

With a great deal of difficulty, I recaged my resistant erection inside my undershorts, folded the towel, and replaced it on the rack, smoothing it to match the one beside it.

Careful to turn off the light, I quietly exited. Heart pounding, resisting even a glance at the beckoning aperture to the bedroom, I slipped quietly back down the hall. Although it was still throbbing, my mutinous member had momentarily retreated into an uneasy truce.

I was standing by the sink, working on a double shot of the Tennessee sipping whiskey when Melba came back into the kitchen.

"Mere alcohol doesn't thrill me at all . . . ," Sinatra confessed my secret to the world.

"I just love Old Blue Eyes," Melba purred. "Did you find the powder room okay?"

The titillating idea that she might have known I was watching and had been putting on a tease sent a new wave of aggression surging through my unruly nether region.

Her smile was as inscrutable as the Sphinx.

She had changed into a pair of silky lounging pajamas of a delicate lilac shade—the perfect shade to compliment her almost silver-blonde natural color. The pants were tightly fitted over her hips and thighs all the way down to just above her knees, where they flared in wide bell-bottomed swishes to her ankles. The bolero top was off her shoulders, revealing an enticing cleavage. Dropping straight down from the points of her breasts, the skimpy top left her navel shamelessly exposed.

Gwyneth Paltrow doing Marilyn Monroe.

Quite obviously she wasn't wearing a thing underneath. Her nipples stood out in minute detail—even the tiny little bumps that circled the large areolae showed through the light silky knit. With a gravity-defying upward tilt, unconfined, her breasts jiggled and bounced underneath the fabric with an energy all their own. The image of her on the bed with her legs up against her chest left me weak.

"Do you like Sinatra?"

"Uh," I croaked, my throat dry. I took another sip and nodded, afraid to speak.

"Sorry I took so long. I wanted to get out of that dress and freshen up."

I finally understood the meaning of freshen up.

I just might write a book.

She handed me her glass. "Go light. I have champagne in the fridge to go with dinner. Don't you just love champagne?"

"Uh-huh." Still at my loquacious best, I turned to get the ice.

Busying myself with her drink, I felt a sudden blast of hot air as she put the half-baked potatoes in the preheated oven. When I turned back, she was standing closer.

"Whoa! Careful, don't get me tipsy. I'll never get our dinner." She giggled as she watched me absently slosh in the gin.

As she reached across to take the drink, I caught her delicate scent.

The erotic image of her touching the glass perfume stopper to her breasts and her perfect bottom flashed across my brain.

"I'll never be the same . . ." From beyond the pale, Sinatra was reading my mind.

She melted against me. Lips parted, her chin tilted up with an air of expectancy. The tiny currents of her breath were feathers against my face. She touched the tip of her finger to my tongue. Without taking her eyes off me, she reached around and set her glass on the counter, breasts pushing softly against my arm. With just the slightest hesitation, she raised up on her tippy-toes and, eyes wide open, she rested her lips lightly against mine.

Blindly, I set my own glass on the counter behind me. We stood, lips barely touching for a lingering moment.

"Round and round I go, down and down I go, caught in a spin . . ." Frankie swirled around us.

Our bodies scarcely brushing, my hands found her. I let them rest lightly at her bare waist, just below the edge of the bolero top—her abdomen was incredibly flat and firm. Taking my hands, she guided my hands gently upward until the tips of both thumbs touched the underside of her naked breasts beneath the loosely hanging blouse.

The conical baby teat nipples were erect.

When I lightly massaged them, she gasped. Inside my mouth, the flutter of her breath made me weak. A frisson of excitement rippled across my skin.

Her responding shiver was electric.

Sighing, she made a tiny pleading sound.

Now, she was leaning heavily against me, and I moved to steady myself against the kitchen counter. When her thigh touched the bulge of my swollen penis, she began grinding her upper leg back and forth with such a force I had to push her back. The curious pleasure-pain of the engorging blood pushing against the confines of my imprisoned member was unbearable.

"Don't you like it?" she asked, bewildered.

"I love it," I murmured, reaching down trying to free my penis. "But . . . this . . . damned thing has to go somewhere," I said, gasping between the words.

"Oh, poor baby. Here, let me." she breathed, dropping to her knees.

Kneeling on a little hooked rug emblazoned BLESS THIS HOME, she fumbled with the fastener of my slacks.

Helpfully, I reached down and undid the tab.

Before the slacks slid all the way to the floor at my feet, her fingers were already freeing my chiseled-marble phallus.

Released from its imprisonment, the eager warrior snapped straight upright.

"Oo-o my," she admired, giving it a kiss.

She clutched my throbbing member in both hands, and her mouth greedily closed over it. My hands went around the back of her head and held her motionless for perhaps a minute, fighting back from the brink of orgasm. After the initial intensity passed and I could stand the pleasure again, I pushed away and gently urged her to her feet.

"Come on," I said, my voice unrecognizable to my own ears. Forgetting I was fettered by my slacks, still encircled around my ankles, I tried to take a step and almost fell.

"Oops!" She giggled and bent to help.

Steadying myself on the counter, I stepped free. Without a word, she gathered up my clothes and turned off the oven.

"I hope the potatoes will be all right," she worried.

"Forget the potatoes," I croaked.

"But we're definitely going to need food later," she giggled again. Taking my hand, she pulled me toward the door.

"Won't matter. We're about to have a marvelous double suicide," I muttered, unbuttoning my shirt as I followed along.

In the bedroom, she turned toward the closet looking for a hanger. I pulled her back and tossed my shirt on the floor at the foot of the bed.

I dropped to my knees in front of her; her wispy pajama bottoms slid easily down her legs. She held onto my head now as she stepped free.

"Oh . . . oh, there." She took the back of my head now and widened her stance to give my busy tongue its way.

I'd barely begun, it seemed, before she stiffened and pulled my mouth sharply against her. She shuddered violently, struggling to pull away from my insistent attentions. My tongue persisted with its busy work, and she quickly gave in to me again.

No matter how I probed, I still couldn't get my tongue far enough inside her.

Far enough? A conundrum? Curious time to think of that.

"No, wait. I want you in me." She moved back and helped me to my feet.

Turning, she sat on the bed and collapsed back across the sheets. Perfect legs spread wide apart, she completely opened herself to me.

"Hurry . . . put it in me, now." I could feel my swollen tip enter her softness, but her maidenly tightness resisted penetration.

Despite both our efforts, the yielding of her passage was exquisite torture. Pulling roughly down, Melba hooked her feet behind my buttocks. One hand clasped hard around my neck, she forced her tongue inside my mouth, devouring.

In almost no time at all, I had to pull back and rest, as I was heading toward the brink.

Just as we began to make headway again, the bedside phone broke the silence with a raucous ring. "Oh spit!" she gasped.

"Can't we turn off that freaking bell?"

"No, I've got to take it. I'm on the beeper." She gave me a quick kiss and, scooting around, picked up the cordless just as it began another ring.

"Melba Noyes." All business now, she disengaged herself from beneath me, sat up, and turned on the light.

"Yes. I'm the nurse on call. Who is this?"

After a moment, she looked over at me and gave me an apologetic smile. Listening patiently to the caller, she covered the phone and whispered, "I'm sorry. Be right back."

Her perfect bottom bounced as she left the room and walked down the hall. I could hear her talking earnestly as I rolled over, reached down, and picked up my slender leather wallet, which had tumbled out of my trousers when I'd tossed them on the floor.

Right before my eyes, my son stared accusingly from a snapshot in my billfold.

Guiltily, I rolled out of the bed and slipped it back inside the pocket of my trousers.

As I gazed around the room, my eyes came to rest on a snapshot of me standing with Melba, tucked into a corner of her mirror. I remembered she'd had one of the secretaries take the photo at a coffee break during a recent business call at the clinic.

351

I realized that, over recent months, a sort of intimacy had blossomed between us. From time to time, I'd complained to her about my marriage. Had she misread my intentions? Reflecting on her innocence, I was ashamed.

I sat staring blankly into space as the guilt of my selfish charade earlier at Top Notch came flooding back over me. I stood and slowly gathered my clothes. When Melba came back in the room, I had dressed and was moving for the door.

"What?" Her face fell when she saw me dressed.

"I'm sorry. I can't go through with this." I spread my hands in despair.

"I don't understand. What's the matter? I'm sorry about the phone. Rotten luck, really. That's the first time I've had a call after-hours in a month. I've already called one of the other girls and had my calls forwarded. I promise it won't happen again."

"No, it's not the phone call. I just can't . . ."

She squeezed my hand and looked down to the diminished bulge at my crotch. "Don't worry, we can fix that in no time." She reached down and gave my bulge a pat.

I stopped her. "No, no. It's not that. We just can't—I mustn't—"

"But why? I don't understand. I thought you wanted me." Standing there almost naked, she looked bewildered—on the verge of tears.

"Oh, Melba, please don't. I more than just want you." I couldn't help myself and pulled her close. "You deserve better than this. It doesn't matter that my marriage stinks. I'm not about to give up my son. I don't want to just use you like this. Please understand."

"No wait!" She pushed me back. "You dumb jerk! It's you who doesn't get it. I know you're married. It doesn't matter. It's me who wants to abuse you!"

"But you're so—no. We just can't."

"Give it a rest! Come here and shut up. Maybe you won't respect me in the morning, but I've dreamed about this. Relax, you poor idiot. I'm not scheming to introduce you to my parents. No promises asked, no promises given."

"But—"

"You know something? You talk way too much." She lifted up on her toes and kissed me, her tongue busy as a hummingbird.

In almost no time at all, she pushed back, laughing at the embarrassing evidence of my total lack of character.

"You may say you value me only for my intellect, but your animal instincts betray you." Now, she was slowly undressing me. When I was fully naked again, she pushed me back on the bed. Straddling me on her knees, she wet me with her mouth and mounted me, struggling to impale herself on my throbbing organ. Straining against each other, we sweated and panted until finally, inch by inch, her yielding maidenhood eagerly admitted me all the way. Joined at last, we began moving in a measured rhythm against a lovely clinging, sucking tension.

She clenched her fists, arched back and raised her arms high above her head, the tight walls of her passageway contracting violently, driving me to the brink.

I felt myself disintegrating—cell by cell, my entire essence began rushing out of the end of me—as my brain imploded, pulling me inward in a blinding white light.

Afterwards, I thought I would never lose my erection and that she would never tire. I lost count, but she kept coming . . . over and over. And, unbelievably, at the very end, I came again.

Not in my wildest dreams, had I ever imagined anything could be like that.

CHAPTER THIRTY-NINE

I dozed.

I dreamed I heard a phone and gradually roused.

Straining to hear, I couldn't catch a sound.

I closed my eyes again . . . drifting.

"Logan, wake up! That was your wife, Logan. Wake up, baby, that was Rose! Wake up!" A hand was vigorously shaking my shoulder.

I made out a shadowy shape silhouetted against the dim outline of the doorway. Melba was standing above me, still clad in only her lavender bolero top.

"What?" I blinked against the darkness.

"Wake up! Damn it, Logan!"

"I am awake! What's going on?" My head was fuzzy. I'd had a lot to drink.

"That was Rose . . . your wife! My god! Please, Logan, honey, wake up!"

"Rose?" I sat bolt upright.

"Yes! Listen. I'm telling you, that was her on the phone. You've got to get out of here."

"What do you mean?" She wasn't making sense.

"Come on, damn it. Get dressed." She turned on the lamp. "Rose is at the hotel. She says she's coming here."

"What? That's a bunch of crap. Are you crazy? Rose, at the Greenbrier? No way. Somebody's pulling your leg." I still couldn't quite comprehend, but the urgency in her voice got my adrenaline flowing.

I swung my legs over the side of the bed. Groggily, I moved across and grabbed my pants off the floor.

"I'm serious. You should've heard her." Melba plopped on the side of the bed, watching me struggle into my trousers. When I looked back to her, she was sitting, shoulders slumped over, hugging herself, softly sobbing.

I walked across, put my hands behind her head, and pulled her face gently to my abdomen. "Come on now, Melba," I crooned. "It's a joke. I'm telling you, somebody's putting you on."

"No, you should've heard. She called me a slut . . . a goddamn whore. I've never had anyone talk to me like that. She said she was coming over here. Said she was going to scratch my . . . my . . . fucking eyeballs out," Melba sniffled.

"Look, baby, calm down. I know Rose. She never in her life said anything like that. Besides, I talked to her on the phone around six-thirty tonight." The clock beside the bed showed 10:33. "That's barely four hours ago, and she's in Melas. You know, outside Roanoke. I assure you it would take her at least three hours just to drive. She couldn't leave our son. Besides, my wife doesn't know White Sulphur Springs from Budapest. I'm telling you someone is playing us a dirty trick."

"But who?" She looked up at me.

In an instant, I came fully awake.

"Ginny!" I said, remembering her snub at the party.

Melba slowly nodded.

"Where're my shoes?" I asked.

"Living room. I found them in the kitchen."

She went to the closet and took out the hanger with my coat and tie.

"Okay, baby, just calm down. This is a bad joke. It's got to be that bitch Ginny. She's got a grudge against you. She was raised in an orphanage in my hometown. She has an old resentment against Rose too."

She wiped her tear-stained cheeks on the insides of her sleeves. "Ginny has a grudge against your wife?"

I nodded, walked to the vanity, and brought her a Kleenex.

She blew her nose and sat up straight, considering. "You're right. She does hate me. She put someone up to this?"

"Of course. You said yourself, she got one girl fired. She was pissed at you because her precious Cleveland had eyes for you tonight in front of all those people. Ginny's jealous. She—," I began, then stopped. I didn't dare tell Melba about last night.

"It's just the sneaky kind of thing she'd do. She's such a bitch."

"I'll fix us a drink. It's just a bad joke. The bitch may be watching the house, expecting me to run out of here. We can't let her ruin our evening."

"I don't know. I still don't want her making trouble for me at work. She's got a nasty mouth. She tried to make trouble for me once before, but Dr. Robothom stopped her. She got poor Nell Hernandez fired because she thought that Cleveland was trying to date her."

I led her into the kitchen and got a tray of ice.

"You can make mine a stiff one now," she laughed shakily.

I handed her a muscular drink, poured myself a double shot of the Black Jack, and tossed it back.

Despite the early hour, I was a little more than slightly hungover. My mouth was as dry as a debutante's meatloaf; my head felt like a balloon.

The secret to managing hangovers lies in the fact that the cause and the cure are the same. A true alky may die with a bad liver, but he never gets hangovers.

I took a deep breath and waited.

In less than the time it took Rush Donald to tell a lie, I was feeling better.

Nothing like a little hair of the proverbial dog.

Encouraged, I poured the double Old Fashioned glass nearly half full again.

This time I took a normal swallow.

Melba had stopped sniffling. Even with her eyes red and slightly puffy, she looked good enough to make the pope forget his vows.

She had put on bikini panties with the bolero top.

My anatomy responded with admiration. The old highwayman was not dead by a long shot.

"What did she say?" I asked, my mind already wandering to more pleasant things.

"When I first picked up the phone, she asked to speak to Logan Baird . . . smooth as honey. I first thought that it was that New York woman looking for your boss. The one who took a bite out of his penis." Melba giggled, feeling better. "Anyway, whoever it was took me by surprise. My god, I almost told her to wait and I'd go wake you. But thank goodness I caught myself." She took another swallow of her drink.

"For chrissakes!"

What if the caller really had been Rose?

My stomach did a turn.

"Don't worry. When I got my wits, I just said, 'Who?' Then she started in on me. She said, 'Don't play dumb with me. You know who. I know he's there, you whore.' It got worse. When I could get a word in, I told her that she was mistaken. She yelled that she was in your room at the hotel and if she found out where I lived, she was coming over here to get you. She was screaming at me. I told her that if she didn't leave me alone, I'd call the cops."

"What'd she say to that?"

"She said she'd see who called the cops."

"She may call back," I said. It occurred to me that Ginny might. "Don't worry. If she does, then call her bluff. Tell her that I'm too nice to fool around and besides you wouldn't go out with a married man anyway. Play along and hold the phone away from your ear. I want to listen."

"No way. If the phone rings again, I'm not about to answer it," Melba protested.

"If you don't, whoever it is will let it ring all night. You don't want to put up with that, do you?"

"Well . . . no."

"Besides, you're on call. Come here." I put down my drink and held out my arms.

She moved closer and leaned into me. I turned up her face and kissed her, probing deeply.

She stirred, and I let my hand slide down over her buttocks and pulled her close. Slipping my hand inside her top, I massaged her nipples

Her tongue got very busy in my mouth. I could feel myself getting hard again.

Reaching down, she forced her hand between us and squeezed my stalwart. Pulling back, she unzipped me and took me in her hand.

"You said I'd killed you," she admired.

"I lied."

"Are you really an ordinary earthling?" she murmured affectionately.

"Just little ol' me." I stuck my tongue in her ear. "My people only want plutonium for our space ships and microchips for our children."

She shivered, stepped back, pulled her top over her head, and quickly stepped free of her panties. "Come in the living room, I want you on the sofa. Leave me some memories for when you're away."

Making plans already?

Naked now, she skipped across the room.

I marveled at that absolutely perfect ass.

Sitting on the sofa with her legs in a sort of lotus position, shamelessly she invited me. I shucked out of my clothes again and dropped to my knees in front of her.

"Oh, honey." She arched her back against the sofa and stretched her arms high over her head. After awhile she pushed my head gently back. "Wait. I don't want to come that way again. I want you in me."

She moved around so that she was bent over on her knees facing away with her elbows resting on the back of the sofa. "Do me now." She took her hands and guided me into her from behind.

Sinatra crooned, "One for my baby and one more for the road . . ."

The perfection was destroyed by the jangle of the phone.

"Shit!" I muttered.

"Just let the damn thing ring," she purred as I reached around and cupped her breasts, struggling to keep the rhythm.

After a half-dozen rings there was no sign of stopping.

"I better get it. I handed off my call, but I'm still on backup."

"No, it's just Ginny again, I'd bet anything."

"You really think? Oo, I love that," she purred, making no attempt to move.

I lost count of the rings.

"Damn." She pulled away. "I'll have to take it. It could be Dr. Robothom."

Reluctantly, I rolled aside. "Hurry. Let's not lose our place."

She twisted, leaned across, and started to pick up the phone.

"Wait," I whispered. "Hold it up, so I can hear it too."

"In the kitchen, on the wall by the door. Pick up when I answer. Be careful not to let them hear."

I stepped over to the pass-through and nodded for her to pick up.

"Hello." I listened as Melba answered, covering the mouthpiece with my hand.

"Let me speak to Logan Baird. Quit playing games, I know he's there, you bitch."

My gubernaculum contracted violently.

Rose! No mistake. She sounded very drunk.

"Look, I'm sorry, ma'am. I already told you, you have the wrong number."

"Listen, you slut, I know that no-good son of a bitch is there. Tell him that his wife wants to talk to him."

"Ma'am, why don't you just go to bed and get a good night's rest. I'm sure you'll feel better in the morning."

"Don't patronize me, you whore. Let me speak to Logan. I'm on to him. Tell him he's a dead duck. Ginny McKim told me he was fuckin' you. I'm waiting right here in his room. He won't get by with this."

"Hang up," I silently mouthed the words and signaled Melba to put the phone down, but she'd turned her back, struggling to reach her drink on the cocktail table.

"Ma'am, I really don't know what this is about, but if your husband is the Logan Baird who works for the pharmaceutical company, I know who he is and I can tell you he wouldn't cheat on his wife. And ma'am, I've never been out with a married man in my life."

"You're not fooling me, you whore."

It was Rose all right—drunk as a hoot owl. I couldn't believe my ears.

"I'm warning you, ma'am. Don't call me anymore. You've made a terrible mistake. You wouldn't want me to file a complaint and embarrass you, now would you? Besides, I'm on to you, Ginny."

"Ginny? Ginny McKim? Listen, you goddamn slut, I'm not Ginny McKim. She's the one who told me. That orphan bitch's trying to get back at me."

"Just fuck off, Ginny. Enough is enough already. Now, good night." Melba hung up. She caught me by surprise. I was left with the open line.

"Bitch? Are you still there? Who's there? Logan, are you listening on this line?" Rose screamed as I gently placed the phone back on the hook.

My knees went weak. Leaning against the countertop to steady myself, I slopped some more Jack Daniels over the melted cubes in my glass and drank it down without waiting for it to chill.

"How was I?" Melba called from the living room. "Now she knows I caught on to her, I bet Ginny McKim is about to shit her panties. Serve the bitch right."

Oh God!

"Come back in here, lover. Don't leave me all turned on like this."

I walked into the room and without a word started putting on my clothes.

"What's the matter?" She looked at me, surprised. Then she saw my face.

"Oh no, Logan. Was that . . . ?"

I nodded.

"Oh, no."

"Gotta go." I already had my loafers on. I grabbed my jacket and tie.

"You sure?"

I nodded again.

"My god!" she whispered. "How?"

I shrugged. "Don't worry, I'll cover our ass. Trust me, shug, I'd die before I'd confess. Rose and Ginny are old enemies. I'll just tell Rose I was out at the Camellia. Charlie Zaharias will cover for me. It's early. I'll go straight out there from here. Take your phone off the hook for an hour or two." My heart was pounding. I kissed her lightly on the nose. "I'll call you at the clinic tomorrow as soon as the coast is clear. Now turn out the lights and go to bed."

"God, suppose she does show up here. What'll I do?"

"Don't worry. I know Rose. She wouldn't do that in a million years," I tried to sound reassuring, but my gut was churning. I was sweating from pure, unmitigated fear.

"Yeah? That's what you said when I told you she had called."

I made no response to that. She had me there.

When I made it back to the main drag, I drove slowly back past the main entrance of the hotel, halfway afraid I'd see Rose's SUV coming out from between the gateposts. Now that I'd had time to think it over, it occurred to me that my story that I was at the Camellia Club wasn't all that great. What if Charlie Zaharias wasn't there? Worse. What if he wouldn't stick his neck out?

Would you, I asked myself. Well?

I hardly knew the man.

"Shit! Shit! Shit!" I banged the steering wheel.

I slowed the car, made a tight U-turn and headed back through town.

> HOT SPRINGS 41
> COVINGTON 25
> ROANOKE 71

I'd seen that sign a hundred times before. Now, it leaped out at me.

I glanced at the gas gauge.

Nearly full.

I pushed the accelerator to the floor.

I wasn't about to lose my son.

CHAPTER FORTY

Even midweek at eleven o'clock at night it's hard to make time over the mountains between White Sulphur Springs and Melas. The road is torturous, but at that time of night at least there is no traffic and, best of all, no cops.

Negotiating the tedious, harrowing drive, I rationalized that, maybe, with all the booze and my sudden fear and guilt at being caught, I'd been mistaken, that the voice belonged to Ginny after all.

I knew better.

I finally pulled up in front of our house about five minutes before the witching hour. I'd covered the seventy-odd miles in just under an hour.

I breathed a silent thank you that the house was dark and the drive was empty. In this tight-assed neighborhood, people were nosy. I cut the lights and got out of the car, careful not to slam the door. Fumbling nervously with my keys, I quietly let myself in the front door.

Even unlit, the house had an eerie empty feeling. My toe hit a plastic toy and sent it skittering noisily across the floor to collide with another toy that had a bell.

Nerves jangled, I closed the door, pulled the drapes, and turned on the light. I anxiously checked the clock—11:59.

Wasting no time, I quickly inspected the rooms.

Empty.

Any last hope that I'd been mistaken disappeared.

The thought of losing Paul brought a numbing chill.

Now or never.

No time to waste.

I knew exactly what I had to do.

Feeling shaky, I retraced my steps into the kitchen and turned on the light. I found the fixings and quickly made myself a Bloody Mary. Gulping a big swallow of the spicy liquid, I refilled the depleted quantity with vodka, took the wall phone off the hook, and dialed my parents' number.

"Dad?" I was surprised when he picked up on the second ring.

"Logan? Where the hell are you?"

The best defense is a good offense.

My dad had taught me that before I caught my first varsity kickoff in high school. I had been thirteen and scared to death then, too. First play from scrimmage, with the ball on our twenty, I threw a pass that went for a touchdown. The coach didn't know whether to hug me or bench me.

"I'm home, Dad. The question is, where the hell is Rose?"

"Home? Rose said you were at the Greenbrier."

"I am. I mean, I'm just heading back there. What in hell's going on?"

"You tell me. Rose called us about eight all shook up. Said some woman called. Said she was going to leave Paul with your neighbor lady, Martha. She asked us if we'd come get him. When we got there to pick up Paul, Martha said Rose was headed for the Greenbrier." My dad stopped and paused for breath.

So far, so good.

I took another swallow of my drink.

"What's this all about? What're you doing back here? Didn't Rose call you? Are you in some kind of trouble? What's this about a woman? I thought I raised you better." Poor Dad was in quite a state.

Dad was straight-arrow all the way. He'd always loved me. But he was right. He had taught me better.

"Woman? Dad, don't be absurd. This is crazy. Sounds like Rose has let her imagination get the best of her," I lied. I was getting pretty good at it. But there was a lot at stake.

My *cajones*, for instance.

"What the devil's going on? Your neighbor said Rose tore out the driveway like a bat out of Hades."

"Beats me. I talked to her about six-thirty. She seemed okay. She was pissed a little about me running into one of our old high school teachers night before last. Now she lives over there. Rose has some old grudge against the woman. I didn't think there was any big deal about it. Women! They're all crazy. Damned if I can figure it out."

There was a pause while my father took it in.

I waited and took a hopeful sip of my drink.

"She said something about a phone call. Isn't that the darnedest thing. She's there to be with you, and you're back here." He still sounded suspicious. "Why'd you come back here, anyway?"

"I left some important papers. My boss was raising hell. I tried to call here, and then I tried to call you and got no answer, so I decided to drive over and get them myself. To tell the truth, I thought I might talk Rose into coming back with me in the morning. That is if you and Mom would keep Paul. A vacation would do Rose good. Now she's already there. Damned if I can figure her out."

"Women! You two must have passed each other on the road. What a mess. Who'd believe it?"

"I'm worried now. Let me call over there and see if she's showed up. I don't know if they'd let her in my room. God, I hope she didn't turn around and start back home. I'll call right back, okay?"

"Yeah. Now you've got me worried too. Mom's asleep with Paul. Go ahead and call. I'll stay right by the phone." He broke the connection.

I took another drink, sucked in my breath, and dialed the Greenbrier.

"This is Logan Baird. I'm in twelve fifty-nine. I—"

"Oh, yes, Mr. Baird. We've been trying to locate you." The clerk sounded relieved.

"Never mind that. Has my wife shown up there? There's been a crazy mix-up. We got our signals crossed," I blurted nonstop.

For the Best Original Dialogue in a Life-or-Death Situation, the envelope please.

"Yes, sir, she's here. She had identification. We let her in your room. I hope that's all right?" the clerk asked anxiously.

"Perfectly all right, just fine. I'm relieved. Will you connect me please?" I held my breath.

"Yes, sir. Of course."

"Uh, hello?" Rose answered tentatively.

"Rose? Would you mind telling me just what the devil's going on?" I said, my voice fairly dripping righteous indignation.

"Logan? You . . . son of a bitch. Where are you?"

"Rose, I'm home, for chrissake. Goddamn it, Rose, I just talked to my father. Have you lost your mind? What the hell's going on?"

Chew on that, you sneaky bitch.

"Home? You mean in Melas?"

"Are you drunk, Rose? What other home do we have?"

Silence.

"Oh, no! You bastard, you can't fool me. You're with that whore. You were listening on the phone. I'm going to kill you, you sleazy bastard."

"Rose, what the hell are you raving about? What's wrong with you?"

I remembered I had left plenty of booze there in the room.

"Have you been drinking, Rose?"

"I'm not drunk, you son of a bitch. Where are you, anyway? Are you still there with that goddamn slut? You just wait—"

"Listen to me, Rose, I just told you, I'm home. I came back to get some papers Rush needed. I was going to spend the night here with you and try to talk you into coming back with me in the morning."

"Oh, don't give me that."

I waited. An edge of doubt was creeping in.

"Logan? Are you still there?"

"Right here, Rose. That's what I'm trying to tell you, honey."

If my skinny ass hadn't been hanging out in the breeze, I'd have laughed out loud.

"Logan, you can't get away with this. I know where you really are."

"Look Rose, let's start over. I'm going to hang up the phone. This time you call me."

"Where?"

"Goddamn it, Rose, you are drunk. I'm at home. Call me back." I hung up.

I sipped my drink more slowly. I wondered how many drinks I'd had since we finished the golf. I'd started again around seven at Scotty Brown's reception. Then there was all the Jack Black at Melba's.

I still wasn't out of the woods, and I was beginning to feel the wear and tear.

Not good. I shuddered, thinking about the result of Rush's two-day binge.

The phone jangled the stillness of the empty house.

"Hello?"

"Oh, Logan, you are home. I don't understand—"

"That makes two of us. What are you doing there when I came over here to get you?"

All at once I felt positively omniscient.

"That goddamn bitch Ginny called me and said, 'Wanna know where your husband is?'" Rose mimicked Ginny with a high pitch. "Then she told me, 'He's fucking Melba Noyes.'"

I didn't say anything. I wasn't about to sound defensive.

"Logan, how could you? I've never been so humiliated in my life. How could you do this to me?" She burst into tears.

"Do what? Rose, you've got to get a grip." I waited for the sobbing to subside.

"I want a divorce," she sniffled.

"A divorce? Rose, I haven't done a blessed thing."

"Don't try to fool me," she said.

"Rose, dammit, listen. Don't you know that anybody can say anything they want about anybody they want to—any time they want to. I can't help—neither one of us can help—what Ginny McKim says. Give me a break." I struck the perfect note of righteous innocence.

"But, why would she say—"

"Think about it, Rose," I interrupted "You told me yourself Ginny hated you. She's just trying to pay you back for whatever it was between you two back in high school. And you played right into her hands. It's okay. I forgive you, babe. Just hang on. I'll be there in about three hours. There's ice and some liquor on the credenza. Fix yourself a toddy and try to get a nap. Okay? No real harm done."

I hoped I didn't get struck by lightning.

"No harm? Oh, God, Logan, I called that . . . that nurse, Melba Noyes, and gave her a piece of my mind. I was so sure." She still wasn't totally convinced.

"You called Melba Noyes? Damn it, Rose, do you know who Melba Noyes is? I'll get fired for sure."

"What? What do you mean? Because she's a nurse? Get real."

"Rose, Melba Noyes is the appointment nurse at the Main Street Clinic, Dr. Robothom's girl Friday. Don't you ever stop and think? What the hell did you do that for?"

"But Ginny said—"

"Rose, stop and think about it. Ginny McKim's the bitch you were warning me about tonight, just a couple of hours ago." I really laid it on. "Okay, okay, never mind. What's done is done." I let a note of resigned doom creep into my voice.

"Rose, when word gets out, I'll be dead around here. Rush will probably fire me in the morning, as soon as Robothom calls Teaneck and complains."

"Rush Donald? Just let him try. I dare him. When I got here tonight, I saw that two-bit Romeo smooching some hussy in the lobby, hanging all over her. They headed for the elevators. Just let him try to fire you, and I'll give his precious Nadine an earful. Don't worry, I'll take care of Mr. Rush Donald."

"Oh, Rose, don't jump to conclusions. That woman was probably the research chemist from the foundation. She was embarrassingly drunk earlier, and Rush was probably trying to help her to her room. You know drunks. He was just trying to do a good turn and keep the poor woman out of trouble." This was getting way more complicated than I'd bargained for. "Besides, Robothom will call Teaneck. He's an old friend of Gert Kearns."

"Can't you just go to Robothom and this Melba person and explain? Tell them everything. They'll understand."

"Maybe. Of course, you're going to have to apologize to Melba Noyes."

Easy boy! Best quit while you're still ahead.

"I couldn't. You don't know what I said. I called her twice. I just couldn't." She was sobbing again.

"Don't worry, hon. I can probably go back to work at the paper." I exuded self-sacrifice.

"We can't live on a reporter's pay. We'll never get a new house," she wailed.

I felt a twinge of conscience, but after all, I was fighting to keep my son—not to mention my overactive *cajones*. Rose would have them bronzed for sure unless I played out my hand.

"Calm down and stop crying. I'll never get back there if I don't get off this phone. And Dad is probably going crazy wondering what happened to me. I promised I'd call right back."

My watch showed 12:25 now.

"Go to sleep. I'll see you sometime after 3:30." I didn't want her to realize the drive was shorter than she'd thought.

"Be careful. And please hurry. I've really made a mess. I'll never get to sleep."

"Just try to forget the whole thing, Rose. It'll all work out."

"Can you ever forgive me?" Now she was sobbing again.

I felt a tiny twinge of guilt. I didn't want to punish her, but my whole life was on the line.

"Fix yourself a toddy, Rose, and you'll feel better. It's not the end of the world. I'm going to hang up now, or I'll never get back there." I hung up softly.

Without replacing the phone, I dialed again.

"Dad?"

"Yeah? Is everything okay?" Poor guy, he was thoroughly confused.

"Uh-huh. I got Rose. She's safely there. Women . . . they're all nuts. I'm heading back now. Thanks for coming to Paul's rescue. We'll call tomorrow, okay?"

"Okay. Are you sure everything's all right?"

"Really, Pop, I'm sure."

"All right. Be careful, son."

"Not to worry." I replaced the phone.

I turned out the kitchen light but hesitated at the front door. I went back into Paul's bedroom and turned on the light. The faded press pass with Sam Snead's signature was on Paul's mirror. I turned out the light. An unexpected welling of emotion brought me to the verge of tears.

On the way back down the hall, I stopped and groped my way into the spare bedroom that doubled as my office. I found the box with the unfinished manuscript of my novel and thought about John Paul's letter.

Backing out of the drive, I absently hummed the refrain from the old Ledbelly chain gang song, "Make a long-time man feel bad, Lawdy, Lawdy . . . when he don't get a letter from home."

THURSDAY, THE WEE SMALL HOURS

CHAPTER FORTY-ONE

Heading back across the mountains, I shuddered to think how close I'd come to letting Rose catch me with Melba.

It certainly would have destroyed our marriage. I would have lost my son.

But I was breathing easier now. So far, so good—my brilliant scheme was working like a charm.

Still, I really didn't want to hurry. I was pretty sure Rose believed my story. I knew she wanted to. But, if I got back to the Greenbrier too soon, I'd just stir up her suspicions again.

After I crossed the last mountain and passed by the shadowy cluster of majestic old brick ruins at Sweet Chalybeate Springs, I was surprised to see a youngster walking disconsolately along the road. He was wearing new jeans and a clean chambray work shirt. In his right hand, he was carrying a canvas gym bag.

I slowed and moved toward the middle of the narrow two-lane to give him plenty of room in case he was drunk, but as I drew closer I saw that he was steady enough on his feet.

When I pulled abreast, he turned his head and half-heartedly stuck out his thumb. I flicked my headlights up and caught a clear glimpse of his face. He looked young. I guessed fourteen or fifteen at the most.

Guiltily, I passed on by and glanced up at my rearview mirror, wondering what a young boy was doing out in the middle of the night. He kept trudging right along, looking forlornly at my taillights.

On impulse I pulled to a stop and beeped the horn.

As he broke into a sprint, I checked to see if my doors were locked. Ordinarily I never would have stopped, not even in broad daylight—not when suicide bombers terrorized the world and decent men walked city streets filled with fear. But pondering Jean Paul's death and thinking how close I had come to losing my son were doing funny things to my judgment.

By the time he came jogging up beside me and tried the door handle, I had already lowered the window on the passenger side a few inches.

"Where you going?" I asked through the crack in the window, keeping my hand firmly on the door release.

"White Sulphur . . . Covington. Unless you're going to Charleston or Richmond maybe. I just want the nearest bus station." He peered in at me wistfully.

"I'm going to White Sulphur. That okay?"

"Sure, that's great."

"Get in," I said and released the lock.

He opened the door, put the gym bag on the floor, and scooted into the seat.

"Man, I'm evermore glad to see you. I figured I'd have to walk all the way to White Sulphur. That's the closest. The early bus to Charleston leaves at seven. At this rate, I'd never make it."

"Buckle up," I said and took a closer look at him.

As young as he looked, he had attained almost his full growth. He looked a little older than I had originally guessed. Up close his right eye looked puffed; his lip was bruised and slightly swollen.

My heart started thumping.

I had second thoughts.

"What happened to your face?" I didn't want to start the car rolling and have any unpleasant surprises.

It was night.

I was alone.

"My stepdaddy's drunk. Slapped the snot out of me. Last time for him though. He'll never lay another hand on this ol' boy."

"Oh? Why's that?" The implication sounded ominous. I turned, trying to prepare myself for anything.

"I'm gone. Outta here. Never coming back," he said. "I'm sick of his sorry shit. The drinking and beating. He's always beating on me and Mama. She won't leave. She drinks with him now. Wasn't always that way though, leastways not when my real daddy was still around. Anyhow, I stuck it out with her as long as I could. She's welcome to the son of a bitch. I already finished high school. If I can't find work, I'm gonna join the army. My real daddy was in the army."

"How old are you?"

"Eighteen in two weeks."

I looked him over. Freckle-faced with tousled copper hair, he reminded me of John Paul.

I relaxed.

"Shut the door," I said and let the car roll forward.

I set the radio low on a country music station. Not a word passed between us until we were past Crows, where Route 158 forks east toward Covington.

"Where's your real daddy?" I finally asked to break the silence. I turned up the AC a notch. I was getting a little drowsy now.

"Dead . . . in the war."

"Oh." I thought that over. "Where? Beirut? Desert Storm?"

"Naw, Bosnia. And after two tours in Nam. Ain't that a real kick in the head? Anyway, SOB Lester just married my mama so's he could drink up my daddy's life insurance. I was twelve when my daddy went off to war. My daddy taught me things. My daddy was real good to me."

I couldn't think of anything to say. I remembered how my father had taught me how to throw and pass and kick a football. He used to take my brother and me to ball games and fishing.

"You ever in the military?"

I swallowed hard. My throat felt dry.

"Army," my voice cracked.

We drove through the tunnel of night, the lush, forested mountains towering above us on one side and the steep creek bank dropping off on the other. It was easy to trace the crooked path of the stream with the moon sparkling off the rippling water. I thought about my son's namesake, my brave buddy Lt. John Paul Silver, and the war. This ghostly road reminded me of a road north of Sarajevo, except most of the trees there had been blasted or burned away by artillery and rockets the last time John Paul and I had laid eyes on it.

"My real daddy didn't drink no liquor, wouldn't allow it in the house. My granddaddy still won't, but it don't matter. Granddaddy's on his last legs now. Your daddy drink much?"

"No. When I was real little he'd have an occasional beer. He used to umpire professional baseball. He quit drinking the beer when my brother and I were old enough to understand. Said he didn't want to set a bad example."

"Mostly Lester drinks beer, too, but it don't matter. Liquor or beer, it's all the same what it does to him. Did your daddy get mean when he was drinking?"

"No. My father doesn't have a mean bone in him." Thinking it over, I laughed and added, "He still doesn't curse much in front of me."

"My real daddy neither."

"I was in Bosnia. I'm real sorry about your father. Over there we had a saying that everybody has a bullet with their name on it. I was pretty lucky, I guess."

He mulled that over. Finally, he asked, "You got any kids?"

"One. A boy, John Paul. He's five, almost six."

He brightened. "Good! You play with him much, teach him things?"

"Not as much as I should, I guess. I travel for a living. I'm gone a lot." It occurred to me now that I might change that if I really wanted to.

"Oh, sure, everybody's got to work. But I bet you're good to your kid. A boy ain't got a damn chance without a daddy." His voice hoarsened at the end.

I couldn't look at him now.

In the headlights, the sign marking the West Virginia line loomed ahead.

I remembered I'd been meaning to buy Paul a kite. I'd always wanted to try a box kite. They looked interesting. Now, it came flooding back over me how my daddy used to make my brother and me kites—big solid three-stickers. Sonsabitches needed a stiff breeze to get 'em up, but once they were up there, they'd fly forever. Took a strong man to get 'em down.

Funny time to be thinking about that now.

His laugh broke the silence. "You know, I think the hardest part was having to leave my mangy old hound dog. Your kid got a dog?"

"No, but I'm working on it."

My throat hurt, and my chest was as empty as downtown L.A. on Sunday morning.

In White Sulphur Springs, I stopped in front of the all-night place next to where the Trailways stopped.

"So long and good luck," I said.

"Thanks," he replied, reaching for his duffel.

He got out and stood beside the car, waiting for me to start moving.

On impulse, I fished in my pocket, found a twenty, and let the window down.

"Here." I reached across and stuck it in his hand.

"Oh, no! I can't take that mister. You've got your own family—"

"Go on, take it. Maybe pass it on someday." My voice broke.

"But—"

I lost his words as I rolled up the window and let the car start rolling.

In the mirror, I saw him look down at the twenty. He looked up and gave a wave.

"Good luck," I breathed into the empty darkness.

I didn't even know his name.

I slowed as the entrance to the Greenbrier appeared.

So far, so good. Rose would be blissfully asleep. Her suspicions about the memorable Melba would be only a disturbing dream by morning.

But why was I missing that old exhilaration that always came after I'd walked unscathed through certain disaster?

Did I believe that crap about having a bullet with your name on it? I was getting to be a world-class expert at dodging bullets. After all, any man worth his salt made his own luck.

Nothing ventured, nothing gained.

But I still couldn't shake this damn ache in the back of my throat. And my chest felt like it had a big hole in it with a cold wind blowing through.

I wondered why I felt rotten.

CHAPTER FORTY-TWO

My good luck was running full throttle. I found my old space still vacant. Retrieving the box containing my manuscript from behind the driver's seat, I glanced up at the stars and walked through the cool night air contemplating fathers and sons.

And karmic grace.

A mere few hours ago, I had been a condemned man walking his last mile. Now, I had just dodged another bullet—a last-second reprieve by my all-seeing cosmic travel agent.

At night the old hotel, its graceful white-columned facade dramatically highlighted with concealed lighting, looked more like a Maxfield Parrish painting than ever—but, oddly enough, it no longer appeared aloof.

It struck me as nothing short of amazing that what had always been my symbol of unattainability now warmly beckoned me.

I mused tiredly on the chimerical quality of reality.

In the diminishing wake of adrenaline, was it extreme fatigue or a newfound glimmering of self-worth that altered my perception?

In the course of one evening, I had been handed the promise of John Paul's trust fund and Ian Ferguson had put my writing on a pedestal.

Now that I had options, did I even want Rush's job? I knew I could be a *Wunderkind* in Teaneck without breaking a good sweat, but was it actually worth the effort?

Too tired to ponder the imponderable, I shrugged. At the moment, I was running close to empty.

My momentary depression lifted as the night man on the door saluted and smiled when I handed him my keys. To him, odd people at odd hours were hardly out of the ordinary.

"I left it in the same slot." I bid him good night and saluted as I went smiling down the steps and crossed the lobby to registration, wondering if Ferguson might have left word about tomorrow.

"Anything for Logan Baird, twelve-fifty-nine?" I asked as if Logan Baird always checked his messages at three in the morning.

"Oh yes, Mr. Baird. Your wife, she—"

I raised my hand to interrupt. "I know. Sorry for the mix-up. Thanks for handling it."

"Our pleasure. No problem."

"My messages?" I reminded him, still smiling.

"Yes, of course." He handed me a small sheaf of papers from the box.

"Thanks. Have a good night," I called over my shoulder as I thumbed through the squares of paper.

Two calls from Rose: 7:50 and 7:59.

Call Home.

A personal note from Rush—at 12:59 in the morning.

Logan: What's Rose doing here? Call me ASAP.

I struggled to keep from laughing out loud. I could just see him lying up in his room in a pool of cold sweat, staring into the darkness.

There was a tiny envelope with a plain card like the ones that florists use.

9:55 P.M.
I meant it—you really are beautiful. I'll never forget last night. Someday you'll thank me.
Ciao
P.S. Give Rose my best.

No signature—not even an initial.

The vindictive bitch couldn't resist giving the knife a final twist.

Blind-embossed in Helvetica type on the flap, the final envelope bore the legend:

MACKENZIE BROWN
Hidden Beach, Key West, Florida

My breath came faster.

Inside, the heading on the folded note card was blind embossed again:

MACKENZIE BROWN

Dear Logan Baird:

Ian Ferguson suggests you would be a valuable addition to our 10:00 press conference at the Valley View Estate House tomorrow morning. If you could come early, I'm having a few special people in for breakfast at Top Notch around 8:30. I'm looking forward to the opportunity to talk with you.

Best,
Scotty Brown

Scotty Brown and Ian Ferguson.
What did those two have up their sleeves?
Was Jake Chetauga right?
Could Ferguson really be serious?
All at once, my karma seemed to be mocking me.

Heart racing and my knees rapidly turning to Jell-O, I increased my stride, bounding up the wide staircase two steps at a time. In the alcove off the deserted upper lobby, the open elevator stood beckoning.

My Timex showed 3:15 as I quietly let myself into the room.

From the half-open door to the bathroom and a narrower crack in the closet door, twin slivers of light traced soft patterns across the lush green carpet.

Sprawled across the bed, Rose was asleep, her slip crawled all the way up, exposing her delectably rounded bottom. The very picture of womanly innocence, her lovely derrière encased in plain white nylon panties was powerfully erotic—an absolute miracle in my exhausted state.

Tiptoeing across the thick carpet, I carefully placed the handful of message slips and the manuscript box on the lamp table. Crossing back, I slipped quietly inside the walk-in closet and pulled the door quickly closed, careful not to flood the room with sudden light. Hurriedly, I slipped out of my loafers, pulled off my socks, and dropped them on the shoes. Without a sound, I hung my jacket on a hanger, looping the tie across its shoulders.

Looking down to unfasten the tab of my slacks, I stopped cold. Where I'd tried to wash away my earlier flood of juices, it had dried into one scabrous patch of crusty, white residue.

Wriggling free, I carefully rolled the slacks into a tight wad and quickly shed my underwear. My briefs were crusty too. Without even bothering to look, I removed my shirt, wadded everything into a hotel laundry bag, and placed it behind my duffel on the back of the closet shelf. Searching my suitcase for clean underwear, the thought occurred to me that I should sniff my hands.

Melba's muskiness was intensely erotic and arousing.

I crossed quietly into the bathroom, closed the door, and started the shower. Without waiting for the water to run completely warm, I stepped in. Teeth chattering, I started to lather myself. Giving little thought to caution now, I scrubbed as if I'd been contaminated by atomic fallout. If I awakened Rose, at least I'd be free of the evidence before I had to get close enough to incriminate myself.

When I finished, I reentered the bedroom wrapped in the luxurious oversized bath-sheet.

Rose stirred fitfully and raised up on one elbow, rubbing her eyes.

"Logan? Oh, honey, I'm glad to see you. What time is it, anyway?"

"Almost three-thirty. I tried not to wake you."

"Oh, I'm glad you did. There's coffee in the carafe." She waved sleepily toward the dresser. "Juice too. I ordered it after you called." She swung her legs over the side of the bed and walked over to me.

I took a closer look.

This was the mother of my son—the realization moved me deeply.

And, despite being thirty and the mother of a soon-to-be-six-year-old, Rose always took good care of herself. She remained a desirable figure of a woman.

Without a bra, her heavy breasts under the satin slip reminded me of Elizabeth Taylor in *Butterfield Eight*. Hair tousled and rubbing eyes heavy with sleep, without even trying she was probably as sexy right at this moment as anything I'd ever seen.

I stirred anew.

Had I been visited by a pituitary anomaly, some wellspring of supercharged testosterone?

"I'm so embarrassed. I really showed myself tonight." Rose sounded subdued and wouldn't look me in the eye.

Still, I kept my guard up. I didn't trust that I was out of the woods so easily.

I decided to play the martyr. "Don't worry about it. It'll work out."

"I hope so." Sleepily, she kissed me again. "I'm glad to see you."

"Me too." In a perverse way, I was. I kissed her back.

"Did you take a shower?" she said, drowsily. "You smell delicious."

Score one for the finest Castile toilet soap money can buy.

"Mmm . . ." She tasted me again.

Amazed, I felt my insubordinate manhood stirring against her.

"Wait. I have to pee. I'm about to pop." She pushed away and padded into the bathroom. Without bothering to close the door all the way, she lifted her slip, pulled down her panties, and sat to pee.

I walked over and poured her a coffee from the thermos carafe.

My edge was fading fast. My own renewal clearly demanded something more therapeutic. I found a carafe of orange juice in a little tub of half-melted ice. Locating a glass, I uncapped the bottle of vodka and poured the glass half full. Scooping ice from around the juice carafe, I dumped it in and topped it off with a modicum of the OJ.

Turning up the large water glass, I gulped half of its contents without taking the glass from my lips. With a deep breath, I finished the rest and waited for a miracle.

When I reached for Rose's coffee cup, I saw John Paul's letter was lying open on the dresser top.

My instantaneous welling of irritation gave way to fear.

I had a sinking feeling.

I should have known she'd search the room.

What else had she seen?

My eyes found the pile of doodles and scribbled notes I'd left beside the phone.

When I heard Rose flush, I turned to see her brushing her teeth.

What had I done with Ginny's note from my box this afternoon?

Scooping up the scraps of paper, I quickly sorted through them but didn't see Ginny's number among my scribbles. I put the notes back into a careless pile where I'd found them.

Too late to wonder if housekeeping had emptied the trash before Rose arrived.

Rose finally came back into the room and walked slowly over to where I stood.

I made a deliberate show of putting John Paul's letter back in the envelope. I wanted her to know I was damned unhappy.

Righteous indignation or bearding the lioness? Either one a reckless death wish.

"I was half-crazy looking for evidence," Rose shrugged. Clearly she had no intention of making a further apology.

"You disappoint me, Rose. I've nothing to hide." I hoped I sounded unconcerned.

Rose picked up the coffee cup.

Out of the corner of my eye I caught Ginny's note among the messages I'd left carelessly protruding from under the edge of the box with my manuscript.

So much for the question about death wishes.

She gave me a chilly stare. "Of course, you can't accept John Paul's offer."

"I really haven't had time to think about it. I did talk to the attorney, Prueffer, though. He wants me to come up there for the reading of the will. It could be an opportunity—"

She raised her hand to cut me short.

"But, Logan, don't you see, it's just a cheap trick. Just a tawdry way to take care of his mistress now that he's dead. You'd be insulting his wife, his family. Certainly you wouldn't be part of that."

"That's an arrogant assumption, Rose," I snapped. My fear of her snooping vanished in a cloud of indignation that she would so superciliously devalue my right to choose my friends.

"But he was cheating—"

This time, I raised my hand.

"John Paul Silver was my friend. Are you telling me that marriage robs a man of his right to dispose of his property in the way that he sees fit? How do you know he still loved Cathy? Or even that she was a good wife? You—neither of us—ever met the woman. Besides, if I did decide to take the offer, it would only be because I saw it as an opportunity for me, for you, and for our son."

"I can answer for me and Paul right now. Don't do it for us."

I gritted my teeth against rising resentment.

I turned away to conceal my exasperation at her conceit.

"And just what the devil gives you the right to answer for our son?" I said, struggling to control my exasperation.

"I'm his mother. You hardly ever see him," she announced self-righteously.

Recalling my conversation with the kid I'd just left at the bus station, I was visited by a fleeting spasm of guilt.

"Rose, be reasonable. I guess I might as well tell you now; I may be offered another opportunity. There's a famous doctor from Cambridge who wants to talk to me this morning about medical writing. Starting some new enterprise, I think."

"Cambridge? You mean England?"

"No, Boston. You know, Harvard University?"

"Forget it. God! That's even worse. I'd never get to see my sisters then. Why are you always looking for something else? Can't you, just for once, be satisfied with your life? Wait your turn for Rush Donald's job. We're doing fine right where we are. Besides, I won't move. I thought I already made that clear. You'd have to go without us if it meant living in . . . where was John Paul's attorney? Ohio? And I certainly wouldn't even consider Boston. What do we care about Harvard, anyway?"

"Ferguson might be going to New York—"

"New York would be worse than Boston. You're such a snob," she snorted.

"I'm not sure how I feel about it yet, but I warn you, it's all very interesting to me. But there's no use discussing it tonight. Why don't we just both get some sleep."

"I've said all I have to say. I don't want you to take another job."

"Getting back to that, after tonight, I just may not have my current job. In about three hours, I've got to try to clean up your fine mess. I'm not looking forward to that."

I turned, picked up my empty glass, and poured some more of the vodka.

"Stop that! You've got no business drinking at this time of morning! Rush Donald is a bad influence," she whined.

"What's Rush got to do with it? I've had a rough night. We both have," I amended. "This whole trip has become a goddamn nightmare."

"You're right about that. But I've begged you not to take the Lord's name in vain." She walked over to the chairs by the window, put her coffee cup on the table, and rested her feet on the manuscript box.

The corner of Ginny's note was in plain sight.

Bending her head, she slowly started to tremble.

"Oh, Logan. Can you forgive me?" she asked, quietly sobbing.

"What's done is done." I steeled myself—tears usually reduced me to a ninny.

"Could you actually lose your job?" She stopped sobbing, and her mouth tightened into a line.

Straightening, she wiped her cheeks with her forearms and stared at me.

"You just tell Rush if he makes a fuss, I'll tell Nadine what I saw last night."

"Calm down, Rose. You really don't know what you saw. Besides, haven't you jumped to enough conclusions for one night? Anyway, things may not come to that. I'll try to catch Melba—Miss Noyes before she goes to work. Maybe we can smooth things over. Rush wouldn't have to know. We could meet Miss Noyes for breakfast and you could apologize."

My skulking death wish again. What was it I loved about living on the edge?

Besides, I couldn't let her off the hook too easily. And, after all, she'd already said she wouldn't do it.

"I told you, I can't. I'm too ashamed. You don't know the things I said. I'd be mortified to have to face her. Just tell her I'm sorry. Explain that I'm not really like that," Rose pleaded.

"We'll see." I took the remaining swallow of my drink. "Let's try to get some sleep."

"Is that that disgusting book?" She saw the manuscript box and wheeled. "What did you bring that for? Oh, I get it now—John Paul's letter. You know I hate that book. I thought you put it away forever. I don't want you writing about our making love. What will our friends think?"

Over her shoulder, the corner of Ginny's note was glaring.

"Forget the book, Rose. Let's go to bed." I walked to where she sat, reached out my hand, pulled her to her feet, and kissed her.

She kissed me back, letting her mouth go open. Nuzzling my neck, she rubbed her belly against me.

"I was so worried when Ginny told me what you were doing with that woman. I kept thinking about how good you make me feel."

"Rose." Amazingly, I felt a stirring in my groin.

"Never ever leave me," she said between wet kisses.

"Rose, today's just Thursday. We've got the whole weekend ahead. Save all this 'til we've had some sleep. You're here now. Stay over. We'll have a second honeymoon."

"Oh, no." She pulled back. "I can't stay. I don't have a thing to wear and no makeup." Rose was strictly an Estée Lauder girl—even under the threat of nuclear extinction.

"No problem. Go shopping in the boutiques tomorrow. I have to take Rush to the airport Friday morning early. Make a list; I could pick up some stuff for you. We'd have 'til Sunday."

"No, I can't." She started to turn back toward the manuscript box.

I stopped her, stifling her protests with a tender kiss. Instead of pulling away, surprisingly, she responded again in a very suggestive way. Quite likely out of pure self-preservation, I was rock hard now. After a moment, she gently pulled me to the bed and lifted her slip over her head.

Clearly suicidal, I moved to help.

When she'd wiggled out of her panties, I knelt in front of her, lowered my head between her legs and began slowly licking.

"Driving over here, I thought about your doing this to that woman. It made me so hot." She was grinding hard against my mouth. She arched her back and came with a shudder.

I lightened up my tongue and continued to graze the inside of her labia. In no time she began to respond again. Twisting lengthwise on the bed, I had her vagina exposed above my face. Those enormous breasts were just begging to be squeezed.

"I almost died thinking about you doing this with another woman. I couldn't stand to lose you. Oh . . . you are driving me insane."

She was hot again, and I was too busy to answer.

She came with another violent bucking spasm.

Quickly now, she pulled me down on top of her. "Come inside me. I love it when you come inside me."

She pulled her knees up against her shoulders, urging me in as far I could go. "Come on now, give it to me."

Her eyes went wide with abandon as she started to respond anew. In no time, she began to convulse again.

I tried to slow down to let her know I was going to come, but that only egged her on.

Now she had driven me beyond the point of caring.

I surrendered to the universe.

Blissfully unaware of the diminished state of my juices, my Friday girl came again.

I didn't have the heart to remind her it was still only Thursday.

When Rose finally drifted off, I got up and tucked Ginny's note safely out of sight.

So much for living dangerously.

Back in bed, I firmly resolved to get a grip.

Tomorrow I would join a cult and spend the rest of my life copying the *Rubaiyat* in Sanskrit—a fitting end for a short, happy life.

The damn bullets were getting too close for comfort.

But all's well that ends well. I breathed a grateful sigh.

CHAPTER FORTY-THREE

When I struggled awake, my watch showed 5:12. Light was just showing around the edge of the drapes, and Rose was coming out of the bathroom.

Fully clothed.

"What's going on, hon?" I rubbed my eyes.

With only a little over an hour's sleep, the alcohol had kept me mellow.

"I've got to go. I just remembered Maryanne and Cookie are here. I can't let them see me this way. Except for my compact, I don't even have any makeup. Anyway, I promised your parents I'd get Paul before lunch. I didn't have a chance to call the nursery school."

"Rose, that's all bullshit and you know it." I swung my legs over the edge of the bed and stood up, naked.

"No, Logan, that's reality. That's the trouble with you. You don't have any sense of responsibility. All you think about is parties and playing golf," she sniffed. "I have to deal with real life. Besides, I don't like this place. It makes me feel like a phony. We don't belong here. After last night, I don't want to ever come back here again. We can't afford places like this. People who come here can afford it. We don't belong. Maryanne and Cookie can afford to come here. Their husbands are doctors. They go to New York and shop."

"I don't feel like a phony. I'd take you when I go to New York if you'd go. God knows I've offered. I take you to Richmond to shop, and we stay at the best hotels. This doesn't have anything to do with who's paying the bill. You have just as much right to be here as anyone. That's a right you have to give yourself. The people who operate this hotel don't judge us. They don't care if we're not the Kennedys or movie stars. If they did, they wouldn't solicit these meetings here."

"See? You've already forgotten who you are."

"Rose, what's the matter with you? I know who I am, and being here doesn't make me feel in the least inferior."

"It does me. I'm sorry. I'm leaving. It was nice just now, and I do love you." She kissed me, started toward the door, then turned back. "I really hate to leave you to straighten out my mess, and don't worry too much about the job. There are always other jobs. Call me as soon as you've talked to that nurse. Funny, I still hate her. Ginny really did say some awful things." Rose lowered her eyes. "I imagined you making love to her—doing all those things we do. I hated her. I don't think I could ever face her without thinking about it. Ginny said that woman was . . . was fucking you blind."

Now that I thought about it, my vision did seem a little fuzzy.

"It was all your imagination. I've got more than I can handle at home." I smiled reassuringly. At the moment, it didn't feel like a total lie. "What did you plan on doing anyway? I mean why did you want to drive over here? Why didn't you just throw my stuff out in the front yard and change the locks?"

"I don't know. I guess I just wanted the satisfaction of telling you what I thought of you. You can't imagine the speeches I rehearsed on the way over."

"Me? I thought you were after her."

"Maybe. But I wanted the satisfaction of scratching your eyes out, too. It makes my blood boil now, just thinking about it. I still think I might just scratch your eyes out." She smiled and dropped her head. "I don't trust you any farther than I can throw you."

"Sounds like you were enjoying the idea of getting rid of me."

"Why wouldn't I? Except for bed and making the money, I hardly have a husband. You've never loved me. Don't think I don't know it."

"Rose, be fair. If I . . . if you didn't think I loved you, why did you marry me?"

"You had me fooled at first. You are smart. Everyone said so. My mama said you had the highest I.Q. in the county. Everybody loved you. I thought you were going places. I thought that would be enough. And you were different then.

You still went to church. Until you met John Paul Silver and then Rush Donald, your hero. You copy everything about him—same clothes, same music. It makes me sick to think of the trouble you went to to get those Gucci loafers. They don't look a damn bit different from the ones you were already wearing."

"Listen, Rose. Rush is no saint, but he's older and he's been around. I've learned a lot from him." I didn't want to expand on that. "And listen, lady, if I still want it, he's going to be my ticket to stardom. Wait and see. Besides, what does that have to do with anything? I wouldn't be doing any of this if you hadn't pushed me into it. You're never satisfied. You nagged me to quit the paper. And now that I might have a better opportunity, you tell me you don't want to move. Do you think that I'm so damn brilliant that the mountain is going to come to Mohammed?"

"Hardly," she sniffed. "I just don't want to wind up with Paul growing up in a strange place and you gone all the time."

"Oh, come on. Other women do it. What makes you different? You just got through telling me you thought I was going places. And that you loved me. Don't you love me anymore?"

"I guess I do, but you've changed. You don't love me. You don't love anyone, not really. Don't forget I know you. You can't love anyone because you're afraid."

"Oh crap! Afraid? Afraid of what?"

"Afraid you'll have to give something of yourself."

"I give you every damn thing."

"Yeah, you give me things. You don't give me any intimacy. We don't share anything. Trouble is, you can't find anyone who can love you more than you love yourself."

"Rose, that sounds like it came out of some dumb magazine. Put a copy of *Cosmo* in your hands and you're a danger to yourself and others."

"Just because you're a genius, don't think I'm dumb. You don't really love Paul and me. You can't help it. You're so arrogant, you don't really respect anyone. You just use people. You're really just a cynic. Most likely a real live sociopath."

"Sociopath! For chrissakes, Rose! I'm canceling all your subscriptions."

"It's true."

"Be fair. You know I love you and Paul. Why do you think I'm chasing around doing all this garbage? If I were selfish, I'd just quit and get back to writing books."

"Yes! You and your dirty books. And I'm still not sure about tonight. You could have pulled a fast one. I wouldn't put it past you."

"If you still had doubts, why'd you just make love to me?"

She didn't say a word.

"Well?"

"Maybe I just wanted to remind you of what you'd be missing."

"You did that, all right. Come here." I moved toward her, but she stepped back.

"What does the bitch look like anyway?"

"Who, Ginny?"

"No, the other one, the nurse. You can't trust nurses."

"Rose, you're a nurse, remember?"

"That's how I know. What does she look like?"

"I don't know. Not sexy at all. She wears a nurse's uniform. I've never really given her a second look. She looks like most nurses. Like she has antiseptic in her veins. I always hated that you had to wear 'em, remember?" It was true. I hated uniforms of any kind.

"That's not what Ginny said," Rose insisted.

"Ginny? Listen, any bitch who'd pull a stunt like that would make up anything. She must hate you a lot."

"Yeah. She's orphanage trash. I fixed her good in high school. Spread the rumor she was the orphanage whore. She's not likely to forget it. If you run into her today or tomorrow, what are you going to do? You just stay away from her. She's crazy. We don't want any more trouble than we've already got."

"Don't worry. If I can smooth this over with the nurse, I don't want to mention any of it ever again. Wait a second, and I'll slip some clothes on and walk you down." I was anxious for her to leave now. If she stayed, there was no telling what might happen.

"Okay. I would feel better if you walked down with me. I feel like everyone in this snooty place knows all about what happened. It'll be all over the hotel by breakfast."

"Don't worry. You may call them snobs, but the Greenbrier staff would never deal in cheap gossip. That's trashy."

"I hope you're right. But it doesn't change the way I feel. And I'm not trash. I know how to behave. The trouble with you is, you're a snob."

I wanted to explain that she was the snob, but what was the use?

I moved to the closet, took a pair of khakis off the hanger, and grabbed a golf shirt. When I'd dressed, I slipped into my loafers without bothering to put on socks and grabbed my key.

As I jammed it into my pants pocket, I felt a folded slip of paper.

Ginny's message from this afternoon. Rose had overlooked it.

I really did lead a charmed life.

"Ready?" I breathed a sigh of relief.

She nodded and headed out the door.

"By the way, Rose, about that beagle puppy—" I began as we located her fancy SUV.

"I told you, Logan. Forget the puppy!" she snapped, climbing into the yuppie truck.

Safely buckled in her Tahoe, Rose rolled the window down and smiled a little. "I really do love you, but I wish you'd get over all this phoniness. This place . . . it's not real. And, Logan, forget New York and London."

"I love you, too. And it's Cambridge, Rose." Despite her bitchiness, I couldn't help but laugh.

"I'm serious about moving. I won't go to Teaneck or Boston or even Ohio. I want to stay right where we are. You're going to get Rush's job, and you can play Mr. Big Shot. I can have a new house, and you can join the new country club with your doctor buddies." She leaned out and pulled my head down and stuck her tongue in my mouth "If you want more of what you just had, remember—get it at home. I'll fuck you cross-eyed."

I laughed. She wrinkled her nose at me as the car started rolling, and I almost let her run over my new Gucci loafers.

My watch showed 5:29 as I stood in the lavender light of the dawn, watching the taillights of her Tahoe disappear. She'd be back in Melas by 8:00 at the latest, I guessed.

I thought about Rose's ultimatum.

What would she do if I decided to leave Severance for a job somewhere else?

I couldn't stop her.

But what about me? Did what I want matter, anyway?

And what did I want, really?

Turning back to the hotel, I was thinking about Scotty Brown's invitation.

Under the portico, I stopped and looked back at the oval and the graceful grounds.

Rose kept insisting that this wasn't real. I knew better. For seekers, it was real all right.

Extracting Ginny's note from my pocket, I looked at the home phone number.

I decided not to throw it away just yet.

It was unpublished, most likely.

CHAPTER FORTY-FOUR

I showered, left a wake-up call for 7:45, and went back to bed. I figured that at this stage, an hour and a half was better than no sleep at all. My watch showed 7:35 when I was startled awake by the phone. I didn't even remember turning off the bedside lamp. Switching on the lamp, I picked up the phone expecting the hotel operator with my wake-up call.

"Can you talk?" Rush whispered.

I wondered what good he thought whispering would accomplish.

"Sure, Rose's gone. She just sneaked over for a quickie. She had to go back home. Paul has to go to nursery school." Technically, I really wasn't lying. "What's up?"

"Last night, in the lobby, I think Rose saw me with Mimi. I wondered if she mentioned it," he asked nervously.

"Oh, yeah, she mentioned it all right. She said some slut was trying to kiss your belly button from the inside. For a moment she thought you were Siamese twins. Rose is not a liberated woman. She was upset. I had to talk her out of calling Nadine the minute she walked in the room." I smiled. I wanted him to know his *cajones* were in my hands.

"Jeezus! Oh, my god, you don't think she'll call when she gets home, do you? Nadine will have my balls." He could hardly speak. "Why the fuck didn't you warn me she was coming?"

Having just come within a pubic hair of my own disaster, I almost felt sort of sorry for him. But recalling how he'd tried to coerce me into falsifying my expenses, I still didn't trust him to live up to his word about paying to fix my company car.

"It was as much a surprise to me as it was you."

"What did you tell her?"

"I think I convinced her that the woman was a fellow research associate who'd had too much to drink and you were trying to rescue the poor damsel before she made a complete fool of herself."

"Jeezus! Couldn't you come up with a better story? Do you think she believed that?"

"I did consider telling her that the woman was your long-lost sister who had been put in a foster home when you were children and you'd been separated for over thirty years. But from the way Rose described what was going on, it would have raised the question of sibling incest. I'm not sure she bought what I told her completely, but I think for this time you're safe. But she did bring up the instance of sexy Hannah Riker and you trying to seduce her at our house that night during the Virginia Medical Society meeting. I think Rose just called strike two on you when she saw Mimi dry-fucking you in the lobby last night. One more strike and you're out of the box, hoss."

"It wasn't like that."

"Why don't you call Rose and explain?"

"Don't be that way, man."

I didn't respond. I was in no mood to put up with his garbage.

"We did get pretty bombed. Mimi said that Ferguson thought I'd lied about talking to Gert. What do you think?"

"Let's just say I think he was more than a little doubtful. By the way, did you ever get up with Gert?"

"I was too far gone. Going to call her right now soon as I hang up and tell her what happened. Gert's okay. She'll cover me with Ferguson. Anyway, why should I give a fuck what Ferguson thinks? He's just here to read a paper. Doesn't really have anything to do with me." It was a brave speech, but he sounded more than a little anxious.

"It's your call. Ferguson said Gert used to work for him. You know how straight-arrow Gert can be."

"Did he say anything about it? After I left, I mean."

I remembered Ferguson's remark about beta-estradiol, but I was tired of trying to save Rush from himself.

"Nah," I said. It wasn't exactly a lie.

"Mimi said I really showed my ass about Snead and Brown. Do you think I did?"

"I don't exactly think everyone had a proper appreciation for your cosmic observations about the true meaning of class."

"So what? Anyway, women are so afraid they'll hurt someone's feelings. Mimi calls 'em 'sensibilities.' "

"I imagine at Hahvahd B they'll call it 'diplomacy.' "

There was a pause while he thought that over.

"Want to meet me downstairs for breakfast?" he ventured.

"Can't. I'm meeting Ferguson at Top Notch for breakfast."

"Ian Ferguson? What the fuck?"

Silence.

"What's that all about?"

"Nothing to do with you. Bobby Johnson told him I'd been a writer, and Ferguson remembered my piece in *Harper's*. Seems Ferguson is starting something new . . . looking for a medical writer. I tried to discourage him, but he insisted. I really couldn't refuse. Besides, he's important. Good politics. Won't hurt to have a cup of coffee. Gert would approve, I'm sure."

"I can't believe Ferguson saw that damn piece in *Harper's*. I didn't think it was all that great." Rush dripped disdain. "Don't take me wrong. You know what I mean."

"No. Exactly what do you mean?"

Eat your fucking heart out, I gloated.

"Oh, come on, now," he sputtered.

I didn't answer. I was anxious to get off the phone.

"I guess this kinda leaves me minding the store, and all the time I thought I was the boss." His whiny voice dripped self-sacrifice.

"Relax. It's all arranged. Don't worry about the booth. Bill Moss will man the exhibit 'til I relieve him, and Al Stamper is coming over from Lynchburg to hold the fort this afternoon. By the way, I got a twelve-twenty-eight for the Old White today. Bobby Johnson wants to play again. He's Ferguson's buddy. I thought you might want to play in my place today since you got shot down by Gert's call yesterday."

"Uh, no. And I don't think it looks very good for us to play every day."

"Rush, I hate to remind you, but you're the one who told me to set us up to play with Max and Sam. I don't understand you at all. Why the change of heart? Make up your mind. I don't think I can cancel on them now, even if I wanted to. You didn't get to play yesterday, so why don't you play with them today? Johnson will make a great partner. After last night, he might help you make amends. Go ahead. Last chance for some fun before you have to go hit the books at Mr. John Harvard's college."

"I know Ferguson is important, but I don't see how knowing someone like Bobby Johnson is such a big deal. So he works for that redneck MacKenzie Brown. He's just a hick who got lucky. Now he runs around buying companies. What does that have to do with anything?"

"Jake Chetauga with *Time* says he's one of the most powerful men in the country. Just look at all the important press that's here for this news conference. You're a young man on your way to Harvard. Ferguson has Harvard ties. Might not hurt to rub elbows with these guys. You never can tell when guys like Johnson and Ferguson can help you."

"You're too easily impressed. Guys like that don't help people. A bit of customer golf doesn't hurt once in awhile. But there's no substitute for hard work. You go ahead and play. It'll be okay, I guess. The company will understand."

Poor Rush. Just couldn't help being a bastard.

"I'm confused. You're the one who had me get you the clubs and set this whole golf thing up. I'm not a mind reader. Why'd you change your mind? Don't you like the clubs?"

"It's not the clubs. I mean they aren't the right swing weight, but that's okay. You did your best. Besides, you misunderstood, got carried away. I just mentioned it might be nice to play a little golf while we're here. I didn't mean to give the impression that we came over here on vacation."

I wasn't about to lower myself to confront his lie.

"Oh, well, I can cancel, make some excuse. Max and Sam are going to be disappointed that they didn't have a chance to get their money back, but they'll get another shot at me back home.

They're skeptical about your mysterious phone call. Thought you were just afraid you'd dump your tee shot in the creek with Sam Snead standing there."

"Did those bastards say that? I don't think much of your doctor friends."

"What do you care what they think? Remember telling me business is just fucking business? Do you know how many Severance Laboratories products those guys use? Sam's on the therapeutics committee at the Alger-Sewell Hospital. It's just business, boss man. Yo' slave is liftin' dat pill and totin' them ampules for good ol' Severance Laboratories. If you don't want me to play, I'll make an excuse."

For the moment, fearless Logan was getting highly fed up.

"No, no. I told you, go ahead. It's too late to cancel. But next time I don't think it's too good an idea for us to be playing golf. We came over here to work. People like Dr. Ferguson have a double standard. It's all right for them to have fun, but they expect us peons to work. I wouldn't want Ferguson telling Gert that we're not serious. Wouldn't sit well with Herman Asbury." He was obviously pouting now.

"Yeah, wouldn't want to make a bad impression on good ol' Herman Asshole," I said. "Of course you're right. We can't be too careful how we act around these people. People like them are always judging a company by its management."

Smoke that, you jerk! I smiled smugly to myself.

"I got to get dressed. Gert Kearns wouldn't want me to keep Ferguson waiting. By the way, if I were worried about keeping Ferguson's good opinion, I don't think I'd forget to call her."

I could feel him glaring into the phone.

"I'll tell Ian you're coming to hear his paper this morning. I'll come straight on back to the exhibit hall as soon as I can get away. See you then."

Fuck you! And while we're at it, fuck Herman Asbury and Harvard, too.

I hung up.

Walk softly and carry a sore dick.

CHAPTER FORTY-FIVE

I'd showered and the clock by the phone was showing almost 7:40 when I took a deep breath and dialed Melba.

"Hello?" she answered tentatively.

"Hi. It's me. I just wanted to tell you that you can breathe easy now. I would have called earlier, but I was afraid you wouldn't answer. It took most of the night, but I convinced Rose that she made a fool out of herself. She left this morning around five. Probably back home by now."

"Oh, God. How? Did Zaharias at the Camellia Club cover for you?"

"No, I changed my plan. It's a long story, but it's over. You're in the clear. I'm really sorry it happened."

"It's not your fault. I knew . . . I know what I'm doing. You told me you had a wife."

"I want you to understand. I think you're very special—" I stopped.

"I think you're way more than special, too. I . . ." She let it hang.

"Take good care. I'll be seeing you," I said.

"Maybe this afternoon. Come by and have a drink after golf?"

"Melba, Ginny's still around. We can't go through that again."

"If you came here, Ginny wouldn't know."

What had I gotten myself into? Estrogen poisoning, a raging epidemic?

Served me right. I hoped I'd learned my lesson.

"Too risky. Besides my boss is mad at me. I have to work," I said. "Just take good care."

I hated to leave it like that, but I didn't wait for an answer.

Labeling the laundry bag, I left my telltale clothes for the valet before I got dressed.

All things considered, I felt okay, better than I had a right to. Still, with two hours sleep, I knew I'd feel like hell later.

Fantasizing about a short nap before our 12:28 tee time, I looked fondly at the vodka bottle and carafe of orange juice wasting on the tray.

With Rush breathing down my neck, fat chance of that.

It was a little past 8:00 when I walked out of the motor entrance, adrenaline flowing. The prospect of meeting Scotty Brown had me higher than the red-tailed hawk circling against the morning sun. Taken with the glorious day, I decided to walk and arrived at Top Notch a few minutes late.

Ian Ferguson met me with a hearty handshake, a large glass of tomato juice in his other hand. "So glad you could make it. Would you join me in a Bloody Mary? After last night, some of us are having a bit of the hair of the dog. We're a rather depraved bunch out of sight of home."

"Sure, why not?"

In the presence of my superiors, I'm easily led.

Dutifully, I followed him down the hall to the huge serving pantry. It was actually a full-blown kitchen. A young barman and a couple of women dressed in catering livery were standing by, eager to satisfy our whims. Low voices drifted in from the direction of the sun porch as, fresh drinks in hand, Ferguson led me out to where Bobby and MacKenzie Brown were standing with a group of five other men whom I vaguely remembered seeing last night.

"Look who's here. Gentlemen, I want you to meet Logan Baird, my new golf partner. Logan is with Severance Labs," Bobby introduced me. They others were lawyers and accountants. Except for Sternweiss and Morgenroth, I'd never heard of any of them.

Scotty Brown shook my hand and said, "Baird. Glad to see you again. Alex Crim says she sees you in Roanoke. I believe you have a mutual friend from Hot Springs? Hope we'll get the chance to talk later."

"Well, yes. Betty Farnsworth. She's a—"

"Yes, we'll chat about it later. Ian, why don't you get Mr. Baird something to eat?" Brown smiled warmly but turned back to continue the discussion with the group.

Logan Baird, a man of great importance and an all-around spellbinding raconteur.

"They're up to their ears. Let's get some food and find somewhere to talk." Ferguson picked up his briefcase and steered me back down the hall into the dining room, where another young woman from the Greenbrier dining room staff was standing guard over a sumptuous buffet. Polishing off my Bloody Mary, I set the glass on the sideboard and helped myself to a cup of black coffee from a small silver urn.

"Grab a bite. If we're to believe our mothers, all sorts of bad things happen if you don't eat breakfast," Ferguson guffawed.

"Thanks, I'll pass. I had a rough night. I'm rarely hungry in the morning, anyway."

I was afraid to tell him that what I really wanted was more hair of that favorite dog.

"How about a bite of melon? We can go back in the front room and have another one of these. They're absolutely chock-full of vitamins." Waving his Bloody Mary, he pronounced it "vit" not "vite."

I gazed upon Ferguson, a veritable Saint Bernard among men, with newfound appreciation.

He filled his plate to overflowing. Fresh drinks in hand, we went into the front room, found two easy chairs by a low cocktail table, and took a seat.

The second Bloody Mary tasted even better than the first.

I barely nibbled at the melon.

Before Ferguson had a chance to say anything, the others came parading out through the room. Still talking a mile a minute, Brown led them, single file, out through the front door.

The last to leave, Bobby hesitated at the door and spoke to Ian. "We're heading on over to Valley View to rehearse. Hope to see you both there later."

"I can't speak yet for Logan, but I'll be along as soon as we've had our chat."

"Sure. Logan, I'm glad you could meet with Ian this morning. I've got to run right now. If I don't see you at Valley View, I'll see you at the golf shop. We go off at 12:28, right?"

I nodded, still wondering what the deal was all about.

"Okay, see you then." Bobby turned and hurried after the others, who were already piling into a limo.

My second Bloody Mary was working. Happily in a state of grace, I sipped my coffee and watched him eat.

Even if I'd never heard Ferguson speak, there was something veddy British about the way he held himself. Mid-fiftyish, I guessed, he made an impressive appearance. When buttoned, his navy double-breasted yachtsman blazer looked a trifle snug. Not actually fat, he certainly was in no danger of malnutrition. Sitting there watching him stuffing his face with groceries, I guessed if I kept a pace like that for long, I'd look positively Pickwickian in a month.

"There, now," he said as he pushed back his plate and shrugged self-consciously. "Usually I'm not such a pig. I barely got a bite all day yesterday, and I'm overcompensating now, I suppose. If I always ate like that, I'd become a rhinoceros within a fortnight, I'd wager."

A young woman appeared and took our plates. In a moment she was back to refill our coffee cups.

"Time's a-wasting. I'm sure you're wondering what this is all about." He extracted a thick file folder from the expensive briefcase at his feet and took out a photocopy of my *Harper's* article. "As I already told you, your essay enchanted me the first time I laid eyes on it."

"Thanks. It's really the only major credit I've had."

"We were curious about that, so I had research dig up some of your other stuff from the newspaper." He waved a pile of photocopied newspaper clippings. "You've quite a way with language. We wondered if you're working on a book."

"No. I haven't written a word in years. Don't have the time." I spread my hands. "I abandoned the great American novel when I left the paper. It was not very good, I'm afraid."

"What a pity. We're standing on the threshold of a fantastic age in medicine and science and culture. More progress in the past sixty years than in the past two hundred . . . two thousand, really. Merely thinking about it boggles the mind. Insulin, sex hormones, polio vaccine, steroid hormones, antibiotics and tranquilizers. At last we've managed to put our martini in a pill and overcome the final barrier to perfect serenity. The priest can have his morning tot, and no one is the wiser." He laughed out loud. "Now, retroactive birth control and drugs for an instant hard-on. Better living through chemistry, a new miracle practically every day. And men like you and I are right in the thick of it. Not many men with your medical background have the gift of words."

Peering up like an eagle, Ferguson paused and regarded me over the edge of his coffee cup. A man afire, he exuded energy. Just listening gave me chills. My grandmother would have called him a spellbinder.

"So, what do you think?" He looked at me.

"Think? About what?" I didn't have a clue what to say. "I don't know quite what to make of all this. I guess I take a lot of that for granted. I guess we all do. As for the writing, I always considered myself ordinary. The piece in *Harper's* is the only publication of any consequence I have to my credit."

I sat there looking at him, completely in the dark about what this was leading to.

"Why do you insist on selling yourself short?"

Reaching across, I thumbed the thick stack of clips from my newspaper column and other features he'd assembled.

"Pretty impressive, wouldn't you say?" he ventured.

"How the hell did you get all these on such short notice?"

"Clipping service. We have our own research staff. I'm putting together a team for a new undertaking. We have been searching for just the right people to fill certain slots. This is a great opportunity for those with talent. One of the things we're going to do is publish an avant-garde magazine exclusively for physicians. Politics, manners, the arts and literature, fashion, sports, and travel and leisure," Ferguson enthused and ran on. "A combination of *Esquire*, *GQ*, *Harper's*, *Architectural Digest*, *National Geographic* . . . the *Atlantic Monthly*, the *New Yorker*, *Sports Illustrated*, and *Vanity Fair* . . . *Entertainment*, *Holiday*, and *Smithsonian* all rolled into one. It will be freestanding.

405

There's nothing like it, an entity all its own. We will offer today's busy, culturally deprived—if not downright oafish—physician, a mirror on the outside world. *Hippocrates*. How's that sound for a name?"

"Great name."

"*Hippocrates* will have the same sort of snob appeal and attract the same advertisers that the *New Yorker* and *Esquire* and *Vanity Fair* do. Just think about it. What a marketplace! It's going to be exciting, seductive. Can't you just imagine!" He paused for breath.

I nodded, still at a loss for words.

"Yesterday when Bobby mentioned your name, something clicked. When we were trying to identify some writers and editors to fit our profile, your *Harper's* article was the model we used to define our concept. You actually planted the seed that grew into my concept for *Hippocrates*. When I found out yesterday you were here, imagine my surprise. This is divinely ordered . . . pure serendipity."

The concept gave me shivers. My mind was abuzz with images of a big slick magazine with grand full-color pages and glitzy ads—a *Vanity Fair* for the medical profession.

"I still can't believe you actually use my piece in your lecture at Harvard Medical School. In-flipping-credible."

He laughed.

"And *Hippocrates*? Just the right touch. It has a very snobbish ring."

"Snobbish! Just the right touch indeed!" He clapped his hands. "We physicians are clods for sure, but we are a snobbish lot."

"I still don't know exactly why you're talking to me. I haven't done any serious writing in over four years. I'm not sure I remember how. If, in fact, I ever really knew. That *Harper's* piece may have been just a fluke."

"You're no fluke. We're sure of that." He waved the thick stack of clippings. "As to what slot you'd fill, right now editorial director is a title that's been mentioned. After all, it was your idea that really spawned the whole bloody thing."

"Me? Editorial director?" I could hardly believe my ears.

Part of me still wondered if all this might not be some kind of elaborate put-on.

"Why not? The concept was yours. Anyway, I'm expecting a decision from our top candidate for managing editor before lunchtime. And of course, if our candidate decides to come aboard, he'd have to have the final say. I already told him about you last evening on the phone. He didn't know your *Harper's* piece, so I faxed him a copy. I asked our New York people to get copies of these clips to him. They've been quite busy assembling files of a number of other people's work, too. Naturally he withheld comment until he'd seen your stuff. We're assembling a crackerjack staff . . . the *New Yorker*, *Vanity Fair*, *Publishers Weekly*. A lot of talent will be coming with us. It'll be a great learning experience for a bright young man like you. Think of what you'd learn. Just think of the credentials it will provide for your future. In a year or two, you could go anywhere you wanted. What do you think? Doesn't the idea excite you, old chum?"

Old chum? I wanted to pinch myself.

"Sure, but I still think you've overestimated me. All this over one lucky article. I wrote that piece right off the top of my head. It started when I was doing a series of interviews with doctors for the *Stars and Stripes* in Bosnia. All they knew was medicine. If you tried to talk to them about art or music, or hell's bells, even sports—no, particularly sports—all you got was a blank stare. The rest of my writing experience has been at a medium-sized daily paper."

"Look, good writing doesn't depend on its venue to define it. Don't underestimate yourself. I already have a top team in place to run this thing . . . the best. My people say your stuff is out in front. You were nominated for a Pulitzer weren't you?"

"Well, yeah . . . twice. But the paper just threw me in the breech. A Pulitzer nomination doesn't mean anything that serious."

"Pure rot! Goddamn it, man, why argue for your limitations? Doesn't this excite you? I would have thought that anyone who wrote with this kind of fire would be a seething volcano inside.

Not at all the sort to be content peddling pharmaceuticals door to door." He stopped, realizing he might be hurting my feelings. "There's nothing wrong with that, of course, but blast it"—he slapped the table top with a bang—"that's the sort of thing best left for men like your Mr. Donald. I should imagine he does well at it, despite his bluster. From what Gert tells me, he's a great salesman. But not the sort I'd want to take to the Harvard Club. Maybe at Harvard Business they'll rub the rough edges off. Anyway, what do you think? Don't just sit there. Say something."

"Are you offering me a job?"

"Absolutely."

"Editorial director? *Hippocrates*?"

"Something like that. We're not absolutely certain of the title, yet."

"Where? New York?" Rose's ultimatum was fresh in my mind.

"Yes. We considered Boston, but New York's the only place for what we're going to do. We've already taken office space. One of Scotty's minor holdings. Hah!" he guffawed again.

"What sort of money are we talking about? It probably costs three times what I make just to live there. Down here I belong to a nice country club and the University Club, and more importantly, I have the time to use both. I'd be lost in the big city. I'd have to give up my lifestyle. What's the use if I can't play some golf once in awhile?"

I was scared to death that I was in over my head, but the idea had my adrenaline pumping overtime.

"Give up golf? Don't be absurd. Our people are well compensated, and most live in the suburbs and belong to clubs just as you do. Come on, old chum, we're not offering you an oar as a galley slave. And there are other compensations. When's the last time you saw a Broadway play or your wife went shopping on Fifth Avenue? And there will be the best private schools for your son. You're young; there's a whole world out there. Don't tell me you're just as dull as the doctors you wrote about?"

"Maybe I am at that," I laughed. "You still haven't told me what kind of money we're talking about. I have a wife to deal with. I can hardly expect to talk this over with her and tell her I don't know what the salary is. She's dead set against moving anywhere. I already know that."

"Oh, yes. Well . . ." Ferguson opened his briefcase and took out a sheet of paper. He gave it a quick look and made a check mark in the margin with his pen. "This is the range for the top slots. You'd be in there. Near midrange to start. We'll furnish you an Audi or Mercedes, or Cadillac if you prefer American. The expense and entertainment account in this job is unlimited—as long as it isn't abused. And there'll be a corporate membership at Westchester and a membership in one of the best downtown athletic clubs. Scotty always insists his people go first class."

When I looked, I caught my breath. Including perks with the car, the figure was almost four times what I was making, even if I were top man in my division.

It was over twice what I knew Rush would be making when he was reassigned to Teaneck headquarters. I could already see myself driving out the Long Island expressway in a shiny silver Audi convertible.

"And MacKenzie Brown's the backer?"

"Scotty Brown, Bobby Johnson, the entire team. This is all part of a major undertaking they're to announce in a few minutes. Come along if you're interested. I assume you'd have to be."

"Sure. I'm speechless really," I stammered. "But I need time to think it over. This is overwhelming. I . . . when would you want me to start?"

"Would two weeks be acceptable? We need you on board yesterday. Of course, I expect you'd need to take a few days. You'd probably want to give notice, but you wouldn't have to actually. We'd make it right with Severance. We want to hit the street with the January issue in mid-December. And have February already in the can. That doesn't give us much time. We're moving along."

"Two weeks? I'd need time to take Rose up to find us a place. There's a lot to consider."

"Certainly, but plenty of time for that after you start. We'll put you up in a hotel and fly you back and forth to see your family. You travel anyway. It won't be a lot of difference now, will it?"

"Guess not."

He placed the clippings and file folder in his briefcase and snapped it shut.

He saw me give the case an envious look.

"Dunhill. A gift of the corporation. How would you like one just like it?"

"I'd kill for one just like it," I croaked. My heart was pounding.

"Good. There's nothing like an appreciation of the finer things to keep a chap working at top speed. Come along, it's almost time for Scotty's big announcement. We wouldn't want to miss it, now would we?"

"Not in a million years," I breathed as I followed him to the waiting limo, my spirits passing just over Mount Everest.

THURSDAY . . .
AND BEYOND

CHAPTER FORTY-SIX

By the time Ferguson and I arrived at Valley View Estate House it was 9:25. I knew Rush would be in a bad mood when I showed up late at the booth, but now I savored the idea of a confrontation. Rush would turn green with envy when he found out about the deal Ferguson had just offered me.

I'd seen Valley View before, but always from a distance. Situated atop a hill west of the outdoor pool and tennis complex, Valley View Estate House overlooked the Greenbrier golf course. I'd always assumed it was an exclusive hideaway for visiting VIPs of the controlling CSX railroad. In my travels through the area, I sometimes had seen their private railroad cars sitting on the special siding at the quaint station just across from the hotel entrance. I was familiar with the vestiges of feudal status and privilege that the railroads once afforded their corporate barons.

Valley View Estate House was larger than Top Notch. An instant replay of last night's cocktail party but on a much grander scale, the present scene was crackling with excitement. An army of people, including last night's media crowd, was tightly packed inside. The size of last night's mob had doubled at least. The overflow spilled out onto the porch and terraces on the upper level and the private terrace off the boardroom on the level below.

Below us, a quartet of photogenic women returned volleys from the automatic ball machines at the tennis complex.

The area around Valley View was swarming with people. Outside, a sprawling burgundy-striped tent with an MBI logo had been set up, and gasoline-powered air conditioners were running full blast. Leaving the limo, Ferguson and I approached the bustling venue on foot.

I could hardly wait to tell Rose the news. She'd pitch a fit at the prospect of moving to New York.

So be it. Just let her. It was way past time she grew up.

It was impossible to ignore such an incredible opportunity. It was more than a mere opportunity, it was a fairy tale—a once-in-a-lifetime dream come true.

And who could tell? A change of scene might give us a chance to get our marriage back on track.

Above, a jet aircraft traced a pencil-straight white contrail high in the morning sky.

When we were passionately coupled together this morning, I'd wistfully recalled echoes of the bittersweet intensity of our honeymoon.

Rose was right. I didn't know much about love, but if I could, I'd gladly settle for that.

Deftly, Ferguson steered me past the crowd. A cadre of mess-jacketed bartenders was randomly stationed inside and out, doing a lively choreography, pacifying the restless crowd of working press, who were no doubt nursing monstrous hangovers from last night's bash at Top Notch. The scene reminded me of a news clip of FEMA rescue workers at a disaster area, uniformed attendants busily dispensing emergency treatment in the form of Bloody Marys, screwdrivers, and champagne cocktails.

Talk about hangovers. I could write a book.

We made our way around to the rear and entered through the kitchen. Inside I could see a battery of silver coffee urns. Rows of juice carafes stood guard beside a lavish continental brunch buffet of grapes, melon, and pastries, all laid out in the spacious dining room.

I recollected that a reporter never turns down the opportunity for a free meal or a free drink.

Raw meat for rapacious lions.

When my dad—and mom, too—heard the news, they'd be so proud. They'd hate to see me leave Melas, but they'd celebrate and cheer me on. Of that, I had no doubt.

I caught my breath. Right in front of us, holding fast to Bobby Johnson's arm, was Lesley Stahl.

"Lesley, dear, I want to present Logan Baird. Logan's going to be the new force among the New York magazine crowd."

"May the force be with you," the lovely Lesley purred, then moved on.

Bobby looked back and winked.

I could barely nod.

Spielberg, Gwyneth Paltrow, Matt Damon, and William F. Buckley, Jr., were standing near the terrace bar.

Ferguson saw my mouth fly open and grinned.

I searched the crowd, hoping to locate Jake Chetauga and Pete French among the sea of faces.

What would that pair of crusty cynics say if they knew they were addressing the new editorial director of *Hippocrates* magazine? I tried to comprehend the power of that. Remembering the late nights during my salad days, trying to freelance my stuff to the magazines, I knew that even pros like Chetauga still feverishly chased the dream of major magazine ink. Would first-rate journalists like Jake and Pete try to impress me with their abilities now?

Frantically, TV crews were trying to move equipment through the unruly army of people. From the looks of the setup, I surmised that the grand announcement was going to be made here on the upper terrace level, adjacent to the covered porch off the dining room. At a corner of the terrace, a walnut lectern was dominated by its bristling a collection of oddly shaped, oversized microphones sporting the alphabet letters of all the major networks. Behind the lectern, there were two large easels. One—firmly anchored against vagrant summer breezes—had a maroon-colored drape concealing whatever earth-shattering secrets it contained. The other held an oversized poster or blackboard, I surmised.

In a twinkling, my world was turning into a carnival, a heady new perspective. Overnight, my fondest dream—the not-too-certain prospect of superseding the tarnished Rush Donald as division manager—had become an uninspired ambition.

I was awash in a tsunami of career possibilities.

Even if Ferguson and his advisors thought I was such hot stuff, I didn't want to be too quick to dismiss John Paul's foundation as a possible course of action. I resolved to fly to Cincinnati to see Paxton Prueffer III, Esquire, and give John Paul's posthumous offer serious consideration. Perhaps I could still live in Melas. If the money were enough, I could probably convince Prueffer that the fund could be administered from anywhere—an easy undertaking for a bright young man with a creative flair.

I'd be under no real pressure to do anything but write my own books and administrate.

That might present Rose with an appealing option. She could hardly argue if she didn't have to move.

Beyond the pool, a chauffeured dark green Rolls Royce Silver Cloud was debarking a foursome of golfers at the golf club.

Across the room, a young man spotted Ferguson and pushed his way through the crowd, waving to get his attention.

Ferguson saw him and returned the wave.

Sweating with exertion, he made it to where we were standing. "Ian! What a zoo! Scotty says to bring you down to the boardroom."

When he saw me, he shot Ferguson a look.

"Forgive my manners," Ferguson apologized, "Abe Stein, I'd like to present Logan Baird. Logan is currently with Severance Labs."

"Logan Baird?" Stein wrinkled his brow, then brightened. "Of course, the *Harper's* piece. You're our editorial director. I'm honored."

He stuck out his hand.

His proprietary "our" had a heady sound.

"Abe's my long-time assistant at Cambridge. Can't do anything without him. He's the force behind the launching of *Hippocrates*," Ferguson explained.

Dumbstruck, I nodded.

May the force be with you, too, Abe, old sock.

I stood there looking at the two of them talking, trying to take it in.

With the booze and no sleep and the high stress of my long, insanity-driven night, the entire morning was taking on a surreal quality. In this carnival-like setting, time flowed like gooey strands of taffy spilling from mixing bowls on the midway of some cosmic county fair. Head reeling from the hullabaloo, I was a trifle lightheaded. My mind was having trouble working.

I took a closer look around. Were my eyes playing tricks?

Were Andy Rooney and Walter Cronkite standing just over there with Oprah Winfrey?

No tricks.

Malcolm Forbes, Jr., was joining them. And William Safire.

I looked enviously at a woman sipping on a dewy screwdriver.

Editorial director, *Hippocrates* magazine. The kind of job that I'd always thought existed only in movies starring Nick Nolte or Robert Redford. I tried to picture myself walking down Madison or Park Avenue on the way to work. Having lunch with Norman Mailer or Tom Wolfe. What the hell, I'd commission pieces from guys like Dominick Dunne, perhaps even George Will.

Ed Bradley? With a Bloody Mary? I'll just be bloody damned!

The place was crawling with celebrities, all of them poised to report the big story.

Could I still write? What would be my lead?

A good opening sentence?

I drew a total blank.

Logan Baird, impostor.

I'd just been offered the title of editorial director at a fancy magazine and I couldn't even come up with a decent sentence for a lead line. Hell, who was I fooling? I hadn't written a word that counted in four years.

Headline: *HIPPOCRATES* MAGAZINE DUMPS LOGAN BAIRD

Publisher Ian Ferguson says, "Baird over his head in the big leagues."

"Stick around, you're going to like it. I promise. I'll find you later at the hotel. Right after I present my paper. We have a lot to talk about." Ferguson gave my arm a squeeze and left with Abe.

As soon as Ferguson was out of sight, I grabbed a screwdriver off a passing tray and gulped it down.

I dumped the empty and grabbed another.

Within seconds, I began to breathe again and my vision cleared.

Good old C_2H_5OH—ethyl alcohol, the unsung miracle drug.

Just before half past the hour, the crowd quieted and there was a rush to the rows of folding chairs that had been reserved for the major wire services, big city dailies, and network broadcast people.

Brokaw, Rather, and Matt Lauer were all sitting in the front row.

Ben Bradlee had come down from the *Washington Post*, and James J. Kilpatrick himself took the seat beside him.

MacKenzie Brown's wealth and the Greenbrier.

All these high and mighty moths fascinated by the eternal flame.

A couple of rows behind the superelite, I spotted Jake and Pete. Behind them, here and there, were other vaguely familiar faces that I couldn't put a name or place to; most were from network TV, I guessed.

In the distance an exuberant car radio echoed Tony Bennett's "Fly me to the moon . . ."

A waiter passed through with the ubiquitous tray of screwdrivers.

I snagged a booster, just in case. Might as well be drunk as the way I was.

Good old orange juice! A man should get his vit—not vite—amins.

Ian Ferguson—bless your stuffy British ass—ain't you proud?

I sniggered a bit boozily. From across the way, Paula Zahn frowned disapprovingly.

I raised my glass and winked.

She frowned again and looked the other way.

Behave, I chastised myself. You'll wind up just like Rush last night.

A technician moved to the lectern and tapped one of the mikes, making a sharp popping sound in the portable speakers that had been set up on tripods.

"Testing . . . one . . . two . . . testing."

A butterfly perched on the CNN mike, slowly waving its wings.

Special effects by Disney or just an alcoholic hallucination?

The speakers blared and screeched with feedback from the overkill of microphones. A second technician with headphones made a quick adjustment at a console.

The screeching stopped as quickly as it began.

From nearby trees, a cardinal answered the sweet trill of a mockingbird.

Growing impatient now, the rowdy group whistled and shouted some mildly obscene suggestions as to what he could do for an encore.

I reddened—there were a lot of women present.

Shirtwaist dresses, tailored pants with mannish blouses. I recognized the look—career journalists, most of them. Some were still young and most were fairly attractive, but I noticed that many had developed tiny lines at the corners of their mouths. In no time, these women would become unflinching thick-skinned veterans, completely inured to the foul language that flowed like piped-in music to the newsrooms in the minutes before deadline.

At once, the low buzz of conversation stopped. The tension was electric.

Far off, there was a half-heard, half-imagined rumble of thunder. In a virtually cloudless sky?

Momentarily, I wondered about the afternoon. Our tee time was 12:28.

Looking around for Bobby, I found him at the lectern with Ian.

Beside them were two of the men I'd met back at Top Notch. I couldn't remember who they were or what they did.

Without preamble, MacKenzie Brown appeared and nodded to Bobby, who stepped to the lectern and cleared his throat.

"Good morning. I'm Robert Johnson, executive vice president of MBI. Before I introduce Scotty and the rest of our group, I want to thank you all for coming."

An expectant murmur. I stole a glance at Brown.

As studiously rumpled as he had appeared yesterday, now he projected the image of a man accustomed to the limelight. No longer the bumpkin in wrinkled chinos and rolled-up sleeves, he was attired in an expensive lightweight suit of suntan khaki. His button-down, blue oxford shirt was complemented by a silk tie with a regimental stripe.

"Before I turn this over to Scotty, I'd like to introduce some other players on the team. Ian . . ." Starting with Ferguson, Bobby made brief introductions of MBI's board.

In the distance, the drone of mowers manicuring the golf courses as the sun climbed higher in the morning sky.

"Now a bit of housekeeping. To save everyone extra questions at the end—and particularly for those who aren't familiar with MacKenzie Brown and MBI—instead of boring you all with a recitation of ancient history, I'll point out that there are plenty of press kits to go around. They contain complete outlines of everything you'll need: background data, including current and proposed corporate organizational charts and bios of all the key players, and copies of all the visuals we have up here this morning. The kits will be on the tables when you leave. Each kit has eight-by-ten color glossies of the key players—it's all there. And for those who were too busy at the bar and missed the news, there are more than enough phones with data ports set up in the air-conditioned tent to accommodate you." He turned and grinned at Brown and the others. "So, let's get on with the big news. I'll turn this over to my boss and old friend, MacKenzie Brown. Scotty, it's all yours."

There was a polite round of applause.

Behind the lectern, Abe appeared at the easel and gave the maroon drape a tug; it floated to the terrace.

The large visual was emblazoned:

***

THE HIPPOCRATES GROUP
subsidiary of
MBI
***

The headline HIPPOCRATES was done in open-face Augustea.

The Augustea typeface had a classic sculptured look.

Augustea was actually a Roman alphabet, but I was sure old Hippocrates would've forgiven the confused ethnicity—the ancient Greeks may have had a lot to say for themselves in art and architecture, but their alphas and omegas and the sharp-angled look of their alphabet have never been among their strong points.

H. Logan Baird, Editorial Director would look impressive in Augustea.

Brown waited, letting the audience consider the card in silence.

From the golf course there echoed a clear cry of, "Oh shit!"

An embarrassed spasm of laughter ran through the assemblage.

"A magic moment," Brown smiled down at the crowd.

The group exhaled an honest laugh.

Brown waited patiently for the laughter to subside before he began.

"We're here this morning to announce a new MBI undertaking: the Hippocrates Group—a conglomerate of free-standing enterprises, all related to the advancement of modern health care. Hippocrates will have autonomy with its own central management, which will orchestrate a cohesive thrust to the overall MBI mission. Our intent is for the Hippocrates Group to be the leading force in national health care and health care abroad as well."

Behind him, Abe removed the top card and sat it, blank side out, on the empty easel standing on the other side of the lectern.

The next card was a complex chart of the corporate family tree, listing an array of companies dealing with all aspects of health care. There was a large national hospital chain; a well-known leader in the manufacture of bandages, sterile dressings, and first-aid products; two leading electronic instrumentation firms; several nursing home chains; a national group of psychiatric hospitals; and on and on.

One by one, Brown quickly explained the roster of his holdings in the health care field.

In the distance, the muted pop-pop-pop of skeet guns at the Kate's Mountain Range.

Abe removed the card and transferred it to the second easel. The new card read:

COMMUNICATIONS
***
HIPPOCRATES MEDIA
***
Hippocrates Press
***
Hippocrates Films
***
Hippocrates Magazine

Hippocrates Magazine 'R US. That was me!

"The entire Hippocrates Group will be anchored by two divisions. The first is Hippocrates Media, consisting of a book publisher, Hippocrates Press; a film production company; and a magazine—all diverse and far-reaching. Our press will have separate divisions ranging from the field of scientific textbooks to fiction for children and adults. The power of Hippocrates Media will enable the Hippocrates Group to influence . . ."

In the distance a horse-drawn carriage transported a group of guests up the scenic mountain trail. The wayward breeze wafted the aroma of horse dung mingled with honeysuckle.

Instantly, it all came clear. MacKenzie Brown was entering the medical arena in the same way a revolutionary orchestrates the overthrow of a government.

First you take charge of the radio and TV stations and the press.

In time of revolution, it's axiomatic: Control the minds, and the bodies will follow.

" . . . and in just over three months, on December 15th, the first issue of *Hippocrates* magazine will hit the stands.

Hippocrates will be a major lifestyle magazine. Entirely supported by advertising, it will be mailed as a free subscription to every doctor and medical student in the USA and Canada."

Romantically, I imagined myself as Gregory Peck in *The Man In The Gray Flannel Suit*, the old Sloan Wilson classic.
 I remembered Rose naked in bed this morning.
 Rose even looked like Jennifer Jones.
 If you used your imagination.
 I'd find a place out of the city, one of those small towns in suburban New York. Westchester, or in Connecticut. Or Long Island, maybe. I could most likely afford them. I would carry one of those fancy Dunhill cases and work on my novel riding into the city on the commuter train. The salary—the club memberships with the expense and entertainment account—seemed enormous. Which was best? Some young sophisticates lived in Manhattan in brownstones and high-rises. My cousin Pat Saunders lived at the edge of the village in a new high-rise. One of the big network news anchors lived in her building. I'd had Bloody Marys—actually, the anchor had a chocolate shake—with her one Saturday morning in the spring when we were all up on the roof taking the sun. The anchor and her hubby had young children . . . two, I recalled. That might be okay for city-raised, show biz folk, but I couldn't see Rose trying to raise Paul in the middle of New York City.
 A few hundred yards below us, golfers were walking the fairways of the Greenbrier course.
 "And now for the grand announcement." It seemed that the sound on the PA system had been turned up. I almost expected an accompanying tantara of trumpets.
 Abe removed the media poster to the other easel, and my eyes followed, mesmerized by the headline *Hippocrates* Magazine.
 The blare of the PA speakers snapped me back to attention. "Yesterday afternoon, MBI formally acquired controlling ownership with the holding of sixty-nine percent of the common and fifty-seven percent of the preferred stock of Severance Laboratories of Teaneck, New Jersey."

Severance. I caught my breath.

No shit!

From the group a sharp gasp, then murmurs of surprise.

Here and there, a scattering of reporters rose and hurriedly made their way off the terrace, clasping laptops and cell phones and grabbing press kits on the way to the data phones.

"I hasten to say that there will be no immediate changes in the day-to-day management of Severance Laboratories. There will be the immediate calling of a meeting of the board. By sundown, MBI intends to vote its stock to elect Dr. Ian Ferguson as chairman of the board and CEO of Severance Laboratories. Effective immediately, Dr. Ferguson will also join the board of MBI."

No shit, indeed!

I took a sip of my screwdriver, trying to absorb the latest developments.

Rush's drunken scene with Ferguson at last night's cocktail party flashed before my eyes. The whole thing was incredibly ironic. Standing at the mike, the ordinary-looking old gentleman whom Rush and I had passed as he trudged the lonely country road was now our boss.

Fate hangs by a fragile thread.

What effect would this have on Rush's plans for Harvard B?

Behind Brown, Abe was removing the corporate chart for Severance Laboratories and placing it on the sister easel.

Remaining on the main easel was a blowup of a full-page ad in the *Wall Street Journal*. Dated for the following day, the ad's headline shimmered in the morning sun: MBI MAKES ONE-TIME OFFERING FOR SEVERANCE STOCK.

I was too overwhelmed to read the entire text, but the offering was substantial. Scotty Brown was certain to obtain virtually all the outstanding stock.

There was a visible break in the crowd. Cameras were flashing, and reporters were trying to ask questions. Here and there, more figures with laptops were rushing to grab press kits and head for the data phones. Any second it was going to become a complete madhouse.

"Gentlemen . . . ladies . . . please . . ." Scotty Brown looked back at his supporting players, shrugged, and laughed.

After a short wait, the movement subsided.

"Ladies and gentlemen, as most of you know, there is an important medical conference going on here at the hotel this week. Dr. Ian Ferguson, who will be the new chairman of Severance Labs, is one of the foremost authorities on steroid chemistry . . ."

He pronounced the word "stir-roid" in the traditional American way.

I glanced at Ferguson. His mouth silently formed "stee-roid" as he looked my way and shook his head.

You and me forever, Ian, old chum!

Brown went on, "In about twenty minutes Dr. Ferguson will be reading the featured paper on his recent landmark work with Severance Laboratories' new miracle drug for male erection enhancement, Virecta. You will find an advance copy of Dr. Ferguson's paper in the press kit. Full-sized copies of the tear sheet for tomorrow's ad in the *Wall Street Journal* are being distributed in all the meeting rooms and throughout the hotel's exhibit hall."

I looked from one easel to the other and then to the men standing at the front of this formidable gathering.

Either way I looked at it, no matter whether I took the *Hippocrates* offering or not, for the time being, at least, I was working for Ian Ferguson. And Bobby Johnson, my golf partner, had just become a board member of my company.

I didn't know whether to laugh or cry.

At this very moment, Rush was probably being handed a copy of the *Wall Street Journal* ad. I figured he'd head straight for his room. I couldn't blame him. He probably had some liquor there.

My pang of sympathy for his new vulnerability was fleeting.

In the end, we all coped the best we could.

Still dazed, I turned and made my way back through the crowd. As I left, I picked up four copies of the press kit.

MBI
✳✳✳
HIPPOCRATES GROUP

Was that my future blind-embossed into the fancy cover?

CHAPTER FORTY-SEVEN

I was mistaken in assuming Rush would be hiding in his room. When I arrived back in the exhibit hall, everywhere I looked, men and women—doctors and company representatives alike—were holding the tear sheet of the *Wall Street Journal* ad.

Sitting in our booth by himself, Rush had the ad spread out on his lap.

Around the large hall, groups of twos and threes were talking about the announcement. Some were still reading. Others were dangling the paper limply from their hands. From time to time, they glanced over at Rush sitting alone in our booth. They were uncertain what the takeover meant to us but afraid to ask.

Change is a scary thing. To the people in this room, this monumental move affected a lot of lives. It was a sobering event.

Lately, there was a nervous climate in the industry. The high cost of pharmaceuticals was under government scrutiny. Old liberal politicos like Ted Kennedy and new ones like the aspiring female from New York were making noises. With the aging population, the prospect of semisocialized medicine was a political expedient, too seductive to overlook. Now the government was starting to look the other way when the small houses infringed on the patents of the big research companies.

"Hi, Rush. I brought you something." I handed him one of the MBI press kits.

"Thanks." He took the folder, staring at it dumbly.

"I brought copies for Bill and Al. Did he show up yet?" I waved the extra copies.

"Huh? Oh, yeah, Al's here. They were both pretty excited. I let 'em take a break."

"I'll just leave these here. Don't forget to tell them." I put two of the folders behind the exhibit backdrop and kept the other for myself.

"What do you think this means?" he asked.

"I'm not sure. Wonder what the company is going to tell the men in the trenches?" I looked closely for a clue about how he was holding up.

Sometimes the corporate line could rival the constant stream of garbage spewed forth by the best White House spin doctors.

"We already got the word. Herman Asbury arranged a big closed-circuit TV hookup to all the division managers around 9:20. I took it in my room."

"And just what did old silver-tongued Herm allow?" I asked.

Old Herm was VP sales. And, like Rush, notoriously full of shit.

"Mr. Asbury says business as usual, no major change. He says the reason MBI acquired us in the first place is because we're well managed, have the best people and the best research."

He glanced my way. A look of curiosity crossed his face.

"By the way, what did Ferguson want with you . . . about the writing, I mean?" He was clearly uncomfortable. I represented an unknown quantity now.

"Oh, he was all pumped about *Hippocrates* magazine. Can you imagine? He told me that my *Harper's* article had inspired the *Hippocrates* concept. Ferguson actually thinks I'm somebody. Wants to make the magazine a status symbol for physicians and their wives. Big snob appeal. A manual for the sophisticated physician lifestyle, I guess you'd say."

I didn't mention Ferguson's offer. I still had an uneasy feeling that I'd wake up and it would all be just a dream.

"Did he say anything about your future . . . with Severance, I mean? Ferguson's the big cheese, chairman of the board and CEO now. And, can you believe it? Our new owner is that Scotty person . . . MacKenzie Brown. The same old gentleman we tried to help on the road coming over with the . . . uh, quaint old golf bag. No wonder those bellmen and porters down at the club jumped when he drove up. The help around a place like this can spot real class when they see it. Good thing we turned around to help him the other day," Rush said, shaking his head.

"You just never know," I shrugged, amused at how quickly he could change his tune.

"You're not saying much. Did you meet him too? Brown, I mean. C'mon, you're awfully quiet. What happened?" Fidgeting, he stood up and self-consciously folded the tear sheet of the newspaper ad. "Some souvenir, huh?"

"Yeah, it really is," I smiled.

"Aren't you going tell me about it? Is it a secret?" Rush shuffled his feet nervously.

"Not much to tell. I did see Brown, and Bobby Johnson was there with the other members of the MBI board. They were busy with the last-minute details about the press conference. The main reason Ferguson invited me was because he'd been using my *Harper's* piece at Harvard Med to tell the incoming classes of budding doctors that they should stop and smell the roses. He said my essay inspired the entire *Hippocrates* concept, especially the magazine. Can you believe it? Wait 'til Rose and my parents hear that."

"Guess that puts you in solid, huh? Did he say anything about a job? A promotion? I thought he was looking for a medical writer."

"He sort of danced around it. Wanted to pick my brains about *Hippocrates* magazine. Say, listen, it's not too late to take my place in the foursome this afternoon. It's okay. Give you a chance to rub elbows with Bobby Johnson. I need to go take a nap anyway. How about it?" I knew he wouldn't take me up on it, but I really didn't care if he did. I'd just as soon have the nap.

"Oh, no. Hell no. But maybe I could just show up at the golf club and have a drink with you guys when you finish, like yesterday, huh? Wouldn't hurt to get to know Johnson over a drink."

"Sure, that'd be fine. Christ, I'm a zombie. I don't know how the hell I can play. We should finish around four-thirty, quarter to five. You can watch us when we play up eighteen."

"Great idea. By the way, about your car, did you get the estimate yet?" He looked at me anxiously.

"Yeah, forty-eight hundred twelve bucks and change." I shook my head, sadly.

"Jeezus! Wonder if it'll be cheaper in Roanoke?"

I stood my ground. "I don't know, but with you heading out for Boston, I don't want to waste any time. Whoever fixes it will want their money . . . cash. You can't expect me to cover it, and I don't know how I'll be able to get in touch with you. I'm not about to hedge to the company on this."

"Oh, c'mon now." He reached across and dusted an imaginary speck from my jacket and smoothed my lapel. "You don't really think I was serious about playing cozy with your expenses? Listen, you know me better. I'm a stand-up guy. I'd never do a thing like that."

"You said—"

"Oh, no. That was just a joke. You know me, I always kid around a lot. Don't worry. Listen, what the hell, I'll just write you a check for forty-eight twenty-five right now. Okay?"

He walked over, reached behind the display backdrop, and retrieved his briefcase.

It was a nice case but definitely not a Dunhill.

"Look, if it runs more, then I'll send you a check for the rest, all right?"

What a difference a day makes.

I nodded. I could hardly believe my ears.

He wrote the check and handed it to me with a shy grin.

"My squirrel account. Nadine doesn't have any idea it exists. If the cost runs more in Roanoke, just let me know."

"Thanks, I will." I looked at the check and put it in my pocket.

"Say, I almost forgot." I pointed to my watch. "Ferguson was scheduled to start reading his paper about two minutes ago. You going in?"

"Jeezus, yes. Slipped my mind. Wonder if I can still get a seat up front. Never hurts to make brownie points." Still holding the briefcase, he grabbed a scratch pad and pen from the giveaways on the display table. He called back over his shoulder as he started off. "If I miss you here, I'll see you this afternoon at the golf club, right?"

"Right," I murmured, watching him go.

Things were moving fast. Ferguson would be looking for me. They'd promised me I could have until Wednesday, but I knew he would be pressing me for an answer.

Before I talked to Ferguson again, I needed to talk to Paxton Prueffer III, Esquire, about John Paul's will.

I surveyed the room to see if Bill and Al were anywhere in sight and spotted them at the back of the hall. Retrieving the extra Hippocrates press kits, I set out in their direction.

Handing over the press kits, I bid them adieu and headed for my room.

CHAPTER FORTY-EIGHT

When I called, Paxton Prueffer's secretary rang me straight through.

We got right to the point about the details of John Paul's legacy.

"There will be plenty of money, and you're the sole legal administrator. You'll have the power to fix your own salary . . . within ethical bounds, of course. It's all duly incorporated in the state of Ohio as a tax-exempt foundation. There are established by-laws, and it's clearly spelled out that the foundation must be audited and will function as a legitimate grants-in-aid institution for supporting young writers. The funding is in a separate trust, not part of the regular estate. When I discussed it with John Paul, the salary figure we had in mind was in the ninety- to hundred-thousand range. You could provide yourself a car, plus health insurance and all expenses, of course. It would give you a pretty nice income by anyone's standards. When John Paul was granted full tenure, he was raised to forty-nine nine. Nowadays bank VPs are topping out at seventy to seventy-five," he emphasized the point.

I couldn't argue. Rush was making about fifty-five or sixty, and after Harvard would be raised to around seventy . . . eighty tops, I figured.

The *Hippocrates* salary Ferguson dangled was over one hundred grand plus the perks . . . and all the power.

"I'll make reservations to fly in Sunday, late afternoon or early evening, depending on the flights. Sunday night okay for you?" I asked.

"Sounds great. Call as soon as you know your flight number and times. I'll meet your plane."

"Fine. By the way, what about establishing a headquarters? Would it have to be up there in Ohio? I mean, it would seem that it wouldn't matter. Could I run things here just as well and fly up to consult with you when I had to?"

"I don't know. The whole thing revolves around providing for Maggie Walker and her kids," he said. "You'd have to work it out with her. I guess there aren't any rules. John Paul didn't express any strong feeling about having the foundation operate out of here, but Maggie lives here. And it is founded under Ohio law. On the other hand . . ." He stopped and there was a lengthy silence on the line. "Now that I think about it, all things considered . . . I mean with the initial grant going to Maggie . . . it would be better not to have it here. There's probably going to be a stink with the wife and sister. It might just be worth looking into moving the corporation out of state. Maybe someplace like Delaware that is sympathetic to incorporation, if you get my drift."

"Yeah." I was pretty sure I was going to be in for some unpleasant questions from the wife and sister when the will was read. "Can we set up a meeting with this Mrs. Walker, Sunday night or Monday after the will is read?"

"I don't see why not. Maggie is as anxious to meet you as you should be to meet her. I'll let you know when you call me with the flight information, okay?"

"Fair enough," I said. "I'll call you back as soon as I make my reservation."

My watch showed almost 11:00. That left me an hour and a half before I had to show up bright-eyed and bushy-tailed to play golf.

I undressed and hung up my clothes. A shower would help.

When I finished toweling dry, I felt revived, but even though I was in the perfect win/win situation, I still had miles to go and promises to keep.

Woodenly, I moved to the dresser, put on clean undershorts, poured a healthy slug of vodka into a tall glass, and rescued the carafe of orange juice from the ice bucket.

Sure enough, the housekeeper had replaced the ice.

Ladies and gentlemen being served by ladies and gentlemen, the brochure said.

It occurred to me now that I'd been living on adrenaline and alcohol for the past thirty-six hours. The realization was disturbing. I had to get off this treadmill sooner or later. But I knew it wasn't going to happen right this minute. For the moment, my coveted nap was out of the question.

I took an unhealthy swallow from the glass and replaced the volume with pure vodka.

Too late to stop the train right now.

Drink in hand, I made my way over to the easy chair, found air line companies in the yellow pages, and dialed USAir. In less than five minutes, I had a reservation.

I called Prueffer again to confirm the times. "I'm booked out of Roanoke on USAir to arrive in Cincinnati around two Sunday afternoon."

"Maggie will be with me when I meet your plane," he said, the perfect model of efficiency. "By the way," he added, just before he hung up, "don't feel too sorry for Cathy and Jean. John Paul's doctor's attorney just called offering to settle my threat of a malpractice suit. Their insurance company is talking humongous bucks. The wife and sister will come out okay."

With that good news, I hung up the phone feeling much better.

Pacing myself slowly on the atomic orange juice, I placed the drink on the table beside my manuscript. I opened the box and lifted out a sheaf of thirty or forty coffee-stained pages.

With a tug of regret for my abandoned promise to John Paul, I began.

Henley Logan Baird
125 Hurst Avenue
Melas, Virginia

A POSTURING OF FOOLS
a novel

Whooomp! The mortar shell hit close enough to cover him with dirt.

"You never hear the one that has your name on it," the British army captain had told them in the briefing. At the moment U.S. Army correspondent Lt. Randall Carter fervently wanted to believe him . . .

434

Time eluded me as I became lost in the words. The phone rang just as I was beginning page twenty-five.

"Logan? Ian Ferguson here. Glad I caught you before you headed to the golf course. Bobby, Scotty, and Abe have decided we have done about all we can do here. Time's a-wasting, so we're flying out this afternoon around three. Since Bobby has to cancel the golf, I wondered if you might be willing to forego the game with your pals and grab a bite of lunch with us here at Top Notch before we go? Time is of the essence now, and I want to make sure we understand each other before I leave. We'll be needing an answer from you no later than the middle of next week."

"Sure. What time?" I readily agreed.

"The sooner the better. It's almost eleven-forty now. How soon can you get away?"

"Be there in thirty minutes, okay?"

"See you then."

Without putting down the phone, I dialed Sam's room.

"Maryanne, is Sam still there?"

"Hold on, he's just going out the door."

When Sam came on the line, I made my excuses and offered to call the golf shop and explain that he and Max would be looking for a pairing.

"No need. I know someone. Just tell them we'll be there with four." I thanked him, called the pro, and confirmed the change. Reluctantly putting my manuscript aside, I dressed and headed out the door.

At Top Notch, everyone had changed into casual clothes. Porters were already busy moving luggage into limos. Ferguson and Abe met me at the door, apologizing for having to ask me to cancel the golf.

"No matter, really. To tell the truth, you did me a favor. I didn't get much sleep last night. When we're finished here, I'm going back to my room and take a nap," I reassured them.

"You remember Abe? Meet Abe Stein, boy publisher, *Hippocrates* magazine. Abe's your new boss as of about two hours ago."

"Congratulations," I nodded and shook Abe's hand.

435

"Let's grab a bite and go out and sit under one of those umbrellas." Ferguson pointed to a sandwich buffet laid out in the dining room, then steered me in ahead of Abe and himself.

Glancing around the room at the expensive luggage, I'd bet the $42,500 gross income on my last year's tax return was probably less than MacKenzie Brown paid his yardman in Boca.

Brown and the others were already seated in a group on the sun porch sipping drinks, engaged in a very convivial discussion.

"There you are, Baird. What did you think about our little show?" Brown asked.

"Quite impressive."

"Ah, yes. By the way, I haven't had a chance to tell you I'm glad you're aboard." He stood and extended his hand.

"Thanks . . . Mr. Brown." I was uncertain how I should address him.

"Scotty, please," he said. "By the way, thanks for coming back to pick me up the other day. I'd gotten myself in a quite a fix."

"It was nothing. But tell me, that car you were driving when I passed you on the road, it had a Massachusetts tag."

"My son's." He smiled. "Mac graduated medicine at Harvard. Everyone here knows that old jalopy. Mac's a resident at MCV in Richmond now. I usually stop off to visit when I'm down this way. He loans me the car so I can visit an old friend in Roanoke on the way here. And he lets me borrow his golf equipment, too. I leave my clubs in Boca. My golf bag looks slightly better than his," he chuckled.

"Not much! Sam Snead has given up. He calls it Scotty's refugee bag from a yard sale," Bobby interjected.

They all laughed.

"Anyway, it's a good deal for Mac. For the loan of the car, I fly him over here. Next week he'll spend a long weekend here with his new wife, and they'll drive his car back home."

I nodded.

"How do you feel about all our big news?" Scotty asked me.

"It was quite a surprise to learn about the Severance acquisition. It's too new for me to digest completely. But, when you were making the announcement about Hippocrates Media, I couldn't help but be struck with the notion that you planned this the same way revolutionaries map out a coup d'etat." I paused for effect. "Control the minds and the bodies will follow," I intoned theatrically.

He turned to the others. "That's it exactly! That's how it has to work. You have to win the public's tacit permission." Brown slapped my shoulder. "When you come on board in New York, I'll be looking forward to hearing more of your observations. Glad to have you with us, Baird. See you soon." He turned back to the others.

Brown was the genius here. Who was I to quibble?

On the terrace, Ferguson got down to business. "By the way, we have a bit of good news. Our first choice for managing editor, Sherrill Bobbitt, called and committed less than an hour ago. Do you know who Bobbitt is?"

"Sorry, no."

Perhaps I should reconsider my limitations before they realized I was a cheap impostor.

Don't fly too near the sun on waxen wings.

Ferguson shrugged. "Me either until a few days ago. Sherrill Bobbitt's currently at *Esquire* as executive editor. He's the best. By the way we had a messenger take him copies of your *Harper's* piece and he saw your clips. Said your stuff put him in mind of a cross between Mark Twain and Tom Wolfe. The man's impressed and pleased that you'll be with him."

"He actually said that? That's pretty heady company." I almost licked his hand.

"The bottom line is that Sherrill is high on you. All we need is your answer. How much are you making at Severance?"

I was tempted to fudge, but I knew better. I was certain he had the answer to the very last penny.

"Depends on bonuses, but I'm counting on paying taxes on a little less than thirty-eight thousand, plus my car and all expenses. In lifestyle, that probably translates to about seventy to eighty K in the big city. And even then, there are certain things I have that I can't buy up there, not at any price."

I wanted to be sure he understood that I valued my lifestyle and that little things meant a lot to a peon like me.

He smiled and looked to Abe. "How about it, Abe? We can't expect Logan's answer unless he knows what we're offering. Tell the man."

"Eighty, huh?" He raised his eyebrows and glanced at Ferguson. "That's a lot of lifestyle even in New York, Ian."

I just gave him a stare.

He looked at me and back at Ferguson.

"I told my wife one hundred." I couldn't believe it was my voice I was hearing, but after two days of Rush's insanity, I was sick and tired of being jacked around.

Abe looked at Ferguson again. Ferguson shrugged.

My heart sank. Had I overstepped the mark? I didn't want to shoot myself in the foot before they made me an offer.

"You think you're worth it?"

"If I'm not, then you goys don't know what you're doing." The slip was fatigue, not Freud.

Everybody laughed.

Abe more than the rest.

"We don't want to play with you. Including expenses, we budgeted one-fifty to start. It does cost a lot to live in New York and raise a family. You don't have to tell me about that. I won't sell you short. Bobbitt says you're green but you're a pro. He likes your stuff, and he says he's looking for people who are fresh . . . people who won't muddy up the carpet with a lot of cliché and other bad habits. We'll pay you one hundred base, plus car and expenses, and the title will be executive editor. That's Bobbitt's idea from his *Esquire* days. How's that sound to you?"

I was about to wet my pants. I'd left home two days ago fighting with my wife over an air conditioner and now, within the last two hours, I'd been given two separate chances to more than double my gross income. "Sounds okay to me, but, of course, I'll still have to consult my wife. Rose has the responsibility of raising our son. I couldn't give you an answer unless she agrees. Could we fly up and take a few days to look over the area?"

"Has your wife been to New York City lately? Say, in the last two or three years?" It was Ferguson asking.

"Once," I replied.

"We'll pay the expenses you require to relocate. Take a month, take two or three. Bring your wife and the boy. We'll put you up in a hotel and provide you with a car and baby-sitting. We'll have someone drive her around while you spend your days putting this damn magazine together. Anything you require, but only after you tell us yes. I don't see the need for your wife to go make sure she remembers what New York looks like. It's the biggest, most cosmopolitan city in the world. I'm sure with the money she'll have, she can find a place to make a good home for you, with good schools for the boy. After all, we want you happy." Ferguson took a bite of his sandwich. "That's fair, don't you think?"

I didn't have to think that over.

"More than fair," I said. "I'll need a day or two. I won't get home until Saturday night . . . that's two more days." The trip I'd planned to Ohio was heavy on my mind.

"No later than Wednesday morning, and that will make you among the last. All the other key players will be moved in and working by then."

"Of course, but surely the others had more time. After all, I was the last you asked." I was through being pushed around. As fast as my heart was beating with excitement, the adrenaline was wearing off, and my fatigue went all the way to the bone. Besides, I reminded myself, John Paul had dealt me an ace in the hole. I still had Paxton Prueffer waiting in the wings.

"Touché," Abe said and smiled. "But I need an answer by Wednesday . . . noon. Sorry, but that's the way it is. Besides, you don't have to wait 'til you get home to start dealing with your wife. That's what phones are for."

"Yeah, but you don't know my wife. She invented eestrogen poisoning." I watched Ferguson break into a wide grin. "It's difficult for her to make a decision about the next movie we see, much less a major change in our life."

"Wives! We all have our crosses," Abe sighed. "Anyway, if you can make it sooner, you are hereby released from Severance without having to give notice. Goes without saying, Ian will clear that."

Ferguson interjected, "Why are we quibbling about this? We all know you're coming with us—wife or no wife—don't we? Go ahead as soon as we get back, Abe. Start making all the arrangements. Make airline reservations and get Logan and his wife a suite at the Plaza or the equivalent beginning next Thursday. Arrange for a limo. Make sure Mrs. Baird has everything she needs to go house-hunting to her heart's content. And, Abe, I should think Logan will need an operating advance. He's going to need some walking around money until he can get his family relocated and his salary starts coming on time. How's fifteen thousand sound? I think that should do rather handily for openers. Just keep receipts. Go ahead and have the check cut, Abe. Wednesday will be the official day."

As far as Ferguson was concerned, it was a decision, not a question.

Fifteen K . . . just for walking-around money. That was two years on my mortgage.

Scotty Brown stuck his head back inside.

"So long, Logan. Glad you're aboard."

I gave a wave.

"See you Wednesday," Abe said companionably. He got up and handed me a shiny new Dunhill case and a heavy folder. "Here's some stuff to look over. Nothing like a flying start."

I made no protest. I wasn't into jousting windmills.

"Hate to eat and run," Ferguson said. "If you need anything, just call. There's a list of the private numbers and policies in the folder. Goodbye and thanks."

I watched him go.

"Take your time, finish your lunch. The check will be in the mail. I'll be waiting for your call." Abe shook hands and followed Ferguson back inside.

I grabbed my beer and headed out through the back gate.

To hell with lunch. I might change my mind, but I wanted to get out of there before they had a chance to change theirs.

CHAPTER FORTY-NINE

Back at the hotel, I headed straight for the elevator, hell-bent on catching a snooze. I was determined to tell the switchboard to hold my calls and put the do not disturb sign on my door for the rest of the afternoon.

The elevator doors opened and Rush brushed by me, almost knocking me down.

He stopped and turned. "I thought you were playing golf. What happened?"

"Canceled. Bobby couldn't play. Flying back with Ferguson and Scotty and the rest. These guys don't waste time. What's up with you? Where're you headed with that stuff?" He had a briefcase and a package in his hands. There was a golf scorecard with the map of the Old White Course on the back sticking out of the breast pocket of his blazer, now emblazoned with the Greenbrier crest.

He saw my stare.

"Real touch of class, eh?" he said, grinning like a chimp.

I gave the package he carried a closer look.

"Greenbrier golf shirts," he smiled proudly. "You should get some while you're here."

"I guess." I glanced down at his briefcase. "Going somewhere?"

"Yeah. I'm glad I caught you. I left a message for your room. Herman Asbury called, wants me to fly to Teaneck Sunday. I'm on my way to Roanoke now. I hate to leave this way, but I have to get back tonight. Herman needs me there to do some planning next week. I'll probably go straight on to Harvard B from there. My stuff's packed and sitting outside. I ordered a rental car."

"Okay. All the best. I know you'll dazzle 'em in Boston. Too bad you didn't get to play some golf." Nothing more I wanted to add.

"By the way, I know Ferguson must think I'm a horse's ass. I heard his paper, but I didn't get a chance to speak with him. I don't expect that you'd plead my case, but you know he's our chairman now. Did he say anything about last night?"

"Nah, I wouldn't worry." It was mostly true.

"If you get a chance, put in a word . . ."

"I will. And, seriously, I wouldn't sweat last night too much."

"No sense in losing sleep. C'mon, walk out with me and say goodbye." He turned to leave. I noticed he was walking a bit stiff-legged.

"Leg bothering you?" I had to ask.

A born troublemaker to the end.

"Not bad. An old sports injury. I hardly notice it." He straightened up his stride.

"Life can be hard for old sports sometimes." I couldn't help but grin. I could just hear him pleading his caught-it-in-my-zipper story with Nadine.

"By the way, does Mimi know you're going?"

He gave me a suspicious look.

"Sure. She's quite a gal. Talking about coming up for a weekend while I'm at Harvard B, but I don't think I'm going to encourage it."

"Let's face it, Rush. You're just plain hell with the ladies."

At the curb, a brand-new dark gray Cadillac stood waiting. The bellman was loading his luggage.

"Some rental," I whistled.

"Nice, huh?"

"No one ever said you didn't like to go first class."

I really didn't want to be too hard on the man—I'd learned a lot from him.

Not all of it positive though.

Reminded of the last time I'd seen John Paul—the night we said, "So long, stay in touch" in New York, six years ago—I realized I might not see this man again.

Sometimes things end sooner than we think.

"Goodbye again," I said and gave his shoulder a friendly pat.

That was about all I could think to say.

"By the way, thanks for getting the clubs. I know you went to a lot of trouble. Pretty nice sticks, really. Sorry we didn't get to play. I think I'll try a set when I get settled in Teaneck. Nadine is going up to look at houses next week."

"Good luck." I sounded like a broken record.

"I really am sorry about your car . . ."

"Not to worry," I smiled.

"I'd best be getting on." He turned to the bellman waiting beside the car.

The old mahogany-colored attendant stood waiting with his hand resting lightly on the gleaming trunk deck. Two rings with massive diamonds sparkled on the fingers of his hand.

"Be careful of your rings, George," Rush cautioned him sharply. "This isn't just some damn jalopy."

"Don't you worry, Mr. Donald. I'm always very careful. I got one at home jus' like this. I buy me a brand new one ev'y year. Give las' year's model to my daughter up in D.C. jus' las' week. My new one's jus' like this, 'ceptin' mine's a Fleetwood. At my age I needs a little extra room. And mine's a nice dark blue. Yes, sir, I'm real proud of that automobile." He lifted his hand carefully. On his wrist was a genuine Rolex, a lot fancier than Rush's.

A flush crept up the back of Rush's neck as he took a big roll of bills out of his pocket and peeled off a twenty.

"Well, now! Thank you, kindly, Mr. Donald, sir. It's always a pleasure to see you back heah."

"Drive safe," I called.

"Sure has been a bitch of a three days," Rush offered lamely, reluctant to leave.

I grinned. "I don't guess either one of us will forget this one for a while."

"About last night. I hope Rose won't mention anything to Nadine . . ."

It was getting truly awkward now.

"Don't sweat it. Get rolling before you miss your plane," I said with an offhand wave.

The elderly black man and I watched as Rush and his rented Caddy rolled out of sight.

"That Mr. Donald, he a touch o' class, all right," the old gentleman said, folding the twenty and stuffing it into his breast pocket.

I winked. "I guess."

"It sho' 'nuf be one fine day, Mr. Baird. Sho' 'nuf one fine day."

I didn't dare ask how he remembered my name.

CHAPTER FIFTY

Tired as I should have been, the exhilaration of the meeting at Top Notch had left me with a supercharged adrenaline afterglow. I was reluctant to go back to my room just yet.

"Can you find my car keys? I gave them to the night attendant early this morning," I asked the ageless major-domo.

"Yes, sir, that's the new Buick with the messed-up side. The dealer came yestiddy and did a estimate. Be right behind them trees. Can I have 'em get it for you?"

"Could I just go get it myself? It's a beautiful day. Thought I might take a little spin—see the country."

"Sho' 'nuf be a right pretty day. Yes, sir, jus' let me get the key, an' Mr. Baird, suh, you just call me Obadiah."

I found the car, drove slowly out the gate, and turned right, which took me west on U.S. 60 toward Lewisburg.

When I topped the rise just past the Lewisburg town limit, I had no trouble recognizing where Ginny had turned Tuesday night. In the bright sunshine it looked less storybook than it had two nights ago.

A lot had transpired since then. My mood was decidedly different now.

In front of Ginny's cottage, I slowed. There was no car in the drive, and the house had an empty look. Edging to the curb with my motor running, a tiny ache blossomed in my chest as her words came back to me.

"You were so beautiful. You reminded me of a Greek god. Now you're such a beautiful man," she had breathed in my ear.

It had been the loveliest speech a man could ever want to hear.

"Lies, lies, lovely lies. Promises, promises, promises," I'd replied.

Served me right, I guess—I'd been so eager to believe.

"What ya think you're doin' back here, Baird?" Clyde Goins's growl shattered my reverie.

"You got a good memory, deputy." The oafish rent-a-cop had snuck up beside me and rolled his window down. I attempted a smile, without much success.

"Why don't you move on before I run you in for blocking traffic?"

"Sure." I started rolling my window up.

"And, Baird, a piece of friendly advice. I don't think I'd come back here if I was you. Miss McKim don't want to see you no more."

I was tired of his insolence, but I took the pressure off the brake.

"Not ever again. You hear me now?" he prodded.

I saluted as I swung around and headed out slowly, back the way I came.

"Don't get your pantyhose in a bind, asshole," I breathed half-aloud to his image in the mirror. I wished I'd had the *cajones* to tell him to go do unspeakable things to himself.

He followed me all the way back to White Sulphur Springs. When I came abreast of the railway station across from the Greenbrier gates, he pulled off and watched me continue in the direction of the tiny business district. Then I saw him turn and head back west again.

At the street where Melba lived, I turned and drove between the well-ordered old houses. Children were playing on the quiet, tree-lined street. I watched a woman digging in her flowerbed while her neighbor raked pine straw. When I approached the old place with the garage apartment in back, Melba's yellow Beetle was gone.

I sighed and drove on past without slowing. Making a sweeping turn at the cul-de-sac, I headed back the way I'd come.

It occurred to me that I'd never learned anything worthwhile if there wasn't a lot of chaos attached.

My way . . . the hard way.

What had the last three days taught me, anyway?

I was too tired to pursue the implication.

I guessed that somewhere down the line, I'd figure it out.

I tried to remember who said, "The thing that makes life so sweet is that we will never come this way again."

Good thing we can't see the future. I marveled at my brilliant philosophical insight.

Anyway, things seemed to have a way of working out.

At the hotel, I parked, strolled to the front entrance, and handed the old gentleman back the key. Pressing a twenty in the old man's hand, I winked.

"Buy yourself another Fleetwood, Obadiah." I grinned.

"I just might at that Mr. Baird. Hee-hee." I left him shaking his head.

Still too restless to think about a nap, I walked down the arcade, browsing the expensive shop windows. I wondered what I'd say to Rose. She'd throw a fit.

I loved New York. I'd traveled there several times a year since I'd been with Severance. I loved the music and the lights.

Bobby Short was there in June. And Donald Harrison had been at Sweet Basil on Bleeker, doing that groin-grabbing New Orleans eighties sound. And the Algonquin, the Knickerbocker . . .

Caught up in the reverie, I fantasized walking in and out of Barneys and Saks Fifth Avenue.

Lunch at P.J. Clarke's. Everyone would know my name.

I'd eat it up.

Henley Logan Baird, executive editor, could handle the big city. I'd bet on that.

Still not ready to go back to my room, I walked purposefully up the wide stairs, through the upper lobby, and into the exhibit hall.

Wistfully, I took a final look.

The room was virtually empty. Only a few nongolfing physicians still wandered aimlessly about. A handful of night security guards was already in place.

"Henley Baird?" a voice trespassed on my reverie. Except my mother, no one had called me by that name in almost twenty years.

I turned to face a well-dressed gentleman who, standing only a few steps away, looked to be a few years my senior.

He was wearing a physician's badge.

Watching me screw up my brow trying mightily to place him, he broke into a grin.

Then, still grinning like a crocodile, he leaned slightly forward and took the pleats of his well-pressed silk trousers between his fingers at mid-thigh and, daintily, like a schoolgirl, stepped out of his expensive Italian loafers. Slowly, he raised his trouser legs above the tops of his dark-gray silk opera-length socks and pirouetted completely around.

I raised my eyebrows, wondering if he were drunk as a shithouse rat.

"No holes in my socks now, you see," he chortled.

"Melvin? My god, is that really you?"

In a twinkling, I was transported back to my childhood.

Melvin Long was several years older than I was, but his brother Charlie was in my grade when I was just starting school. The Longs had about eight kids at home, and Melvin and Charlie's daddy had been laid off from the railroad. During the early eighties, with struggling coal miners and railroad mergers, times were hard. Mr. Long had been out of steady work for quite some time. My mother was always sending my brother and me over to the Longs' with clothes my daddy's family had sent. We carried them extra food we couldn't use.

The Longs were a proud family. It wasn't that they weren't willing to work. Mr. Long was always looking for the chance to earn his family's daily bread.

"Melvin, ain't you ashamed to wear socks like that?" My first year at high school I had thoughtlessly rebuffed poor Melvin one day when he came up to me and tried to be friendly while some of my football teammates were standing around. I was big for my age and already making a name for myself on the playing field. I thought I was something special. I didn't want my new teammates to think this raggedy bumpkin with holes in his socks was someone I knew.

I had hardly finished the hurtful question before Melvin hit me flush in the mouth and knocked me clear over a bench down by the practice field.

Melvin was several years older, but I had already grown taller and heavier. I had a mean reputation on the football field, and I'd already whipped his ass pretty convincingly at the school bus stop once before when he'd tried to pick on a smaller kid.

Melvin knew damn well I could do it again, any time I chose.

Lying on my back looking up at him that day, my daddy's words had come back to me. "Mr. Long does the best he can. Lots of folk looking for work. No shame in that."

The shame was mine; the cold truth had come pouring over me like a winter rain.

And more, I had admired Melvin's courage.

Everybody had come running, looking to see a good fight, but I had known I was wrong. I just brushed myself off, walked over to Melvin, and said, "Sorry, Melvin, I was outta line."

I had offered a handshake instead of wiping up the pavement with him.

Fully prepared to take his lumps, Melvin had shaken his head in open-mouthed amazement and walked away.

"Chicken," an anonymous voice had come floating out of the crowd.

"Step out here and say that," I had challenged and stood my ground. I was in the mood for a good fight then—but not with Melvin.

No one had stepped forward.

"How do you feel about it now?" my daddy had asked me that night. I'd been hurting pretty bad deep inside, and I couldn't figure out why.

"I guess I felt ashamed that I said what I did about his socks. He can't help being poor. But it was hard not to beat his butt for hitting me in the mouth. Still, I knew I had it coming." I looked down and kicked a rock halfway across the road.

I'd been pretty confused. But I'd known I wasn't scared of Melvin.

"I'm proud of you," my daddy had said and walked off. I was going on thirteen and was second-string quarterback—too grown-up to hug.

That was back in the eighties. Not long after that Melvin went off to join the marines. He'd gotten blown out a window in a bombing in Beirut. When he came home, he went back to high school and finished in my class.

By then I was a star, my name in all the papers.

Nobody paid Melvin much attention.

But seeing his quiet dedication to his studies taught me that it takes more than scoring touchdowns to be a real man.

I had lost track of Melvin after high school. After college, I'd gotten married and eventually found my own war in Bosnia.

I stepped forward and read the tag: Melvin J. Long, M.D., Richmond, VA.

"Melvin? My god, is that really you?"

He grinned and shrugged, then hugged me unashamedly.

Laughing, we both fell to asking questions. Turned out that he was a professor at the Medical College of Virginia.

He looked at his watch and apologized. "I'm driving back to Richmond. I have to meet the wife and some friends for dinner."

I made him show me his fancy socks again. Those elegant silk stockings and his handmade Italian loafers spoke of everything between us.

I was tempted to tell him about my sudden celebrity, but I was afraid it might sound all wrong . . . or change my luck.

Besides, it wasn't all decided, anyway.

Bone-tired, I took his card and through misty eyes watched him as he left the hall and made his way into the broad gallery.

When he was gone, I found my handkerchief and blew my nose.

When I left the hall, Melba was standing in the empty gallery, looking lost.

I pulled up short. I'd hoped I wouldn't have to see her—not right away at least.

"I saw you talking to the man and waited. I was thinking about you all day. It's my day off," she said. She was wearing a heartbreaking little summer dress. It should have been against the law.

"How're you feeling?" I struggled to control my breathing.

"I'm fine. Are you okay?" Except that she looked tired, she seemed all right.

"Oh, sure. Well, no, that's a god-awful lie. I've been going on nervous energy and screwdrivers ever since I left you around ten-thirty last night. I was just heading up to crash. If I don't get some rest, I think I'll probably fall right over."

"I'm sorry. I guess I could use a nap myself. I was just headed home."

"I'm sorry, too, about everything. In the end it worked out okay, I guess." I rummaged for the right words, but words had left me.

"I hope you don't h-hate me," she stammered, fighting tears.

"None of that. You mustn't feel bad about us. It was good."

"More than just good." Trembling, she touched my arm.

I nodded, afraid to speak.

"I hope you mean it." She looked at me hungrily.

"You know I do. It was . . . I thought we were something special."

God help me, I couldn't help but say it.

"For me it was the absolute best." She lowered her eyes. "I guess we can't ever have it back again."

"Wouldn't be very smart, I'm afraid."

We were walking slowly back through the wide gallery now.

"No, guess not." She tried to smile. "When do you have to leave?"

"I'm stuck until Saturday. A lot's happened. One of my best friends died, and I have to fly to Cincinnati Sunday. No rest for the weary."

"You wouldn't want to come back and have your steak? Tonight, I mean."

The memory of her naked on the bed was overpowering.

"I want to very much, but I'm not going to. We can't. It just has to be that way. You understand, I hope."

"I guess I do, but sometimes I just don't want to understand everything that I know is true."

She quickly turned away and brushed aside a tear.

"Yeah, sometimes I feel the same."

We'd reached the top of the stairs.

"I've got to go. Be very good to yourself. Take care . . . get some rest."

"It was really the best. I'll never be the same. I mean it." Her voice broke at the end.

"Me too." It sounded like the truth.

"About tonight . . . you sure? Maybe tomorrow, if you're too tired tonight?"

"No, no. We really can't." I hoped I sounded convincing.

"All right, but it isn't fair. I purely hate it."

"Take care," I said and gave her a clumsy hug.

The feel and scent of her turned me inside out.

Watching her walk away, I felt the ache in my throat again.

At the elevators, I looked back. She was still standing at the top of the stairs.

"Melba, it isn't because I don't want to," I called across the empty lobby and waved again just before I got on the elevator.

I knew it was against the rules to feel that way.

But I did.

And that was just a goddamned fact.

CHAPTER FIFTY-ONE

Early Saturday morning I made arrangements with the hotel staff for crating and shipping our display. Afterwards, I hung around my room debating whether or not to call Melba. I had tossed and turned all night. She stirred me in a way I thought I had forgotten.

Or maybe I'd never known existed.

Yet I knew I wouldn't leave Rose. There was no way that I would give up Paul. Finally, I heaved a sigh, packed my bags, and called the bell captain's desk.

By 11:45, I had checked out and stood watching Obadiah oversee the bellman's loading of my car.

When he finished, I took care of the bellman, then pressed a picture of Mr. Jackson in the old man's palm. "You take good care, Obadiah."

"Yes, sir, Mr. Baird. Can't be too soon you come this way again. You are a fine genamen, sir. Drive safe now and come back to the Greenbrier right soon."

After he closed the door, I waved and wasted no time heading out.

At the top of the oval I pulled over and looked back one last time.

Rose was right. I was a snob. I loved this place.

But, after all, what were snobs if they weren't people who appreciated something better.

It didn't matter that Rose could never understand.

The Greenbrier would be mine forever.

The day was absolutely perfect.

I took my time driving back over the crooked mountain roads.

After I'd passed through Newcastle, the harsh light of the afternoon sun in the countryside brought back memories of my boyhood on the farm. I stopped beside a long, gently sloping hillside that had recently produced a crop of corn.

I got out of my car, removed my tie, and tossed my jacket across the seat before I closed the door. Then, bemused, or perhaps bewitched, I jumped the roadside ditch and scrambled up the weedy bank to the fence.

Some things—like riding a bicycle, they say—are never forgotten. Climbing expertly through barbed wire fences is, for a former farm boy, a trick that is undoubtedly imprinted on the genes.

Moving gingerly, I emerged undamaged on the other side of the treacherous wire.

Stretching before me, the spiked stubs of the newly harvested cornstalks stood like toy soldiers in neat rows rising up the slope. As my eyes moved upward, I could see where, three-quarters of the way to the summit, the cultivated field gave way to a narrow tangle of wild blackberry brambles. A few yards beyond, there was the beginning of a towering forest that crowned the hill.

Overhead, except for a line of thunderheads on the rim of the distant horizon, the sky was virtually cloudless. A lone hawk was a tiny speck, drifting in effortless circles against the sun-faded, almost colorless sky.

Moving closer, I could hear the soughing of the breeze stirring the treetops. Far off, a half-imagined rumble of thunder whispered echoes of my long-lost innocence.

Those woods beckoned me.

I began climbing.

I was transported back in time. The summer I was twelve, with my younger brother, Jim, and a neighbor's son, Carl—who was several years older and came daily with a phlegmatic dappled-gray plow horse named Nell—together we'd made a crop of corn on an eight-acre piece of rocky Virginia hillside, which looked a lot like the one I was climbing now.

That summer's inglorious labor had been an altogether uninspiring fate for a suppressed romantic male. Each morning I'd awoken to the endless prospect of undistinguished days. Beginning at the top of the dusty hillside, we'd plowed and hoed our way, cornstalk by cornstalk, down the dusty, rock-strewn slope. Laboring under the relentless sun for most of the summer, the three of us had worked like automatons, struggling vainly to keep the indomitable scourge of morning glory vines and farmer's wiregrass away from their mindless lusting to ententacle the cornstalks in a death embrace.

To my pubescent melodramatic mind, our labors had called up images of Dante's *Inferno*.

Rats on a treadmill, top to bottom, each cycle had taken perhaps two weeks. Each time we reached the bottom row, there was no celebration. We had simply turned and marched, numb and resentful, back to the top to begin again.

Then, one hot day—just as unceremoniously as our labor had begun—without fanfare, it was over.

My brother and I had shouldered our hoes and watched Carl unhitch old Nell. In a few days, the grownups had come, harvested the scraggly crop, and hauled it off.

That summer's labor had felt totally unredeeming. Even the morning glories and wiregrass appeared driven only by pure meanness. The land was totally unsuitable for growing anything but weeds. Once the crop was harvested, even the weeds had appeared to lose interest and languish. And, in the end, the corn was destined to be fed to the livestock anyway—a rather pointless objective to my pragmatic way of thinking, since it would be my brother and me who eventually had to spend the winter carting the sorry corn and fodder to the chickens and cows and hogs.

At the close of that summer, I had put away forever most of what was my childhood. A few weeks later I would begin riding the school bus five miles into town to enter the big consolidated county high school in Melas where I would demonstrate my skills in kicking and throwing balls of every shape and size.

And discover girls.

Now I climbed awkwardly in my polished Italian loafers. When I reached the topmost rows, I found a clutter of lunch bags and candy wrappers mixed with soft drink bottles and cans at the edge of the maze of blackberry brambles. Two rusting tins labeled "Pork and Beans"—and several smaller ones that had contained potted meat and Vienna sausages—had been carelessly tossed aside to lie rusting in the sun. This rude litter was a reminder that crops of corn do not make themselves. I walked along the border of the blackberry thicket to where I could see the almost invisible trace of a narrow beaten-down track leading through the tangle to the deeper shadows at the edge of the trees.

Feeling a tad foolish, a professional man headed for his destiny in New York and not at all dressed for this adventure, I picked my way carefully along the clutches of the bramble-strewn pathway toward the trees. When I finally threaded my way into the leafy overhang of branches, I looked back down the hill. My car looked like an abandoned toy.

A freshening breeze mixed a heavy scent of honeysuckle with cooler breaths of the approaching storm.

I felt strangely astraddle a chasm in time.

My memorable twelfth year had been a confusing time for me. For reasons I didn't understand then, I had been skipped ahead in school. I was large for my age and, unlike the sons of our farmer neighbors, I usually left the swimming hole early and put in a lot of serious practice at passing and kicking a football. And, that seminal summer, I suffered a plethora of euphoric hormonal influences. My voice played tricks on me, and I began sprouting dark hairs in all those funny places. In the evenings, I found myself reading less of Robin Hood and Captain Nemo. Already, I'd been caught sneaking copies of *Tropic of Cancer* and *Lady Chatterley's Lover* out of my aunt's library.

After dark, on the pretense of playing Old Dead Mule with the neighborhood gang, I discovered the perfect excuse to spend a lot of time hanging around the teenage girl across the river.

She thought I was fourteen. And I was content to let her go on believing this cheeky invention. One night, crossing the moonlit surface of the torpid river in a leaky old rowboat, she brushed her mouth against my cheek and whispered that I was beautiful—hungrily, she'd tasted me.

After that, I was never the same.

But I had still daydreamed about being a pearl diver on a South Sea island or a movie star or a dashing jet pilot, and I sometimes slipped off alone to play out these romantic fantasies in the woods at the top of our sorry cornfield. There, shadowed by the fear of discovery, I would self-consciously don a homemade loin cloth, cut the thick grapevines at their roots, and go swinging through the trees, playing a solitary game of Tarzan.

As I took in the sweeping vista out across the sunlit country landscape, the memory of that summer was seductive.

I took another look at my car and stepped through the leafy drapery. It was as if a curtain had closed behind me, shutting away the lively chorus of birdcalls and insect sounds.

Enthralled, I picked my way to a giant grapevine hanging from a towering oak and tested it tentatively with my full weight. That ropey vine would swing a long way out over the slope of the clearing. A good ride for an adventuresome lad; the idea captured my imagination.

Emitting a peculiar green luminescence filtering down through the leaves, any forest encompasses a universe all its own. The timeless, fairy-like setting of leaf-strewn mossy carpets, towering trees, huge vines, and lacy ferns is unforgettable.

The first time I'd seduced Rose, we'd been at a cabin party just on the other side of this very mountain. That drizzly afternoon deep in the dripping woods back of the cabin, we'd found a gigantic boulder, perhaps ten feet high and flat on top. Covered by a big plastic raincoat, stark naked in the fine silver mist, we'd shut out the world.

I was fifteen.

There would never be another time like that for me.

But, Melba, you were very special, you really were. God help us both. I whispered my anguished confession to a curious mockingbird sitting on a hickory limb.

After a time, I threaded my way back through the trees and brambles. I looked out over the broad valley. High above a barn and farmhouse, a red kite was floating in the wind—flying free, as high as the hill. I traced the line to a small boy and a man. They were tiny figures in a homespun tapestry. The man's hands helped the boy hold the cord. Together they intently watched the kite dance on the breeze.

After a moment, I reluctantly made my way back down the hill and drove away, wondering if there would be woods with grapevines and places for flying kites in the suburbs of New York City.

On the outskirts of town, I took the shortcut that went by my club. When I pulled to the rear of the golf shop, the head pro was consulting with one of his young assistants over a disabled golf cart standing partially disassembled on a canvas tarp.

"Hi, Charlie . . . Lou," I called and moved around the car to extract the bag with Rush's borrowed sticks from the trunk.

"Wait, Mr. Baird, I'll get those." Lou, the young assistant, came around the car to help. He stopped cold in his tracks when he saw the damage to my car. "Man! You hit a train?"

"Not really, but it's a story I'd just as soon forget," I said and watched him shoulder both golf bags and move into the storage area at the back of the shop.

"Did your boss like those Pings? Think he might like a deal?" Charlie asked.

I spread my hands in futility. "Don't hold your breath, Charlie. He didn't even play." I opted not to tell him about Rush's charade.

"At the Greenbrier? Are you serious? Has he ever played the game?"

"Not much, Charlie, and that's a sorry fact," I said.

"I suppose that spoiled your trip."

"No, not at all. I played with Max and Sam. The golf course was unbelievable. Those turkeys will be looking for my hide when they get back. I'd rather let them tell you. I think you understand?" I winked.

He laughed.

"You wanna play? Bennie's in the clubhouse looking for a game. Nobody out there to bother you this time a day. The last money players left over an hour ago." He looked at me. My jacket and tie were still on the car seat.

"Not today, Charlie. I'm anxious to get on home. Thanks again for the loan of the sticks." I waved and got back in the car.

As I headed down the street to my neighborhood, the tops of the trees were swaying gently in the wind.

It was still early enough to take Paul shopping for a box kite. It would be a damn shame to waste a fine breeze like that.

Epilogue

Perched on the front steps of the house next door, casually watching the movers as they loaded our furniture, I extracted an envelope postmarked Cambridge, Massachusetts, from a stack of mail that was mostly three weeks old.

September 6
Harvard B

Dear Logan:
It's Sunday in Boston and I'm stuck up here for Labor Day weekend because we don't have time for anything but work.

I've tried to call you several times but have received no answer. I'm sorry Herman Asbury gave the promotion to fill my slot to someone else—you had my recommendation.

Next week Nadine will be moving our household from Charlotte to a wonderful place she found in Englewood, NJ. It's really not that much different from Charlotte, except that the yards are smaller. Our teenagers love it. We took them to NYC. They love being near a big city again. San Francisco spoiled them forever, I'm afraid.

By the way, I went over to call on Ian Ferguson and caught his first-year lecture at Harvard M. Damned if he wasn't telling the truth about using your *Harper's* article for his text. I guess you're in pretty tight with him, huh? I'll never forget our days in the Hotel Roanoke, solving all the world's problems over a bottle of Jim Beam—love that old square bottle. When I get reassigned to Teaneck in January, I'll see if I can find a slot for you at the home office. You can be my protégé—you always were my best pupil, but you've still got a lot to learn.

Warmest regards,
Rush

P.S. If you're tight with Dr. Ferguson, how about putting in a good word for me? Old buddies should hang together.
R.D.

I replaced the memo in the envelope and tossed it on top of the stack.

"And my best to you too, Rush, old chum. I'll put in a word all right. And, speaking of hanging, when you hang, I hope you and Herm Asbury hang together," I said to myself as I gave Humphrey Bogart, Paul's new beagle puppy, a friendly pat on his wiggly behind.

Turning my attention back to the mail, I found a short note from Paxton Preuffer III.

Henley Logan Baird
Director, Chairman of the Board
John Paul Silver Literary Foundation
125 Hurst Avenue
Melas, Virginia

Dear Logan:

Your idea to let Maggie do the actual running of John Paul's foundation was dead on—she's definitely taking charge. I know John Paul would celebrate your decision to invest your director's salary into a rehabilitation hospital for Bosnian children crippled as the result of the war. Will you approve the foundation's paying for Maggie's (and my) expenses to come to New York? We'll need to hold a board meeting.

Best wishes for *Hippocrates* magazine. I can hardly wait to see the first issue.

Sincerely,
Pax

Absently returning the note to the envelope, I caught sight of one of the movers carrying the box with my manuscript to the van.

461

"Wait, let me take that," I called. I walked over and rescued the box. Returning to my perch, I collected the stack of outdated mail and stuffed it and the manuscript in my new Dunhill briefcase.

When I looked up, Rose was coming out of the house with Paul tagging behind, holding his new box kite. "We'd better hurry. You don't want to miss your plane," she said and walked down the drive to the curb.

"I was just coming to find you." I followed them to the car.

At the airport, I surrendered my ticket to the sidewalk check-in and walked back over to the car. "I'll be at the Algonquin, same room. Call there or my office when you get to Tarrytown, and I'll try to run up Wednesday night and join you for dinner. If the beds are set up and we can find sheets, maybe I can spend the night in our own bed."

"I'll call. Thursday might be better. Let's give Daddy a big kiss, Paul." Rose leaned out the window and gave me a solid smack.

Paul stuck Humphrey Bogart out the window for a kiss, then planted a fleeting peck of his own on my cheek.

Lately Paul, Humphrey, and I were having a fine time being buddies.

Buddies don't kiss a lot.

"Be safe," I said and added, "Are you sure you're going to be okay?"

"With Arlene along, we'll be just fine. We're spending tonight at the Hampton Inn in Charlottesville and leaving there tomorrow morning. We're going to drive all the way tomorrow and spend the night at the Hilton outside Tarrytown. The movers say they'll move us in on Wednesday morning. We'll be waiting for them. Shopping in the city is awesome. It's hard to imagine being able to shop at Bloomingdale's. And they are reviving *The Music Man*. Arlene can hardly wait."

"Great," I said, for the moment glad Rose had sisters.

When I'd checked my bag and passed through security, I could see my airplane through the wide expanse of windowed wall. It was Sunday. From Roanoke, flights to New York were usually crowded. Walking over near the door, I waited, trying to cool off in the air-conditioned room before I had to board.

"Hi. I'm Pru Sharpe from the Greenbrier spa. We met at the pool a few weeks back. Remember?" When I turned, she was standing at my elbow. Absolutely striking, and her smile was radiant.

"Yes, of course I remember. I'm Logan Baird. I used to work for a pharmaceutical house, calling on the doctors in the hotel clinic." I shifted the book I held and shook her hand, recalling how she'd looked in the skintight tank suit.

"You taking USAir to New York?" she asked.

I nodded.

"Me too," she said. "I'm going to visit Melba Noyes, an old friend who just moved there last week to work for Hippocrates, a big new medical company. You may remember Melba. She used to be head nurse at the Main Street Clinic in White Sulphur Springs."

"I remember Melba very well."

"Do you go to New York often?"

"I work there now."

"I'll be sure and tell Melba," she said as the attendant called our flight. "It's a small world, isn't it?"

"It is at that." I picked up my briefcase when they called for first class passengers, and she noticed the book I carried.

"*Carpe Diem*. That's the book everyone is raving about. I can hardly wait to read it."

"I just finished. Here, please take it as a gift. You can read it on the plane." I handed her the book.

"How nice of you. Are you sure?" She gave my arm a flirty squeeze.

"I'm sure," I smiled.

Carpe diem, John Paul, old sock. I'm doing the best I can.

ACKNOWLEDGMENTS

My deepest appreciation to my publishers, Carolyn and Al Newman of River City Publishing, and Ashley Gordon, Gail Waller, Lissa Monroe, William Hicks, Lovelace Cook, and the rest of their tireless, competent, professional staff.

I am especially indebted to Sharon Rowe and Raymond J. Hoffman for offering their uncomplaining expertise in my dedication to do justice to the grandeur of the Greenbrier. They deserve all the credit for the accuracies. Any errors or omissions are my own.

Special credit goes to John Miller, author and friend, whose unwavering belief in this book was an inspiration.

Thanks to C. Terry Cline, Jr., George Garrett, Sally R. Jones, Judith Richards, James Harris Robertson, Les Standiford, Pat Saunders, Dr. Sue Walker, Rick Robotham, and Jay Qualey for their support.